A SHOT OF OAKIES

THE OLDE ROSIE CHRONICLES

A SHOT OF OAKIES

VOLUME I

ALEX BENNETT

Library of Congress Control Number:		2023900640
ISBN:	Hardcover	978-1-6698-6265-9
	Softcover	978-1-6698-6263-5
	eBook	978-1-6698-6264-2

Print information available on the last page.

Rev. date: 03/02/2023

To order additional copies of this book, contact:
Xlibris
844-714-8691
www.Xlibris.com
Orders@Xlibris.com
849456

To Mom for dealing with my artistic side,
the ladies who taught me the lessons I needed to learn,
and all my regulars for making this possible...
Thank you!

Acknowlegements

Trisha Charlotte Albano—Star of the cover
Instagram: @trishaalbano

Stephen Gardner—Cover art
Website: www.gardnerillustration.com
Instagram: @gardnerillustration

Melissa LoBianco—Proofreading
Website: wanderingpathremedies.godaddysites.com

Aine McGillycuddy—Translations.
Facebook page: The Irish Skinny

Gregg Obodzinski—Map compasses
Website: www.GreggsDeepColors.com
Facebook page: Gregg's Deep Colors—Paintings and Artwork
of Gregg Obodzinski

And last but not least—All the people who read my work and
gave me feedback. Your input was invaluable!

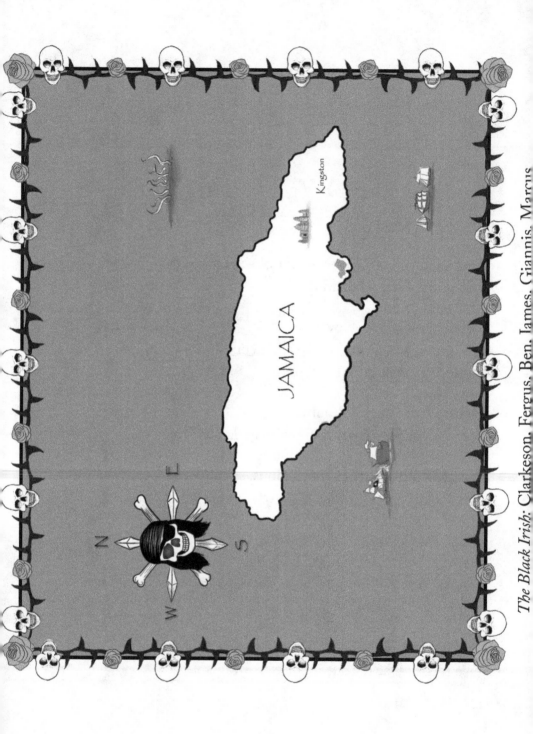

The Black Irish: Clarkeson, Fergus, Ben, James, Giannis, Marcus

Chapter 1

October 1, 1785, Kingston, Jamaica

With a spark, the burning switch lit the fresh wick atop the beeswax candle on the mantel behind the bar, and though a dozen lanterns already illuminated the room, the sweet aroma immediately brightened the entire space. While a thin white melting rivulet began meandering through the ten metal pins inserted down the left side of the stick, Sarah blew out the switch and, continuing the tradition her grandfather had established forty-three years before, tugged on the knotted rope dangling from the bell tower over her head. Despite the tropical storm battering the island, she heard the familiar clear peal announcing Henry's was open for the evening, took a deep breath, and turned to face the familiar coarse squeak of a stool being pulled out.

"Hello," she said to an old sea captain taking the spot farthest on her left, where the hand-crafted mahogany top spanning the width of the room met the exposed white brick wall. The moment he sat down, lightning flashed through the gaps in the wooden shutters covering the arched windows flanking the front door, and as he scooched forward, it sporadically flickered to the ensuing rumble of thunder. Forced to wait out the clamor,

Sarah smiled and held his bright blue eyes until she could follow up, "What can I get for you?"

Slowly stroking his long white bushy beard, he looked to the three different-sized casks in the cradle beneath the mantel and asked, "What do ye have?"

Hooking her right thumb toward the largest, a hogshead at the far end with a capital H branded above the tap, she began, "The big one is lager. I still brew it using the same recipe my grandfather developed back in 1742." Nodding to the barrel in the middle, bearing a scripted vermillion *CLT*, she furthered, "The next in line is claret. The Dutch captain who ships it to Jamaica says it's the finest wine produced at the finest estate in the entire Bordeaux region of France, and believe it or not, he swears it gets even better after a couple months at sea."

"Oh, I believe ye," the old sea captain attested, his voice booming in the confined place, "only I'm afraid I'm not much of a wine drinker."

"That's not a problem," she went on, tapping her knuckles on the third, last, and smallest cask in the row. "This little firkin is the best spiced rum made in Barbados, and—" she added, with a wink, "they import it to Kingston specifically for me."

Still stroking his beard, the old sea captain muttered, "Rum from Barbados. My good friend George favors rum from Barbados."

"Would you like an ounce?"

Vigorously shaking his head, he held both palms forth and asserted, "No, I drank my fill of rum durin' my time in the Royal Navy, and I'd be perfectly happy to never drink it again." His gaze shiny and clear, he revealed, "To be sure, I was hopin' fer a shot of Oakies."

"A shot of Oakies?" Sarah repeated to another burst of lightning and another roll of thunder. "I've never heard of such a thing. What is it?"

Letting out a long happy sigh, he looked to the burning candle on the mantel and suggested, "Fer simplicity's sake, we'll call it an ounce and a half of the greatest whiskey the world has ever known."

Frowning, she leaned forward and told him, "Then you must be new to the Caribbean. This is rum country. You'll be hard-pressed to find any good whisky in these parts."

Raising his big white bushy brows, the old sea captain countered, "Although I always hesitate to tell a bartender she's wrong, I feel compelled to mention I've sailed the world round and I've tried every whiskey in every port of call to have it and I can promise ye, I've never had one better than the one I had the last time I sat on this very stool." Digging his fingertips into the smooth timeworn wooden top, once a captain's table salvaged out of a sunken Spanish galleon, he closed his eyes and murmured, "Bein' here again, I can almost taste it—uisge beatha."

Suddenly, a bolt of lightning crackled nearby, the thunder bellowed overhead, and a heavy downpour began echoing off the roof. The previous night, a hurricane had reached the southern Atlantic, and in unleashing a series of intermittent storms on Jamaica, it effectively closed the Port of Kingston. While Sarah had opened for lunch earlier in the day, Henry's had remained empty, so she had taken advantage of the weather and gone home for the afternoon. In the evening, however, she had returned to Tony waiting with Rags at the door and Nancy, her serving maid, arriving a few minutes later.

Now, seven spots separated the old sea captain and Tony, who had pulled out his stool and stood with his left foot resting on the brass rail running six inches off the floor. Like always, he had used a red silk bow to tie his wavy graying black hair in a ponytail, waxed his dark mustache straight off the corners of his lips, and trimmed his dark goatee into a point on his well-defined chin. His white silk blouse and red leather vest were only buttoned halfway, exposing the sizable Spanish gold coin on the sizable braided gold chain in the midst of the curly hair blanketing his chest, and his black velvet pants were tucked into the tops of his muddy knee-high black leather boots. To his left, Rags sat on the second to last stool before the end. He wore a simple black blouse with tan pants and a small silver crucifix on a thin silver chain. His gray skin was wrinkly, his gray eyes were watery, and his few remaining strands of wispy gray hair were slicked back in an attempt to cover his bald head. Facing them both, Nancy, who was dressed in the same white shift, black waistcoat, and black bow tie as Sarah, stood in the gap leading behind the bar, and they all quietly chatted together.

The thunder faded in the background, and looking at the old sea captain, Sarah said, "I'm sorry, I couldn't hear you. What was that?"

"Uisge beatha," he repeated, smiling wide, "It's Gaelic, and literally translated, it means 'water of life.'" Covering his heart with his right hand and raising his left index finger, he declared, "And I've witnessed many a person who either couldn't speak the language or, fer some reason wouldn't speak it, utter the phrase upon takin' their first sip of Oakies. It was like magic. Ye just couldn't help yerself."

"If it was that good," she asserted, tilting her head to the left, "I'm surprised I never heard of it. Do ye know where my grandfather got it?"

Chuckling softly, the old sea captain replied, "If only there was an easy way to answer such a simple question." Seeing her cross her arms, he opened his palms and quickly followed up, "To be sure, I'd be getting into a story."

Uncrossing her arms and placing her hands on her waist, she repeated, "A story? What story is that?"

"Some call it the legend of Old One-Eyed Clarkeson," he got out a moment prior to a particularly vicious clap of lightning and angry bout of thunder.

Without flinching, Sarah arched her brows and remarked, "Old One-Eyed Clarkeson? I've never heard of him. Who was he?"

Slowly stroking his beard, the old sea captain explained, "Well, he wasn't a he, fer Clarkeson was a she, and fer those who didn't know any better, they'd say she was the most beautiful pirate to ever sail these seas."

Picking up on the conversation, Tony shifted from one foot to the other and, leaning their way, inserted, "I'm sorry to interrupt. However, I was born on this island, and in my childhood, I heard all the stories about all the pirates of the Caribbean. I don't recall one named Clarkeson either." A gleam in his dark-brown eyes, he tugged on the left side of his mustache and, with the candlelight sparkling in the large ruby set in the large gold ring on his pinky finger, added, "And I'm sure I would, especially if she was as beautiful as you say she was."

Taking him in, the old sea captain stated, "That doesn't surprise me. Her story begins in the early 1740s, right around the time Henry first opened and probably long before ye were born. Anymore, I doubt there's very many of us still livin' who do remember her."

"That doesn't matter," Tony asserted, waving his finger. "My ancestors built our first warehouse on the docks of Port Royale well before the English captured Jamaica in 1655, and when the earthquake destroyed the city in 1692, they went on to help establish Kingston in the months thereafter. Between listening to my father and my grandfather, there isn't a pirate I haven't heard about."

"That's because Clarkeson isn't real," Rags contended. He poked his head forward and, glaring at the old sea captain, continued, "And don't bother trying to fool me. I was sitting on this stool back then. It sounds like you're trying to tell one of those tired old fables that'll end with the pirate turning out to be Anne Bonny."

"Ye may have been sittin' on that stool back then," the old sea captain retorted, "but both yer memory and yer numbers are fuzzy. Where Anne Bonny was a redhead, Clarkeson's hair was jet black." Pressing his left index finger to the bar, he went on, "And in 1720, when she was sentenced to hang at Gallows Point, Anne Bonny was already twenty-four years old. Even if ye believe she escaped the hangman's noose, she would've been close to fifty durin' Clarkeson's reign. If somehow she was still alive, she was most likely old and gray."

"If Clarkeson wasn't Anne Bonny," Sarah interjected, "who was she?"

Spreading his arms wide, the old sea captain answered, "She's the one who made Oakies famous."

"Ah, this is all a bunch of hogwash," Rags growled. "I never heard of this Oakies either. Just like now, nobody drank whisky back then unless they had to. It's too harsh."

Patting Rags's shoulder with his left hand, Tony said, "My friend, I know you think you know everything." He waved his right hand toward the old sea captain and added, "But maybe this man has a different tale to tell." Looking at Sarah, he noted, "And maybe it would be nice to listen to something different for a change."

In a soft voice, Nancy inserted, "It would be." Her long dark hair was tied in a single thick braid that wound around the right side of her neck, and her full pouty lips spread wide into a gleaming white smile. Casting her cheerful almond-shaped dark-brown eyes on Rags, she told him, "This sounds like a pirate story even I would like to hear."

Beaming, the old sea captain looked from Nancy to Tony to Sarah and warned, "If yer lookin' fer a pirate story, ye'll be disappointed, fer Clarkeson was no pirate. She was a warrior in the spirit of Joan of Arc. Although, in reality, she preferred to maintain an almost mythological existence and that nobody knew exactly who or what she really was." Lowering his voice, he tilted his head forward and whispered, "In fact, she happily let people believe she was a faerie."

"Oh come on," Rags scoffed. "You're not going to tell us she was some sort of water sprite. What's next, she rode the Loch Ness monster all the way to the New World?"

"Of course not," the old sea captain dismissed. "Clarkeson was more human than any of us. Fortunately, I was lucky enough to know the truth."

"And how could you possibly be so lucky?" Rags snapped.

Letting out a long sigh, the old sea captain slowly stroked his beard and solemnly stated, "Because my skipper was the only man she ever loved." Placing his hand back over his heart, he put forth, "And fer all the sunrises I've seen, I can truly say I never saw one redder than the one on the mornin' of the day he departed to hunt her down."

"Hunt her down?" Nancy exclaimed.

"Aye, hunt her down," the old sea captain repeated. "By then, Clarkeson had caused enough trouble to capture the attention of the Royal Navy and with the war escalatin' in Europe, they were of no mind to risk an Irish lass sparkin' a rebellion in the New World." Tapping his chest, he followed up, "To be sure, they tried sendin' others, yet in the end, my skipper proved to be the only man noble enough to complete the task."

"So you caught her?" Sarah asked.

With the rain slowing to a pitter-patter, he answered, "I suppose ye could say she caught us. But, I should warn ye, to honestly answer yer question, I'd be startin' a tale taller than the ships anchored in the harbor and longer than the storm keeping them in port."

Patting Rags's shoulder again, Tony widened his eyes and insisted, "That's fine, your tale couldn't be any taller than most of his, or longer." Picking up his glass of wine and sweeping it toward the old sea captain, he declared, "Sarah, I'd like to buy this gentleman a lager on the condition he begins his story, for I don't see the weather breaking anytime soon and I could use a novel yarn to pass the time."

Sarah filled a glass mug and, as a bit of foam ran over one side, she set it down on the bar for the old sea captain. He scooped it up, took several healthy swallows, gave Tony a nod, and said, "Thank ye kindly, good sir."

Suddenly, the front door opened, and in unison, every head turned to see two couples enter and watch the two gentlemen carefully remove their partner's wet cloaks. Though the ladies were both tall and slender with dark-brown eyes and long black hair, the first had a bronze complexion and wore a form-fitting maroon dress while the second had an olive complexion and wore a comparable green one. The men hung the sodden cloaks on the pegs to the right of the entry and then went on to remove their own. The same age, they had light skin, brown eyes, bare cheeks, and short silvery-blond hair. Their vests matched the color of their companion's attire, and they were each clad in black pants with yellow shirts and had similar blue-green amethysts set in the silver bands on their left ring fingers. Paired up, they all strode down the center aisle separating the five tables abutting the walls on each side of the room and chose to sit at the one behind the old sea captain.

He silently waited until they had settled in and Nancy had filled their order. Once she had returned to her perch in the gap leading behind the bar, he tugged on his beard and admitted, "To be sure, sometimes the hardest part of tellin' a story is figurin' out where to begin." Setting his bright blue eyes upon the flickering orange flame atop the melting beeswax candle on the mantel, he went on, "Nevertheless, I have to start somewhere and I'm thinkin' it may be best to go back to this very day forty-two years ago, fer on that day, Clarkeson took her very first ship and the legend of Oakies was born . . ."

October 1, 1743, west of Jamaica

A black patch covering her right eye, Clarkeson held a brass spyglass to her left and focused on the British merchantman heading due west off the bow of her brigantine, *The Black Irish*. Her long dark hair blowing wildly in the wind, she let an evil smile cross her lips and, with a harsh cackle, declared, "*The Empire's Reach*." Her feet planted firmly at the fore of her helm, she told the tall burly redhead guiding the wheel, "Well, Fergus, it appears the time has come to introduce Oakies to the world."

Dressed in all black, Fergus carried a pair of daggers tucked into his belt on his right hip and a pair of flintlock pistols in cross-draw holsters on his left. Additionally, he had a five-foot Scottish claymore strapped to his back with the foot-long cross guard behind his neck and the leather handle rising eighteen inches to the diamond-shaped pommel above his head. Both his flaming-red ponytail and his flaming-red beard bore streaks of gray, and as he squinted in the midday sun, deep furrows set in at the corners of his bright blue eyes. Noting their quarry featured a distinct pear-shaped hull and two masts supporting the spars for three square sails, he stated, "Even at this distance, I can tell she's a fluyt, but the seas are full of 'em." His voice raspy and low, he looked at Clarkeson and asked, "Are ye sure she's the one we want?"

"I'm sure," she said, lowering her spyglass. Turning around, she offered it to him and followed up, "Go ahead, see fer yerself. I'll take over."

They switched places, and after locating the other ship through the lens, he zeroed in on the bright red Cross of England stitched into the mainsail on the mainmast. Following the rigging down to the hull, he read the brass nameplate below the fluttering Union Jack at the stern, scanned the length of the main deck, and settled upon the waterline sitting heavy in the rolling aquamarine sea. "I'd say she's a good eighty feet long," he calculated, "and judgin' by her displacement, she's fully loaded. Do ye know what she's haulin'?"

"Not only do I know what she's haulin'," Clarkeson revealed, "I know the captain came to Jamaica with a load of slaves to trade fer molasses and indigo to take to the colonies. I also know he's on his way to Belize Town fer some logwood to bring to England. Had he been able to keep his big fat mouth shut, he maybe would've had a chance to make it."

"Does he have any gold aboard?" Fergus wanted to know.

Her eye gleaming malevolently, she cackled harshly and responded, "Not unless ye count the Oakies, though if all goes accordin' to plan, at the end of the day, men will lust fer Oakies more than they do fer any shiny metal coin."

Directing his attention to the top of their foremast, Fergus pointed to the bright green flag with the black shamrock in the center and warned, "That's because after today, every captain in the world will fear the sight of yer Jolly Roger." Lowering the spyglass, he collapsed the tubes and, presenting it to her, posed, "We have yet to commit any crimes, and if we stop now, we can return to our normal lives." When she grasped it, he held on, met her gaze, and added, "If we don't, there'll be no goin' back."

Sneering, Clarkeson snatched her spyglass out of his hand and insisted, "Until the cause is won, I don't want to go back. Trust me, in many ways, I'm more excited to introduce Clarkeson to the world than I am Oakies."

Taking over control of the wheel, Fergus reminded her, "Keep in mind, the more trouble we stir up, the more likely the Royal Navy will commission someone to come find us."

"It won't go on that long," she retorted. "In the next six months, the prince will land in Scotland, and the war will end before anyone is the wiser."

"Given the prince is in Rome," Fergus remarked, "I still say we're startin' prematurely and it would be wise to plan fer somethin' to go wrong and fer someone to figure out the truth."

A black vest covered her ample bosom, and while she slid her spyglass into the pocket over her right breast, she simultaneously drew a thin silver flask out of the pocket over her left. On one side, the flask was etched with a rose having two buds on the stem above the word *FIAT*, and unscrewing the metal cap, she stated, "I'll worry about the truth comin' out when I meet a captain smart enough to figure me out."

"We both know of one," Fergus reminded her, "and it sounds like he's gainin' quite the reputation in the Mediterranean. If he keeps havin' success, they could send him."

Scrunching her face and gnashing her teeth, she snarled, "It sounds like he's a pompous ass, especially with that name he's goin' by. I hope they send him. He has to know what they did to me father. I can't believe he still serves those scum. He's a traitor, and fer that, I'm lookin' ferward to drivin' me dagger through his heart." Handing Fergus the flask, she ordered, "Now, let's focus on the task at hand. To the king across the sea."

"To the king," he repeated and took a healthy swig. He swallowed, let out a slow "Uisge beatha," and asked, "All right, tell me what we're up against."

Arching her brows, she glanced at the fluyt and began, "I have good news and bad news. The good news is that other than the officers, most of his sailors are native to Africa or these islands and he treats them like slaves. It's more likely they'll fight fer us than against us." When a sharp reflection from the other stern momentarily blinded them, she immediately swapped the flask for the spyglass and, upon raising it, spotted a man staring back at her. His long black hair hung down over his glittering steel breastplate, and with a gauntleted hand, he stroked his scruffy chin. Seeing several more similarly armored warriors gathering at his sides, she inhaled deeply and went on, "The bad news is he has two dozen Spaniards aboard."

"Spaniards?" Fergus questioned. "Why would a Brit have Spaniards aboard?"

"They're mercenaries," she explained, "and if he didn't hire them, he'd face a mutiny every time he set out, particularly if he's transportin' slaves." Behind the soldiers, she found the English captain, who was noticeably shorter and pacing to and fro. He wore a triangular gold-trimmed black hat that made up the difference in height and a navy-blue shirt under a bright orange vest stretched over his pudgy belly. Tracking his movements, she continued, "He also claims that flyin' their flag from his bow keeps the Spanish privateers at bay."

"While that may be savvy on his part," Fergus acknowledged, "he won't escape a battle today." Nodding to their own crew, milling around the five overturned skiffs strapped to the main deck of their brigantine, he noted, "With most our men bein' former slaves, they won't show the Spanish any mercy."

"With the way the Spanish have treated these people," she replied, "I doubt they'd expect it. Thank God we don't need them to survive. Fer the plan to succeed, we just need to capture a few of the British officers and the captain. Especially the captain. I'm lookin' ferward to makin' an example out of him." Shivering, she curled her lips and snarled, "I haven't even told ye what a disgustin' pig he is. In the pubs, he looks fer every opportunity to put his paws all over the servin' maidens, no matter their age. It's pathetic. And do ye want to know the worst of it?"

"What can be worse?"

The gleam in her eye ablaze, she hissed, "When it comes time to pay, he argues about the tab and doesn't believe he should have to throw in any extra."

"He stiffs them?" Clenching his jaw, Fergus shook his head and determined, "Fer that alone, he gets what he deserves."

Close to sixty feet long, *The Black Irish* had two decks with two masts and a single shiny white skull embedded on the tip of her bowsprit. Three successively smaller square sails climbed the foremast, while off the main, a single large trapezoidal gaff sail jutted over the helm. Though she was only eighteen feet at her widest point, she fielded ten twelve-pound cannons per side, a half-dozen multibarreled swivel guns on her railings, and a pair of nine-pound chasers stationed in her stern. Absent any other cargo, she was light in the water, and fortunate to have the wind at their back, they made up enough distance in an hour to make out the individual sailors aboard the fluyt without the aid of a spyglass.

Searching *The Empire's Reach* for open portholes, Fergus asked, "Besides the mercenaries, what else do we need to be wary of?"

"There's a couple of sixteen-pounders on both sides of the stern," she filled in, "and a big twenty-pound chaser, so we can't attack her rear. We'll have to concentrate on her bow and waist, at least in the beginnin'. I think we should stick with loadin' chains on our port side and canister shot on our starboard. I'm afraid if we fire any cannonball, we'll punch a hole large enough to sink her and defeat our entire purpose."

"Even worse," Fergus picked up, "there wouldn't be anythin' to salvage fer the compound. Livin' on a deserted island is one thing, sleepin' in a tent every night is another. I'm lookin' forward to tearin' that ship down and havin' somethin' solid over my head, especially durin' the stormy season." Meeting her eye, he followed up, "What's the plan?"

Squinting, she stated, "Let's come along her starboard and take out her sails with a volley from our port. Once she's dead in the water, we'll circle back around her stern to cross her bow on our starboard and then, when we're in position, ye'll lead the boardin' party over in the skiffs while I'll provide cover with a barrage of shot down her deck."

"Are ye sure? That could very well kill the captain."

"He's a coward," she insisted. "I'm sure he'll keep his head down." While quickly braiding her hair and tying it in a bun on the top of her head, she continued, "Since this is the first the world will hear of us, I think it'll make fer a better story if we use overwhelmin' force."

"No warnin' shots?"

"Why bother? It's a waste of ammunition." Producing her flask, she shook the contents and concluded, "I'm goin' to give the boys some liquid courage. Bring us within earshot and let's give those Spaniards somethin' to stew about."

Clarkeson left the helm and passed her flask among her men. Wading through the throng, she called to them by name and patted their shoulders or nudged their arms. Their countenances concealed under long hair and shaggy beards, they too were dressed in black, and though some had ebony skin, most were various shades of brown. Upon reaching the waist of her brigantine, she could hear the Spanish captain aboard the fluyt relaying orders to his troops. Stepping between the bulwark and the middle skiff, she stared at the other vessel and, in Gaelic, commanded, "SEAS AR AIRE! [Attention]."

Immediately, her crew faced *The Empire's Reach* and formed into five ranks of ten assembled into three rows of three with a leader in front. Clasping her hands behind her back, Clarkeson watched the sunlight sparkle off the mercenaries taking up defensive positions. "I know only a few of ye understand what it's like to live under the iron fist of a king like the pig on the throne in England," she started, "but most of ye do know what it's like to have yer lives stolen when pigs like that captain over there ripped ye from yer homeland and brought ye across the ocean." Spinning around, she pointed at them and shouted, "Which means ye know what it's like to be chained to a hull, ye know how it feels to be sold at a market, and ye know what it means to live under Spanish rule! If fer some reason ye don't remember, go ahead and touch the scars crossin' yer backs!" Silently, she let them glower at the other vessel for a count of thirty, then holding up two fingers on each hand, she went on, "At this very moment, there's two dozen of those bastards over there, two dozen dogs who beat, tortured, and enslaved yer people." Smiling wide, she screamed, "And today's yer day to exact some vengeance!"

"FAUGH A BALLAGH! [clear the way]," Fergus boomed.

"FAUGH A BALLAGH!" their crew repeated.

"That's right!" Clarkeson followed up, spreading her arms wide. "Faugh a ballagh! That's our battle cry! And as ye go down the deck, clear those Spaniards off it! FAUGH A BALLAGH!"

"FAUGH A BALLAGH! FAUGH A BALLAGH! FAUGH A BALLAGH!"

Her smile harsh, she waited until their shouting subsided, raised her left index finger, and ordered, "The sailors, however, are another matter. Many are no different than ye, and fer our cause to succeed, we'll need more real men to take it up. Remember, yer not pirates, yer warriors, and ye fight fer a greater purpose. When the Spanish are slaughtered, the killin' must end." Lowering her voice, she sneered and seethed, "More than anythin', I want that captain brought to me alive. His punishment will announce my reign to the world! FAUGH A BALLAGH!"

While the chanting repeated anew, Clarkeson returned to the helm and relieved Fergus of the wheel. Taking charge of the boarding party, he ordered, "SUIDHEACHADH [ready positions]," and the sailors in the first rank took up stations in the rigging, while three of remaining four ranks climbed down the ladders to the gun deck. The fifth stayed topside, and in pairs, they checked the ties holding the skiffs. At her cry of "CASADH AR CHLE [left turn]," the big gaff sail swung to the right, sending *The Black Irish* hard to the port on a course toward *The Empire's Reach*. Once they closed to within range of their cannon, she brought her brigantine alongside the fluyt, tightened her grip on the wheel, and shouted, "SCAOIL URCHAR! [open fire]"

Simultaneously, the ten cannons on their port side erupted, rocking *The Black Irish* far enough for the sea to splash over her starboard. With a high-pitched whine, thousands of iron balls connected by chains twirled through the shroud of thick acrid smoke, randomly tearing through canvas, rope, steel, and tissue. Crumpling almost instantaneously, the mainsail and its blood-red Cross of England disappeared under the black haze.

"CASADH AR DHEIS! [right turn]," she cried, and the big gaff swung to their left, turning *The Black Irish* to its starboard side. Keeping their distance, they circled around the fluyt's stern and sailed along her port. Though the battered vessel's sails hung tattered from their spars, the momentum carried it out of the smog.

Joining Clarkeson at the helm, Fergus watched the surviving mercenaries cut at the canvas draped over the deck and concluded, "She'll be dead in the water soon. It's time to get ready to board her." Meeting her eye, he made his way to the nearest ladder and added, "We're goin' to be exposed on the way over. I'm countin' on ye to make sure I'm not a martyr."

Watching him disappear down to the gun deck, she called out, "Don't worry. I've got yer back."

As *The Empire's Reach* glided to a stop, Clarkeson brought *The Black Irish* across her bow and ordered, "CUIR NA SCIFEANNA SAN FHARRAIGE! [launch skiffs]" Immediately, the men tending the skiffs launched them into the sea off the port side and kept them tied in a line along the waist. Her gaze to the starboard, she watched the Spaniards hurrying to clear their deck of the remaining debris, and with a cruel smile creeping over her lips, she tightened her grip on the wheel. When a swell lifted her brigantine higher than the fluyt, she ordered, "SCAOIL URCHAR! [open fire]"

This time, the ten cannons on the starboard side erupted and a fusillade of tens of thousands of tiny lead balls blasted through the armor protecting the mercenaries on the way to the flesh underneath. Under the blanket of smoke, Fergus led two ranks to the main deck. Each man carried a ten-foot length of rope slung over his shoulder, a cutlass (a broadsword with a slightly curved blade) at his waist, and a buckler (a little round shield) covering a fist. Quickly, they climbed into the skiffs and cast off. The fourth rank, holding flintlock rifles, stood in three rows of three along the bulwark under the command of their leader. He was short with light-brown skin, a wide chest, stubby legs, thick arms, and graying dreadlocks on his balding head long enough to blend in with those of his beard.

"Yer up Ben," Clarkeson told him. "Make sure they keep their heads down."

"If they don't," Ben replied, "they'll lose 'em."

The boarding party on their way, Clarkeson ordered, "CASADH AR DHEIS! [right turn]" and slowly she brought the starboard side of her ship along the starboard side of the fluyt. Seeing a glittering Spanish helmet through the smog, Ben ordered, "CUSPAIRICH! [fire at will]"

With a loud pop, the first three muskets discharged, and to a sharp ring, the helmet flipped into the air. As the mercenary wearing it collapsed to the deck, the first row of musketeers vacated their positions and fell to the rear of the line. The second row immediately stepped up, took aim at another adversary, fired, and dropped back. Following the same routine, the third took their turn, and by the time they pulled their triggers, the first was ready to go again. The medley of metallic clangs, heart-wrenching screams, and grisly spurts of blood affirming their deadly efficiency, the riflemen kept a steady stream of fire on the hapless fluyt. Clarkeson checked on the progress of the boarding party. Having reached the other bow, they began casting their ropes over the bulwark and climbing up the hull. "COINNIGH SIAR D'URCHAR! [hold your fire]" she yelled to Ben. He repeated the order and the flintlocks quieted.

Leading the way, Fergus scrambled over the side, raised his claymore, and cried, "FAUGH A BALLAGH!" Repeating his call, the rest of his men formed a tight wedge bristling with sharpened steel around him, and as a unit, they moved in the direction he pointed his sword. A few Spaniards attempted to fight but were mercilessly chopped down, and recognizing their hopeless situation, the final six retreated to the helm with their leader.

Crashing the wedge into their defensive line, Fergus swung his giant sword at the Spanish captain, smashing away his opponent's raised saber and cutting off the top third of his head. The rest of mercenaries scattering, they were quickly surrounded and, in succumbing to the vicious blows, their cries of pain resonated over the crescendo of ringing steel. As they fell one by one to the deck, the sounds of the battle faded until the English captain, sobbing heavily, cowered alone at his wheel.

Still at her helm, Clarkeson noticed the sun reflecting off several armored bodies being tossed into the sea, and untying her braid, she let her hair tumble down about her breasts. Her crew quickly tethered the starboard side of *The Black Irish* to the starboard side of *The Empire's Reach*, and she climbed up the lanyards the boarding party had cast. Landing in a crouch on the other deck, she picked a single steel helmet rolling around the bow, and tapping the circular dent deep in the forehead, muttered, "Welcome to a new world," before throwing it into the water. Picking her way through the battle damage, she found Fergus at the stern, guarding the bound and gagged English captain. Another half dozen British sailors were huddled along the bulwark, and looking them over, she declared in Gaelic, "That couldn't have gone any better!"

His bright blue eyes shining, Fergus wiped his forehead, leaving a red smear, and replied, "Aye, the trainin' really paid off!"

"Now that our men know they don't have to fear the sight of Europeans anymore," she followed up, "they can be confident goin' up against British marines. Ye should've seen the helmet I found. Even if the shot didn't kill whoever was wearin' it, he had to be out cold when ye slit his throat and threw him overboard."

"If he was out cold," Fergus mentioned, "we didn't bother to slit his throat."

Cackling harshly, she responded, "Even better. What about our casualties?"

Pointing his claymore toward a row of feet sticking out below a bloody remnant of canvas, Fergus reported, "A few of those Spanish bastards fought to the bitter end."

Frowning, she asked, "How many did we lose?"

"Six dead and the same amount wounded. Luckily, none of the injured are unconscious and nobody lost an arm or a leg. The surgeon says, beyond sewin' their cuts, his biggest worry is infection."

Biting her bottom lip, Clarkeson remarked, "Worryin' about an infection is enough. We better expect to lose a few more. I hope we find some new recruits. Where's James?"

Still using his sword, Fergus directed her attention midships to three men circled around a fourth and said, "Already workin' on it." Standing in the middle, James was tall and skinny with dark skin and long thin dreadlocks tipped in gray.

"Perfect," Clarkeson remarked, switching to English. "Then let's get this over with. Where's Ben?"

"Searchin' fer the manifest," Fergus told her. He kicked the captain at his feet and went on, "We tried askin' this pig nicely to give it to us, but he just kept blubberin' on and on. It got so bad nobody could understand a word he said."

No longer wearing the gold-trimmed black hat or the bright orange vest, the Englishman strained against the chains binding his hands to his ankles and the torn piece of sail stuck in his mouth. Little black holes tinged in red peppered his navy-blue tunic, and a steady stream of blood flowed out of a gash above his left temple. Squatting down, Clarkeson bored her dark gaze into his soul and asked, "Is there somethin' yer hidin'?" His eyes wide and wild, he shook his head and let out several muffled screams. Giving the gag a little tug, she asked Fergus, "What happens if I take it out?"

"He'll probably cry like a little girl again."

Clarkeson held up her left index finger and waved it until the English captain settled down. While he took several short gasps of air through his nose, she calmly inquired, "Now is that true? If I take yer gag out, are ye goin' to start cryin' like a little girl again? Because bein' a grown woman, I can assure ye, nobody cares." To his several muffled, high-pitched "nos," she glared at him and warned, "God forbid yer lyin', fer if I have to put it back, ye better take the deepest breath ye can. Rest assured, it'll be yer last."

Callously, she slid the rag clear of his mouth, and immediately, the English captain sputtered, "Why did ye . . . why did ye . . . why did ye destroy my ship? Whatever the cost, I would've paid your ransom!"

"Well, Johnny boy," she began with her evil smile, "I destroyed yer ship because ye christened it *The Empire's Reach* and I want the world to know that ends where I stand."

"How did ye . . . how do ye . . . how did ye know my name?"

Slowly shaking her head, she disclosed, "I know more than yer name. I know where yer from, I know where yer goin', and most importantly, I know everythin' yer haulin'." Snapping her eye toward the rest of the British prisoners, she told them, "And I know the same about all of ye. Should I ask ye a question, ye better be honest."

"If ye already know all that," Captain Johnny cried, "then ye know I don't have any gold aboard. There's nothing ye could possibly want!"

Arching her left eyebrow, Clarkeson returned, "I think I'll be the judge of that." Seeing Ben emerge up the ladder behind the helm, she rose from her haunches and, baring her teeth, growled, "Well, well, well, Ben, yer timin' is impeccable. He just told me he's got nothin' we could possibly want. What do ye think?"

Solemnly, Ben shook his head, handed her the manifest, pointed to an entry, and stated, "I think he's a liar."

"WHAT!" Captain Johnny screamed.

Ignoring him, Clarkeson read the entry and followed up, "I think he's a liar too."

Gasping desperately, Captain Johnny insisted, "No, no, I'm not lyin' about anything! There's no gold aboard!"

Gnashing her teeth, she looked at Ben and suggested, "Either he doesn't know what gold is or he thinks we can't read."

Holding her gaze, Ben suggested, "Or maybe he just thinks we're stupid."

"I don't know what yer talking about!" Captain Johnny cried.

In a single swift movement, Clarkeson crouched down, held the manifest before his face, and with the middle finger of her right hand, pointed to a single line. "What does this say!" she yelled. Watching his eyes move across the page, she scrunched her face and went on, "Ye better tell the truth!"

His lips quivering, he stated, "It doesn't say anythin' about gold!"

Through the manifest, she smacked him with the back of her left hand hard enough to bounce his head off the deck. While he writhed in pain, she placed her finger to his nose and sneered, "I told ye to tell the truth. It's only goin' to get worse if ye lie to me again." Returning the paper to his face, she ordered, "Now answer me question. What does this say?"

Blinking, he followed her finger across the page and recited, "9/29 . . . two barrels . . . Whiskey."

"It's called Oakies!" she screamed and snatched it away. "Now tell me, how many slaves did ye trade fer two barrels of me Oakies?"

"None," he divulged, shaking his head, "I couldn't trade in slaves. I had to purchase them in gold."

"Purchase them in gold?" Clarkeson repeated, tilting her head to the right. "I thought ye said ye didn't have any gold."

"I don't anymore," Captain Johnny whimpered. Straining against the chains, he attempted to cover his face and divulged, "I used all I had to buy those barrels."

She took a deep breath, let him relax, and backhanded him with her right hand. Her blow broke his nose, and blood splattered across the manifest. She crumpled it up, threw it away, and leaning forward, held her index finger to his chin. "I knew ye were lyin'!" she exclaimed. "Any whiskey good enough to make a cheap bastard like ye willin' to spend all yer gold must be worth more than the gold itself! Personally, I call Oakies liquid gold, fer there's nothin' I value more in the entire world!" Though his features were still frozen, she continued to scream, "Let me ask ye another question. Since I'm at war with Britain, tell me what would happen if the Royal Navy gave me Oakies a try and decided to ration it to their sailors instead of rum. I'll tell ye what would happen: they'd grow some balls and be willin' to fight! Believe me, as much as I love killin' the English, it sure is satisfyin' to see them tuck their tails and run like the cowardly dogs they are."

Suddenly, James tapped her shoulder and, in Gaelic, noted, "I hope we didn't miss the show." Nodding to his gaunt companions, he gave her a wink and added, "They would've been disappointed if we had."

Leaving Captain Johnny to hover in and out of consciousness, she rose and responded, "Tell them the best is yet to come. Does this mean they've joined the cause?"

James shrugged and admitted, "Well, I'm not sure if they understand what cause it is they're joinin' or if they even care, but they do understand if they fight fer us, they'll have a place to sleep and get three meals a day. Look at how skinny they are. Given the assurance they'll simply be fed was the only convincin' it took."

Crossing her arms, she asked, "Do they know they could end up dead?"

"They pretty much already are. Fer men like these, any sort of existence is better than the alternative."

"Then introduce them to me," she ordered.

Gesturing to the tallest of the three, a man with light-brown skin, curly black hair, and bare cheeks, James said, "This is Alifoe. He's one of the Ewe people. Those tribes are always on the move around Ghana, so it's hard to pinpoint exactly where he's from." Raising his eyebrows, he predicted, "And I'll bet he has a hard time growin' a beard."

"That's fine," Clarkeson returned. "We need people to do more than fight. We'll find somethin' fer him. What about the other two?"

Nodding to their second recruit, who had dark skin, a round head, and a sturdy frame capable of holding significantly more muscle, James went on, "That's Alvaro. He's a Kongo, and I doubt he'll have any problem growin' a beard. Plus, he claims to already know how to fire a musket."

"Perfect," she followed up, "then he can learn how to fire a flintlock. What about the last one?"

Shorter than the other two, the third recruit had straight black hair, tan skin, and a stout body. Shrugging, James had to admit, "To be honest, I'm not really sure what his name is. I think it's somethin' along the lines of Manicatoex, although the other two simply called him Mo."

"Ye don't speak his language?" Clarkeson asked. "I thought ye knew them all."

"While I know most of the African languages and those from Europe," James stated, "he's a Taino and native to these islands, and I haven't learned his yet. I hope we can teach each other."

"Do ye think he'll be able to sail in Gaelic?" she asked.

"Actually, he's not a sailor," James replied. "He's a cook."

Grinning wide, she exclaimed, "Now that's good news indeed. The chef has needed an aide ever since his last one ate a poisonous frog and died. Once we get home, we'll turn him loose on our island and see what he finds."

"I'm all fer that," Fergus chipped in.

Clarkeson patted his shoulder and determined, "I'm sure ye are, but we're gettin' ahead of ourselves. Let's finish what we came here to do." Over Captain Johnny whimpering at her feet, she addressed the British prisoners huddled at the stern. Starting in Gaelic, she proclaimed, "Fer those of ye blessed to understand my sacred tongue, this is yer chance to join a meaningful cause and get some purpose in yer life, unless, of course, ye prefer breakin' yer back to make fat pigs like this one even fatter. If ye sail with me, ye'll always have a roof over yer head, ye'll always get three meals a day, and," producing her silver flask, she went on, "ye'll always get a daily ration of the best whiskey the world has ever known." Bringing it to her lips, she took a healthy swallow, let out a sigh, and announced, "If that life sounds better than the one yer currently livin', then this is the only language ye take orders in. Let the dogs answer to the pagans."

She put her flask away, turned her thumbs to her chest, and switching to English, declared, "My name is Clarkeson and the Caribbean is my sea!" Nodding toward the shredded remains of the Union Jack, she vowed, "And from this day ferward, any vessel sailin' under those colors is subject to search, and any captain I catch with a barrel of me Oakies aboard will be sentenced to death." While Captain Johnny's whimpers turned to sobs, she ignored them and, spreading her arms wide, furthered, "I suppose I could mete out the same fate to the rest of ye, but in a testament to me mercy, I won't. Instead, I'll grant ye the chance I didn't receive, the chance to survive." Pointing east, she put forth, "Jamaica is no more than a day away. We've loaded a skiff with enough food and fresh water to make it. Whether ye do or not is up to ye." Letting her wicked smile cross her lips, she followed up, "And just to prove there's no hard feelin's, I'm even givin' ye a couple firkins of me Oakies. Once ye give it a taste, ye'll understand why any Englishman lookin' to purchase it had better be ready to pay in blood." Placing her hands on her hips, she concluded, "Now, get up and be gone. I could still change me mind."

Of the six British sailors huddled on the deck, four followed her orders and left in the waiting skiff. Offering the other two her hand, Clarkeson stated, "Eirigh agus bi linn [rise and join us]," and they climbed to their feet to stand beside her. She then squatted down and, patting Captain Johnny on his forearm, told him, "Since I'm not sinkin' this ship, ye won't be goin' down in it, but don't worry, I've got somethin' more suitable fer ye." At that, Fergus and Ben picked him up under his armpits, chained him to an empty skiff, and sent him over the starboard side. Waiting in another skiff already in the water, James tethered the two little boats together, towed the condemned man to the rear of *The Black Irish*, and cut him free. Standing at the bow of

The Empire's Reach, Clarkeson raised her left hand and called out, "Any last words?"

Bobbing up and down in the waves, Captain Johnny screamed, "I hope you burn in hell, you Irish cunt!"

Cackling harshly, she murmured, "So much easier this way," and dropped her hand to her side. With the released prisoners watching, a single chaser fired an entire canister of shot—obliterating both man and skiff—and a swirling mishmash of wooden splinters, bone fragments, and blood disappeared under the sea. . .

The Scottish Rose: Mairi, Connor, Angus
The Wasp: Mark
The Hornet: Mathew
La Bonita Senorita: Ricardo DeLogrono

CHAPTER 2

October 1, 1785, Kingston, Jamaica

As the first inch of the beeswax candle on the mantel behind the bar melted away, the first metal pin fell from the left side of the stick and rattled about in the brass drip catcher. Looking to the bright orange flame, the old sea captain slowly stroked his bushy white beard and, to a roll of thunder fading in the distance, concluded, "While I suppose ye could say that fateful day was the start of it all, the legend of Oakies was actually conceived the previous summer, when King Louis XV of France sent his master of horse, a Scot named James Butler, on a tour through England."

Squinting, Rags put forth, "That doesn't make any sense. What would a tour through England by the master of horse for a French king have to do with a whisky in the Caribbean?"

To his left, a man sitting on the last stool before the corner interrupted, "You know, heh-heh, I served aboard many a vessel during those years." He had arrived halfway through the story, quietly occupied his usual spot, and silently, Sarah had poured his usual glass of claret. Though wrinkles lined his face and his eyes possessed a peculiar glossy shine, he still had a full head of silver hair and perfectly straight, gleaming white teeth. Dressed in a black suit with an ivory blouse, he kept his jacket on and his pants pulled up to his navel in a feeble attempt to hide his portly torso. On his left ring finger, he wore a chunky gold wedding band and, on his right wrist, a thick gold link bracelet. To its clattering off the bar, he set down his wine and went on, "Of course, heh-heh, we all served in some capacity back then. I was a sailor, heh-heh, but if you weren't a sailor, then you were a pirate or a privateer, heh-heh. I may have been a privateer at one time or another, heh-heh, but I was never a pirate, heh-heh. At a minimum, I made certain the captain of every ship I sailed on was issued letters of marque, heh-heh."

Raising his hand between them, Rags snapped, "Jesus Christ Jack, would you get to your point?"

"Well, heh-heh, this reminds me of the stories us sailors used to tell of the return of Anne Bonny, heh-heh."

"Jack," Rags declared, holding his palm high, "I swear on my mother's grave, that's exactly what I said. Only none of them will believe me."

Waving his right index finger, the old sea captain insisted, "That's because yer both mistaken. Anne Bonny was a pirate, plain and simple. Like Grace O'Malley, Clarkeson was a noble warrior fightin' fer a cause, and had Butler had not gone to England, her legend might have never been born."

"Why?" Tony chipped in. "What did Butler have to do with Clarkeson?"

The old sea captain took a healthy swallow of lager, set his mug down, and turned upon his stool to face the entire room. "Fer those of ye too young to recall," he began, "it really started in 1740 after the death of Charles VI, who, at the time, ruled the Austrian Habsburg monarchy and was, accordingly, the Holy Roman Emperor. Since he didn't father a son, he had no direct heir and he tried to leave everythin' to his oldest daughter,

Maria Theresa. Unfortunately, the rest of the powers had their own ideas about how his inheritance should be divided, and in the way of kings, fightin' soon broke out over his successor. Seein' that England and Spain were already goin' at it in a war limited to the Caribbean, whatever that is, they were only too happy to have a reason to go all out on the mainland and they forced the rest of Europe to choose sides." Juggling his hands, he furthered, "With ties to both countries, the French did their best to stay neutral. Nevertheless, in the course of time, it became more and more apparent they'd be joinin' the Spanish, until in 1743, they finally did. Hopin' to end it quickly, King Louis XV hatched a plan involvin' the Scots." Raising his left index finger, he noted, "Ye see, despite the French givin' up on James Francis Stuart, also known as the Old Pretender, following his failed rebellion in 1715, they did foster him in Rome, where he successfully set up a court in exile and had a son, Charles Edward Stuart, five years later."

"Wasn't Charles Edward Stuart known as the Young Pretender?" Tony picked up.

"That he was," the old sea captain replied, smiling wide.

"I thought he was known as the Bonnie Prince Charlie," Sarah put forth.

"That is true as well," the old sea captain confirmed, nodding her way. "And havin' been raised with a firm belief in the divine right of kings, he grew up believin' the British throne to be rightfully his. By twenty, his demeanor had earned him quite the reputation in France, fer they called him the Young Chevalier, and confident in his burgeonin' Scottish prince, King Louis XV decided to, once again, fund a Jacobean restoration."

"You still haven't told us what any of this has to do with Butler," Rags interjected. "Yeah, heh-heh," Jack concurred, "what does this have to do with Butler?"

Picking up his drink, the old sea captain remarked, "I'm gettin' to it." He downed the rest, wiped the froth from his lips, and setting the empty mug on the bar, went on, "While his plot did seem well thought out, the French king had one big problem—thirty years had passed since the Old Pretender's defeat and the Young Pretender had never actually set foot in Scotland, so there was no way to know if he would garner any support. To find out, Butler was sent to England that August under the guise of purchasin' new bloodlines fer the royal stables, and in October, he delivered his report. Satisfied that enough acrimony still existed to stir up trouble, the king decided to go ahead and put his plan in motion. First, Charles was given the title of Prince Regent and granted the authority to act in the name of his father. Then in December, he secretly left fer France, where the famous French general Maurice de Saxe waited with 10,000 men at Dunkirk." Widening his bright blue eyes, the old sea captain concluded, "To be sure, given her feelin's fer the English, the moment Clarkeson caught wind of a possible invasion, she was only too happy to take up the fight."

"That's impossible," Rags pointed out. "It takes at least two months for news to travel across the Atlantic, and if she took her first ship on October 1st, it means Butler hadn't even returned yet. I don't care if she was some sort of water sprite. There's no way she knew of any impending invasion."

"Of course not," the old sea captain allowed with a shrug, "she wasn't made privy to everythin'. But she had heard firsthand accounts of the Young Chevalier, she was told the name Maurice de Saxe was bein' bantered around, and most of all, she was well aware of Butler's travels. Knowin' the contempt many Jacobites felt toward the British king, especially among the highland clans in Scotland, she was certain his visit would secure the necessary aid."

At the table behind the old sea captain, the man in the red vest sat next to the aisle, with his back to the bar. Turning to his left to listen, he inserted, "Knowing a few Irishmen, I get why Clarkeson took up the cause. Yet I don't see why she made such a big deal out of the Oakies."

Sitting directly across, the man in the green vest followed up, "Yes, it's one thing to seize a ship. It's quite another to execute the captain in cold blood. She'd have to know if she were caught, she'd be executed. I can't believe there has ever been a whisky worth the hangman's noose at Gallows Point."

Nodding their way, the old sea captain asserted, "Now there's a keen observation." As the rain began to echo off the roof, he picked up his mug and swallowed the few drops of lager that had gathered in the bottom. Setting it down, he went on, "And to be sure, the shortest answer I can give ye involves telling a longer story."

"Since the last one was worth a pint," the man in green put forth.

"We'll be glad to purchase his next," the man in red offered.

"Put it on our tab," they both said together.

Tilting his head their way, the old sea captain returned, "Thank ye kindly, good sirs." While Sarah refilled his drink, he glanced between them and noted, "Ye two look alike. Are ye related?"

"We sure are," the man in red confirmed. "We're twins. Just like the islands we were born on. I'm John."

"And I'm Luke," the man in green followed up. "We grew up on Nevis and now live on Saint Kitts."

"May I ask who these lovely ladies are?" the old sea captain inquired.

Proudly, the brothers answered, "Our beautiful brides." Luke held the woman in red's left hand, showing off the large rose-cut diamond on her ring finger, and stated, "This is Lina."

His arm around the woman in green, whose stone was fashioned in the traditional old mine style, John added, "And this is Ginevra."

"They make us the luckiest men in the world."

"We came to Kingston to celebrate our marriages," Luke divulged.

"Regrettably, this hurricane has put a damper on things," John conceded.

"At least ye have beautiful company to survive it," the old sea captain posed. Giving them a wink, he furthered, "And if it were me, I'd thank God fer this storm."

Suddenly, to a burst of wind, the door opened and every head turned to watch a man in a long black cloak duck under the entry. At his arrival, Sarah instinctively poured a mug of lager and set it down before the stool to the left of Jack, where the newcomer would be able to look down the length of the bar. Once he had settled in, she met his dark-brown eyes and mentioned, "Good to see you, Brass, you came at a good time. The gentleman at the other end is telling a pretty good story."

His skin light brown, Brass kept his head shaved bald and trimmed his beard into thick sable muttonchops meeting at his mustache. Two silver hoops pierced his left ear lobe, several silver skull-shaped rings adorned his fingers, and a bracelet of tiny silver skulls wrapped around his right wrist. With his tight black sweater accentuating his well-defined muscles, he directed a surly look at the old sea captain and, in a menacing voice, asked, "What's his story about?"

"Heh-heh, a pirate," Jack offered.

"Anne Bonny," Rags insisted.

"Neither," the old sea captain corrected, shaking his head. "To some, it's called the Legend of Old One-Eyed Clarkeson, to others it's the Story of Mairi."

"Mairi?" Tony repeated. "Who's Mairi?"

Beaming, the old sea captain smiled and asserted, "Mairi was the only person strong enough to tame the spirit of whiskey." Picking up his fresh mug, he took a quick swig, turned to face the room, and over a steady pitter-patter of rain, began, "She was a young Scot born in Port Glasgow who was only ten years old when her mother's death forced her aboard her father's ship. Through her teens, he taught her both how to sail and the business of sailin' on the way to seein' her become a captain of her own accord. Those who dealt with her insisted she was the real brains behind Oakies, though they never did so in her presence. Fer, to be sure, the moment she heard Clarkeson had bestowed that name upon her whiskey, she made it a point to let the world know exactly what she thought of it . . ."

Mid-October 1743, off the southern coast of Culebra, an island just west of Puerto Rico

With her head covered under a bonnet woven in a red, white, and blue tartan, Mairi drank her coffee alone at the bow of her schooner, *The Scottish Rose*, and watched the fiery-orange sunrise brighten the horizon to her right. Barefoot, she wore tan breeches and a baggy long-sleeved kelly-green shirt that partially obscured the thin black leather belt strung through a canvas pouch on each hip. At the sound of a clumsy shuffle behind her, she directed her attention forward to the emerald island emerging out of the shadows and stated, "Good morning, Connor, come join me. It's time ye learn all about my favorite Irishman, Paddy, and his pub on Culebra."

Clad in a dingy white shirt hanging loosely off his torso and bell-bottomed tan trousers a bit too short for his long gangly legs, Connor leaned over and rested his long gangly forearms on the railing atop the bulwark to her right. Along with everyone else working at the distillery, his flaming red hair was cropped close to his head and his baby face was clean-shaven, although he had only began sprouting peach fuzz on his upper lip sometime in the past two weeks. Following her gaze toward their destination, he cast his light blue eyes across the white sandy beaches lining the shore and inquired, "Are ye sure anybody even lives here? It looks deserted."

"I'm sure," Mairi confirmed. "Ye just can't see his place right now."

Frowning, Connor followed up, "Then how does anyone know it exists?"

Her mug between her hands, she used it to point out an opening taking up almost half the southern seaboard and explained, "That's the entrance fer a deep-water harbor protected to the north and east, makin' it quite possibly the safest location in the entire Caribbean to weather a storm. During a hurricane, it doesn't matter who's at war, ye'll have ships of every nation shelterin' inside under an informal truce, at least until the worst has passed." Lifting her mug to her lips, she asserted, "And the moment ye enter, ye can't help but notice Paddies. In the short time he's been here, he's already gained regulars from every part of the world." A three-masted polacca flying a red flag embroidered with the golden Lion of Saint Mark holding a Bible ventured out through the gap, and identifying the vessel's colors, she went on, "See, there's a Venetian."

"Are there any other settlements?"

She took a sip and, shaking her head, replied, "Not yet. This little island is considered a part of Puerto Rico, and since the Spanish didn't find any gold, they left it uninhabited."

"Do they know about Paddies?"

"They do."

"Why do they let him stay?"

"Because over the years, the harbor has also provided a refuge fer the pirates and privateers raidin' the treasure galleons sailin' out of San Juan," she filled in, "and Paddy convinced the Spanish his presence would bring the traffic needed to keep them at bay."

"How did ye meet him?"

She cackled happily and responded, "Pure chance. He originally left Boston bound fer Kingston and just happened to walk into Henry's on the very same mornin' I was makin' a delivery." Patting the canvas pouch on her right hip, she carried on, "Like I do fer anyone I meet, I poured him a dram out of my flask, hopin' he'd order an ounce. Except he claimed that it was my lucky day and told me to give him passage, sayin' an Irishman would bring me good luck and he was the luckiest of all."

His voice cracking and popping, Connor asked, "And ye agreed?"

"In case of a fight," she mentioned, "my father always had a few Irishmen in his crew, and to that end, Paddy is no exception, so quite honestly, the second I heard his accent, he reminded me of home. Still, I didn't actually agree to anythin' until I heard his plan. I'm not goin' to lie, at first I thought he was mad and it didn't stand a chance, especially seein', beyond the gold, the Spanish didn't find any fresh water here either. Yet he was payin' in coin, and considerin' Henry was my one customer at the time, I figured if Paddy was lucky enough to pull off his crazy scheme, then I'd be lucky enough to have a second one." Dumping the dregs in her mug overboard, she concluded, "In the end, I decided why not, I didn't have anythin' to lose."

At close to sixty feet, *The Scottish Rose* warranted two masts and though the foremast was shorter than the main, each employed the same single large trapezoidal gaff sail extending toward the stern. Because of a headwind, they uniformly swung side to side, and on a zigzagging course, the schooner continued into the harbor. At the entrance, however, the coastline wound back to the northwest in a large half circle, and following it, the small craft approached three large vessels anchored in a hidden cove directly opposite the mouth.

With the morning light reflecting sharply off a little white pier sticking out from the beach, Connor covered his brows and asked, "What was his plan?"

Producing a spyglass out of the pouch on her left hip, Mairi raised it to her right eye and returned, "Do ye remember me tellin' ye how the Kingdom of Naples and Sicily stayed neutral durin' the current war?"

"I thought ye said the Royal Navy sent a fleet to Naples with orders to bombard the city if they didn't."

"That's correct," she confirmed with a nod, "so I suppose they didn't really have much choice. Regardless, they accepted the terms, and to this day, they allow any ship, no matter her flag, access to their ports. Bein' in the middle of all that trade has made both the cities of Naples and Palermo very rich, and knowin' there wasn't any equivalent in the Caribbean, Paddy came up with the idea to provide one. Havin' heard of the aura already surroundin' this place, he figured it would be a perfect spot to give it a try and wanted me to bring him to see it. All it took was a single walk across the white sand, and that was that. I dropped him off in San Juan to do what he needed to do to make it happen."

"I take it his plan worked out," Connor determined.

"It has so far," she replied, lowering her spyglass, "and since two of those men-of-war are British sloops and the third is a Spanish galleon, it looks like it still may be." Tracking a thin wisp of smoke down until it disappeared into the darkness of the tree line, she went on, "But I've learned to expect the unexpected at Paddies, and it's quite possible we'll arrive one mornin' to a bunch of dead bodies strewn about." Nodding to the helm of *The Scottish Rose*, she ordered, "Come on, let's go talk to Angus. It's best to have a plan of our own."

Being fifteen feet at the widest point, her schooner had very little room aboard for the full barrels of whiskey they intended to deliver, let alone all the extra empties they picked up along the way. Forced to climb around casks of all sizes stowed in every available space, Connor had to wait until they were midships to inquire, "How does he do it?"

"Do what?"

"Keep the peace."

Turning her palms over, Mairi asserted, "Paddy's got this air, and fer some reason, people are willin' to respect his three rules."

"Three rules? What are they?"

"Well, first off, he doesn't allow any steel to be brought ashore. He says if the fights are kept to bare fists, it's unlikely any real blood will be spilt and doubtful things'll get completely out of hand."

Raising his eyebrows, Connor glanced at her left wrist and asked, "Does that mean ye won't have yer dagger?"

Sliding back her sleeve, she exposed a slim black leather handle strapped to the inside of her forearm and revealed, "Oh no, I've got it. I've always got it. I'd rather be safe than sorry. Make no mistake, no matter how else these men may seem, every one of them is dangerous." Snapping her fingers, she continued, "And in a second, all hell can break loose."

"Then why do they bother listenin' to him at all?"

"His second rule," Mairi stated, "which is really the key to everythin'. He gets a cut out of every deal made at his bar, which puts his business squarely in the center of everyone else's, and, as my father used to say, when people are makin' money, they rarely mess with business. In fact, the last time I stopped in, he said business had gotten so good that he no longer worries they'll start fightin' the war. If anythin', he's afraid it'll end."

Tilting his head, Connor admitted, "That somehow makes sense."

Letting out another happy cackle, she commented, "It's all a part of Paddy's way. Now, remember yer role. Yer not to speak unless yer spoken to. Yer to listen in on every conversation, no matter how insignificant ye think it is. Ye never know, you may hear somethin' that may one day save our lives."

Connor gave her a curt nod, and as they continued on, he asked, "What's his third rule?"

"His third rule," Mairi repeated, bobbing her head, "hmmm, when it comes to his third rule, Paddy tends to be a little . . . Irish."

"What's that supposed to mean?"

"Well," she explained, "his third rule is that on his island, everyone must go barefoot. He claims these beaches have magical powers."

"Magical powers?" Connor questioned.

"Aye," she responded, rolling her eyes. "Despite bein' Catholic, he never forgot his lore and he insists there's fairy dust sprinkled in this sand and if ye walk barefoot over it, ye lose yer will to fight. He says it happens to him all the time."

They arrived at the helm and gathered around Angus at the wheel. Taller than Connor, he had the same bright blue eyes and short red hair, except the sleeves of his white shirt were tight on his arms, and if Mairi would let him, he would happily grow a full flaming-red beard. "Two Brits and a Spaniard," he observed in a low voice. "Paddy looks busy today."

"He does at that," Mairi agreed. "I hope it's quiet because they're still sleepin' and not because they're dead."

"I don't see any signs of a battle," Angus noted.

"Maybe we just can't see the damage," she advised. "Ye know how Paddies can get. I don't want to make any assumptions."

"Then what do ye want to do?"

Gesturing to the galleon, she told him, "Come alongside the big one first, and if everythin' checks out, we'll take a quick peek at the other two. No matter what though, the entire time I'm gone with Connor, I want ye to keep our ship at the ready. Paddy may be confident he can keep everythin' under control, I prefer to be confident we can leave in a hurry."

Sparkling in the morning sun, the Spanish vessel was one hundred twenty feet long with a trio of decks and a trio of masts that supported a fighting platform in between the spars for their two gigantic square sails. At her stern (carved to resemble a brick turret, painted red, and inlaid with gold), oversized bronze letters spelled out the name *La Bonita Señorita* below a flag consisting of one bright yellow horizontal stripe in the middle of two that were crimson red. Along her inwardly sloped hull and high forecastle, the carving morphed into a springing lion until, at her bowsprit, its gaping maw opened to a figurehead of a naked woman holding the pole for a white flag with a burgundy X. To the piercing cries of the seabirds perched amid the rigging, *The Scottish Rose* passed close enough for Mairi to count the swivel guns mounted at ten foot intervals on her bulwarks. Yet not a single sailor or officer came topside to issue them a challenge.

Whistling softly, Connor said, "If she were in the Royal Navy, she'd be a first-rate ship of the line."

"That she would," Angus put forth. "I counted forty-five cannons on her port."

"Me too," Mairi concurred, "givin' her a total of ninety, plus the six chasers in her stern. That means her crew numbers at least four hundred, if not closer to five."

"I wonder where they are," Connor remarked.

Shrugging, she offered, "Well, it is sunrise, and the Spanish aren't known to be early risers." Looking to the other two ships, she followed up, "Let's go see who else is here."

Both eighty feet long, the British sloops sported two decks and two masts having the same pair of triangular fore and aft sails common to vessels originating out of Bermuda. From their bows, they flew a white flag bearing a scarlet cross of England. Down their sides, they were armed with sixteen cannon and a dozen swivel guns. At their sterns, the Union Jack lazily fluttered between two chasers mounted above their iron nameplates, but like their Spanish counterpart, they appeared to be empty.

Pointing to the one to his left, Angus said, "That's *The Hornet*. I remember she was settin' out the moment we arrived in Kingston a couple of deliveries ago. I think we figured she has over thirty cannons and close to two hundred men. Since they look like sisters in design, I'm guessin' the other one is *The Wasp*. I've heard their captains are brothers."

"They are," Mairi verified. "Henry has told me they're a bit on the wild side. I guess we'll see today. Drop anchor close to the pier. With this sort of mix, if we don't see Paddy come out, it may be best to move on."

They had barely lowered their skiff into the water when a man materialized out of the shadows at the forest edge. Short and stout, he had slicked his thick black hair back over his round head and let a dark scruff fill in on his meaty cheeks. Dressed in a forest-green shirt under a black vest with wide lapels and black shorts cut off at his knees, he furiously waved his arms while he marched barefoot out to meet them.

Taking up the oars, Connor looked back over his shoulder and asked, "Is that him?"

Letting out a happy sigh, Mairi confirmed, "That's him."

"Does he live here alone?"

She shook her head and, nodding to the skeletal remains of a ship run aground a hundred yards down the shore, explained, "In San Juan, he purchased that old carrack to salvage fer wood and all the Tainos and Caribs he could afford, figurin' they'd already know how to survive on an island like this and could help him run his place."

His eyes wide, Connor asked, "He relies on slaves? Isn't he worried they'll rebel?"

"Not really. Paddy is savvier than ye'd think. Not only did he purchase the men, he purchased their wives, and if he doesn't need them to work, he's happy to leave them alone with their families. He even tries to give them all at least one day off a week to help raise the kids. He says happy wives lead to happy lives, and if ye ask me, his people live better than most of the Irish who are indentured servants in the Caribbean."

"Still," Connor pressed, "if they turned on him, he wouldn't be able to do anythin' to stop it."

"That may be," Mairi acknowledged, "but they also know should anythin' happen to Paddy, they could all end up back at the slave markets in San Juan, or even worse, Port-au-Prince."

"How many does he have?"

Crossing her arms and narrowing her eyes, she admitted, "I don't know and he won't say, which is a little surprisin' since he usually can't keep a secret to save his life."

"Why does he keep this one?"

"He says it's in the interests of national security. Ye see, when a fight starts, he says it's best no one knows how many men he can summon to break it up." Raising her eyebrows, she furthered, "He also prefers to create a certain mystique to it all, fer at his whistle, they all seem to appear at once, and after order has been restored, they all seem to disappear just as quickly. Rumor has it he's got fifty, although I'd be surprised if there's more than a dozen."

"He'd have to form a settlement if he had fifty," Connor determined, "especially if they all have families."

"Which he can't do unless he finds fresh water," she added.

"If the Spanish didn't find any, how does he expect to?"

Chuckling, she shook her head and began, "Accordin' to Paddy, the reason the Spanish weren't successful is because they've become too pious and forgotten their lore. He believes it's here, somewhere, and if he makes the fairies happy, they'll happily lead him to it."

"Then how does he survive in the meantime?"

"Well, first and foremost, he built a large reservoir to capture rainwater, and second, he relies on people like us." Waving her finger between them, she asserted, "At Paddies, uisge beatha takes on a whole new meanin', fer whiskey really is the water of life."

Smiling ear to ear, Paddy tugged on his lapels while waiting at the only slip available on the pier. Mairi tossed him a length of rope, and quickly, he tied it around a stanchion. Helping her step up, he declared, "I had a hunch ye'd be showin' up. Not only did I put some honey in the porridge I left out fer the fairies last night, I also placed me last few drops of whiskey in a cup next to a pail of fresh water. This mornin', I woke, saw me whiskey was gone, and I knew it'd be me lucky day!" Wrapping his thick, hairy forearms around her waist, he picked her up and proclaimed, "Thank God yer here! I went to sleep afraid I'd have to survive the morrow drinkin' rum!"

"God forbid that should ever happen," Mairi returned, hugging him back. Raising her eyebrows, she asked, "Yer already out of whiskey? That was quick."

He set her down and, waving his hands toward the English vessels, replied, "It's those Brits. They took a likin' to it and drunk me dry." Noticing Connor joining them, Paddy looked over her shoulder and inquired, "Who is this mighty lad?"

"Angus's younger brother Connor."

Rubbing his chin, Paddy muttered, "I thought I noticed some resemblance."

"He needs to start learnin' the trade," she added.

"Does he now?" Paddy remarked, extending his right hand. "Then it's me pleasure to meet ye."

Turning bright red, Connor accepted his offer and mumbled, "Thanks."

Tightening his grip, Paddy insisted, "Ye should consider yerself to be the luckiest lad on earth, fer there's no soul nobler than Mairi's. If I've said it once, I've said it a thousand times: ye never need to worry whether her whiskey'll pass proof."

"And ye never will," she assured Paddy. Squeezing his shoulder, she directed him down the pier and slid her right arm into the crook of his left elbow. "Where is everybody?" she wanted to know. "It's so quiet I was afraid of what we were arrivin' to."

"How many times do I have to tell ye," he replied, "none of these boys really want to fight. Last night ended a little late is all, and believe me, had ye been here, ye'd still be sleepin' too."

"What about yer workers?" she followed up.

"I had a feelin' it'd be a lazy morning," he disclosed, "and I told them to take it off. Not only did the festivities go on a little late, they got a bit out of hand, and I'm sure my people could all use the break."

"I gather yer still keepin' the peace in yer own special way," she noted.

"As long as business is good," he countered, "the peace keeps itself. It's simply that I occasionally must remind everyone of how happy we all are." Tilting his head closer, he whispered, "And with the turn the war is takin', I sure couldn't be happier."

"Why?" she asked. "What happened?"

A gleam in his eyes, he smiled and said, "In Europe, the fightin' has gotten a lot more serious, and they're worried it'll spill over to this side of the world."

"If I remember correctly," she mentioned, "it all started on this side of the world back in 1739."

Shrugging, he remarked, "Ah, not really. Sure, in the beginnin', everyone was rarin' to go and then they fought a few battles, got a taste of reality, and may I say unsurprisingly, they all happily let it fade away, especially once no one could remember what they were fightin' fer."

"I believe it began over the severed ear of an English captain named Jenkins," she recalled.

With a snort, Paddy blurted out, "Who the hell was Jenkins, and what would make his ear worth dyin' fer?"

"I don't know," Mairi responded. "Fer some reason, a Spanish captain cut it off, and it gave them the excuse they needed to start killin' each other."

"It sure doesn't take much, does it?" Paddy commented. They stopped at the end of the pier, and turning to face her, he confided, "Last night they said now that the royalty is wholly involved, the war is bigger than ever. I should warn ye, the news came late and none of them were makin' much sense anymore, but it sounds like some king doesn't want Austria to succeed, though fer the life of me, I couldn't find out what Austria is tryin' to become successful at."

Raising her brows, Mairi asked, "If the royalty has gotten involved, aren't ye worried yer island will one day become a battlefield whether ye claim neutrality or not?"

"Nah," Paddy shot down, waving his hand. "Beyond how good business is, I've got them all believing this place is a vacation paradise and the perfect place to kick back and relax."

"A vacation paradise?" she repeated. "What the hell does that mean?"

Smiling, Paddy tugged at his lapels and explained, "It means ye come here to take yer mind off yer troubles and enjoy life fer a while."

Scrunching her face, she asked, "Where the hell did ye come up with that crazy idea?"

"I stole it from Shakespeare," Paddy stated. "A Venetian friend of mine was watchin' one of his plays in London, and thinkin' of everywhere he's been in the world, he decided if he wanted to go on a holiday fer a week, this would be the best place to do it."

"I've read the play he's referrin' to," Mairi retorted, "and I don't think that's what Shakespeare had in mind."

"I don't care what Shakespeare had in mind," Paddy asserted, "and to be honest, I'd be surprised if any of these idiots know who he was anyway. All that matters is they understand killin' each other is their job, and when they take a vacation, they're not supposed to do their job." Tugging at his lapels, he surmised, "Ergo, they're not supposed to kill each other."

"That's ridiculous."

"That may be," he confessed. "However, it sounds official and they're buyin' it, at least fer now. Ye know how kings can be, the next ship could bring us news a treaty was signed a few months ago and everyone is friends again." Shrugging, he asked, "Given that's the case, wouldn't it be stupid to die today fer a war that ended yesterday?" Smiling, he concluded, "And the moment they realize that yes, their death would be fer nothing, it makes it easy to convince them to kick back, relax, have a drink, and enjoy themselves. Why fight if ye don't have to?"

"I still think yer puttin' a little too much faith in a single word," Mairi suggested, "regardless if Shakespeare came up with it or not."

Raising his finger, Paddy replied, "Then ye need a reminder of me third, and may I say, most important rule," before opening his hand toward the beach and offering, "Go ahead, be me guest."

Stifling a smile, Mairi took a deep breath and set her right foot onto the soft, powdery white sand already warm in the morning sun. Closing her eyes, she followed with her left foot and, letting her feet slowly sink in, murmured, "Ye know, Paddy, there may be somethin' to yer magic. Not only does it drain the fight out of me, it makes me want to sit and rest fer a bit. Unfortunately, I get so caught up in work that I do forget it's good to take a break once in a while."

"I'm tellin' ye, and people can call me crazy all they want, there's fairy dust sprinkled on these islands." Leaning toward her, he proposed, "Ye know, if ye'd like, ye can quit work and take a permanent vacation. Business has been good enough to make me think it's safe to marry me a wife and start a family."

Meeting his gaze, she asked, "And have a bunch of little Irish boys?"

Tugging at his lapels, he grinned and responded, "Somethin' like that."

"Then I'm not the one to be yer wife," she retorted, "fer if I'm goin' to raise a family, I aim to raise a clan of Scottish men." Looking to his public house appearing in the morning light, she determined, "The vacation is over. Show me around. It looks like ye've expanded since the last time I was here."

Doing a double take, Paddy let out a long sigh, smiled sheepishly, and said, "Yer right. I have. Behind the bar on the beach, I've added a great room fer the sailors to gather." He led them toward a building constructed using the remains of the carrack, with the divided masts providing the pillars for a frame following the same curvature of the old hull, minus the bow and stern. A sloping circular thatched roof covered the top, and at each corner, a large window afforded an unobstructed view of the sea. Pointing to them, he went on, "Not only that, I've added a couple private rooms fer the captains to rent, should they not want or be able to return to their ships. That's where they slept last night."

While the little group walked past the carcass of a roasted pig on a spit over a smoldering firepit, Mairi asked, "What about the sailors? Where are they?"

"Out back," Paddy answered, "in a clearin' between here and the Caribbean. I converted the sails of me vessel into tents and rent out the space underneath. Fer a little extra, they can even sleep on a cot instead of the ground."

"I'll give ye credit, Paddy," Mairi noted. "Yer on to somethin' here. No wonder business is good."

The sand cooling in the shadow of the walls, Paddy brought them to the middle section of his former ship and stepped onto a deck shaded by the recessed eaves of the roof. Underneath, two wooden arches leading to the great room flanked a ten-seat bar built out of weathered oak planks. It had an additional stool on each end and mirrored a second bar that served the inside. In between, a large cradle held seven casks of different sizes with a waist-high shelf covered by neat rows of upside-down wooden cups. Walking around the left corner, Paddy revealed, "I'm actually thinkin' of addin' another floor, it's only a matter of figurin' out if I have the wood to salvage to do it. I'm tellin' ye, I've got no complaints other than the way the tropical sun burns me skin up. I'm startin' to think I should marry a native girl so the same thing doesn't happen to me children."

"Then yer kids wouldn't be Irish," Mairi remarked.

"Sure they would," he insisted. "Unlike ye Scots, we say ye just have to have a little Irish in ye to be Irish. There's safety in numbers, ye know." Reaching for a cup, he said, "Let's have a drink. I'm parched."

Joining him, Mairi left Connor in the gap and produced a thin steel flask out of a pouch on her belt. Shaking the contents, she divulged, "I have a surprise fer ye today. This is out of a special barrel. It's one of a kind."

Snapping his head toward her, he accidently knocked several cups off the shelf and, squatting to pick them up, replied, "Is it now?"

Watching him fumbling around at her feet, she continued, "Aye, so ye can't fall in love with it, at least not yet."

He grabbed one and, staying on a knee, confessed, "If only that was possible." His hands trembling, he held it forth and followed up, "Ye may as well ask me to swim the Atlantic."

She unscrewed the cap and, pouring him a healthy sploosh, warned, "Well, yer goin' to have to find a way. I won't have any ready fer some months, and when I do, it won't come cheap. Still, on the day I first tried it, I thought of ye and had to bring a taste."

"One more reason I tell everyone there's no soul nobler than Mairi's," Paddy asserted. Looking from his whiskey to Connor, he advised, "I hope yer payin' attention, young laddie."

"He's payin' attention," Mairi assured Paddy, tapping her flask to his drink, "To yer fairies," she offered, "and yer lucky day."

Paddy stood and, closing his eyes, savored his first sip for several moments. Upon swallowing, he curled his lips into a tight circle and, exhaling slowly, let out, "Uisce beatha. Good God, Mairi, this really is the water of life. On me mother's soul, I can't figure out how ye do it."

Smiling, she suggested, "Let's just say it takes a special kind of magic."

Meeting her gaze, he countered, "Ye don't really expect me to buy that, do ye? Whatever me beliefs may be, I'm smarter than yer givin' me credit fer. In fact, I already know one of yer secrets."

"Really," Mairi responded, crossing her arms, "and what secret it that?"

"Corn," Paddy stated, tilting his cup toward her, "go ahead and try to deny it." Without waiting for her reply, he spread his arms wide and furthered, "Me people know all about it. It's been a staple in their diets fer generations. What do ye think is the main ingredient in me porridge every mornin'?" Swirling his drink, he waved it under his nose and lamented, "I just wish I could figure out how to make it into whiskey."

"Leave it to a Scot to figure that out," she contended. "After all, we made whiskey first."

"Oh, Mairi," Paddy dismissed, "ye may have tamed whiskey's wild spirit, but ye can't change history. Everyone knows the Irish made it first." Seeing her shake her head, he quickly added, "I do have a secret I was goin' to keep, only now that ye've given me this taste, I feel obliged to let ye in on it. I've started growin' corn right here on me island, and if I must, I'll hire someone who knows how to distill it. Then, I only need to discover where Oakies gets its woody finish, make it meself, and ye'll have some real competition."

"Oakies?" Mairi repeated. "What's Oakies?"

"That's the name Clarkeson gave yer whiskey."

"Clarkeson? Who's Clarkeson?"

"Ye haven't heard of Clarkeson?" Paddy questioned. "This past week, Clarkeson has been the biggest story comin' out of Kingston."

Turning her palms over, Mairi replied, "When we were there, Henry didn't say anythin', and the day we departed, we got caught in a storm that blew us off course."

Frowning, Paddy mentioned, "Huh, yer the first person to report a storm in these parts."

"Well, ye know how it is in the Caribbean," she reminded him. "Storms can crop up out of nowhere and be gone in an hour. With my luck, we may have been the only ship in the vicinity. Now, tell me more about this Clarkeson. Who is he?"

Beaming, Paddy set his cup on the bar and, tugging on his lapels, began, "He is not a he, fer he is a she, and it sounds like she's a pirate more beautiful and mysterious than Anne Bonny. She wears a black patch over her right eye, lets her long dark hair blow wildly in the wind, and with a redheaded banshee at her side, she commands a crew of dark-skinned natives who speak Gaelic. Accordin' to the stories, they're half man and half beast, and they fight with the strength of a thousand warriors." Raising an index finger, he boasted, "The day she took her first ship, they swept the deck clean of fifty armored Spanish mercenaries hired to protect it."

Her mouth agape, Mairi echoed, "Fifty Spanish mercenaries? What'd she do to the captain?"

Slowly shaking his head, Paddy told her, "Once Clarkeson found out he had her Oakies aboard, she accused him of smugglin' and sentenced him to death."

"Sentenced him to death?!!?"

"Aye," Paddy continued, "they chained him to a skiff and towed it behind the stern of her brigantine. Standing at the bow of the captured vessel, she gave the order to fire a full canister of grape shot. The witnesses say hardly anythin' remained to sink."

"Did she execute anyone else?"

"Apparently not. In fact, she gave the sailors who spoke Gaelic a chance to join her crew and gave those who didn't a couple of firkins of whiskey to survive on until they made it to Jamaica. Ye want to hear the craziest part?"

"How can there be a crazier part?"

"The Dutch merchant who rescued them said they were disappointed they didn't speak her language and they couldn't join her. He claims, to a man, they all vowed to learn how, should they ever get the opportunity to again."

"That's completely insane!" she exclaimed.

"Insane is one way to put it," he agreed. Lowering his voice and looking over his shoulders, he whispered, "But if ye ask me, I'd say she cast a spell over them."

Crossing her arms, Mairi shifted her hips and followed up, "Why do I have the feelin' this is a part of the story that came up late last night?"

"I'm tellin' ye the truth," Paddy insisted, picking up his cup. "If she didn't cast a spell over them, then she did on yer whiskey, fer it seems like every time a sailor hears of her tale, he wants to give it a try. More than anyone, she's the reason I ran out. She's makin' Oakies famous."

Keeping her arms crossed, Mairi glowered at him and snapped, "Don't ever say that name again."

His eyes darting back and forth, Paddy responded, "Don't ever say what name again?"

"Oakies. Don't ever call my whiskey Oakies again."

Spreading his arms wide, he asked, "Why not? That's what everybody's callin' it."

"Because it's my whiskey," Mairi declared, "and I'll say who can buy it and who can't. It's already hard enough to do business in this world of rum. I don't need some pirate makin' it worse."

Leaning forward, Paddy whispered, "What makes ye think she's a pirate?"

"If she's not a pirate, what is she? A privateer?"

"She's not that either. In fact, I don't think she's human at all. If ye ask me, she's a water sprite."

Rolling her eyes and shaking her head, Mairi retorted, "Oh, come on, now ye really are talkin' nonsense."

Stone-faced, Paddy replied, "Think about it. Her crew is made up of natives who all speak Gaelic."

"Lots of people speak Gaelic. In Inverness, they speak it openly."

"Inverness is in Scotland, not the Caribbean."

"Well, if she's a water sprite," Mairi countered, "why would she need a ship?"

"It's a part of her guise," he put forth. "If she's to inspire humans to take up her cause, she needs to take on a human form."

"And what cause would a water sprite want us to take up?"

"Freedom of speech," he stated, tugging at his lapels. "It's said Gaelic is native to the land of the faerie and there's nothin' they find more soothin' than the sound of their tongue on our lips. If ye've been payin' attention to what the English have been doin' in Ireland over the last hundred years, then ye know they're usin' the penal laws to wipe out our culture, startin' with our language. Ye watch. Ye Scots are next."

"They haven't banned Gaelic in Ireland," she reminded him. "Ye can still speak it anywhere ye want."

"They made it illegal to do business in Gaelic, and that was the first step," Paddy shot back. "The next thing ye know, they'll tell us we can't teach it to our children. Clarkeson came over to make sure such a travesty never occurs."

Touching the fingertips of her right hand to her forehead, Mairi asked, "Are ye tryin' to tell me, in an effort to make sure Gaelic would always be spoken in Britain, a fairy sailed all the way across the Atlantic to spark a rebellion in the Caribbean?"

"She didn't sail over here," Paddy corrected, waving his finger. "She didn't have to. She came through the portal. To be sure, it's the portal that makes the whole thing possible."

"Portal? What portal?"

Nodding past the ships in the cove, he told her, "The one on Vieques, an island to the south of here. The Spanish call it Isla Nena, and according to the captain of the galleon, there's a narrow entrance on the southern coastline to a small bay where the water glows in a livin' green, especially durin' a new moon. Of course, bein' so pious, he says it's the work of the devil." Pointing his thumbs to his chest, Paddy insisted, "But I know better. The truth is this bay is the portal Clarkeson uses to go back and forth between the Old World and the New."

"Has the captain seen this portal fer himself?" she wanted to know.

"Aye, and fer months, ye could see the terror in his eyes every time he spoke of it."

"He's the captain of that humongous man-o-war. I'm surprised he's afraid of anythin'."

"I can assure ye he's not afraid of anythin' on this planet," Paddy testified. "Yet somethin' from another world is a different story, and to this day, he swears *La Bonita Señorita* will never go near that place again, lest she be tainted by an evil spirit."

"*La Bonita Señorita*," Mairi repeated. "Quite an interestin' name fer such a vessel."

"Well, he's Spanish."

"What's that supposed to mean?"

"Trust me," Paddy assured her, with a wave, "when ye meet him, ye'll figure it out."

Giving him another sploosh, she asked, "What does he drink?"

Smiling, Paddy lifted his cup to his lips, took a sip, and answered, "Mostly rioja, unless I run out, then he switches to rum."

"What about whiskey?"

"He won't touch it."

"Why not?"

"He can be the one who tells ye that," Paddy replied. "I may be a bit mad but I'm not stupid."

Looking at the two sloops, she followed up, "What about the Brits? I met the captain of *The Hornet* in Kingston. I hear he and the captain of *The Wasp* are brothers."

"They are. Twins, actually, and I can't believe ye met one and not the other. They're never far apart."

"*The Wasp* had already set sail, and *The Hornet* was preparin' to when we docked alongside her. I only had a moment to say hello. I'm not sure I even remember his name."

"Mathew," Paddy said, "and between him and his brother Mark, ye've found some good customers."

"If they're English," she mentioned, "I'm surprised they don't prefer gin."

"If they were English, they might, only they were born on Nevis or Saint Kitts, I'm still not sure which, and they're Scots by heritage."

"What are they like?"

"Well, they're twins," Paddy said, "and I always say, if ye like one, ye'll like the other. If not . . ."

"If not," an elegant, baritone voice picked up, "then you'll find each just as annoying as the other, and together, exponentially so."

Exclaiming "Jesus," Paddy flinched and turned to his right to face a man leaning against the arched threshold.

Taller than Connor, he had tied his curly black ponytail with a burgundy silk ribbon, waxed the ends of his mustache straight off the corners of his mouth, and trimmed his goatee into a point at the base of his dimpled chin. Wearing a burgundy vest accentuated in gold thread over a white silk blouse, he left both unbuttoned to his chest and a gold coin dangled freely at the end of a gold chain in the midst of a copious amount of dark hair. Casting his vivid brown eyes upon Mairi, he purred, "Perdon, bella doncella. I did not mean to frighten you. Required to go barefoot, I find, like a feline, I tend to sneak up on people. My name is Captain Ricardo DeLogrono. It is my honor to meet you."

"While I appreciate the compliment, I'm not sure I should be called a maiden," Mairi returned, "and while ye may have snuck up on Paddy, I had heard ye movin' around."

"You didn't hear me," DeLogrono groaned. "You heard them." Rolling his eyes toward two brothers bursting through the arched threshold at the opposite end of the bar, he continued, "And not only did you hear them, I heard them, the men in the tents out back heard them, the fish swimming in the cove heard them, the sailors on the ships crossing the Atlantic heard them, and why, it is quite possible the good people back in the my region of Spain heard them, for I'm not sure how one could have not."

Identical in appearance, the siblings donned red and white sleeveless shirts tight on their brawny torsos, with black breeches rolled halfway up their well-defined calves. Their rugged features bronzed, they kept their cheeks bare and let their wavy bleached blond tresses flow past their shoulders. One wore a bluish-green aquamarine in a bezel setting on his right pinky; the other wore a matching one on his left, and noticing DeLogrono, they both cast their bright green eyes upon him. Raising his middle finger, the first grinned mischievously and slid an ornate gold ruby ring down to the second knuckle. Wiggling it, he hailed, "Hola, el capitano."

"That would be Mathew," Paddy whispered to Mairi. "He's the one ye met."

"Or is it 'Buenos dias, mi amigo'?" the second chipped in.

"And that's Mark," Paddy followed up. "Respectively, they are the captains of *The Hornet* and *The Wasp*."

"Listening to the way they defile my good language," DeLogrono bemoaned, "they would be better suited as butchers. I have to imagine Cervantes is rolling in his grave."

Slipping the ruby ring on the rest of his fingers, Mathew pointed out, "Look, it's too small fur any of them. It won't even fit my wee one." Passing it over to Mark, who also tried and failed, he added, "Look, neither can he."

"The Spanish must have little hands."

"Maybe that's why they need such big ships."

Ignoring them, DeLogrono offered his palm to Mairi and murmured, "The only redemption to waking at such contemptible hour and to such wretched company is the beautiful view of such a magnificent sunrise."

Accepting his gesture, she waited until he gently placed his lips on her knuckles and noted, "The sun rose some time ago."

Looking up from under his brows, DeLogrono responded, "That is a matter of perspective."

Holding his gaze, she ordered, "Tell me somethin'."

"Anything."

"Why is the name of yer ship *La Bonita Señorita*?"

Wielding two rows of sparkling white teeth, DeLogrono proclaimed, "Why, I would think the answer is obvious."

"What do ye mean? Are ye tryin' to imply I'm stupid?"

Straightening, he twirled his left hand and began, "Not at all. Perdon my manners, for I must answer your question with one of my own. At the crux of it all, what is the primary function of a warship?"

"To kill men."

His eyes sparkling, he followed up, "And what weapon is more effective at killing a man than a beautiful woman?"

"A dagger driven into his heart."

His mouth open, DeLogrono pressed both hands to his chest and gasped, "Paddy was right. You do live up to the namesake of my noble vessel. Here we've just met, and you've already slayed me once."

Rolling her eyes, Mairi suggested, "Be grateful I'm just usin' my words. If my hands get involved, it'll get agonizin'."

Keeping his chest covered, DeLogrono declared, "Oh my, you've done it again. How many more blows can one man suffer?"

Leading his brother behind the stools, Mark interrupted, "Hey, before yu go shove off into the great blue yonder, would yu happen to have another ring yu could lose? It'd be nice to have a pair."

"Aye," Mathew followed up, "that way we won't have to keep passin' this one back and forth."

While the twins settled on the last two spots in the row, Mairi directed her attention to DeLogrono and asked, "Was that ring yers?"

In the process of sliding onto the stool at the end between the corner and the gap leading behind the bar, he sighed, "It was." Placing his elbows on the wooden top and his head in his hands, he revealed, "My grandfather gave it to my cousin who in turn gave it to me. Growing up together in the vineyards of our family's estate, we considered ourselves brothers, and prior to my departure to Puerto Rico, he gave it to me as a reminder of home."

"If it meant that much," Mairi replied, "why would ye gamble it away?"

"It wasn't me," DeLogrono grumbled. "It was the rum. It almost made me forget I'm Spanish. I was doing fine until Paddy ran out of my prized rioja. I never should've switched. I should've stopped drinking right then."

Shaking a pair of six-sided dice, Mark inserted, "Maybe we should pick up where we left off."

"Aye, even if yu don't have another ring," Mathew continued, "I suppose yu do have somethin' of value. How 'bout yur ship?"

"Not that we want to sail it per se," Mark let him know, "we just want the prize money the Royal Navy would pay us fur it."

"Not that we think it's worth very much," Mathew followed up. "Just because it's big doesn't mean it's effective."

"And yu can keep yur crew," Mark went on. "They aren't effective either."

"But the Union Jack would be a welcome sight flyin' from that mainmast," Mathew determined.

"Aye, and we wouldn't have to kill anyone to make it happen," Mark concurred.

"The only way the Union Jack will ever fly from *La Bonita Señorita*," DeLogrono growled, "is if it is wrapped around both your necks and tied to my bowsprit."

Wiggling the ruby ring on his middle finger, Mathew replied, "If yu kill us, yu can't win this back."

Rolling a pair of dice on the bar, Mark added, "Not that yu have any chance of winnin' it back anyway." One came to a stop on the three, the other came to a stop on the four, and snapping his head toward the Spaniard, he noted, "Would yu look at that? Lucky number seven. Come on, el Capitano. What do yu think?"

Turning to face Paddy, Mairi inquired, "What are they talkin' about?"

"The English play a dice game called Hazard," he filled in, "and last night, they taught it to DeLogrono."

"The only thing I was taught," DeLogrono sneered, "is that to have any success at that idiotic game of chance, one needs to be British."

"Yu don't have to be British to win," Mark retorted. "We explained the rules a thousand times."

"Aye," Mathew said, "yu just have to know yur numbers."

While Mairi looked between them, Mark explained, "Yu see, the roller calls the main."

"It's gotta be a number between five and nine," Mathew continued.

"And if he rolls the main, he nicks," Mark went on.

"Or wins, yu could say," Mathew clarified.

"But if he rolls a two or three," Mark warned, "he loses."

"Now here's where it gets tricky," Mathew picked up, "because if he rolls an eleven or twelve, it all depends on the main."

"With a five or nine, he's out on an eleven or twelve."

"With a six or eight, he's out on an eleven and nicks on a twelve."

"If it's a seven, he nicks on an eleven and is out on a twelve."

"Are yu with us so far?" Mathew asked Mairi.

Biting her bottom lip, she replied, "I think so."

"Good," Mark began anew. "Because, yu see, if he neither nicks nor rolls out, then his role becomes the chance."

"And it gets a bit trickier, because he rolls again."

"Only this time, if he rolls the chance, he wins."

"If he rolls the main, he loses."

"And if he doesn't roll either, he keeps rollin' until he wins or loses."

"Once he loses three times, he's out."

"And then the dice go to the next man."

Taking a deep breath together, they both concluded, "See, simple."

"It's just that some people"—Mark carried on as Mathew whistled three high-pitched notes and hooked his thumb toward DeLogrono—"get confused rather easily."

"It must not take much brains to join the Spanish navy," they simultaneously concluded.

Moaning, DeLogrono buried his forehead deeper into his hands.

Offering her flask, Mairi told him, "Maybe ye should've switched to whiskey."

"Only pagans drink whisky," he declared.

Frowning, Mathew posed, "I'm not sure I like the sound of that."

Immediately Mark added, "Aye, I think yur tryin' to offend us."

Slowly turning his head, DeLogrono met their eyes and responded, "Perdon me, and please, allow me to clarify any misconceptions. For the record, there shall never be a time when I am not trying to offend you."

"All those pretty words," Mathew remarked, "and yet yu still can't figure out yur numbers."

"Aye, yu may have a big ship," Mark chipped in, "but there's still two of us and only one of yu."

"Yes, there are two of you," DeLogrono allowed, "and you have two tiny ships, *The Wasp* and *The Hornet*, aptly named for two tiny pests. Personally, I believe they would be better called *The Flea* and *The Tick*, for it would take barely a swat to sink one of you off my port side and the other off my starboard."

"Now, now, now," Paddy interjected, "it's too early in the day fer anyone to start talking about sinkin' anyone. Besides, I gave me people the mornin' off. If this goes any further, I'm goin' to make all of ye walk the beach. I was tellin' Mairi how I need to figure out if there's enough salvageable wood left on that old carrack to add another floor, and I'm sure if the three of ye were to put yer heads together, ye could do it fer me." Waving his finger, he cautioned, "Today's me lucky day. Don't ruin it."

"And let's not ferget yer all on vacation," Mairi picked up, "and ye don't work when yer on vacation. So if yer goin' to start killin' each other, go elsewhere to do it, preferably somewhere far, far away, because I don't want to see it. I get squeamish at the sight of blood." Producing her flask, she turned to face Paddy and offered, "Let me buy these gentlemen their first drink of the day. Get me three cups."

After he did her bidding and she measured out three ounces, she set one in front of each captain. Smiling, the twins picked theirs up and simultaneously asked, "What are we havin'?"

"Whiskey," Mairi announced.

Holding his palm to his drink, DeLogrono broke in. "Tempting though it may be, I must forgo your offer, for my culture will not allow me to consume something so . . . unrefined."

Meeting his eyes, Mairi countered, "I consider this whiskey to be the product of my blood, sweat, and tears."

"Making it even more painful to decline," DeLogrono lamented, covering his heart, "for I fear, under the influence of your passion, I may forget my heritage." He glanced at Paddy and groaned, "For the first time in my life, I truly appreciate Adam's predicament. If only I merely had to face a naked Eve holding an apple."

Oblivious, Mark swirled his cup under his nose and asked, "This is whisky?"

"It's whiskey," Mairi corrected. "I say it k-e-y."

"I thought Paddy ran out last night," Mathew tacked on.

"I did run out last night," Paddy insisted. "Luckily, Mairi arrived early this mornin'. She's the one I told ye about, the one who tamed the spirit of Oakies."

"What did I say about that name?" she snarled. He opened both palms to her and stepped back. Turning to the twins, she followed up, "And I better not hear it come from yer lips either. Should I, I may have to rip them off."

Holding their palms forth, they assured her, "Wu're happy to call it whatever yu want."

"To us, the name is unimportant," Mathew picked up.

"Aye, it's more important yu teach us how to make it," Mark carried on.

Shaking her head, she answered, "I can't do that."

"Sure yu can," Mark maintained. "Our grandfather owned a distillery in Scotland until the tax of '25 wiped him out and he was forced to cross the Atlantic."

"And since he couldn't find any suitable grains," Mathew went on, "he resorted to makin' rum instead."

"Or sugar water as he used to call it," Mark furthered.

"Which we had to switch to last night," Mathew bemoaned. Looking inside his cup, he concluded, "And I must say, it's nice to start the day drinkin' somethin' with a bit of a kick to it."

In unison, they took a healthy swallow.

"Uisge," Mathew offered.

"Beatha," Mark followed up.

Raising his left eyebrow, DeLogrono looked to Mairi and inquired, "Water of life?"

Raising her right eyebrow, Mairi tilted her head and returned, "Ye speak Gaelic?"

"My province was first settled by the Phoenicians over ten thousand years ago," DeLogrono related, "and being so close to the border, it has been a route for travelers ever since. To this day, my people still provide goods and services to the pilgrims passing through on their way to one of the many holy shrines in Spain." Letting a grin cross his face, he settled his eyes on hers and purred, "Consequently, in my youth, I was exposed to a variety of tongues, and no matter how exotic they may have appeared, I found I had a gift, or may I humbly say a blessing, for picking them up rather easily. Personally, I've found adding a little Spanish flair to a foreign language can be quite . . . rewarding."

"Yer not the only one who knows yer history," Mairi asserted, "and while the Celts may have spoken Gaelic across Europe centuries ago, it's been a long time since anyone outside Ireland or Scotland understood it." Leaning forward, she whispered, "And given Britain has never conquered Spain, I'm curious to know how ye learned it."

Throwing his shoulders back, DeLogrono puffed out his chest and boomed, "Well, it's not like it's a secret or something. In my service to the crown, prior to being dispatched to San Juan, I had the pleasure of transporting an Irish brigade fighting for the Spanish Empire. Quite a quarrelsome lot, they were whisky drinkers themselves, and out of spite, they refused to speak anything other than Gaelic. Thus, I had no choice but to learn it." Flaring his nostrils, he noted, "I find it to be rather . . . primal. Wouldn't you agree?"

"I can't answer that question," Mairi revealed. "To keep his crew from fightin', my father forbade it aboard his ship, and the only words I know are the few his sailors taught me." Waving her right index finger, she asserted, "Don't get excited. I have no intention of havin' that sort of conversation with ye."

"Perhaps a nice meal and glass or two of my prized rioja would change your mind," DeLogrono suggested.

"Ye prefer a girl who drinks wine?"

"Of course," he murmured, "the nectar of the noble tempranillo grape only sweetens their souls, among other things." Leaning closer, he pressed, "Perhaps you would even be willing to remove your bonnet and allow your locks to cascade down around your shoulders."

"Don't get yer hopes up," she replied, "fer there aren't any locks to cascade. In a distillery, the threat of a fire is greater than it is on a ship, and in the event one starts, I require my workers keep their hair short and their cheeks bare to reduce the chance their faces will burn off. Sharin' the same risks, I follow the same rules and shave my head too." Widening her eyes, she touched his hand and uttered, "All the same, if ye were to meet a girl who prefers whiskey, would ye give it a try?"

Curling his lips and slowly shaking his head, he replied, "No, I would expect a girl who prefers whisky to want to fight like the boys who prefer whisky, and in such moments, I always say why fight when you don't have to?"

Tugging at his lapels, Paddy inserted, "That's exactly what I always say."

"Have ye ever found out what happens once the fightin' ends?" Mairi continued.

Stroking his goatee, DeLogrono confessed, "No, I can't say that I have."

Narrowing her eyes, she stated, "What a shame. After all, the girls who prefer whiskey are most likely those who speak Gaelic, and I would imagine any reconciliation would be rather . . . primal. Wouldn't ye?" Giving him a wink, she took a swallow and asked, "Now are ye sure ye don't want that taste?"

His mouth and eyes wide open, DeLogrono leaned back and covered his heart with both hands.

"We can speak Gaelic," the twins pitched in together. "Our grandfather taught us how."

Brushing them off, Mairi turned to Paddy and determined, "This vacation has gone on far too long. I need to finish up. My flask is almost empty, and I told Henry I'd save him a taste."

"Henry?" Paddy complained. "Why would ye save him some?"

"Why wouldn't I? He's a good customer."

"He's English."

"I don't care what he is," Mairi asserted. "He pays in coin." Seeing Paddy cross his arms and begin to turn red, she shook her right index finger and cooed, "Easy now, or I'll make ye take a walk on yer beach." Spontaneously, laughter erupted out of everyone seated at the bar. She waited for it to die down and followed up, "I want to be off. Where are yer empties?"

"Well," Paddy began, biting his lip, "most of them are out back."

"Most of them?"

"At least a couple of them."

"A couple of them?" she repeated. "I need all of them. I told ye that the last time I was here and ye took a few extra. I even made it a point to repeat myself."

"Oh, that's right," Paddy remembered, rubbing his chin. "I must've forgotten what ye said."

Glaring into his soul, Mairi asked, "Are ye sayin' ye don't have all my barrels?"

"It's not a big deal," he contended. "I've got plenty of other barrels out back. Yer welcome to take them all."

"How many times do I have to tell ye," she exclaimed, "I can't use any old barrel to make my whiskey!"

"I'm sorry I forgot," Paddy apologized, holding his palms toward her. "It was an honest mistake. Ye can't kill me fer it, at least not this time."

"Then tell me where my barrels are!"

"Well," he muttered, "I may have sold them yesterday."

"Sold them?!!?" she repeated.

"It was an offer I couldn't refuse," he blurted out.

"I told ye before," Mairi snapped, "if ye want to sell my whiskey, ye have to empty it out of my barrel and put it in a different one."

"That's what I wanted to do," he whined, "only the captain wouldn't agree to the deal if I couldn't guarantee it wouldn't change the flavor."

"Then why would ye agree to the deal?"

"I already told ye," Paddy reminded her, "it was an offer I couldn't refuse."

"So ye went ahead and sold my barrels anyway," she followed up, crossing her arms, "which means ye lied to me."

"Lied to ye?" Paddy repeated. "I'd never lie to ye!"

"Ye just did when ye said he made ye an offer ye couldn't refuse! It means ye knew better and ye still sold my barrels anyway!"

Opening and closing his mouth, Paddy stammered, "I ah, I, I ah . . . it wasn't that I lied as it was I just fergot in the moment." Smiling feebly, he tapped the side of his head and posed, "Ye always get here early in the morning and I'm not used to bein' up at this time. My brain wasn't clear yet."

"Are ye now sayin' ye remember bein' told not to sell my barrels?" she asked.

"Of course," he answered, "how could I forget?"

"And yet ye went ahead and did it!"

His eyes widening, he leaned back and stuttered, "Ah, he, ah, I, ah . . ."

"Enjoyable as this is," DeLogrono chimed in, "I feel compelled to point something out. Paddy, the more you speak, the deeper you get. Perhaps you should just stay silent."

"Isn't that the truth," Mairi agreed.

Smirking, DeLogrono furthered, "Because of my elite education and my extensive experience, I also feel compelled to provide my assistance in finding a reasonable solution to your predicament. What is the issue with taking the remaining barrels?"

Uncrossing her arms, Mairi turned to Connor and ordered, "Go see if there's any out back that we can use for an example, and we'll let them figure it out."

While Connor exited through the arches leading to the great room, Mathew announced, "We wur just thinkin' . . ."

And Mark followed up, "What happens if Paddy doesn't have enough empties to replace the ones he sold? Will yu sell him any more?"

"Not if I can't trust they'll be here the next time I come around."

"Well then, would yu be willin' to trade directly with us?" Mark asked.

"Aye," Mathew concurred. He held up the ruby ring and posed, "We have this."

"How many could we buy?" they wanted to know.

Watching the sun sparkle of the stone, Mairi replied, "Oh, I imagine we can work out somethin' . . ."

"No! No! No! No! No!" Paddy bellowed. Placing himself between Mairi and the twins, he roared, "Yer all fergettin' rule number 2! I get a cut out of every deal made at me place, and there's no exceptions to the rules."

"We just want to trade her this ring," Mathew started.

Suddenly, Paddy snatched a shillelagh from below the bar and cracked Mark upside his head. "Shut yer bloody filthy stinkin' mouths," he yelled, "ye filthy stinkin' drunken sots!"

Rubbing his left temple, Mark cried out, "What'd yu hit me fur?"

"Aye, I suggested it," Mathew acknowledged.

Smacking him behind his right ear, Paddy screamed, "'Cause I knew whatever was comin' out of his mouth next would somehow be even dumber than what ye had said." Alternately whacking them both, he continued, "Now I'm not goin' to suffer any more stupid talk of tradin' no more rings fer no more barrels of whiskey, ye hear me?" Breathing heavily, he pointed the tip at each one and warned, "I already told ye I gave me people a break today. Don't make me whistle."

"Oh, I do love it when he whistles," DeLogrono commented. "Who knew such a shrill melody could resonate so sweetly within my soul? Personally I would prefer he did it more often."

Breaking the tension, Connor reappeared carrying a rundlet under the crook of his arm and gave Mairi a nod.

"Set it on the corner between them all," she directed. "Let's see how long it takes until they get it."

He placed the little barrel on the bar and pulled the bung free from the hole in one side. Immediately, a horrific stench caused Paddy to cover his mouth and the twins to turn in opposite directions. DeLogrono stood tall and, pulling at the end of his mustache, inquired, "Would you please kindly seal it up again? Your point has been made."

"So ye understand now?" Mairi asked him.

"That the barrels all smell like rotting fish?"

His mouth covered with his sleeve, Paddy mentioned, "I think there were oysters in that one."

Her eyes on DeLogrono, Mairi numbered off on her fingers and related, "Rotting fish, rotting oysters, rotting crabs, pickled herring, pickled eggs, or even just pickles. More often than not, the right kind of barrel can't be used because of whatever was previously inside it."

"Can't yu scrub them out?" Mark asked.

"Aye, or even soak them under the sea," Mathew suggested.

"We've tried scrubbin' them out, we've tried soakin' them under the sea, and we've even tried scrubbing them out while they're soakin' under the sea, but nothin' works. The lingerin' odors always ruin the taste of the whiskey."

"I can empathize," DeLogrono let her know, "for we must sell our rioja to pilgrims in leather boda bags, and invariably, they affect the integrity of the wine. Fortunately for purchasers, the spirit of the tempranillo is bold enough to withstand the invasive flavors." Tapping his knuckles to the side of the rundlet, he advised, "In this situation, however, I would think something so rancid would be too much for even the noble Spanish grape to overcome. In my opinion, you should burn this one and move on."

"If I could I would," she told him, "and if the day comes I don't have to keep track of my barrels the way I do now, I will. Until then, I'll be takin' every one I find, no matter how bad it is because sooner or later, I'll figure out a way to use them." Facing Paddy, she ordered, "Now, tell me the name of the ship and the captain ye made yer deal with. With any luck, I can catch him."

Frowning, he rubbed his chin and answered, "The ship is *The Sea Lion*, I know that fer certain. As fer the captain, I can't remember his name. I meet too many people to keep track of them all."

"Did he tell ye where he's headed?"

Lowering his head, Paddy informed her, "He's off to the British Virgin Islands, Tortola to be specific, and then to the colonies."

Staring at him, she sneered, "Which means I have no chance of trackin' him down. Paddy, I'm not goin' to tell ye again—my barrels are not fer sale. If ye ever sell another one, ye'll never see my sails enter yer harbor again."

"I got it," he replied, crossing his heart, "and ye have me word, I don't make the same mistake twice." Still hanging his head low, he buried his hands in his pockets and inquired, "What about today? I was hopin' to get an extra few." Pointing to the twins, he insisted, "They're not fer me. They're fer me customers."

"Only if ye promise one more thing."

Smiling wide and tugging at his lapels, he responded, "Whatever it takes."

"If ye want extras, ye'll start tellin' me six months in advance. Otherwise, I can't guarantee anythin'."

His features squishing together, Paddy repeated, "Six months? How am I supposed to know what business will be like in six months?"

"Ask the fairies," she suggested to another burst of laughter. "It's October right now. Tell me what yer goin' to need next March."

Rubbing his chin, he glanced to the twins, smiling their identically goofy smiles, and decided, "Ye better bring another dozen."

She squeezed his right cheek with her left hand and remarked, "See how easy that was." Casting her eyes out to the cove, she announced, "It's time I get back to my ship and my crew and have Angus teach Connor how to fill yer order. Who'd like to walk me out?"

Arm in arm with Paddy, Mairi strolled across the warm, white powdery sand to the bright white pier jutting into the turquoise water. To the tramping of bare feet marching behind them, they walked down the wooden planks to Connor, who waited at her skiff. Turning to her Irish friend, she said, "I guess it's time to say slán [goodbye]."

He wrapped his arms around her waist, picked her up, and stated, "No day is ever luckier than the days I cast me eyes upon ye. How long until I do it again?"

She waited until he set her down and returned, "Like always, I should be back in a couple months, so look fer me around late November or early December."

Holding his palms forth, he gingerly inquired, "Is there any way I could get a few extra barrels then? I came up with the idea to have a party on December 31ˢᵗ to celebrate the comin' New Year and I want to be prepared. Ye should join us. It'll be a blast."

Sighing, she replied, "I'll see what I can do." She looked over his shoulder and, individually setting her eyes on Mathew, Mark, and DeLogrono, added, "Can I expect to see all of ye?"

"If yur here," Mathew started.

"Wu're here," Mark concluded.

Embracing them one at a time, she warned, "Between the storms, the sea, the pirates, and the rest of life, it's hard to commit to anythin' that far in advance, but this is my favorite stop and I can't think of a better place to celebrate a new beginnin'."

"Don't be concerned about the pirates," Mathew insisted.

"Aye, we'll protect yu," Mark assured her, "and yur whisky."

She moved on to DeLogrono and slid her arms around his lower back. He pressed against her body, buried his chin into her bonnet, and moaned, "Though Paddy claims this island is a vacation paradise, it is only an illusion, for all its natural beauty cannot compete with yours."

Hugging him, she tucked her head into his chest and replied, "Ye know, my father always warned me of the Spanish and their lovely tongues."

"It goes with the language," he whispered, "for to speak it properly, one must roll their *r*'s. Not only is the sound pleasing to the ear, I've discovered the skill offers other unintended and much more fervid pleasures."

"I can only imagine," she murmured. "Would ye like to know what else he used to say?"

"Of course," DeLogrono purred, "for he sounds as wise as you are alluring."

"Are ye sure? I'm warnin' ye, it takes a brave man to hear these things."

"We fight bulls in my homeland."

Smiling, she closed her eyes and hummed, "Mmmmm, if ye insist. He told me, if necessary, it's always best to use a claymore to cut it out."

Though DeLogrono instinctively flexed, she braced his arms, keeping them tight around her waist and waited for him to relax again. Falling back into her, he whimpered, "Ah, the fourth time today. I'm starting to believe it would be much less painful if you went ahead and drew a steel dagger. May I personally row you out?"

Letting him go, Mairi whispered, "It sounds temptin', but I must decline fer the same reasons you declined my whiskey— I'm afraid I'd forget who I am." Standing on her tiptoes, she gave him a peck on the cheek and, with a Gaelic edge to her voice, breathed, "Ricardo DeLogrono, I am happy to have met ye, El Capitan. You are a most interesting man."

Immediately he closed his eyes, shivered, and covering his heart, murmured, "The fifth time. Please, stop, I can take no more."

She climbed into her skiff, turned around, and announced, "Gentlemen, this is the greatest place in the world to enjoy a vacation, and if the day ever comes I get the time off to take one, I'll be plantin' my bottom on this very beach."

Watching Connor cast off and row away, DeLogrono proposed, "Should I die before that time, would one of you please cremate my body and mix my ashes in the sand?"

"Only if yu'll do the same fur us," the twins responded.

Tugging at the end of his mustache, DeLogrono furthered, "It's not that she makes me forget I'm Spanish, it's that she makes me want it so." Putting his hands to his hips, he pushed out his chest and asked, "Did you hear what she said?" Without waiting, he raised his chin and followed up, "She said I was interesting."

Planting his left hand onto the side of his head, Mathew groaned, "Oh geez, here we go. Look at him, gettin' all puffed up like a tiger fish."

Nudging his brother, Mark rattled the two dice in his pocket and suggested, "Maybe he's puffed up enough to try his luck. That galleon is a big ship. He's got to have another ring on it somewhere."

Watching Mairi climb aboard her schooner, DeLogrono responded, "I heard you promise to keep her whisky safe from the pirates. Shouldn't you be out hunting them? In fact, I've heard of a new pirate who declared war on the English. I've also heard she dwells on Vieques. Vieques is not too far away. Perhaps the two of you should go see, for that is Spanish territory and therefore Spanish waters. Perhaps I will follow, for without a truce to honor, the opportunity to sink you both may prove to be irresistible, and even I may be willing to return to that accursed place. . ."

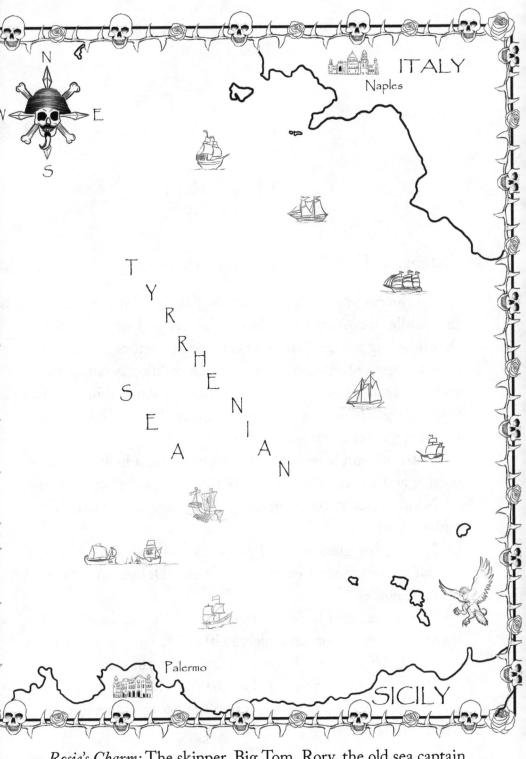

Rosie's Charm: The skipper, Big Tom, Rory, the old sea captain

CHAPTER 3

October 1, 1785, Kingston, Jamaica

To the ringing of the second pin falling from the side of the candle, the old sea captain cast his bright blue eyes upon the flickering orange flame and concluded, "Strong enough to tame the spirit of whiskey, Mairi found it child's play tamin' the spirit of men." Turning to face the room, he covered his heart with his right hand and, raising his left, declared, "To be sure, I certainly never stood a chance."

With the rain barely an echo overhead, John looked to his brother and asked, "We've heard of those twins, haven't we?"

Nodding, Luke confirmed, "Aye, I believe our grandfather told us about them."

Raising his glass to his lips, Tony followed up, "And I remember my grandfather saying the name DeLogrono at one time or another."

"Well, I've never heard of any of them," Rags insisted, "and there was never a pub on Culebra either." Letting out several deep, grumbly chuckles, he nudged Jack's forearm and growled, "If there had been, you can bet the old Ragman would've known about it. Paddies sounds like the perfect place to take a married date."

"Yeah, heh-heh," Jack commented, "I don't remember a pub on Culebra either, heh-heh. I do remember the truce though. I remember one time I was on a ship, heh-heh, and the captain held a letter of marque, heh-heh, or I should say, sort of held, heh-heh. He was never actually issued it, heh-heh. We had taken the ship that had been, and he took the previous captain's name, heh-heh."

"Jesus Christ Jack," Rags interrupted, shaking his head, "get on with it."

"Well, heh-heh, we sheltered out a hurricane at Culebra with two vessels from France, three from England, one from the Dutch Republic, one from Spain, and quite a few privateers who really weren't sure what side they were on, heh-heh. The entire time, we all pretty much played cards, and once the storm passed, heh-heh, we all went our separate ways."

Ignoring him, Sarah put forth, "Well, there's currently not a place on Culebra, that's for sure. What happened to Paddies?"

Raising his eyebrows and his mug, the old sea captain warned, "If I were to tell ye what happened to Paddies, I'd be gettin' way ahead of myself. Now that's truly a story fer another day."

In his low, raspy voice, Brass inserted, "I think the old men are right. I don't think Paddies ever existed. In fact, I don't think anythin' yer tellin' us is real." Casting a harrowing gaze down the bar, he asked, "Where were ye when all this was goin' on?"

Meeting his dark eyes, the old sea captain replied, "Now there's a fair question, my friend." He finished his lager and, setting the mug down, explained, "When Clarkeson made her debut, I was a commissioned officer in the Royal Navy and I had recently been reassigned to join my skipper aboard his unrated sloop of war, *Rosie's Charm*. At the time, the main fleet was at Hyeres, enforcin' a blockade of the Spanish squadron sheltered in Toulon. Attached to the high command, our primary duty was to deliver messages between the admiral and the British naval bases scattered around the Mediterranean."

"Then how could ye possibly know what was goin' on in the Caribbean?" Brass followed up.

"Another fair question," the old sea captain acknowledged, "and to be sure, the news of Clarkeson's exploits wouldn't cross the ocean until December, a good two months after she took *The Empire's Reach*. It was my last night in London, and out in the pubs, I met a few sailors who had arrived from Kingston earlier that day. They told me her story, and without knowin' any better, we all assumed she was a pirate, fer the truth wouldn't come out until much later."

"How much later?" Brass wanted to know.

"Several stories later," the old sea captain divulged, stroking his beard, "a good many of which involve a man who reminds me of ye, right down to favorin' those muttonchops." While lightning flashed outside and thunder rolled overhead, he shuddered momentarily and asserted, "More than anythin' though, he wore that same terrible, intense look in his eyes, eyes that saw stories too terrible to tell. Had Sarah not had yer drink ready by the time ye reached yer stool, I would've sworn I was seein' the ghost of Big Tom."

Glaring at him, Brass repeated, "Big Tom?"

"Aye, Big Tom," the old sea captain confirmed. "Only the skipper had the right to call him Tomas, and to be sure, it wasn't until I went above and beyond the call of duty that I was afforded that same sort of respect."

"Let me guess," Rags interjected. "You saved his life in the battle of Toulon."

"Yeah, heh-heh," Jack followed up, "you saved his life in battle."

"Actually, no," the old sea captain corrected, "Fer I can assure ye, there was never a time when anyone saved the big man's life in battle, although there were quite a few when he saved mine." Picking up his empty mug, he looked inside and continued, "No, it had more to with the almost religious connection he had to whisky and I first had to prove I truly understood the meanin' of the phrase 'uisge beatha.'"

Locking his eyes on the old sea captain, Brass announced, "Ye should know, if I buy yer next one, the story had better be good."

On cue, Sarah refilled the empty mug, and slowly stroking his beard, the old sea captain determined, "Well, if my years at sea have taught me anythin', it's that I had better be able to adapt on the fly. So while I may be jumpin' ahead a couple months, I'm thinkin' it's best to take us back to my first night at sea aboard *Rosie's Charm*." With the rain beginning to fall in an easy patter, he looked to the bright orange flame burning atop the candle on the mantel behind the bar and declared, "Fer anytime my life's been on the line, I've found there's nobody I can count on to save my hide like old Charmin' Al . . ."

Late December 1743, between Naples and Sicily

"This isn't the first time I've heard of an Irish pirate named Clarkeson," the skipper responded to the conclusion of my story, "except he and his sons never took anythin' more than a few barges loaded with barley headin' down the river near his bog." Though he stood only a few feet to my left, I could not see him speak, for we were well into the darkest hour of the night, and because of a cloud cover chasing our ship, the sky was completely blacked out. "A beautiful one-eyed water sprite," he went on, "leadin' a redheaded banshee and a wild band of

Gaelic-speakin' natives in the slaughter of a hundred armored Spanish conquistadors certainly paints a much more fearsome picture."

We had originally met two days prior, at sunset, when I reached the top of the gangplank leading to his ship at the very moment he was disembarking for an evening of revelry. Initially, our rendezvous was scheduled to take place at the naval base in Port Mahon but terrible storms in the English Channel had delayed my journey and he was unable to wait. In light of Naples being on his itinerary, he had secured my passage on a merchantman, and arriving a week early, I had bided my time in the picturesque Italian port watching for his vessel. Having been made quite aware of his reputation during the three years following my graduation from the Royal Naval Academy, I knew of his eccentricities and, upon receiving my transfer, felt suitably prepared to make his acquaintance. Still, despite my confidence, I found his appearance to be far more farcical than I had imagined, and it was a struggle to maintain my composure. Granted, the Royal Navy had yet to adopt any formal uniform standards. Nevertheless, I kept my hair short, my face clean-shaven, and—like the majority of my colleagues—favored a traditional navy-blue broadcloth jacket with white facings and white breeches.

The skipper, on the other hand, had donned a royal-purple jacket accentuated by gold buttons and gold epaulettes over a gold blouse with a kilt woven in a purple-and-gold tartan. Furthermore, his long curly white wig dangled in front of his eyes, his blond mustache was waxed into horns at the corners on his lips, and his goatee was tied into a ridiculous thin braid that reached the middle of his chest. Returning my laughter, he had introduced me to Tomas, a towering Scot who trimmed his beard into thick dark muttonchops that met at his mouth and let his shaggy brown mane grow well past his shoulders. Dressed in a similar ensemble and carrying a cutlass on his hip, he had directed a most harrowing gaze my way and, crushing my outstretched hand, insisted, "Call me Big Tom." Once they were gone, a somewhat disagreeable little Irishman named Rory showed me to my bunk, and I settled into my new home.

Returning the next morning, the skipper had ordered us to prepare to leave later in the day and retired to his cabin. That afternoon, he reappeared in all-black attire, including a black vest covered in pockets, and had removed the wig to reveal his short blond ponytail. While his mustache had been combed out, his goatee had remained braided, and giving it a tug, he had cast his bright green eyes toward a storm approaching through the rugged Apennine Mountains in the background of the city. "There's a cold front movin' in," he had let me know, "and at this time of year, ye can catch a gale that'll propel ye all the way to Sicily. If ye want some advice, in the Mediterranean, it's always wise to take advantage of any good wind ye get." Pointing to *The Roja Capote*, an old Spanish galleon exiting the harbor, he had followed up, "See, her captain is thinkin' the same thing."

"I wonder if she's goin' to Palermo," I had absentmindedly speculated.

With a wink, he had given me a shrug and replied, "I guess we'll find out."

We departed after supper, and the skipper spent our first hours at sea teaching me the basic principles to operating our vessel. Eighty feet long, *Rosie's Charm* had two decks and two masts that, unlike most of the ships in the Royal Navy, both featured a pair of triangular fore and aft sails. Although I was wary of such novel rigging, I picked up its fundamentals rather easily and was summarily impressed with its contributable improvement to our maneuverability. Because of our role, speed was the top priority, and therefore, only half of the ten portholes lining each of her sides were outfitted for cannon—the other half, should the weather be calm, were reserved for the use of oars. The cold front making them unnecessary, we had battened down the hatches to reduce any drag, and it seemed our sloop almost skimmed atop the open water. Darkness set in, and in the course of explaining the overlapping fields of fire for the dozen swivel guns mounted to the bulwarks, the skipper decided to take a break. Returning to the helm, we joined Big Tom at the wheel, and I was asked if I knew any good stories. Thinking it highly improbable they would have heard of Clarkeson, I recited her tale as it was told to me.

Now, in the pitch black, the rigging strained against billowing sails above our heads, and the wooden deck groaned rhythmically beneath our feet. "It sounds odd to hear that name out of someone else's mouth," the skipper divulged, "fer with the exception of a few people under my command, everyone who knows of my Clarkeson is dead."

"This is not the same Clarkeson," I assured him, "and durin' my last night in London, it seemed like all the sailors I talked to were caught under her spell. Indeed, a few headin' to Kingston the next day asked me to teach them a bit of Gaelic, should they be lucky enough to encounter her."

Behind me, Big Tom grumbled, "She's probably Anne Bonny."

"I doubt it." the skipper responded. "Anne Bonny had red hair, and Clarkeson's is black. What's more, even if ye believe Anne Bonny escaped the hangman's noose, she'd have to be almost fifty."

"Clarkeson's not close to fifty," I insisted. "If she was, she'd be worn out and gray." Based on his seasoned looks, I calculated the skipper to be a good eight to ten years older than me, putting him at or near thirty, and I proposed, "I'll bet she's not even yer age."

"One can hope," he returned, "fer in my experience, young ladies prefer older men. Isn't that right Tomas."

"I'd rather talk about the whisky," the big man growled. "I've never heard of this Oakies."

"Ye haven't heard of Oakies?" the skipper remarked. "I've thought ye've tried every whisky in the world."

"I've tried every whisky in every port I've ever heard to have it," the big man confirmed, "and since I've never heard of anythin' other than rum to drink in the Caribbean, I've never seen any point in crossin' the Atlantic."

"I've crossed it many times," the skipper said, "and now that ye say that, yer right. Durin' my journeys over there, we didn't drink anythin' other than rum. In fact, the only crop I remember seein' planted at the plantations was sugarcane. I'm not sure what they'd use to distill whisky."

"Whisky is grain alcohol," Big Tom reminded him, "and barley is native to Britain. There has to be a grain on that side of the world that'll work." While I couldn't see him, I felt his harrowing gaze upon the back of my head when he asked, "Did they mention what Oakies tastes like?"

"Well, I talked to two Scots who sailed with a Venetian," I mentioned, "and accordin' to them, it was smooth with a hint of buttered corn, whatever that is."

"I do know what corn is," the skipper picked up. "It's a long cob covered with kernels and native to Mexico. We ate it durin' a stop in Belize City. The locals called it maize."

"Is it sweet?" the big man inquired.

"It is."

"Then it has sugar in it," Big Tom stated, "and it can be used to ferment the yeast. Did they say how smoky Oakies was?"

"They didn't," I answered. "They just raved on and on about the woody finish."

"If I were to guess," the big man put forth, "they probably burn oak planks in their kiln to dry out the corn. Should this whisky end up bein' real, it may finally be worth takin' the trip."

Rummaging through his pockets, the skipper suggested, "While I agree a whisky smooth enough to be worth a man's life would make the journey worth it, I would also say the beaches in the Caribbean do so alone." To the pinging of liquid inside a metal container, he asserted, "Clarkeson may not be a water sprite, but I do believe there is somethin' magical to those islands." There was a pause, and his voice resonating toward the west, he noted, "Hmmm, the Royal Navy does have a base at Port Royale. Maybe it is time we find a message to deliver to Jamaica."

Noticing a small lantern bobbing in the darkness off our bow, Big Tom interrupted, "We have more important things to take care of first. There's the *Capote*."

"That was quick," the skipper determined, and coinciding with a muffled pop, he ordered, "Considerin' it's not quite dawn yet, let's hold our current course and keep our distance."

Realizing I had never been apprised of our current mission, I wasn't prepared for the prospect of an engagement, and his command caught me off guard. Fearing the crack in my voice was audible, I asked, "Are we goin' to take her? With ten cannon and a hundred men at our disposal, won't we be outnumbered two to one?"

"At a minimum," the big man grumbled.

The skipper swallowed, let out a happy sigh, and added, "Probably closer to three."

"Is our crew eager to face such odds?" I inquired.

Whistling softly, the skipper told Big Tom, "Boy, his reputation really did precede him. Here, take yer swig so I can put this away. It's way too early to give him any." Perplexed, I tried to ask him to clarify his answer, but he immediately turned to me and continued, "We're not goin' to take her. I know, I know. We're expected to uphold the motto 'The Royal Navy never runs from a fight,' except in this case, I don't think it'd be very wise to go lookin' fer one. Ye see, King Charles is havin' a hard enough time keepin' his kingdom out of the war, and he would have no problem closin' his ports to a British captain huntin' Spanish vessels sailin' in the waters between them. More importantly, ye have to keep in mind this is a messenger ship. Our primary duty is to ferry whatever needs to be ferried to wherever it needs to be ferried as quickly as possible. Should we engage enemy merchants along the way, we may not arrive in a timely manner, or even at all, and then we'd fail our mission. Honestly, and I know it may disappoint ye to hear this, it's usually best we avoid any fightin'."

"Unless there's pirates," the big man seethed.

"Unless there's pirates," the skipper confirmed.

Furrowing my brows, I suggested, "I didn't think pirates were a problem anymore. I was under the impression the bombardments of Tripoli and Algiers, plus the treaty with Tunis, put an end to the attacks on English shipping."

"In times of peace, that's true," the skipper concurred. "However, plenty of slave markets still exist on the western coast of Africa, and because of the war, the conditions are ripe fer piracy to thrive. Beyond the letters of marque the Spanish and Dutch have been issuin' to the privateers, there's been an influx of captains to this sea who have no honor, know no treaties, and are willin' to take any ship regardless of her colors.

At every opportunity, we have a moral imperative to capture or kill them."

Hearing a sardonic tone in his voice, I began to feel my heart beat in my chest, and already possessing my daily pint of rum, I patted down my pockets to find my flask. Taking it out and unscrewing the metal cap, I asked, "Do we expect to encounter any?"

Over the big man letting out a low growl, the skipper replied, "Ye never know. Fer now, we just happen to be followin' *The Roja Capote* to Palermo, which is a good idea in this part of the Mediterranean. At any moment, that helpful tramontana wind we caught out of the Apennines could turn into a libeccio coming off the Corsican coast, and havin' survived a few libeccios in my time, I can tell ye the seas will get rough and the squalls will get violent."

Lifting the flask to my lips, I asked, "How long till we get there?"

"Maybe an hour."

Quickly, I took several healthy chugs. Sugary and sweet, it had enough of a burn to ensure my voice remained even and I felt confident asking, "If we see some pirates between now and then, should I expect a fight?"

Chuckling, the skipper asked Big Tom, "Do ye believe this mate?" Directing his attention back to me, he followed up, "Don't worry. If we see some pirates, ye can expect a fight." At another growl from the big man, he determined, "Yer right, it's time. Take us to port, full speed." On command, the two gaff sails swung to our right, and our vessel turned hard to the left, taking us on a course due east. Silently, I watched the lantern at the stern of the galleon disappear into the darkness and debated having another drink. Suddenly, the skipper touched my right shoulder and asked, "Have ye seen any combat yet?"

Flinching, I felt my mouth go dry, and without hesitating, I finished half my rum. "No," I finally managed, "most of my service has been spent patrollin' the coast of Britain, and the few smugglers we caught never put up any resistance."

"That's fine," he assured me. "We all have to face our first. We'll help ye survive it." He gave me several enthusiastic pats and, addressing Big Tom, continued, "I'm going below to get Rory and have him rouse the men. Keep the *Capote* to our starboard side and make sure the sunrise stays at our backs."

Thirty minutes later, to the first rays of light cresting the horizon, the skipper returned, gave the big man a two-handed Scottish claymore, and took over the wheel. Rory, dressed in his usual black wool sweater, emerald-green kilt, and blood-red scarf, accompanied him to the helm and gave me a most menacing look. Though he barely reached the height of my chin, his muscles were well defined, and his contentious demeanor made up for his slight stature. While his sandy-brown hair resembled a disheveled mop, his face was perpetually bereft of any sort of stubble, and the years at sea had weathered his boyish features. Armed with a pair of flintlocks holstered in each of the two belts crossing his chest, a cutlass at his right hip, a boarding axe on his left, a pair of daggers in both boots, and the flared muzzle of a blunderbuss jutting over his shoulder, he clutched four additional pistol belts in his left hand and a second cutlass in his right. Casting his angry brown eyes up at me, he held the weapons forth and, in a heavy Irish brogue, demanded, "Axe or sword?"

Thinking smartly, I replied, "I prefer the pistols."

"That's not what I asked ye," he sneered. "Answer me friggin' question."

Bristling, I held his gaze and responded, "Sword."

Giving me his extra cutlass, he muttered, "I figured. Most of the fledglin's do." Once I strapped it to my left hip, he handed me two of the pistol belts and added, "Wear 'em like me, and remember the flintlocks have lanyards tied to the holsters, so don't worry if ye should drop 'em as we go."

"As we go?" I questioned.

Slowly turning his head toward the skipper, Rory asked, "Ye didn't tell 'em the plan?"

Shrugging, the skipper answered, "I was goin' to wait until it got light out."

"What plan?" I wanted to know.

Ignoring me, Rory gave the other two pistol belts to Big Tom and posed, "So we really are thowin' the fledglin' into the thick of it, eh, Cap'em?"

Smiling, the skipper countered, "Sometimes that's the best way to learn. Besides, I want to see if the stories are true."

Frowning, I inserted, "What stories?"

"Well, make sure he's aware of me job," Rory went on. "I want 'em to know it's a direct order."

"Yer job?" I interrupted. "What's my job?"

Suddenly, a loud report echoed from our starboard side, and we all glanced to our right, still dark under the twilight sky. The claymore harnessed to his shoulders and the other two pistol belts across his chest, Big Tom took control of the wheel. Free to search the pockets of his vest, the skipper produced a flask, and with a muffled pop, he removed the wooden stopper. Widening his eyes, he uttered, "Here we go," and took a healthy swallow. Letting out a happy sigh, he passed the flask to Rory and ordered, "LAIMH CHEART! [turn right]." Amid our sloop turning in the direction of *The Roja Capote*, the skipper told me, "I probably shouldn't've let ye go on about Clarkeson the way ye did and taken a few minutes to fill ye in on how we expect this mornin' to go. Had ye not been such a good storyteller, and it not been such a good story, I probably would've."

My eyes as wide as his, I returned, "Feel free to do so now."

"We'll get to that in a bit," he assured me, tugging at his braid, "first, there's somethin' else I need to explain. Coincidentally, like Clarkeson, when we head into battle, we also command our crew in Gaelic. Anticipation is the key to survivin' a fight at sea, and since very few people outside Britain understand the language, it's impossible fer our enemies to predict our next move. It may seem trivial. Still, in moments of life or death, experience has taught me it's often the little things that make the difference between livin' and dyin'."

Well aware of the penal laws in Ireland, I felt compelled to reply, "Given the way the English have persecuted that language, I'm surprised the Royal Navy permits it."

Creasing the lines on his forehead, the skipper crossed his arms and noted, "Ye know, it never occurred to me to ask fer permission. Maybe it's time I should." Looking to the left and right, he put forth, "Does anyone see the Royal Navy?"

His stare bitterer than Big Tom's was harrowing, Rory handed me the flask and stated, "I sure don't."

"Well then, I guess we'll worry about what the Royal Navy thinks later," the skipper concluded. "Ultimately, the outcome of a battle at sea can likely make it so it won't matter anyway."

Though I had grown up speaking Gaelic, I took pride in being an officer in the greatest naval force in history, and apparently unlike my present company, I felt obliged to set the proper example for those under my charge. Fuming, I accepted the flask and, in an effort to disguise my contempt, took a healthy swallow. Only I discovered it didn't have the typical sweet sugary burn I had become accustomed to during my service, and instead, it was smoky and raw with a wild spicy flavor that somehow reminded me of home. Warmed the instant it hit my belly, I felt my heart begin to slow, and I couldn't help but smile.

"Aye," Rory muttered, "there's that look we heard about."

Still tugging at his braid, the skipper determined, "It makes me think the rest of the stories are also probably true." Frowning again, I went to speak except he held his palm forth and continued, "Anyway, I figured since yer from Stornoway, ye shouldn't have a problem commandin' the ship in Gaelic."

Passing the flask on to Big Tom, I remarked, "I won't."

"Then too bad fer Rory, he won't get to do his favorite thing," the skipper suggested.

"Want to wager on that, Cap'em?" he asked, "The fledglin's always ferget their part of the plan."

"What plan?!!?" I demanded.

Looking ahead, the skipper pointed to *The Roja Capote* emerging from the darkness between us and the coast of Sicily. Her sails furled, she floated helplessly at the mercy of a pirate ship stationed across her bow. The second vessel one hundred feet long, it had two decks, plus a quarterdeck and a poop deck at the stern, and three masts supporting three spars with a fighting platform at the midpoint of the mainmast in the middle. A hybrid galley, she also employed a bank of oars on each side of her waist, and methodically dipping in and out of the water, they kept her in position.

"Well, well, well, what do we have here?" the skipper murmured, raising his spyglass.

Already holding his to one eye, Rory announced, "I count twenty cannon on her starboard and four chasers at her stern."

"What of her colors?" Big Tom wanted to know.

"Her flag is navy blue with bright orange horizontal stripes across the top and bottom," the skipper told us, "and a big orange D in the middle."

His face contorted, the big man squeezed the handles on the wheel and, his forearms bulging, snarled, "*The Sabre.*"

"Well, Tomas," the skipper posed, "we have a chance to catch Kemi Dakit and earn some prize money to boot. What do ye think? Is it worth the risk?"

Through clenched teeth, the big man repeated, "Kemi Dakit."

"Kemi Dakit?" I picked up.

"Aye," the skipper responded, sliding the tubes of his spyglass together and handing it to me. "I guess ye could call him the last of yer Barbary corsairs. Born in Tripoli, he makes his livin' huntin' fer slaves along the coasts of mainland Europe and, when the price was right, has raided hamlets on the shores of Ireland and Scotland."

The galley's bow facing us, I found it through the lens and watched a steady stream of pirates begin climbing into a row of skiffs gathered at the stern along her port side. "I can't believe the Spaniard doesn't put up a fight," I contended. "I'd think they'd have close to the same firepower."

"Not *The Roja Capote*," the skipper divulged. "The captain is an old man and keeps to the relatively safe route between the major cities in the Kingdom of Naples and Sicily. Anymore, he hardly has the sailors to man the riggin', let alone any cannon. To Kemi Dakit, this is like findin' a pot of gold at the end of a rainbow."

"They're castin' away," Rory interrupted.

"Then I guess we'd better hurry," the skipper concluded.

With the sun rising at our backs and the tramontana at its peak, *Rosie's Charm* hummed over the water, and soon I no longer needed the aid of a spyglass to watch the action aboard our foe. Still peering through his, Rory reported, "I count ten skiffs."

"Whew," the skipper let out, "that's a relief. Figurin' there's eight men in each, we'll only have to face a little more than half his crew."

Feeling my heart begin to thump, I quickly did the math and determined, "That means his crew has to number at least 160."

"More like 200," the skipper informed me.

"Two hundred?" I blurted out.

Lowering his spyglass, Rory glared my way and sneered, "Aye, 200. Is that a problem? Because even if we wipe out half of them, at five pounds a head, the rest should still add a good amount to our prize money." Scrunching his features, he glanced at my breeches and followed up, "Yer not goin' to wet yerself, are ye? If ye want, I'll get ye me extra kilt so it won't be obvious ye've pissed yer pants."

Though I did feel pressure building in my bladder, I disregarded his comments and told the skipper, "I was afraid we'd outnumber them and what fun would that be." My voice trembling, I cleared my throat and furthered, "But even if all we're facin' is half her crew, we'll still need all hands to even the numbers."

"It's about time ye tell 'em the plan," Rory groused. "We're gonna be on 'em soon."

"Oh Rory, I suppose so," the skipper relented, turning to me. "It is time ye heard the plan. There's only a few more things you need to know."

"Make sure ye explain me part in it," Rory insisted.

"I will, Rory, I will," the skipper promised, rolling his eyes. "He really likes his part. It's a thing." Patting his stomach, he nodded toward the big man and followed up, "Tomas does too. Ye know that feeling you have in yer belly right now? He loves it. He thrives on it. In fact, ye could say havin' that fire burnin' in his guts is the only time he's truly happy."

"Better give the orders, skipper," Big Tom muttered.

"Right, let's come in fast and split *The Sabre* from the boardin' party. Load canister shot at half charge into our starboard cannon and at full charge into our port. On my first command, we'll fire the starboard side and take out the skiffs. If there's any remainin', I'll use the swivel guns to clean them up. On my second, we'll fire the port side at point-blank range into *The Sabre* and, hopefully, put enough shot through her hull to clear out her gun deck. In the confusion, we'll board her." Looking to the big man, he concluded, "I'll leave ye to give the order fer the final round of swivel guns."

Observing the other boarding party bearing in on the galleon, Rory determined, "They've gone a quarter of the way. Get to the fledglin's part."

Letting out a long sigh, the skipper put his right hand on my shoulder and explained, "We may be outgunned, but we do have a few advantages, the first bein' the element of surprise." Sweeping his left arm toward the haphazard row of little boats, he continued, "Comin' out of the sun the way we are, there's a good chance they won't notice us until it's too late and we'll have more than a third of the pirates trapped in the open water."

"We'll still be outnumbered when we board their vessel," I reminded him.

"Aw, Jesus," Rory muttered.

"Don't worry," the skipper assured me, "we have plenty of friends on the inside willin' to help us."

"Friends?" I asked.

"Aye," Rory followed up, "the best friends we could ask fer."

Gesturing to the waist of the galley, the skipper calculated, "Between the two sides, there's a total of forty oars. If he's usin' two slaves per oar, it means we have 160 people who'll join us. At three per oar, there's 240. Either way, the odds are good enough will survive the initial barrage to help overwhelm the rest of Dakit's men." Taking his hand off my shoulder, he placed it on my chest and stated, "That's where ye come in. Yer to free them."

Feeling my groin tighten, I exclaimed, "Free them? How am I to do that?"

Smiling, the skipper suggested, "Easy. Do everythin' Rory tells ye to do. See? Simple." My eyes widening again and my mouth completely agape, I tried to speak, only to choke on my words. Chuckling, he arched his brows and asked, "Have you ever heard of the Spartans?"

Blinking several times, I tilted my head and answered, "The Greek warriors?"

"Oh good, ye have. That'll make explainin' things easier." Forming his hands into a triangle, he put forth, "In case ye don't remember, they fought in a phalanx, or essentially a big wedge that moved forward, killing everything in its path. Given how effective it was, we went ahead and copied the idea." Nodding to the big man, he added, "The moment we tie up to a ship and our boardin' party gets over the side, Tomas holds up his mighty sword and yells, 'FAUGH A BALLAGH!'"

"Faugh a ballagh," I echoed. "Clear the way?"

Bobbing his head back and forth, the skipper surmised, "Clear the way, clear the decks, it's not a perfect translation, but it's got a nice ring to it and it's easy to teach so it's a good rally cry. Anyway, every time he calls it out, the rest of our men respond in kind and form up around him. Those on the outside carry cutlasses in one hand and bucklers on the other, while those on the inside are primarily armed with flintlocks and bows." Hooking his thumb to the two-handed claymore strapped to the big man's back, he conceded, "To be sure, that thing is a bit unwieldy in this sort of fight. However, it's easy to see and the best substitute we have fer a standard to guide the formation around."

"If I'm carryin' pistols and a sword," I inquired, "where am I supposed to be?"

"Right in the middle," the skipper stated. "The whole purpose of the wedge is to get ye to the nearest ladder and then down ye'll go."

"Dow-dow-down I'll go?" I stammered. "What do ye mean 'down I'll go'?"

"What do you mean what do I mean?" he asked. "Don't make this harder than it is. Ye and Rory will take five other sailors down to the galley deck and free the slaves. Remember, the men yer leadin' are also armed with four pistols apiece, givin' ye a total of twenty-eight shots, minus any misfires. It's best to keep track along the way."

Sliding the blunderbuss off his shoulder, Rory chipped in, "Don't ferget about the twenty-ninth. Of 'em all, it's the most likely to save yer skin." Smiling, he shook the barrel and added, "It's loaded with a new type of pellet. I can't wait to see the effects."

Much to my relief, the skipper handed me his flask and carried on, "The key here is speed. Don't let anythin' slow ye down."

"What if we meet resistance?" I asked.

"Aw, Jesus," Rory muttered.

Turning his palms over, the skipper said, "You shoot them and move on."

"What if we have to stop to fight?"

Shaking his head, the skipper asserted, "You don't stop to fight."

"What if we have no choice?"

"Aw, Jesus," Rory spat.

Tugging at his braid, the skipper posed, "I imagine if ye stop, yer dead."

"I see," I managed and took a healthy swig.

"Don't let it worry ye," the skipper went on. "Our volley should create enough chaos that they won't realize what yer doin' until it's too late."

Feeling the whisky running warm through my veins, I met his stare and asked, "Won't our volley kill some of our friends?"

"Oh, I'm sure it will," he confirmed, "and I'm sure the galley deck won't be a pretty sight. A bit of advice, don't look down. Anyway, they count on the shackles to keep the slaves in line, so there shouldn't be very many guards to contend with. Kill them all and search their bodies fer the keys. The officer in charge will probably be close to the ladder at the stern. Usually, he'll have one set and one other guard'll have another. Expect one chain to run through the manacles attached to every oar, and once it's unlocked, the entire row can be freed. After that, ye only have one more set of orders, and if ye ask me, they should be the easiest to follow, yet it seems like they're the most difficult fer every new officer to carry out."

"What's that?"

"Yell SAORSA [freedom] at the top of yer lungs."

"Freedom?"

"No, not freedom," the skipper insisted. "I already told you, we command our men in Gaelic. Yell SAORSA. While I want there to be a bloodbath when those slaves come topside, I don't want any of our men to get caught up in it. Tomas will be relyin' on ye to give him the warnin' they're on the way."

"Right, yell *saorsa*," I remarked. "That does seem easy enough. Anythin' else?"

"Get back to the wedge," he explained. "Ideally, it'll still be in position at the ladder ye first went down, and the moment ye return, ye'll meld into the formation and take the ship."

"Tell 'em the rest of me part, Cap'em," Rory grumbled, "and I'll be on me way."

Locking his eyes onto mine, the skipper stated, "Should ye get killed, Rory's first duty is to complete yers. If ye live, then he's to make sure ye always command in Gaelic. If ye forget and switch to English, he has orders to remind ye usin' any readily available blunt object." Putting his hands on both my shoulders, he asserted, "This is a bloody affair we're involved in, and I'd rather have ye get some stitches or lose a tooth than risk the lives of the rest of our men. Do ye understand?"

I glanced at Rory, who smiled happily and, handing the flask to the skipper, answered, "Perfectly."

"Good," the skipper concluded. He gave me several pats and turned his attention to *The Sabre*. It was close enough to emit a repulsive stench of humanity, and curling his lips, he ordered, "Rory, go see to the cannons. Make sure the men know they've only got one chance to get it right."

"Aye, aye, Cap'em," Rory retorted, and quickly, he slid down the ladder aft of the helm.

"I know he is a bit combative," the skipper allowed, "but I don't mind and soon you won't either."

"It looks like we've been spotted," Big Tom reported. Following his gaze to the skiffs, which had now covered two thirds of the distance to the galleon, I noticed a man in the closest standing up and attempting to blot out the sun behind us.

"I see him too," the skipper picked up. "All right, Tomas, I'll take the wheel." Beaming, he took one last drink and told me, "We've done this plenty of times. Should something go awry and make it impossible to complete yer objective, get back to the wedge and retreat to our ship. Although it may cost us the prize money, we can always circle *The Sabre* and pummel her into smithereens. Even if it's not profitable, it'll still feel good to see her roll over and disappear under the sea."

I followed Big Tom to the bow, and we gathered with the forty-one men comprising the boarding party. "Just like the skipper told ye," he reiterated, "the men on the outside of the wedge carry a cutlass and a buckler, and those on the inside carry flintlocks and bows. We've got two dozen pistols, a half dozen musketoons, and a couple more blunderbusses. All together, it adds up to be another thirty-three shots. As soon as we run out, we'll rely on the archers."

My heart pounding in my chest, I took a deep breath and asked, "They don't reload?"

"If ye do yer job, they won't have to," he filled in, "and it's always possible that we'll have suffered casualties and they'll be needed to reinforce the wedge. That's why ye can't let anythin' slow ye down."

With the pressure increasing in my bladder, I clutched the hilt of my cutlass and inspected the men I would be leading. Rory climbed up the nearest ladder and moved unimpeded throughout our cadre. "Look around ye," he bellowed. "These are the finest sailors in the Royal Navy, the finest navy in history." His chest out and arms flexed at his sides, he pointed to several veterans and declared, "Ye've never run from a fight, nor have ye, and nor have ye. Surrounded by me mates, there's no way I'd ever run from a fight. Hell, we're the reason they say the Royal Navy never runs from one!" Going on to nudge some sailors and punch a few more, he continued, "There's nothin' more fun that drivin' a blade into the belly of some pirate scum. Who else is ready to do it? I know I am!" Seeing our sloop close in on the *Sabre*'s bow, he announced, "And on top of it all, she's worth at least a year's pay in prize money! Now who's with me?"

Listening to our men roar in response, I noticed *The Roja Capote* had already unfurled her sails and was setting off for Sicily. Word of our arrival also appeared to have spread through the skiffs, for one sprinted ahead toward the galleon, one attempted to return to the galley, and the rest bobbed somewhere in between. Glancing to *The Sabre*, I watched the pirates remaining aboard swarm over her deck and scramble up her rigging.

"What about ye, Cap'em?" Rory wanted to know. A happy gleam in his eyes and an infectious smile across his face, he snapped me out of my trance and inquired, "What's yer lucky number?"

"My lucky number?" I repeated. "Hmmm . . . since I was born on the twenty-sixth, I guess I'll go with that."

"Twenty-six!" Rory exclaimed. Nudging, slapping, and smacking every man standing close, including the big man, he stated, "Now that's a fledgling boastin' some serious gumption." Thumping my left shoulder hard enough to knock me off balance, he added, "To get to twenty-six, ye better be in good shape. Do ye have a dagger?"

Shaking my head, I answered, "No, I only have the cutlass and pistols."

In a single swift movement, he removed one out of his left boot and told me, "Here, take it. To get to twenty-six, yer probably goin' to need a few more weapons still." Though I tried to decline, he forced it in my hands and insisted, "Don't worry, I've got plenty. Besides, me lucky number is seven. That's all I have to get. If I get seven, I'll be gettin' lucky in Palermo tonight!" Clapping my shoulder again, he put his finger to my chest and said, "So ye better save a few fer me, Cap'em." Wading back among the men, he went on to proclaim, "Aye, we got a cap'em who's got some serious gumption. He wants to get twenty-six! Twenty-six! Here all I want is seven!"

Suddenly, Tomas boomed, "BEIR AIR! [grab hold]" and instinctively I grabbed the forestays attaching the sails to the hull. Directly in front us, the returning skiff disappeared below our bow and—in rapid succession—I heard a loud crunch beneath our keel, the galley's wooden oars shatter, and the skipper command, "TILG PEILEARAN! [open fire]."

To the thunder of our starboard cannons discharging, I caught a glimpse of several skiffs disintegrating in a shroud of metal fragments and black smoke. Immediately, the skipper repeated, "TILG PEILEARAN!" to which the cannon on our port side erupted and an iron rain showered *The Sabre*'s hull. The cries of wounded men rose above the din, and with a heavy thud, the bow of *Rosie's Charm* smashed into *The Sabre*'s waist. The collision a glancing blow, it pitched the larger ship violently to port, shaking the men in the rigging loose and sending several tumbling into the sea.

Our stern whipped back into their bow and both vessels spun, locked in a tight circle. In the haze, our boarding party cast their lanyards over the bulwarks, set the hooks, and tied the two crafts together. Big Tom ordered, "TILG PEILEARAN!" and the swivel guns on our port side sent one last salvo across the other deck. Following the big man up the ropes, I reached the top, leapt to the other side, and landed amid several dead bodies.

Holding his claymore high, Big Tom yelled, "FAUGH A BALLAGH!" and chopped down one pirate trying to rise to his feet. Ripping the blade out of the fresh corpse, he repeated a bloodcurdling "FAUGH A BALLAGH!" and responding to his chant with the same force and fury as the rest of our men, I took my place behind his right flank. Even in the tumult, our crew quickly formed a compact triangle of bristling steel, and commanding "LAIMH CHEARR! [go left]," the big man swung the grisly tip of his sword toward the ladder at the bow.

A few pirates, dressed in dark-blue robes tied with orange sashes and matching turbans, tried to mount a defense. Wielding scimitars, they had their blows parried by the buckler of one sailor and an exposed part of their body pierced by the cutlass of another. A few more armed with spears rallied in a circle around our objective, and to a deafening blast, a blunderbuss tore through the little group. One by one, a trio of pirates climbed up the ladder to confront us, and one by one, they fell to the fire of our musketoons. Hearing the clashing of steel at my back, I hastened a look over my shoulder to see an additional half-dozen pirates attack our rear. Suddenly a second blunderbuss went off, ripping them apart and sending their lifeless bodies sprawling across the deck. A crazy smile on his face, the sailor who fired it quickly shouldered the weapon, drew his sword, and filled in the gap where one of our men had fallen. "STAD! [stop]" Big Tom ordered, bringing my attention forward.

Hitting my arm, Rory cried, "We're up, Cap'em!"

Similar to a traditional galley, *The Sabre* was designed with a flat hull and a bow open to the sea. While I grasped the highest rung of the ladder, Rory and the other sailors slid over the edge and momentarily hung on before dropping to the deck underneath. Sheathing my cutlass, I followed their lead and, my feet dangling over the side, caught one last glance of several pirates at the stern, aiming bows at our formation. To our final musketoons blasting away, I let go.

Landing in a crouch, I looked down the gun deck but it was full of smoke and I couldn't see anything other than the faint orange glow of a fire. A pirate, coughing uncontrollably, came out of the haze with one arm covering his eyes and the other reaching for the daylight. Instinctively, I pulled a pistol and shot him in the shoulder. The impact sending him into an uncontrollable spin, he fell over the bulwark and splashed into the water.

His eyes aglow, Rory leapt to his feet and cried, "Good one, Cap'em!"

A flight of six stairs descended to the galley deck, and two more pirates came up to meet us. The first, swinging his scimitar, hacked off the closest sailor's leg below his knee. Rory fired a pistol, hitting the assailant in the chest and knocking him back into the second one. Together, they tumbled to the base of the steps and landed in a heap. Pointing to a pair of our men, Rory ordered, "FAIRE AMACH! [stand guard]." Smacking my arm, he followed up, "Let's go!" and bounded down to the lower level. Holstering my spent flintlock, I drew another with my right hand and my cutlass with my left. Chasing after him, I jumped over the two fallen pirates, and noticing the second trying to lift the body of the first, I plunged my blade through his ribs. He twisted in his death throes, ripping the sword out of my hand, and pulling my third pistol, I advanced.

The galley deck ran the length of the ship, with an elevated gangway down the middle and benches on both sides long enough for three slaves to sit facing the stern. To my right, a third of the rows had been decimated, and body parts floated amid the splintered remains of the broken oars. When the momentum of the sea momentarily separated the vessels, I caught a brief glimpse of daylight through thousands of little holes in the hull before they slammed back together and water surged through the open rowlocks. To the left, the scene was even more ghastly, for the oars had not been broken and lifeless naked corpses still chained in place eerily swayed to and fro.

A few feet down the gangway, the first guard knelt on all fours with a red slime oozing out of his mouth. Rory plunged his cutlass into the base of the man's skull, and splashing face down into the water, the body pulled the sword out of his hand. Letting it go, he drew a pistol and told the sailor following me, "CUARDAIGH! [search]."

The two of us continued on until another larger pirate holding a scimitar in one hand and a whip in the other confronted us at midships. Simultaneously we shot him. Our musket balls knocking him off his feet, he fell into a row of surviving slaves on our right, and wrapping their chains around his neck, they squeezed out his last breath. Trying to slip past his convulsing legs, Rory tripped and stumbled into the opposite row. Per orders, I carried on to the ladder at the stern and found the officer in charge yelling into the open hatch above. Straightening, I raised the pistol in my right hand, took aim for his head, and pulled the trigger. Only I was met by a loud click. Hastily cocking the hammer again, I pulled the trigger again, to no avail again. Looking over the gun sight, I saw two pirates slide down the ladder and make room for a second pair. Letting go of my useless pistol, I pulled my dagger.

Suddenly, Rory ordered, "SEACHAIN [duck], CAP'EM!"

Intuitively, I dropped flat into the dingy water washing over the gangway. His blunderbuss erupting in the confined space, its blast threw all four pirates back into their leader and obliterated the heads of the slaves seated in the two front rows. Crouched on one knee and cackling out loud, Rory slung his weapon over his shoulder and screamed, "The keys!"

My last flintlock wet and useless, I let it go and dove into the mound of bodies. Together, Rory and I plunged our blades into each pirate and pulled them off the pile. His got stuck in the one atop the leader and ripped out of his grip. Immediately, he released it and started patting around the leader's waist. Finding a large iron ring, he yanked it free and, holding it up, rattled the keys. Abruptly, a hand reached up to grab his wrist, and we both looked down to see a face rise out of the mire. Gasping for air, the leader opened his brown eyes, met ours, and rotated the jagged white bone sticking out of his left shoulder. Wild with fear, confusion, hate, and terror, his gaze went from us to the bloody stump, and as I slit his throat, it settled on me. Hastening his demise, I pinned his head under the murk until his life drained away.

Ripping free of the dead man's grasp, Rory yelled, "Yer up, Cap'em! Give the call!"

"SAORSA!" I cried.

Swinging the keys, Rory smacked my jaw hard enough to both knock me back and knock the dagger out of my hand. Tasting blood in my mouth, I ran my tongue over a shattered molar and glared at him. With shrug, he offered a heartfelt "Sorry, Cap'em!"

"Just free the bloody slaves!" I ordered and screamed, "SAORSA!" again at the top of my lungs.

His smile back on his face, Rory replied, "Aye, aye, Cap'em," and following my lead, he repeated "SAOIRSE!" until we all heard a faint response to our chant.

I let a sailor help Rory unlock the chains and continued our mantra. Oddly, I found the more I shouted in my native tongue, the more it increased my enthusiasm and the more savage it became. Once the slaves were loose, we herded them to the ladder at the stern and retreated to the bow. Realizing I was unarmed, I stopped to place my foot on the back of the pirate Rory had cut down on the gangway and ripped the stuck cutlass out of his body. Looking up the steps, I cried, "SAORSA!"

"SAORSA," the men guarding the gun deck repeated, initiating the cadence with those on the main deck.

At my side, Rory yelled, "Come on, Cap'em. The fun is just beginnin'!"

Offering the cutlass, I said, "I believe this is yers."

"No, ye keep it," he stated, raising his boarding axe. "I've still got this." Waving his finger between the two remaining sailors, he asked, "How many rounds do ye have?"

"Two," the first answered.

"One," the second followed up.

"My last pistol got soaked," I told him. "I doubt it'll fire."

"Yer point man," Rory commanded to the first sailor. "If our men are dead, shoot anybody standin' over them."

To the ringing of steel, we ran up the stairs and found our two comrades besieged by three pirates amid a slew of dead bodies. Immediately, the first sailor pulled both triggers, and the first two pirates collapsed to the deck. The second sailor shot the third pirate and, twisting over the bulwark, he fell into the sea.

Splattered in blood, Big Tom looked through the hatch and cried, "FAUGH A BALLAGH!"

"FAUGH A BALLAGH!" we returned and climbed the ladder. Fourth in line, I reached the top and took the big man's outstretched hand. In one motion, he pulled me up the rest of the way and deposited me on my backside. When our last two men fell in next to me, he ordered, "Get up, it's not over yet."

The wedge considerably thinned, I took a place next to Rory at the very tip and enjoyed an unimpeded view of the pandemonium we had created. Thick black smoke poured out of both sides of the ship, and dead bodies, some naked and some clothed, littered the main deck. Groups of slaves picked up the discarded weapons and attacked the few remaining pirates gathered in a defensive circle around the helm. As arrows streaked from our formation and plunged into theirs, Big Tom pointed his bloody claymore forward and ordered, "AIR ADHART! [forward]." Very few of our men still wielded cutlasses, and even fewer defended with bucklers, leaving the majority of us to employ boarding axes, appropriated scimitars, spears, or anything else we could muster. Moving in concert, we chanted, "FAUGH A BALLAGH," and overcoming our adversaries, I felt a euphoric rush of invincibility. When we reached midships, the smoke lessened considerably, and our chanting rose over the din of the fighting. The seconds slowed to minutes and the minutes slowed to hours and those who surrendered survived—those who didn't perished.

"STAD!" Big Tom commanded, bringing the wedge to a halt at the wheel. Glaring at three pirates cowering at our feet, he demanded, "Where's yer captain?"

Their hands up, they all shrugged and shook their heads.

Behind us, someone shouted, "CARA! [friend]."

Letting out an audible sigh, Big Tom lowered his sword, and a fresh wave of our shipmates surrounded us. One man, covered in soot and streaked with sweat, told him, "We've got it from here. Well done. The whole affair took less than ten minutes. I can't believe it went that easy."

In the midst of our formation slowly breaking up, the big man replied, "I didn't think it did."

"That's because ye weren't standin' where I was. There was never a doubt." Winking, he added, "In fact, I even won a little money on ye."

"Who bet against me?" Big Tom wanted to know.

Grinning, the other man responded, "I'm not tellin'. If I did, there's a chance he'll never do it again." Seeing me, he went on, "And how 'bout that? The fledglin' survived. Rory lost to me too." Noting the smoke wafting out the sides, he added, "I suppose I better go put out the fire. Hopefully, the damage isn't too bad."

Leaving the replacements to gather our captives and fight the flames, Rory joined several sailors already sitting at the quarterdeck with their backs against the poop deck. While Big Tom paced back and forth, I peered toward the bow. Surprisingly, far in the distance, I could make out *The Roja Capote* heading unmolested in the direction of Palermo.

"I think he broke his cherry today," I caught Rory telling the men flanking him. Looking down, I discovered they were staring up at me. "I was tellin' 'em about yer first kill, Cap'em," he informed me, "unless ye had one prior to this mornin'."

Noticing my hands, grimy and covered in a red sheen, I muttered, "No, that was my first." Even more alarming, I was now carrying an axe, although I had no idea where I got it or what happened to the cutlass I had brought topside.

Slapping the shoulder of the man seated on his right, Rory exclaimed, "Ye see, I told ye, and I was there fer it." Hooking his thumb my way, he continued, "Of course, the moment we slipped over the side, the fledglin' went to take the rungs of the ladder and I was lucky he did, fer it was a wee bit more of a fall than I expected and I landed pretty hard. Suddenly, out of the smoke and fire, a pirate with a crazed look like a wild stallion comes wavin' his scimitar over his head and screamin' bloody murder at me." Showing his palms, Rory furthered, "And here I am flat on me back without a weapon in me hand. I thought I was a goner fer sure, only down drops the cap'em and calm as can be, he shoots the pirate dead where he stood." Turning my way, he asked, "Isn't that right, Cap'em?"

Pausing, I took some time to survey the surviving members of the boarding party. Bruised and scraped, they were all bleeding somewhere and covered in the same grimy red sheen I was. Meeting their eyes, I nodded to each man individually and asserted, "That's how I recall it."

His cackle harsh, Rory concluded, "And right then, I knew we'd found a keeper. I don't mind losin' me bet today."

Big Tom put his fingers on my chin and turned my head to inspect the bruise on my right cheek. "It seems he forgot his orders."

"I didn't forget anythin'," I mumbled, "I cried out *saorsa*." Running my fingers over the knot forming on my jaw and my tongue over the jagged tooth, I asked Rory, "Why'd ye hit me?"

Shrugging in the same manner he had during the battle, he claimed, "Force of habit. Yer the first fledglin' to get it right!"

"Why does it resemble a key?" the big man wanted to know.

"It was the only thing I had in me hand," Rory answered.

Throwing his head back, Big Tom laughed out loud, and casting my gaze forward, I saw the smoke turn from black to gray to white. His deafening guffaws fading, I heard a slave untie the sash around the waist of a dead pirate and pull it free. Then I heard the piercing cries of several seagulls circling overhead, and I even made out the gentle lapping of the water against the two hulls. Suddenly, an unexpected rush besieged me, and my entire body trembled uncontrollably.

"Ohhh, he's got the shakes," Rory pointed out. "Don't be alarmed. I'm sure they'll be hittin' me soon too." Reaching into a pocket, he produced a metal flask, removed the wooden stopper, and took a healthy drink. Handing it to me, he said, "Go ahead, ye've earned it."

In raising it to my mouth, I noticed an intense aroma of peat, and at the first sip, a cruel burn seared my lips and tongue. While the flavor was somehow heavier than the smell, it could not entirely subdue a slight piney stickiness and the lingering hint of rotten eggs. Shivering, I forced myself to swallow, and let out a breath like fire. Instantly, however, it warmed my belly, sent a tingle through my veins, and the trembling lessened considerably. My eyes softening, I inadvertently smiled.

"It may not be the skipper's whisky," the big man remarked, "but it sure does the trick."

I handed him the flask and inhaled deeply. Thankfully, the acrid smell of the spent gunpowder combined with the charred wood to overwhelm the foul odor emanating from the galley deck. Glancing to the helm of *Rosie's Charm*, I saw the skipper give me a wave, and in response, I issued a crisp salute. Several thuds echoed below, Big Tom continued to pace, and though I tried to listen in on the conversation Rory was having, everything began sounding like a blur. Then, without warning and without meaning to, I yawned.

"Ohhh, look at that," Rory commented. "He's a sleeper."

Forcing my eyes open, I asked, "What's that?"

"Yer a sleeper," Big Tom told me, "the same as the skipper. At the end of every battle, he'll be fast asleep within fifteen minutes."

Fighting another yawn, I managed, "That's nonsense."

"No, yer a sleeper," Rory repeated. "It affects us all differently. I'm a pisser. I pissed myself the entire fight." Gesturing to the big man, he added, "And ye can bet he's as hard as a rod right now."

"Aye," Big Tom acknowledged, grabbing his crotch. "They're lucky I don't go bugger 'em all."

Rory cackled and I yawned again, this time longer and deeper than the previous two. "Seriously," he warned, "sleepers'll pass out right where they stand. Ye need to take a seat. Otherwise, yer likely to hurt yerself worse in yer fall than I hurt ye with that key."

Resisting the desire to close my eyes, I insisted, "I'll be fine."

"Here," Rory pressed, scooting over to make some room at his side, "ye can curl up next to me and be out of the sun. Don't worry, ye'll be safe." Without any intention of closing my eyes, I took him up on his offer, and in moments, I was out like a snuffed candle.

To metal clanging and hammers pounding, I awoke with a start. Alone, I was now surrounded by firearms lined up against the quarterdeck and set atop the poop deck. His back to me, Rory, examining the blade of a boarding axe, stood next to three piles of weapons. Aware of my stirring, he threw the axe into a pile of armaments in a state of similar disrepair and said, "Well, well, well, it's about time yer awake. We'll be headin' out soon."

I must've been sleeping for a few hours, for the sun had risen well over the horizon and a few clouds lazily floated in the bright blue sky. Yawning, I rubbed my eyes, and with a startle, I opened them to the skipper standing over me.

Smiling, he grasped my hand and put forth, "Ye look like shit." Helping me stand, he continued, "I heard what Rory did to ye. I told you he likes his job. If it's any consolation, as long as yer alive, he won't get to do it again." Grimacing, I ran my tongue over my chipped tooth, gingerly touched the side of my jaw, and felt a steady throbbing settle in all over my body. Handing me his flask, the skipper asserted, "Here, ye deserve it."

His whisky smoky and raw with the wild spicy kick that reminded me of home, I swallowed several chugs and let out a happy sigh.

Laughing out loud, Rory determined, "He didn't appreciate mine like that."

"That's because yers can't be called whisky, or even moonshine," the skipper told him. "Rotgut is the better term."

Keeping his eyes on me, he went on, "I've got good news. Because ye completed yer part swiftly, the fire didn't get a chance to spread and we were able to contain the damage to the gun deck." Sniffing at the air, he followed up, "I'm actually kind of grateful it started. I'll take the smell of charred wood over death any day. Anyway, at Palermo, we'll make the repairs necessary to get *The Sabre* seaworthy enough fer the journey to Port Mahon, where the Royal Navy will assess the amount of prize money she's worth."

Watching our crew readying the captured vessel, I asked, "What are my orders?"

"Your orders?" the skipper repeated, raising his eyebrows. "First off, I'm orderin' ye to go to the cockpit and have the surgeon check ye out." Appraising a dark-red patch soaking my left thigh, he suggested, "It looks like ye may have some wounds more serious than a chipped tooth. Then, once yer patched up, I'm orderin' ye to go to yer bunk and get more sleep. I want ye to have yer wits later tonight. . ."

JAMAICA

Kingston

Henry's

Gallows Point

Kingston
Harbor

Port Royale

Palisadoes

Rackham's Cay

N
W   E
S

The Scottish Rose: Mairi, Connor, Angus

CHAPTER 4

October 1, 1785, Kingston, Jamaica

Over the fading lightning and thunder, the third metal pin fell from the side of the candle on the mantel behind the bar and clattered off the previous two. Casting his bright blue eyes on the steady orange flame, the old sea captain covered his heart and noted, "Of course, as always, the skipper proved to be right, fer in spite of his mistake costin' me a tooth, I'll always hold Rory in the highest esteem." He finished his lager and, tilting his mug toward Brass, declared, "The big man too. It may have been decades since the last time he literally saved my skin, yet I got a feelin' he did so again tonight."

Brass squinted at the old sea captain, nodded slightly, and returned the gesture. Absent the sound of the storm or the story, the room fell eerily quiet, and Nancy seized the moment to check on everyone at the table. While she took Lina's order, a short stout man entered and hung his burgundy cloak on a peg to the right of the doorway. Dressed in a sleeveless white blouse and cobalt vest stretched over his portly stomach, he wore a thick gold band on his left ring finger and fitted black pants tucked into his knee-high black leather boots. Though the dome of his skull was bald, he grew out the scraggly brown hair around the base and it blended in with the scruffy brown beard shrouding his chest. Swinging his flabby arms, he marched to the bar, gave Sarah a quick salute, and pulled out the stool to the right of Tony. Bumping his friend's shoulder, he said, "Hola, mi amigo, boy, am I glad to be here. Once I heard the bell and knew Henry's was open, I had to find a way to sneak out."

Serving him two ounces of rum with a lime wedge, Sarah arched an eyebrow and asked, "Jack, when has a measly little hurricane ever shut me down? Besides, you always swear this is the safest place to weather one out."

"Only because it's safer than bein' cooped up at home with the wife and kids," he grumbled and picked up his drink. Shuddering, he buried the left side of his face into his palm and furthered, "I swear, there'll never be a thunder loud enough to drown out all her yellin'. Go ahead and pour me another. I need it."

"It's a good thing you got away," Tony remarked. He leaned forward and, gesturing to the old sea captain, followed up, "This gentleman is telling us a pretty good story."

With a wave of both hands, Rags insisted, "Ahhh, you would've been better off staying at home. This story is a bunch of nonsense."

"Yeah, heh-heh," Jack chipped in, "this story is all crazy talk." Setting down his empty wine glass, he rambled on, "Of course, heh-heh, in my time sailing the Mediterranean, heh-heh, I may have been aboard a galley or two, heh-heh. Of course, none of them were pirates, heh-heh, and even if they were, they weren't slavers, heh-heh."

Closing his eyes and shaking his head, Rags growled, "Jesus Christ Jack, you never sailed the Mediterranean. Where do you get this stuff?"

Ignoring their conversation, the newly arrived Jack squeezed his lime into his rum and asked Tony, "What's his story about?"

Smiling easily, Tony put forth, "A beautiful one-eyed Irish pirate named Clarkeson and her Spanish hero, Captain Ricardo DeLogrono."

Frowning, Brass asserted, "That's not even close to what it's about. It's about the first mate on a British sloop of war. Ye can call him Big Tom."

"It's not either," John started, "It's actually about a pair of twins, Mathew and Mark—"

"Who kept the islands of Nevis and Saint Kitts safe," Luke finished.

Stamping her foot, Nancy exclaimed, "It's none of that!" With all eyes turning to her, she looked at Sarah and stated, "It's really about Mairi. And Mairi is a lot like Sarah."

"It doesn't matter who it's about," Rags contended. "None of it actually happened."

"Well, I don't care who it's about," Jack announced, "or whether or not it happened." In one gulp, he swallowed his rum, set his empty glass on the bar, and told them, "I just want to listen to somethin' other than a mother fightin' with her three boys. I'll even buy his next round if that's what it takes."

Slowly stroking his beard, the old sea captain waited for Sarah to begin refilling his lager and responded, "Why, thank ye kindly, good sir. They did a pretty good job runnin' through the cast of characters. Is there anyone who interests ye the most?"

"I don't care," Jack wearily replied, "anyone who makes the girls happy."

In her soft voice, Nancy demanded, "Then I think we should hear more about Mairi."

The rain falling in little more than a pitter-patter, Sarah stood in front of the old sea captain and arched her brows. With a bit of foam running down the side of his mug, he met her gaze, nodded, gave her a wink, and proclaimed, "The Royal Navy may have never had a rule the skipper wasn't willin' to break, but that sure doesn't mean he didn't have a few of his own he wouldn't bend, and to be sure, if there was one at the top of the list, it was to always keep yer bartender happy." While she smiled and set his lager down, he looked at the candle on the mantel behind the bar and put forth, "Which means we need to go back a few months to the first delivery Mairi made after her stop at Paddies, fer to be sure, the best place to be next is the very place we're already at, seated here at the bar at Henry's on the mornin' she dropped in . . ."

Early November 1743, Caribbean Sea, south of Jamaica

Wearing a navy shirt with long burgundy sleeves, loose-fitting black breeches, and her familiar bonnet woven in a red, white, and blue tartan, Mairi spent the final moments before dawn silently finishing her coffee beside Connor at the bow of *The Scottish Rose*. Their schooner approaching the southern coastline of Jamaica, they beheld the rising sun creep all the way down the yellow-and-green slopes of the eastern mountains and reflect off the white brick buildings barely visible on the farthest outskirts of Kingston. Near the entrance to the harbor, several tiny islets randomly broke the surface of the water, and off their starboard side, one bore a weathered skeleton bound to a rusty iron cage hanging from a dilapidated wooden scaffold. To the slight creaking of the chains drifting in the wind, she nodded to it and stated, "That's Rackham's Cay, named fer old Calico Jack. Since ye didn't have yer sea legs the last time we were here,

I didn't get a chance to tell ye the story behind it. On November 18, 1720, he was executed at Gallows Point, only rather than tossin' his body to the sharks, they placed it in gibbets and strung it up to rot as a warnin' fer every sailor to see." While a raven letting out several high-pitched throaty squawks landed to the right of the skull, she concluded, "And fer all I know, that's still him grinnin' at us."

Watching the yellowed bones swaying to and fro, Connor noted, "Then he's been hung up there a good twenty years. Would they really leave him that long?"

"Should they make it a point to put ye up there," she acknowledged, "ye can bet they'll make it a point to leave ye up there. He wasn't even all that successful. Do ye know what he's probably best remembered fer?"

"What's that?"

"Bein' married to Anne Bonny." Waving her right index finger to the cadence of her speech, Mairi insisted, "Mark my words, he may have been the captain of their sloop, *William*, but she'll be the more famous of the two. History'll put her right up there with Black Bart and Blackbeard."

"If she wasn't the captain," Connor returned, "why would that be?"

"Because of her very nature," Mairi asserted. "It was well known Anne Bonny dressed like a man, cursed like a man, and fought like a man. In fact, the night they were captured, the defense of their ship was largely left to her and Mary Read."

"Mary Read?"

"Another female pirate who fooled everyone into thinkin' she was a male. Rumor has it Anne Bonny saw past her disguise the first time they met and, some say, took their relationship even further." Shrugging, Mairi suggested, "Whether that's true or not doesn't matter. What does matter is that had the two of them not been abandoned durin' that final battle, they might all still be free."

"Where was Calico Jack?"

Shaking her head and crossing her arms, Mairi answered, "Hidin' in his cabin, too drunk to fight. That mornin', he had invited another band of pirates to come aboard, and they drank the day away close to the shore of Dry Harbor Bay. By ten, many of them were already passed out when an English pirate hunter named Jonathan Barnet used the darkness to sneak up in his sloop, *The Snow-Tyger*, and demand their surrender. In response, Calico Jack fired his swivel guns, so Barnet unloaded with a full broadside, and all the pirates except one went scurryin' below decks. Callin' them a bunch of cowards, Mary Read shot her pistols into the hold and actually killed a crewmate, yet I would say her reaction wasn't nearly as ruthless as Anne Bonny's was." A gleam in her eyes, Mairi asked, "Do ye want to hear her last words to Calico Jack?"

"Sure."

With a cackle more harsh than happy, Mairi put forth, "On the eve of his execution, they were granted one final visit, and standin' face to face, she used it to tell him, 'I'm sorry to see ye like this, but had ye fought like a man, ye need not be hang'd like a dog.'"

Raising his brows and leaning back, Connor mentioned, "Ohhh, she was ruthless. What happened to her and Mary Read?"

"Both were tried, found guilty, and sentenced to die, although they both claimed to be pregnant and pleaded with their bellies to earn a temporary stay of execution. Prior to givin' birth, Mary Read took ill and succumbed to a fever in prison—that much is certain. On the other hand," Mairi went on, turning over her palms, "nobody really knows what became of Anne Bonny's fate. There's no record of her havin' a baby, there's no record of her death, and there's no record of her pardon. It seems she just vanished into thin air."

"What do ye think happened to her?"

"Well, her father was a successful merchantman, and the safe bet is he paid fer her freedom, only seein' he had disowned her fer marryin' her first husband, James Bonny, I doubt that was the case." A sly smile crossing her lips, Mairi suggested, "Instead, since she never had a problem gettin' men to fall in love with her, I'd wager Anne Bonny charmed the hangman right out of his noose."

They reached the mouth of the harbor where, on their right, the Palisadoes, a long thick sandbar providing a natural breakwater to the sea, ended at the remains of Port Royale. Once notorious for being the richest and wickedest city in the Caribbean, a powerful earthquake in 1692 destroyed most of its buildings, and the resulting tsunami washed two thirds of its total land under the sea. Though four of the five British forts had also been lost, given the strategic location the Royal Navy restored the remaining facilities and continued to operate a base. Under the watchful eye of Fort Charles at the very tip, *The Scottish Rose* sailed through the gap and passed Gallows Point—a thin sliver of land at the back of the compound with several nooses hanging above a platform.

Peering over the bulwark at the rooftops submerged forty feet below, Connor said, "It would've been nice to have been safe in here durin' the storm that hit us the day we left Culebra. Either that or I wish we could've returned to Paddies."

"Ye know why we couldn't return to Paddies," Mairi stated, "and ultimately, you were never in any danger at Vieques." Raising her spyglass to her right eye, she scanned the thirty ships anchored near the dozen wooden piers dotting the Kingston

121

shoreline and determined, "It looks like we got lucky today. Hardly anyone appears to be moored right now. We should be able to pay the harbormaster his fee and get right in." Lowering her spyglass, she faced Connor and asked, "Besides bein' seasick, what do ye remember about the last time we were here?"

"I remember a guy and his two sons met us at the dock with a cart led by a couple of horses."

"Albilio," she confirmed.

"And that he doesn't own the pub that sells our whiskey."

"No, that'd be Henry. Albilio owns a warehouse. I sell it to him and then he sells it to Henry."

"Why don't we just sell directly to Henry like we do with Paddy?"

"Because in a city this big, the men who control the docks control the trade," she explained, "and if ye don't do business with one of them, ye won't be able to unload yer vessel."

"Isn't Henry our only customer?"

"Aye, but that has nothin' to do with Albilio. That's part of the deal I struck with Henry."

"Why would ye agree to that kind of deal?"

"Because this is rum country," she sighed, "and when I first came here, I couldn't find a warehouse owner who'd purchase our whiskey, fer fear no one would take it. Only Albilio showed any interest, and even then, he made me find a buyer on the other end."

"Henry was the only one?"

Her voice a growl, she repeated, "Henry was the only one. And I went to every place I could find. At most of them, they shot down me down without botherin' to give it a taste. Fortunately, he had recently opened and needed a way to get the word out. In England, he grew up workin' in a pub adjacent to the shipyards at Chatham and knew that despite rum bein' all the rage, the Scots and Irish still preferred whiskey." Nodding to Port Royale, she noticed a British man-of-war beached on the interior portion of the Palisadoes, and raising her spyglass back to her eye, she went on, "More importantly, he knew the war was gettin' bigger, and he heard the Royal Navy was plannin' to expand this garrison, providin' the potential fer plenty more customers. Aware of my position, he convinced me it'd work out fer both of us if I gave him the exclusive rights to sell my product in Jamaica."

"How so?" Connor wanted to know.

"He argued ye can find rum everywhere in Kingston, but if ye want whiskey, ye'll have to find him. Considering the way sailors talk, he said it wouldn't take long fer every whiskey drinker in the world to hear of Henry's and, consequently, hear of us."

"Has his idea worked?" Connor inquired.

"Well, ultimately, that is how Paddy wandered in," she attested, lowering her spyglass, "and should we hear the crew of this new arrival has been to his place, I guess we'll know fer sure." Sliding the tubes together, she ordered, "Come on, let's go back to the wheel and talk to Angus."

After the war in the Caribbean broke out between Spain and England in 1739, the Royal Navy added several more wharves, warehouses, and workshops to complement the enormous ridge of sand they used to careen their vessels. On the section closest to the base, a ship one hundred fifty feet long had been emptied, and looping tethers around her three gigantic masts, her crew had rolled her far enough on her port side to expose her keel. To keep her stable, they had fastened the ropes to massive brick anchors buried underground, and already in the early hour, they crept over her starboard side, preparing the hull to be resealed with tar. Working in two crooked vertical rows, they went bow to stern, stripping away the barnacles and repairing any damaged wooden planks.

Letting out a long, slow whistle, Angus told Mairi, "Well, there's somethin' ye don't see every day. At that size with two decks, I'd say she got a total of at least seventy to seventy-five cannon."

"I was thinkin' the same thing," Mairi concurred, "which makes her a third-rate ship of the line."

"What do ye suppose a third-rate is doin' over here?" Angus asked.

"Let's hope it's only to tell us they've heard of our whiskey in England," she answered. "If there's anythin' more, I'll be sure to find out."

They paid the harbormaster his fee and tied their port side to the pier closest to Albilio's warehouse. Neat stacks of various casks cluttered the dock and, breaking down the piles, the crew for a brig in the opposite slip loaded the cargo into her hold. The vessel close to eighty feet long, she had two decks, an added poop deck, and a burgundy rectangular stained-glass window running the width of her stern. Along the top edge of the window, the name *MARIANA* was painted in bold black letters, and above the nameplate, a blue flag with a white X fluttered in the slight breeze. Though the spars for three progressively smaller square sails climbed her foremast, she only had two at the top of her main, and at its bottom, a little gaff sail extended over her helm. Despite all the activity in the early morning heat, her sixteen portholes were closed and their curtains were drawn.

Noting her colors, Mairi stated, "She's Scottish. Let's hope her captain has heard of us too." A shrill whistle pierced the air, and every head turned to see a pair of draft horses leading a black wagon toward her. Waving to the man in the driver's seat,

Mairi commented, "Here comes Albilio and his sons already. That was quick."

Albilio brought the wagon to a stop at the bottom of her gangplank and cast his intense light-brown eyes upon her. His dark skin leathery, he kept his graying dark hair short and his black mustache thick. Dressed in a light-blue robe tied with a white sash, he wore a gold band on his left ring finger and, reaching out his hand, admitted in a quiet voice, "I've had my boys looking for you every morning since the start of last week. I was beginning to worry something bad might have happened."

She accepted his help and, climbing up to join him, returned, "A storm blew us off course."

"It hit here as well," he replied, "hard enough to damage a few ships in the port." Pointing to a Dutch fluyt anchored in the harbor, he added, "She arrived two days after it passed, with the survivors of a wreck headed to Tortola, and they said it sprung violently up out of nowhere. Thinking you were at Paddies, I feared you met the same end, if not the same outcome."

"It was violent, that's fer certain," Mairi attested, giving him a hug, "but it'll take more than a tempest to stop me." Settling in, she took a deep breath and divulged, "I must admit I'm glad to have some solid ground below my feet, even if it is just fer the day. I'm sure my crew feels the same. I'm givin' them some time ashore to blow off some steam. They deserve it."

"If you're planning on an extended visit," Albilio began, "I'd be honored if you would be a guest in my humble abode." Gesturing toward his sons climbing out the back, he continued, "You have my word, your safety would be paramount. Plus, my boys would be happy to show you our great city."

One a year older and one a year younger than Mairi, they shared their father's complexion and grew their wavy dark hair down to their shoulders. Adorned in gold jewelry, they wore blue broadcloth vests, white silk blouses, black velvet pants, and shiny black leather boots. On their left hips, they both carried a rapier with a hand guard resembling woven branches bearing ripened olives in scabbards wrapped in dark-blue leather. Unconcerned about the hubbub on the pier, they turned the wagon around and positioned it along the waist of *The Scottish Rose*.

Allowing a slight smile, she responded, "That's so sweet. Unfortunately, I'm afraid I'll have to decline. My schooner suffered some damage in that storm, and we won't be able to leave until I see to the repairs."

Turning over his right palm, Albilio faced her and said, "Maybe you shouldn't leave. Consider it. If you were to make one of my sons the envy of every other man, you would be uniting my brains with your beauty. Working together, we could see a barrel of your whiskey reaches every corner of the world."

Clenching her jaw, she retorted, "Then should the day come I don't want to think fer myself, I'll give it some thought. I'm warnin' ye though, I wouldn't count on it bein' anytime soon. I don't have the barrels to send to every corner of the world, and even when I do, I don't see myself gettin' united to anyone. Now, what's Henry's order?"

Hanging his head, Albilio muttered, "Eight. He wants eight."

"Eight!" she exclaimed, "I don't have eight to sell him! I was plannin' on four, hoped fer five, and held a sixth just in case, but I never imagined eight. Business must be good."

"It is," Albilio answered. "On your way in, I'm sure you noticed *The Yorktown* being careened. It seems half of her crew of three hundred and fifty is either Scottish or Irish, and they've really taken a liking to your whiskey." Grinning, he disclosed, "So much so, I've had other pub owners approach me about purchasing some barrels."

Frowning, she asked, "And what did ye tell them?"

"They'll have to talk to you," he assured her. Tilting his head toward the *Mariana*, he furthered, "I said the same thing to the captain of that vessel the other day. I believe he's currently waiting at Henry's, hoping to see you this morning."

"Well, ye can tell all the pub owners they had their chance," she declared, "because my word is my bond, and in Jamaica, Henry will remain my single customer. In terms of this captain, I guess I'll be breakin' another heart." While they were waiting for the wagon to be loaded, Mairi looked over her shoulder to Port Royale and said, "Although it may be good fer business, the sight of that man-of-war still worries me. Is there a reason why the British have sent a third-rate?"

With an easy shrug, Albilio offered, "There's a war on."

"The war in the Caribbean has been goin' on fer four years," she pointed out, "and she's the first ship that size the English have sent to fight it. What's changed?"

"The war is getting bigger in Europe," he replied, "and there's constant talk of the French taking the other side. Lately, the Spanish have been issuing more letters of marque in the Caribbean, especially around the Indies, and *The Yorktown* was sent to counter the threat."

"I see," she answered, biting her bottom lip. "Now I'm really worried."

"With how closely linked your distillery is to Belize Town," Albilio mentioned, "everyone considers you to be a bayman, and quite honestly, seeing how much his crew loves your whiskey, the captain would face a mutiny if he tried to take your ship."

"It's not necessarily this British captain who has me the most concerned," she divulged. "It's that if war has proven anythin', it's proven when the fightin' ends, the privateers go on to become pirates and are no longer discreet about who they rape and kill."

"And then, like they always do," Albilio asserted, "the powers will put an end to the piracy."

"Unfortunately, until that happens, I'll be in danger every time I set sail," she retorted, "not to mention the threat of raids, which I feel should be a concern of yers. I hope ye have a plan ready."

"Raids?" he repeated. "Why would raids be a concern for me? There are no pirates bold enough to attack Kingston. They'd never get past Fort Charles."

"Maybe not," she concurred, "but Cuba, the Dominican Republic, and Puerto Rico aren't that far away, and if the French get involved, neither is Saint-Domingue. Who knows, the Spanish may realize how valuable this harbor is to the British and decide this city is ripe fer the pickin'." Spreading her arms wide, she continued, "I'm tellin' ye, it was better fer all of us when nobody was really interested in fightin' each other."

"Since the fighting has gone from being over a captain's ear to being over a queen," he said, shrugging again, "we don't have much of a choice. Look at the bright side. War brings prosperity. Because of it, there's another one hundred fifty men in town drinking your whiskey."

Shaking her head, she countered, "War brings opportunity, peace brings prosperity. However nice it is to be makin' some extra money right now, ye better not forget ye'll lose everythin' the day an armada appears in this harbor."

"Such is life. With kings leading us, we have to accept the risks."

"Well, maybe it's time to get rid of the kings and lead ourselves. We couldn't do any worse."

The last barrel loaded, Connor leapt up next to Mairi. Albilio's sons found a spot in the back of the wagon, and exiting the pier, they headed into Kingston. To ease the flow of commerce, the city was designed in a grid based on wide main thoroughfares and interconnecting avenues. Many of the buildings along the walkways abutted one another and shared the same two-story layout with a storefront on the bottom and several apartments on the top. The traffic light in the early hour, the wagon quickly advanced a few blocks down Church Street to Victoria Park and turned right on East Queen Street.

Their destination, at the northwest corner of Lower East Street, was a skinny white brick rectangular tavern with a commanding *"HENRY'S* est. 1742" stenciled in black over the arched double doors. Flanking the entry, a pair of windows came to the same high pitch as the gabled roof, and recessed into the longer walls, a series of similarly shaped stained-glass windows depicted the procession of Christ to the crucifixion. At the back, a white wooden tower rose above the surrounding residences and housed a bell that still rang three times a day— when Henry opened for the evening, when he called last call, and when he closed for the night.

Together, Connor and Mairi hopped down to look inside. The room slightly deeper than wide, each side accommodated five tables able to seat six, and in the middle, an aisle led to the handcrafted mahogany bar. Behind it, three different-sized casks sat in a cradle under a thick oaken mantel with a melted candle on the top and a knotted rope dangling above it. Like the chairs in the room, save one to her immediate right where a man sat alone, the eleven ornate cushioned stools were flipped upside down, and at the gap in the far left corner providing access for the bartender, two more men stood obscured by their overturned legs. Patting Connor's shoulder, Mairi tugged the circular brass handle on the door and stated, "Henry closed last night at one, and here he is already. I'm tellin' ye, I wouldn't want to own a pub. Ye never get any sleep."

His brown hair and brown mustache neatly clipped, Henry wore his black vest unbuttoned with his white shirt hanging untucked over his black pants and a gold band on his left ring finger. Facing a man holding a box of fresh candles, he picked one up and said, "It did work great, except they don't come cheap and I don't think I should have to replace the pins. I don't even know where to put them. You're the one who makes the candles, you do it."

The chandler pointed to ten holes evenly spaced down the stick and explained, "That's what these are fer. Simply reuse the pins from the previous candle, and like last night, when the wax melts, the pins will fall out and you'll know an hour has passed."

"I know how it works," Henry returned, crossing his arms, "I just think if they don't come with the pins in already in place, they shouldn't cost this much. Why should I have to do your labor?"

"Look," the chandler countered, "it's not hard work and it only takes a few minutes."

"Every day I have plenty of things that only take a few minutes," Henry insisted, "and it seems I like I could still use an extra hour to get them all accomplished." Picking up a broom, he held it forth and added, "Here, how about this. If you sweep my floor, I'll be happy to replace your pins. Otherwise, cut your price."

"I'm not cutting the price," the chandler said flatly, "and with nobody else making beeswax candles on this island, ye don't have the choice but to pay it."

"That's not true," Henry pointed out, "I can choose to not buy beeswax candles at all. There's lots of ways to tell the time, and the lanterns provide the light—the only reason I burn these is to freshen the room. Other than my wife's birthday and our wedding anniversary, I'm here seven days a week, fifty-two weeks a year. Do the math. If I decide to make this a nightly tradition, I'll be burning my money three hundred and sixty-three days a year. Quite honestly, I'm not sure if I can stomach watching so much of it go up in smoke." Glimpsing a female silhouette outlined in an aura of sunshine at the doorway, he turned toward the light and proclaimed, "Mairi! I was afraid I wasn't going to see you again!" Keeping his attention on her, he told the chandler, "Decide what you want to do and do it. I've got more important business to attend to."

Seeing Mairi saunter in and stroll behind the bar, the chandler snatched up his box and snarled, "All right, ye've got a deal—at least fer the time bein'. In a year, be ready to renegotiate." He spun around and found himself looking up at Connor. Cautiously, he stepped to his left, and storming down the aisle, made his way out.

Once alone, Henry divulged, "I would've rather he cut the price. He was right when he said it takes a few minutes to replace the pins on a single candle. I can do it while I'm talking to a regular. He must have plenty of time to spare."

Sliding her arms around his waist, she suggested, "And pins. In three months, I'll bet his costs force him to have a change of heart." Letting her embrace linger, she murmured, "I hear business is good."

His chest pressed against hers, Henry confided, "Business is great."

She slipped away and, taking out her flask, followed up, "Then I hate to have to tell ye some bad news. Paddy took more barrels than expected, and I only have six I can sell ye today."

"Paddy," Henry sneered. "I don't see why you're still willing to conduct business with him. You do know he's telling everyone the secret to your whiskey."

Removing the stopper, she remarked, "He is? I wasn't aware I had told him."

Henry reached to a shelf below the bar and, picking up two crystal glasses, noted, "By the taste it's obvious you use corn for the mash. I just don't think he should be blabbing it to the entire world."

"When did I ever deny usin' corn?" she inquired. "Since barley isn't native to these lands, I have to use somethin' grown locally, unless ye know of some other grain I can try." She poured them each a healthy sploosh, handed him one, picked hers up, and declared, "Cheers."

They touched the glasses together, and to the tinkling reverberating in the tower overhead, both took a sip.

Swallowing first, Mairi let out a long, slow "Uisge beatha."

"Whuskee bee," Henry tried to repeat. He turned his drink in his hand and, holding it up to the light, told her, "Being a proud Englishman, I never thought I'd speak Gaelic. However, your whiskey stirs up feelings deep within my soul, and more than it being smooth, it has that special woody finish." Looking through the clear liquid, he furthered, "It is certainly obvious why Clarkeson calls it Oakies."

"Don't call it that!" she snapped.

His eyes wide, Henry asked, "Why not? That's what everybody calls it."

"I don't care," she snarled. "Paddy told me what she did to the captain of that fluyt, and now I'm worried she'll kill my livelihood just like she murdered him. It's already hard enough to sell whiskey in this sea. I don't need some pirate makin' it worse. I'm hopin' the British capture her before she gets the chance to strike again."

Setting his glass on the bar, Henry put forth, "It's too late for that. She took her second ship a week or so ago. Albilio didn't tell you the story?"

"No, he told me of a ship wrecked in the storm on its way to Tortola, but he didn't say anything about Clarkeson."

Lacing his fingers, Henry tapped his thumbs together and explained, "There's more to the story of that shipwreck. Did Paddy admit to selling two of your barrels to the captain of *The Sea Lion*?"

"He did," she confirmed with a nod, "and truth be told, I considered chasin' him down to retrieve them until the weather convinced me otherwise."

"Yes, well, you wouldn't have had to go very far," Henry let her know. "In the storm, they were driven aground and sat helpless on a shoal. Unfortunately for the captain, the moment the skies cleared, *The Black Irish* was the first vessel to appear."

Her eyes wide, Mairi breathed, "Oh no. What happened?"

"Believe it or not," Henry said, "at first Clarkeson actually offered to help the survivors salvage what they could and give them passage to San Juan . . . then she found your whiskey."

Crossing her arms and arching her brows, Mairi stated, "And?"

Inhaling deeply, Henry picked up his drink, finished it, slowly exhaled, and began, "Accusing the captain of smuggling, she dragged him to the helm and, in front of his wife and two daughters, sentenced him to death. Her crew hung him naked and spread eagle in the rigging at the top of his mainmast, ensuring his unimpeded view, and then stripped his vessel of everything of any value they could find. Once they had finished, Clarkeson ordered they douse the hull with all the captured rum, and laughing out loud, she personally set a torch to the sails." Meeting her gaze, he set his glass down and added, "The Dutch captain who found the wreck swears he followed her awful cackle and his terrible screams to the gruesome scene."

"Oh my God!" Mairi exclaimed, covering her mouth. "What'd she do to the family?"

"Honestly, she sent them and the few crewmen who didn't speak Gaelic off in a skiff with enough food, fresh water, and whiskey to survive until they were rescued or they made it to shore."

Putting her forehead in her hands, Mairi lamented, "This is terrible news. Please tell me the word hasn't gotten out yet."

Chuckling, Henry replied, "The second Paddy heard, the whole world did. Except in his version, Clarkeson conjured up the storm. Apparently, he believes she's a water sprite."

"He told me."

"You don't really think that, do you?"

"Of course not," she assured him, "but I do believe if the British don't put an end to her soon, she is liable to make my business disappear, whether she's some sort of fairy or not."

"I wouldn't say that," Henry disagreed. "Oddly enough, whenever sailors hear Clarkeson's story, they inevitably want to try Oakies." Quickly raising his palms, he added, "Their words, not mine. And the thing is, the more popular she becomes, the more they desire your whiskey." Nodding toward the man seated alone at the table, he whispered, "You can be sure that captain is well aware of the risks he's facing, and yet here he is, waiting three days to meet you. He's even willing to pay in coin."

Biting her bottom lip, Mairi asked, "How much did he offer?"

"Enough that I was starting to consider it," Henry lamented. Placing his hands over his ears, he followed up, "At a certain point, I refused to listen anymore. No matter the price he was willing to pay, it wasn't worth the price you'd make me pay."

Cackling harshly, she noted, "Wise words, my friend, wise words. Is there anythin' else ye can tell me of this captain?"

Henry leaned forward and, lowering his voice, whispered, "His name is Stewart—Malcolm Stewart. He's Scottish. He says he's spent his life sailing the Mediterranean, only the war has made it too dangerous on that side of the world and he's hoping it'll be more stable in the Caribbean."

"Didn't he see *The Yorktown*?" she asked.

"He's seen it," Henry said, "and he claims she's part of the reason he came here. He says her captain should have these seas under control in no time."

"Those are bold words to say of a single man," Mairi responded. "What do ye think? Have ye met this British captain?"

"I have," Henry let on. "He's an Englishman named Howe."

"What's he like?"

"Ambitious, determined, excited to earn some prize money. He's looking forward to doing his duty."

"Is he plannin' on conductin' any raids?"

"Raids? Why on earth would you ask about raids? He's not a pirate."

"The British will say Henry Morgan wasn't one either," she reminded him, "but the Spanish have a very different take. Bein' that my distillery is on Spanish soil, I don't need some ambitious Englishman to come burn it to the ground."

Snorting, Henry assured her, "Howe would most assuredly face a mutiny if he ordered his men to burn your distillery. It's more likely they'd claim the island as a part of the British Empire and protect you instead."

Without smiling, she growled, "Then I'd have to pay the same tax to the crown that killed the entire whisky industry in Scotland. Either way, I'd lose everythin' I've worked fer."

Clearing his throat, Henry held her eyes and put forth, "From my understanding, Howe's primary role is to protect

English shipping around the Indies and not to conduct raids off the coast of Belize. Of all your concerns, he should be the least of them. He's looking forward to meeting you. He'll be disappointed he wasn't here today."

Lifting her glass, she drained the contents and commented, "Let him know I hope to see him in the future. Which reminds me, if yer goin' to be wantin' extra barrels, I'll need a six-month notice."

"What about the whiskey in your flask? Can I get a few barrels of it?"

"Not then and I'll tell ye, there's goin' to be less of it than we hoped fer. Count on it bein' expensive."

Crossing his arms, Henry suggested, "That's bad business, Mairi."

"How is that bad business?"

"Because you're treating me like a fool. Even if I don't know all the secrets to your whiskey, I do know all whiskey is made the same way."

"If all whiskey was made the same way, then a single sip wouldn't compel a proud Englishman like yerself to speak a pagan language like Gaelic. There's a difference between what I produce and the rest, and that difference is the time I take to make it."

"That shouldn't change the price. If anything, it should lower it. It's not as fresh."

Baring her teeth, she flared her nostrils and suggested, "If ye want fresh, ye can have some of the heads right out of the still. We'll see if that's plenty fresh enough for ye."

"The heads?" he asked. "What are the heads?"

"What do ye mean what are the heads? I thought ye said ye know how to make whiskey. Ye better not have lied to me."

"I didn't lie," he attested. "I told you I know all whiskey is made the same way. That doesn't mean I know how to make it."

Shaking her head, she crossed her arms and stated, "Well, I'm not here to teach ye. If ye want to know what the heads are, yer welcome to come find out. Just don't be surprised if ye wake up blind."

"We're talking business, Mairi," Henry responded. "You don't need to get testy."

"I'm not gettin' testy," she asserted, pressing her right finger to the bar. "That'd be bad business. Ye just don't appreciate the process. Every time I make a new batch, I don't know how it'll turn out. I've had to dump many a barrel because something went wrong along the way."

Baring his palms, he returned, "Those are the costs we all share. I brew my own lager, and I've been forced to dump plenty."

"That may be true," she shot back, "but ye know at the end of a week how yer lager will turn out. With my whiskey, I have to wait a minimum of six months." When he didn't respond right away, she arched her right eyebrow and followed up, "Ye know what? Don't feel obligated to buy it. Paddy has already told me he's willin' to take it all. Actually, maybe it's time I listen to him and stop comin' here." Glancing to the captain seated near the door, she inquired, "What did ye say his name was? Stewart? Maybe I should sell him the six barrels I have on Albilio's wagon."

"If you do, you won't get them back. He's off to New England and then Scotland. You'll be lucky to see him again."

"It's six barrels," she dismissed with a shrug. "If he's payin' in coin, they shouldn't be too hard to replace."

"I still have your word," Henry reminded her, "and we're still in Jamaica. He has to buy it through me."

"And if I choose to honor my word, I'll ask him to meet me in the British Keys," she retorted. "If he's willin' to wait three days fer me here, what do ye want to bet he'll be willin' to make the trip? I can tell ye one thing, there's no one on those islands who has the deal ye do."

Keeping their arms crossed, they faced each other in silence until Henry finally let out a groan and remarked, "You drive a hard bargain."

Nodding to his glass, she asked, "Does that mean we won't be havin' this same conversation the day this whiskey is available?"

"I wouldn't say that," Henry said. "However, at least we'll both know what to expect."

"Then stop wastin' my time right now," she concluded, "I have more pressin' issues to take care of." Turning to Captain Stewart, she went on, "So if there's nothin' more, it's time I break his heart."

"Should his price change your mind," Henry inserted, "I expect you to honor the same rules you do at Paddies."

"What? Ye want me to go barefoot?"

"No, I want my cut of any deal you reach at my bar."

Smiling, she divulged, "Don't get yer hopes up. Ye were right when ye said I didn't want to lose my barrels. They're too hard to find."

Curling his lips, he shook his head and exclaimed, "I knew it!"

"It doesn't matter. The price of the whiskey is goin' to be what I say it is," she reaffirmed, "and I know Paddy will always pay it."

"Drunken Irishman," Henry groused.

"Call him what ye want," Mairi remarked, "but he's on to somethin' over there. Now, is there anythin' else we need to discuss?"

"Actually," Henry inserted, waving his index finger, "I do have one more thing."

"What is it?"

"Well . . ."

"Spit it out."

"In that case," he started, "I've always given you every empty barrel you've wanted, and I've never expected anything in return."

"And I appreciate ye doin' so," she acknowledged. "Had ye not, I wouldn't have anythin' to put my whiskey in."

"I know, and though I'm happy to continue to help, we need to address a problem." He nodded to the doorway and stated, "Because you see, for every man like him willing to wait a few days to meet you, I've had ten others who wouldn't, and with how generous their offers are becoming, it's getting harder and harder to turn them down."

"That's easy to solve. Drain my barrel and put the whiskey in another."

"They won't buy it unless I guarantee the flavor won't change, especially not at the prices they're all willing to pay."

"Then get to yer point."

"Well, sometimes I'll have a captain purchase a barrel of my lager to take out to sea. To let him know which one is which, I always brand the top with a capital H." Meeting her eyes, he suggested, "I'd like to do the same to the empties I give to you."

"What fer?"

Taking a deep breath, he proposed, "So I could sell them to whomever I choose. Being they were mine to begin with, I think it's only fair that I should be able to without any fear of the consequences."

"The consequences will be your barrels won't be returned," Mairi pointed out, "and that I'll never have any extra to sell you."

139

"You have plenty of my barrels already," he insisted. When she didn't answer right away, he furthered, "I do appreciate your situation, I only ask you to appreciate mine. Right now, it's possible to make enough money to see this place stays open for my grandchildren to run."

Biting her bottom lip, she held his gaze for several moments and reached out to shake his hand. "Fair enough," she consented, "just don't bother cryin' to me once they've all disappeared."

Accepting her offer, he smiled wide and stated, "Don't worry. I'm sure I won't have a problem covering my losses."

"Then go heat up yer brand," she ordered, "and if we find any we can take, they'll be yers to sell the day they're ready." Whistling, Henry left a cheerful tune lingering in the bell tower on his way out the back doorway. Picking up another clean glass, Mairi turned toward the entrance and announced, "We're done here, Captain Stewart. Would ye like to share a taste from my personal cask?"

He nodded, stood up, and walked down the aisle to the bar. Taller than Connor, he let his long brown hair hang well past his broad shoulders and had a thick brown beard brushed out to cover his chest. Clad in a sleeveless maroon vest over a sleeveless black blouse showing off his bulging biceps, he donned a kilt woven in a red-and-gold, green-and-white tartan that exposed his well-defined calves. Adorned in an assortment of gold jewelry (notably a thick band on his right ring finger, a thick rope around his neck, and a thick hoop in his left ear), he was armed with a saber in an ornate red sheath trimmed in gold on his left hip and a flintlock in a cross draw holster on his right. Approaching Mairi, he extended his hand through the gap between the upright legs of two bar stools and began, "From one captain to another, please call me Malcolm. It's my pleasure to finally meet ye."

Gently placing her fingers in his, she replied, "The pleasure is all mine." Waiting until his lips touched her knuckles, she asked, "Is the *Mariana* yer ship?"

"It is."

"It's an interestin' name. I don't suppose yer familiar with Shakespeare, are ye? That happens to be the name of a character in one of my favorite plays."

Beaming, he responded, "I'm familiar enough to know *Macbeth*. My father named me fer Malcolm Macduff, and knowin' my namesake, I try to catch every performance I can attend."

"I wish I could say the same," she confessed, shaking her head. "I'm always too busy to stop and take the time to enjoy one."

Frowning, he asked, "Then how are ye familiar with the characters?"

"My father had a copy of Shakespeare's first folio aboard his vessel," she divulged, "and learnin' to read was a part of learnin' how to be a captain. Anytime he gave me the choice, I preferred his plays to ship logs and manifests."

"Fer my father," Malcolm told her, "if it wasn't a log or a manifest, he didn't read it, nor did I. He did, however, teach me to appreciate good theater. If ye haven't seen Shakespeare live, I can't recommend it enough. It was, after all, written to be performed." Leaning forward, he held her eyes and suggested, "Should ye ever want to see a performance, I'd be happy to escort ye all the way to London, or anywhere else on the globe, fer yer first experience."

Sighing, Mairi poured a sploosh into his glass, slid it forward, and stated, "I'm told ye want to do business with me."

Picking it up, he responded, "I do."

Tilting her flask toward him, she furthered, "I should warn ye, I can drive a hard bargain."

Waving his hand, he attested, "I've bargained in the toughest ports in the world. I'm sure I can handle it."

At Henry's reappearance, she gestured toward him and continued, "He can tell ye I only like to do business with people I respect."

"From what he has said," Malcolm assured her, "I expect nothin' less. I hope to be one of those people."

"I hope so too," she agreed, "which is why I poured ye a drink from my personal cask."

"And it is my honor to accept it," he maintained, tipping his glass toward her.

Holding his gaze, she tapped her flask to his glass and said, "My father always taught me respect goes both ways."

"Of course," Malcolm concurred, "I don't see how else it can work."

"Then if we're goin' to do business," she snarled, "ye need to respect the fact I'm not lookin' to get up yer kilt any more than I'm lookin' fer ye to get in my pants, and if ye try to, I'll know what this conversation really has to do with, and I'll know I can't believe a single word out of yer mouth." Nodding to his glass, she asked, "Now, are ye sure ye want to continue?"

His eyes wide, Malcolm confessed, "Strangely, more than ever." He swirled his glass under his nose, took a sip, and rolled it over his tongue. Upon swallowing, he let out a slow breath and murmured, "Uisge beatha."

Responding in kind, Mairi waited until he took another sip and said, "Henry tells me ye delayed yer departure a few days, hopin' to catch my arrival. Ye must really want my whiskey."

"I do. I've never tasted one smoother than Oakies."

Behind her, Henry anxiously shook both hands at Malcolm. "Don't call it that!" she snapped.

Glancing between them both, he responded, "I'm sorry?"

"Look at me!" she sneered. "I said don't call it Oakies!"

"I thought that was the name."

"That is not the name. That's the name a pirate calls it. I don't like pirates, and I refuse to have my whiskey associated with one. Should ye have a problem with that, ye can leave right now."

His mouth as wide as his eyes, Malcolm held his palms forth and offered, "My apologies. I was wrong to make the assumption."

"Well, now ye know better," she stated, "and I expect ye to spread the word."

"When I set out for Scotland with a barrel," Malcolm assured her, "I'll be happy to call it whatever ye'd like."

Letting out a happy cackle, she noted, "And here I was worried with all that brawn, ye wouldn't have any brains. Unfortunately, we have one little problem. Ye can't set out with a barrel of my whiskey. I can't afford to chance losin' it. Because ye waited, however, I'm happy to fill yer flask fer free."

Stroking his beard with his right hand, Malcolm strummed the fingers of his left on the bar. "Ye know," he finally began, "I'd trade ye a whole load of empty barrels for a single one full of yer whisky."

"It's pronounced with a k-e-y. And do ye have a whole load of empty barrels?"

"Not right now."

"Then it doesn't matter if I'd be willin' to accept it or not," she remarked, "and even if ye did, I doubt ye'd have the right kind."

"Tell me the barrels I'm lookin' fer, and I'll bring them back."

"I'm sure ye would, only I can't tell ye what kind of barrels they are."

"Why? What's so special about them?"

Glancing at his empty glass, she asked, "How about ye answer that fer me? Yer the one willin' to pay a high price."

"I don't know," he conceded. "I wish I did."

"And I don't want ye to know," she stressed. "I don't want anyone to know. I'd rather we say they're my barrels and leave it at that."

"I captain a ship," he reminded her. "I don't make whiskey. The knowledge wouldn't mean anythin' to me."

Crossing her arms, she put forth, "Every Scot knows a moonshiner, and I'm sure yer no exception. With the value yer placin' on my whiskey, I can imagine how much the secret behind it would be worth."

Shaking his head, Malcolm countered, "The last thing I'd do is to break yer trust and tell yer secret to anyone. I am smart enough to know it would be counterproductive to my goals."

"And what exactly are yer goals?"

"To make your distillery a regular part of my every voyage and make us both very rich."

Leaning forward and putting her hand on top of his, Mairi replied, "While that sounds wonderful, ye have to understand I know how dangerous it is every time ye leave port. Let's face it, pirates and privateers are only a small part of the dangers we face, and it's more likely the seas will find a way to kill us. Hell, I almost died in a storm the day I left Paddies." Turning her palm over, she concluded, "So when I say there's no guarantee ye'll be bringin' my barrels back, it's not that I don't think yer a man of yer word."

Without looking away, he asked, "Did Henry tell ye my offer?"

"He said it was very generous."

Smiling, he followed up, "Would ye like to hear it fer yerself?"

Chuckling, she returned, "If the barrels didn't matter, I'm sure I'd be happy to take half as much."

Untying a leather pouch on his belt, he jingled the coins inside and said, "Accordin' to Henry, it was twice as much as he normally pays. What would ye say if I was willin' to double it again?"

Arching her eyebrows, she inquired, "Exactly how much are we talking about?"

"Two pieces of gold fer a barrel of whiskey."

"I'd say yer crazy."

"Then I'd have to ask who's crazier, me for makin' the offer or ye for turnin' it down."

Seeing her head shake, he opened his purse and removed two gold coins. Holding one in each hand, he showed her both sides and placed them in a stack on the bar. Biting her lip, she continued to shake her head. Without speaking, he dug into his purse, found a silver piece, and set it on the top.

"Ye don't understand how hard it is to sell whiskey in the Caribbean," she told him. "Number one, it seems like anytime people hear the word whiskey, they think of moonshine."

"Which is why those of us who know better are willin' to pay more fer it," he interjected and set a second silver piece on the stack.

"There's more to it though," she went on. "The pirates and privateers also play a role. Should I ever be attacked, I'm sure I'll have to dump my entire load to escape."

"All the more reason to sell it to me," he maintained and set a third silver piece on the stack. "It would be a travesty to see it sink to the bottom of the sea."

Touching her left hand to her forehead, she continued, "Ye have to realize a distillery and a ship are two different beasts. At the distillery, I have to manage men, worry about fresh water, and track down the ingredients . . . Do ye know how hard it was to find a substitute fer barley?"

Malcolm placed a fourth silver piece on the stack and stated, "It's corn. Anybody who has ever eaten it can tell by the taste."

"It is corn," she confirmed, "which I had wanted to keep a secret, except once Paddy figured it out, the whole world did."

"I had nothin' to do with that," Malcolm insisted.

Tilting her head, she responded, "I know ye didn't. I simply want ye to appreciate why I can't chance the secret of my barrels gettin' out. It's the only thing I can control. Who knows, there could be a day when the knowledge keeps me alive."

In silence, Malcolm dug through his purse until he produced another gold coin and set it on the stack. As he went to remove the silver pieces, Mairi put her right hand on his and ordered, "Leave them all."

Startled, Malcolm held her eyes and asked, "Are ye sayin' we have a deal?"

"Aye," she relented, scooping up his payment. "We have a deal. It's gotten to the point I would be crazy not to take it. It'll have to be the barrel I reserved fer my crew to drink durin' our return home. They may not like it, but they're goin' to have to survive on rum."

Sighing, Malcolm rolled his head around his neck and said, "Thank God." Leaning on the bar, he pointed to Mairi and declared, "Ye weren't kiddin' when ye said ye drive a hard bargain. I'm glad I won't be courtin' ye. I can only imagine how difficult it would be."

Cackling out loud, Mairi poured another sploosh into his glass and asserted, "I'm certain ye'd need a few more of these to get through it." Turning the coins over in her hand, she looked at Henry and posed, "I figure the silvers add up to be about 10 percent. Is that a fair amount fer conductin' business at yer bar?"

Smiling, he replied, "Fair enough. Feel free to do it again."

Mairi handed Henry his share, turned to face Malcolm, and asked. "When will ye be departin'?"

"The moment I get my barrel."

"Why the rush?"

"Would ye like me to stay?"

"No, I'd just prefer ye set out with a few more ships," she advised, "or maybe wait until *The Yorktown* is ready and leave then."

"Are ye worried about me?"

"I'm mostly worried about my barrel," Mairi remarked, "although I don't want to hear Clarkeson has taken yer ship either. I don't wish to wash yer blood off my hands. The world associatin' my whiskey to yer death would be bad fer business."

"I'd say the opposite is true," Malcolm put forth, stroking his beard, "and the more her legend grows, so does yers. Whether ye like it or not, hearin' her story brought me to you."

"Exactly," Henry chipped in.

Pointing her right index finger at Malcolm's chest, Mairi stated, "If that's true and Clarkeson holds to form, yer skull will be the next one she puts on her bowsprit." Holding her flask up, she asked, "Is this really worth riskin' yer life?"

"Riskin' my life is what makes the risk worth takin'," Malcolm insisted, "and the day I arrive in London, I'll be able to auction off Oakies by the dram." Though Mairi glared at him, he held his glass forth and added, "I'll bet my crew and I could drink half the barrel on the trip home and I'll still come out ahead."

Waving her arms over her head, Mairi exclaimed, "Oh, ye men are mad!" Continually looking between Malcolm and Henry, she went on, "Ye all say we women are crazy, but if ye ask me, it's all of ye who are nuts! This doesn't make any sense. Here I am, lyin' awake at night worryin' about a pirate killin' people fer my whiskey, and here ye are, sayin' I should be sleepin' well at night knowin' there's a pirate killin' people for my whiskey."

"Look, Mairi," Henry interjected, "your fame isn't completely intertwined with hers. Similar to wine drinkers, whiskey drinkers want good whiskey and having had tried the finest produced in every region of Scotland, I can vow there is no doubt this is the best the world has ever had to offer." Raising a finger, he went on, "And the more men Clarkeson kills for it, the more men will be willing to pay for it."

"That makes no sense!" she cried.

"That makes perfect sense," Malcolm interjected.

"Then it's no wonder the world is constantly at war," Mairi retorted. Seeing them both shrug in response, she took a deep breath, exhaled fully, and said to Malcolm, "I have to ask ye to please do me a favor and wait to head out. Sail with a few more ships, Captain. No whiskey, mine or any other, is worth yer life."

"Don't worry about me." Malcolm brushed off with a wave, "The *Mariana* is faster than any ship in this sea, and pirates have always been a part of my life. If Clarkeson were to hunt me down, I already know how to handle her."

"Are ye sayin' yer prepared fer a fight?" she asked.

"Most pirates aren't lookin' fer a fight," he stated, "and no matter what the stories say, I doubt Clarkeson is much different. I'm sure I can make enough noise to scare her away."

"I saw yer ship when I came to port," she brought up, "and I didn't see any cannon. How do ye expect to stand up to her?"

Smiling slightly, he took a healthy swallow and disclosed, "In the Mediterranean, many of the pirates and privateers have eyes and ears in every port. Experience bein' the best teacher, I've learned to keep my defenses a secret, and in the unlikely event *The Black Irish* is fast enough to catch me, I'll set up Clarkeson to walk face first into a volley of canister shot."

"Yer a braver man than me," Mairi submitted, shaking her head. "According to the stories I've heard, she has the firepower to sink yer ship outright."

"She could do the same thing to yers," Malcolm reminded her, "and yet here ye are. Why do ye suppose that is?"

"I suppose it's because she wants to keep drinkin' my whiskey," Mairi determined, "and she's smart enough to leave me alone to make it."

Both men burst into laughter.

Wiping his eyes, Malcolm proclaimed, "Henry said it'd be worth the wait just to meet ye, and ye certainly haven't let him down. I wish I could stay until ye leave."

"If ye can wait until we're done here," she murmured, "I'd be happy to return to the pier together and deliver yer barrel personally. Ye can even show me around yer brig."

"I'd love to."

Arching her brows, she quickly added, "Just don't think I'm lookin' to see yer vessel."

Laughing again, Malcolm covered his heart with his right hand and swore, "Ye have my word, one captain to another."

"Then let's go get yer empties," she told Henry. "I don't want to keep him waitin'." On her way out the back door, she cast one last glance over her shoulder to Malcolm and suggested, "Ye know, patience may prove to be the better part of valor. It'd be a shame if ye arrived in London prior to the legend of Clarkeson."

"I doubt that'll be the case," Malcolm responded. "In fact, I'll wager by the time I reach England, they'll have already heard of Oakies in Sicily. . ."

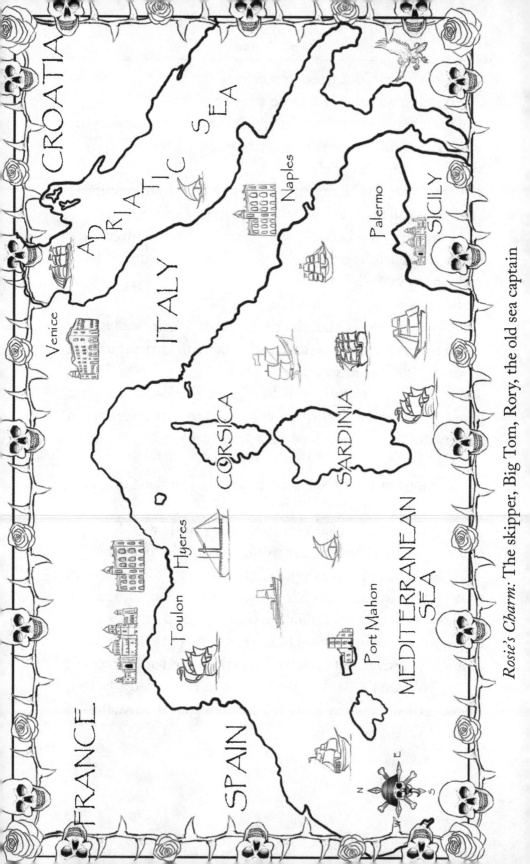

Rosie's Charm: The skipper, Big Tom, Rory, the old sea captain

CHAPTER 5

October 1, 1785, Kingston, Jamaica

As the rain echoed off the roof in an easy patter, the fourth metal pin fell from the side of the candle on the mantel behind the bar and stuck upside down in the wax pooling at the bottom of the brass drip catcher. The orange flame quivered in a sudden downdraft, catching the attention of the old sea captain, and slowly stroking his bushy white beard, he put forth, "Ridin' the high of such a profitable sale, Mairi ignored that little slip of the tongue and went about her business. Old Malcolm, on the other hand, had no idea how prophetic he was, fer on our arrival to Palermo, we came to find out the legend of Clarkeson had already beaten us there." Raising his mug to his mouth, he followed up, "Lookin' back, I suppose that night was the beginnin' of our fateful journey, although to be sure, it would be almost two years until we reached the end, and by then it was too late to stop it."

"This almost sounds like a love story," Lina noted.

"I was thinking the same thing," Ginevra concurred.

"It can't be a love story," Brass chipped in.

"It's a complete bunch of nonsense," Rags insisted.

"Oh, heh-heh," Jack interrupted, "I can't agree with you there, heh-heh. It's not all nonsense. Back in the day, I spent many an hour careening many a vessel at the Palisadoes, heh-heh. Of course, when I was aboard a third-rate, we were pirate hunters, heh-heh, and because pirates didn't have the benefit of Port Royale, they had to careen their vessels on a deserted island, heh-heh." He let out a low whistle and went on, "Oh boy, was it fun to catch them helpless on the beach, heh-heh. It was like watching a bunch of rats scatter, heh-heh, and if they didn't surrender right then and there, we'd burn their ship, heh-heh, and leave them marooned, heh-heh."

"Jesus Christ Jack," Rags interjected, turning to face him, "you never served on a third-rate." Shaking his head, he went on, "Not only that, you came into Henry's back in those days. You know this place was never a whiskey joint, and you know Henry couldn't grow a mustache to save his life."

Frowning, Jack asked, "He couldn't?"

With every head in the room turning toward the old sea captain, he stared at the candle on the mantel and slowly stroked his beard. Sarah glanced at Luke, John, Lina, and Ginevra sitting quietly at the table, then at Jack, Tony, Rags, Jack, and Brass in their spots along the length of the bar. Nancy stood in the gap leading behind it, and giving her a wink, she cleared her throat and asserted, "He had a mustache. I can remember sitting on his lap and pulling on it." To everyone now looking her way, she shrugged and added, "I used to love listening to the sound of him sharpening his straight razor to shave. My grandmother used to say he was too cheap to pay a barber and someday he'd end up slitting his own throat."

"Yeah, heh-heh," Jack inserted, "I remember she was always saying that too."

"This story may be taking place long before I was born," Sarah concluded, "but I sure can't imagine a time when it wasn't there."

Instantaneously, Rags dropped his chin to his chest and the old sea captain exhaled. He smiled at Sarah, turned to face the room, and spreading his arms wide, put forth, "There ye have it, straight out of the mouth of Henry's own granddaughter. Ask yerself who would know better, Henry's own flesh and blood or some random fellow seated at the bar?"

Speaking softly, Lina pointed out, "Whether or not Henry had a mustache doesn't matter. I want to know how the skipper and Clarkeson could have fallen in love."

"Yeah," Ginevra picked up, narrowing her eyes, "especially when they were on opposite sides of a world at war."

Waving his index finger between them, the old sea captain stated, "Now that's very keen of ye both. I'd hate to see what would happen to yer husbands if they were dumb enough to try to sneak somethin' past ye." He swallowed his last gulp of lager, set his empty mug down, and raising his brows, suggested, "I'll wager they'd end up in worse shape than I was after we took *The Sabre*. To be sure, once I was patched up, I didn't have it in me to do anythin' other than follow the skipper's orders and go to sleep." Stroking his bushy beard, he whispered, "It's too bad my wounds hadn't been worse, fer then we might not have had the conversation we had and never crossed the Atlantic."

Over a faint rumble of thunder, Sarah asked, "Why? What were you talking about?"

Twirling his empty mug, the old sea captain replied, "Whisky and pirates, with a bit of Shakespeare mixed in."

"I love Shakespeare," Lina mentioned.

"I do too," Ginevra concurred. "He could make any story a love story. Since there are four of us, do you think it would be appropriate to buy him another?"

When Ginevra nodded, the old sea captain tipped his head toward their table and said, "Well, thank ye kindly, nice ladies." With Sarah filling up his mug and the rain continuing in the same easy patter, he cast his bright blue eyes upon the candle on the mantel and began, "It's written that true love knows no boundaries and I believe it to be true, fer even the oceans aren't vast enough to keep soulmates apart . . ."

Late December 1743, Palermo, Sicily

I awoke to Big Tom's grim countenance cast in the fiery orange glow of the lantern he held in his left hand while he gently shook my shoulder with his right. In the course of the day, the hair on his upper lip had completely filled in, and while I slept, he had trimmed his muttonchops into a pair of thick swooping rolls connecting his sideburns to his mustache. Seeing I was coming to, he repeated my name and said, "Get up. It's time to get ready. Be sure to wear yer finest."

My mind foggy, I blinked several times and tried to ask, "Where are we going?" only to instinctively clench my teeth and gingerly caress the swollen right side of my face.

Somehow able to comprehend me, he ducked to clear the top bunk, stood straight, and answered, "A pub in the old part of the city. We're meetin' the skipper there."

"He's not on board?"

"No, he had to deliver a message to King Charles."

As I touched my tongue to my cracked molar, I mumbled, "I thought the palace was in Naples."

He turned to hang the lantern on a hook next to the hatch leading to the gun deck and replied, "It is, but the king isn't always sittin' on his throne."

"So we followed him here?"

"Somethin' like that."

Feeling the pinch of the stitches holding together the cuts scattered across my body, I slowly rolled onto my right side and, leaning on my elbow, noted, "It must've been an important message."

Meeting my gaze, he responded, "They always are, and more often than not, the admiral personally hands his message to the skipper with orders to personally deliver it. That bein' the case, we'll go to any place we have to go and wait fer however long it takes to get the reply."

"What will we do in the meantime?"

"Repair *The Sabre*," he answered. His eyes aglow, he flared his nostrils and added, "And maybe hunt fer a pirate or two. Now get movin'." On his way out, he gave me one last menacing look and ordered, "Don't shave."

Wider than it was long, the officer's wardroom linked the captain's quarters to the rest of the vessel and consisted of two bunk beds jutting out from the starboard side, with four skinny full-length closets attached to the port. Additionally, we had the benefit of a pair of small circular portholes opposite each other, and having been opened, they allowed the cool fresh nighttime breeze to waft through the space. In spite of the pain, I yawned and, carefully flipping onto my stomach, opened the drawer under my bunk where I stowed my personal belongings. Retrieving my flask, I unscrewed the metal cap and took a long, healthy swig. Though the rum burned initially, I swirled it around until my mouth went numb and immediately chugged another swallow, hoping to experience a similar effect throughout the rest of my body. Feeling a bit woozy instead, I slowly eased my head back onto my pillow, rubbed my eyes, and to the start of a carillon of church bells ringing in the distance, inhaled the sweet saltiness of the sea.

Earlier that day, I had heeded the skipper's command and reported to the infirmary. Known informally as the cockpit, it was always located in the area of a warship considered the most stable—directly under the captain's quarters in the lowest level of the stern. Being below the waterline meant it was completely devoid of any natural light and ventilation, so even in the best of circumstances, the atmosphere was invariably dark, smoky, and stale. Yet after the battle, the intermittent groans of the wounded combined with the smell of death to make the conditions exponentially worse, and indeed, the gory scene did resemble the pit at the end of a night of cockfighting.

In the middle of the room, a young unconscious sailor lay tied down to the operating table with a piece of rope dangling half out his slackened jaw. The surgeon, sweating profusely, dug into the patient's chest and removed a metal fragment. Immediately, a blood trail splattered across his face, and quickly, the surgeon's aide applied pressure inside the incision. Hastily, the surgeon wiped his eyes on his sleeves and, engrossed in his work, remained oblivious to my entrance. A dozen other men were already in his care, and while the few who were out cold had little more than makeshift bandages wrapped around their heads, the rest had been tended to.

Morbidly captivated, I did not see a second aide to my right kneeling on his haunches and tying a splint to the broken leg of a marine. "Sir," he started, "what can I do fer ye?" At my failure to respond, he rose and, stepping in front of me, pressed, "Sir? Do ye need somethin'?"

I snapped out of my trance and, softly touching the right side of my chin, muttered, "I got hit durin' the battle, and the skipper sent me to have the surgeon give it a look. If he's too busy, I can come back later."

"Any teeth missin'?"

"One's been cracked pretty good."

He measured out a half-ounce of rum, gave it to me, and warned, "Go ahead and rinse. Just be careful, this is cask strength and hasn't been cut with water. It'll sting." I did what I was told and he was correct. The instant it passed my lips, it felt like my entire mouth had been cauterized. Once I spit it out, he furthered, "Now, yer welcome to wait fer the surgeon if ye'd like, but I've removed plenty of teeth in my time and would be happy to check it fer ye."

Given I could feel my entire face begin to throb, I accepted his assistance, and because the dim environment made it impossible to see, he took me topside to take advantage of the sunshine. Since I could open and close my jaw and move it side to side, he determined no bones were broken. Unfortunately, because of the swelling, he couldn't do anything more for the tooth, and I'd have to wait a few days to have it extracted. Rather than releasing me, however, he made me strip out of my tattered, filthy, soaking wet clothes and examined my entire body. I was covered in an abundance of scrapes and cuts, especially on my forearms, and had a particularly nasty laceration crossing my left thigh. Biting his bottom lip, he noted, "These all need to be cleaned and stitched, especially this one on yer leg. Should it become fetid, ye'll lose it." Pointing to a barrel of boiled sea water, he ordered, "Climb in."

At the prospect, I clenched my fists and admitted, "I'm hurtin'. Is there any way I can get a bit more rum first?"

When he went to pour another half ounce, I snatched the flask out of his hands and took several heavy pulls. Even somewhat numb, the second I settled into the tepid bath and felt the salt seep into my wounds, I vomited over the side. Losing track of time, I soaked for a seeming eternity and found it quite a bit of a struggle to get out. Delicately, the aide helped ease me onto the deck and, offering a deeply indented six-inch piece of leather, stated, "Ye may want this fer the pain. It's goin' to hurt." In the belief it would be best for morale if the crew was not subjected to my suffering, I slipped it into my mouth and in between my teeth. Awake for the duration of his treatment, I balanced the distress of biting down against it versus that of my wounds being doused in alcohol and sutured. By the end, my hands, forearms, right ankle, and left thigh were bound in fresh white gauze, and even stark naked in the chilly winter air, I was drenched in perspiration.

He shared a final drink with me, and thankfully, used his flask to fill mine. "Impressive," he said. "The odds had ye passin' out."

"Then I hope ye bet on me," I put forth, "although, to be sure, that's exactly what I'm off to do." Grateful for his aid to my quarters, I put on clean clothes, had one last swallow, and fell asleep the minute my head hit the pillow.

Now feeling every ache return, plus a few more, I listened to the church bells reverberate for the ninth and final time. Taking one last deep breath, I finished rubbing my eyes and, warily, rose to don my uniform.

Dressed in my traditional navy-blue coat with white facings and white breeches, I emerged into the gun deck to find the big man waiting alone next to the ladder outside our wardroom. His brown hair brushed out, it covered his shoulders and obscured most of his chest. Wearing the same purple-and-gold attire he did the night I met him in Naples, he reached into the vest pocket over his heart and produced a thin silver flask boasting a single gallant rose etched on the side. Handing it to me, he mentioned, "The skipper left ye somethin'. It's a little walk. Yer goin' to need it."

Conditioned to expect rum in the Royal Navy, I was pleasantly surprised to delight in the wonderful raw, smoky burn and wild spicy flavor that reminded me of home. Realizing it was whisky I was drinking, I happily smiled through the pain and tried to take another belt. Sadly, the big man seized it out of my hands and asserted, "That's more than enough fer now. Come on, follow me."

Watching him scale the ladder, I noticed a cutlass on his hip, and being unarmed, I asked, "Should I get a weapon too?"

"Don't bother," he remarked. "In the shape yer in, it wouldn't matter if I let ye drink yer fill. Ye still wouldn't be much good in a fight."

I wasn't sure what he meant, nor did I care, for the climb proved to be a challenging task and I needed his assistance. Topside, the sky was clear, the stars were out, and the shiny bright white half-moon lit up the vessels anchored in the harbor. Candlelight twinkled in the various buildings outlined on the shore, and a steady parade of people wandered about the public houses along the waterfront. Thankfully, *Rosie's Charm* was moored to a berth and reaching the pier required a simple walk down the gangplank. Letting me set the pace, the big man led the way through the crowd to the gate at the outer wall of the city.

Founded by the Phoenicians twenty-five hundred years before, Palermo had outlasted every ruling party since, including Carthage, the Romans, the Vandals, the Ostrogoths, the Byzantine Empire, the Arabian Empire, the Normans, the Holy Roman Empire, and subsequently, several of Europe's ancient families. With the support of his father, King Phillip of Spain, Charles—then the Duke of Parma—conquered Sicily and Naples in 1735 and united both under one kingdom. Given he had maintained his neutrality in the current war, the port was full, and during our trek, we passed throngs of sailors hailing from every nation. Limping along on the charcoal stone pavers, I did my best to pay attention to the various statues, churches, and monuments the big man used for landmarks. Crafted out of locally quarried marble, they were stout enough to endure the constant upheaval, and some had stood five hundred years or more. Though I tried to remember them all, in the labyrinth of narrow streets and twisting alleyways, I soon became hopelessly lost.

Finally, he pointed to the old wall surrounding the original settlement and told me, "We're gettin' close." Continuing through the maze, we came to an L-shaped piazza overlooking a grand cathedral featuring both a Byzantine dome and a Roman bell tower. Gesturing toward an auditorium on the other side, he told me, "Here we are."

One of the premier theaters on the island, it was built out of wood and large enough to accommodate five hundred spectators for a performance. Sharing the north wall, a second, smaller two-story building filled in the rest of the block. Partially brick, it had a pair of rectangular windows on the top floor and a matching pair on the bottom. In the middle of its facade, twin timber columns supported a peaked archway featuring a carving of grapevines woven around several wine bottles and half-full glasses. Underneath, a heavy oaken door with a scripted *E* carved into the center had a crescent window at the top and a twisted wrought-iron handle on the left edge.

Giving it a tug, the big man said, "Ye made it."

Inside, three bronze chandeliers featuring soft swirls and a dozen rose candle cups lit up a rectangular dining room comprised of ten round tables large enough to seat eight. They were covered in white cloths, and their centerpieces consisted of a beeswax candle amid fresh cut flowers. On a stage in the corner to our left, a string quartet played an Italian concerto, and filling the seats, beautiful local women accompanied a hodgepodge of naval officers representing all the nations at war. Other than because of the big man's costume or my noticeable gimp, I did not think we stood out. Nevertheless, upon our entrance, I felt the din of the conversation lighten and sensed every eye shift our way.

Following a sultry maiden wearing a tight black frock and carrying a tray of dirty porcelain dishes, we wound through a thin circuitous pathway to an alcove around the corner at the far right end. On the side facing our approach, a ten-foot bar constructed of polished English walnut sat in a niche between two metal archways fabricated to resemble climbing grapevines. An identical frame surrounded a rectangular mirror taking up a large portion of the back wall, and below it, three cedar shelves lined with chalices, tumblers, and snifters stepped down to a chestnut cradle housing five different-sized casks. A tall, thin man tending to the dozen people gathered about the eight stools glimpsed our arrival and motioned to a person out of my line of sight. No longer following the server, we angled into the space and were met by a swarthy, slender woman in a form-fitting burgundy gown.

"I was told you'd be coming," she revealed in a husky voice. Her skin a light olive hue, she had dark almond-shaped eyes, red pouty lips, and long straight ebony hair tied into a pair of thick braids coming together in a bow at the base of her neck. Smiling, she wrapped her arms around the big man and said, "It's good to see you alive."

Briefly, he stiffened and replied, "Is the skipper here?"

Letting him go, she returned, "Not yet, but I expect he will be soon." To my surprise, she greeted me in the same manner and, tight against my chest, purred, "My name is Eugenia. It's an honor to meet the hero of the Martorana. If there's anything I can do for you, please ask."

Enjoying her body against mine, I managed to repeat, "The hero of the Martorana?" Regrettably, the whisky had long worn off in the course of our journey, and my injuries making their presence known, I accidentally allowed a groan to escape.

Realizing my condition, she tenderly placed her hands on my chest and mentioned, "I'm sorry, I imagine you're hurting a bit."

"Aye, we both are," the big man answered. "It was a bit of a walk."

Clinging to the two fingers bereft of any bandages on my left hand, she turned and commanded, "Then follow me."

Three square tables sat against the wall opposite the bar, and with the first two already taken, she led us to the third, where two empty chairs faced a bench below a tile mosaic of the Sicilian countryside decorating the wall. Mumbling, "Thank ye," I slumped into the closest. Maintaining a view of the rest of the room, Big Tom took the spot kitty-corner to me, and Eugenia slid in next to him. Leaving his post, the barkeep, clad in a black vest over a white shirt, presented us with a copper flagon, three matching chalices, and an ewer of water. He set them down and, giving us a bow, announced, "Compliments of the king."

Furrowing my brows, I glanced to the big man, who picked up the flagon and poured himself a healthy splash. Smirking, Eugenia tilted her head my way and observed, "He doesn't know, does he?"

"Know what?" Big Tom replied.

"The cargo of *The Roja Capote*."

Shrugging, Big Tom swirled his drink under his nose and said, "It was his first battle and we didn't know if he'd survive, so we didn't see a reason to tell him. I figure I'll let the skipper do it tonight."

"Well, you can explain to your skipper your actions have earned you and your crew some marzipan," she responded. "I'm told the nuns at the Martorana have something special planned." Leaning forward, she went on to divulge, "And that's not all."

The big man asked, "What else is there?" and took a sip. Peering inside his chalice, he swallowed, curled his lips into a tight circle, and let out a slow whistle. Flashing a fleeting grin, he said, "Now that's good whisky."

Patting his knee, she inquired, "As good as the marzipan may be, do you really think a pastry would be reward enough for a clan of Scottish heroes?"

"Eugenia," I felt compelled to say, "you must have us confused with someone else. I'm certainly no hero and I've never heard of this Martorana."

"The Martorana is the cathedral across the plaza," Big Tom filled in. He poured another splash into a second chalice and, sliding it to me, followed up, "Go ahead."

Neglecting to savor the aroma, I took a substantial belt and swished it around my mouth. Slightly smoky, it was surprisingly smooth and, even in my impaired state I was able to discern a light, sweet, fruity yet somewhat floral flavor. Immediately, it numbed my broken tooth and, upon hitting my stomach, did the same to the rest of my body. With a satisfied smile crossing my lips, I slowly let out a blissful moan.

Picking up the ewer of water and filling my chalice, the big man ordered, "Take it easy. This isn't that kind of place."

"I'm only dullin' the pain," I assured him.

Suddenly, laughter erupted in the dining room and progressively headed toward the bar. Staring at the corner, the three of us watched the server we had followed leading the skipper around by his hand. Like Naples, he was bedecked in the same purple-and-gold regalia, with his mustache waxed, his goatee braided, and his long white wig dangling in front of his eyes. Beaming, she escorted him to our table, where he held her in his arms and said, "Ye know, the English language could have a million words in it, and I still don't think there'd be one worthy enough to describe yer beauty." Blushing, the server kissed his cheek, whispered in his ear, and was off. Seeing Eugenia rise to her feet, he proclaimed, "Speakin of beauty! Yer makin' me homesick!"

"Homesick?" she questioned, giving him a hug. "How on Earth could I make you homesick?"

Lingering in her embrace, he began, "Well, one of my fondest memories is the first summer I sailed to the Hebrides durin' the time a Scottish orchid, the dark-red helleborine, had started to bloom along the coasts. Wild and hardy, they're tough enough to actually grow through the cracks in the limestone, yet their soft crimson petals are delicate to the touch and their enchantin' vanilla fragrance magically puts one at ease." Nuzzling the top of her head, he murmured, "Since they only flower fer two months a year, they are a most rare sight to behold, and here in yer arms, I can feel my heart poundin' in my chest the way it did all those years ago."

Grasping him tighter, she responded, "Oh, I forget how much I miss you. You know, I am here all year long. You can always drop in anytime you want."

"Aye and once the seas have been made safe, I aim to," he insisted. "Until then, all I can do is appreciate the few fleetin' moments in your aura that the universe bestows upon me."

A different serving maiden interrupted their exchange, and letting her fingertips slowly slide down the inside of his forearms, Eugenia said, "I'll be back . . . I've got a surprise to tell you."

Taking the seat she had vacated, the skipper poured a splash of whisky for himself and remarked, "Oh, do I look forward to her surprises." He twirled it under his nose and, trying to suppress a sly smile, gave it a sample. Swallowing, he whistled softly and, similar to the big man, peered inside his chalice. "Now that's fine whisky," he declared. "Do ye recognize it?"

"Of course," Big Tom grunted. "It's the one they make in the manor outside of Culloden. With how hard it is to get in Scotland, I'm somewhat surprised to be drinkin' it in Palermo."

"I'm told it's the favorite of Charles Edward Stuart," the skipper explained, "and the king keeps some on hand fer him."

"Charles Edward Stuart," I picked up. "I didn't think he lived in Naples or Sicily. I thought his father held court in Rome."

"He does," the skipper acknowledged, "but the prince is afforded the same protection we are in this kingdom, and as my skipper used to always say, 'If ye want to curry favor out of a noble, best to pour his spirit of choice.' I'm sure King Charles is savvy enough to do the same."

"No matter what the prince may think," I pointed out, "he doesn't rule anythin'. That's why they call him the Young Pretender."

"Maybe King Charles knows there's somethin' to the constant chatter of a Jacobean restoration," the skipper put forth, "and is hedgin' his bets in case it's successful." His smile morphing into a jubilant sneer, he savored another sip and followed up, "Personally, I don't care either way. In the end, it's even more gratifyin' to have the prince's whisky be our reward."

Raising my brows, I inserted, "Eugenia said somethin' about bein' a hero," and nodding to the big man, I went on, "And he says it's up to ye to tell me what she meant. If Kemi Dakit was just a slaver, I don't understand the fuss." Swirling my drink, I posed, "And I can't imagine his head is worth a royal bounty."

"Aye, Kemi Dakit was just a slaver," the skipper concurred. "However, the cargo aboard *The Roja Capote* was somethin' quite different altogether." He sat back and, holding his chalice between his hands, divulged, "I know her captain. He helped King Charles ferry his troops in the war eight years ago, and in return, he was granted unfettered access to all the ports in this kingdom. Therefore, he always follows the same relatively safe route around the Tyrrhenian Sea, and last night, his cargo was two dozen very special passengers. Bein' a veteran to these waters, Kemi Dakit was well aware of his ship and caught wind of who he had aboard. What Kemi Dakit wasn't aware of is that we were aware that he was aware and we intended to stop him."

"Why were these passengers so special?" I asked.

"They were virgins," the big man growled.

"Virgins?" I repeated.

"That's correct," the skipper confirmed. "Twenty-three of them were orphans raised in convents throughout Italy with the expectation they'd eventually take the habit. Havin' reached the age to become aspirants, it was time they progressed to the next step, and they were sent to the Martorana." Holding up a single finger, he furthered, "More importantly, the twenty-fourth is a cousin to the king, albeit several times removed, and the price a virgin of royal blood could fetch on the slave market made too good an opportunity fer Kemi Dakit to pass up."

Turning my palms over, I told him, "Don't get me wrong. It's nice to be of service, except I'm not sure if the Royal Navy would condone us compromisin' our mission to save a group of nuns. I would think someone else would be responsible fer their safety, and if they were kidnapped, payin' the ransoms fer their release."

Shrugging, the skipper replied, "I'm sure the king would've paid fer his cousin. When it comes to the rest, ye never know."

"What about the church," I inquired, "doesn't it have an obligation to save its own people?"

Big Tom clenched his jaw. The skipper gave him a quick glance and explained, "If we had let these girls be sold into slavery, the church would've considered them martyrs and left it to the individual parishes to raise the funds to secure their release. Given they're virgins makes them expensive and given they're orphans means there's nobody to care, pretty much guaranteein' a lifetime of bondage, especially fer one cursed with beauty."

His eyes as haunting as his voice, the big man chipped in, "And even if the ransom gets paid, it doesn't mean they'll be kept safe. Plenty of women have been raped and killed on their return home."

"Which is why," the skipper asserted with a nod, "we don't ask fer permission to save innocent people."

Glaring at me, Big Tom insisted, "And it wouldn't matter if it was granted. We have a moral imperative to kill pirates."

"Keep in mind," the skipper remarked, "the next ship Kemi Dakit seized could have been British, makin' his capture a part of our duty. Of course, had everythin' worked out perfectly, we would be bringin' him to London to collect the price put on his head and see justice served at Execution Dock." Grinning wickedly, he concluded, "Still, I can't say I have a problem with his demise."

Leaning forward, I inquired, "What happened to him?"

"Apparently he didn't trust his crew wouldn't spoil the spoils, so to speak," the skipper began, "and certain *The Roja Capote* would capitulate without a fight, he thought it best to lead the boardin' party. He was in the first skiff to notice our attack."

His chuckle harsh, he set his chalice down and asked, "Do ye remember seein' one tryin' to return to the galley?"

My memory of the battle somewhat hazy, I replied, "Vaguely. I remember losin' sight of it the moment we crashed into the oars."

Smacking his right fist into his left palm, the skipper snarled, "Because that was the very moment we crushed it under our keel." Big Tom's guffaws the same ferocious guttural sounds they were at the end of the battle, he silenced the rest of the room and, though it hurt, for some reason I laughed similarly. A sneer contorting his face, the skipper went on, "Since we never recovered his body, we have to assume Kemi Dakit went down in his little boat. Hopefully, the sharks tore him limb from limb."

"Aye to that," Big Tom concurred and held his drink toward the center of the table. Simultaneously the skipper and I tapped ours to it, and together, we all downed our remaining whisky.

Pouring another round, the skipper continued, "On to even better news. The damage to *The Sabre* isn't too extensive, and in a week, she should be able to sail to Port Mahon."

"How many pirates did we capture?" I inquired.

"Close to fifty," the skipper filled in, "and I'll admit, with the size of her crew, I was hopin' fer more. I guess our surprise worked a little too well and our initial volley killed half of them. The boarding party and the freed slaves combined to take care of the rest."

"What were our casualties?" I followed up.

"Currently, three killed and fifteen wounded," the skipper answered, "although it doesn't look good fer the few who required surgery and we have another four with head wounds who haven't woken up. Thus, the surgeon won't know the final tally until tomorrow mornin'." Raising his eyebrows, he tugged at his braid and clarified, "Fer the record, I didn't consider ye one of the wounded. I figure in a few days ye should be back in fightin' shape."

"I see," I responded.

Eugenia returned and slid into the seat next to me. Looking at the skipper, she asked, "Did they tell you about the marzipan?"

Breaking into a wide smile, he exclaimed, "Marzipan! No, they didn't tell me about the marzipan!"

"What is this marzipan?" I interjected.

"It's a pastry," Eugenia stated, "and the nuns of the Martorana make the best in the world."

"Not only that, they can bake it into any form they choose," the skipper said, "I've seen bears, horses, pigs, turtles, ducks, and frogs." Pressing his left index finger to the table, he furthered, "And then there's the fruit. I'll tell ye now, at first glance, ye won't be able to tell the difference. I remember one time an apple looked so real I had to pick it up and take a bite to assure myself it wasn't."

Furrowing my brows, I inquired, "What do ye suppose they'll make fer us?"

Shrugging, he replied, "I wouldn't try to guess. It could be anythin'. Truly, they can make whatever they want."

Running her fingernails through a curl of hair atop my ear, Eugenia suggested, "I'm sure it'll be something heroic."

Goosebumps covered my body, and involuntarily shivering, I reported, "The skipper told me the significance of the passengers aboard *The Roja Capote*, and while I'm happy to help, I certainly don't believe I'm a hero. I was simply doin' my duty. We have a moral imperative to kill pirates."

Lightly scratching the back of my neck, she shook her head and replied, "The stories in the streets say something different. I hope the king takes his time with his response to your admiral and you get a chance to recover enough strength to see for yourself."

Feeling the best I had all night, I finished half the contents of my chalice and commented, "If ye keep doin' that, I'll be happy to pay fer another flagon and find out a little sooner!"

While it hurt too much for me, the skipper and the big man laughed out loud.

Eugenia waited for their humor to die down and revealed, "That's my second surprise. You don't have to buy anything. The king is sending an entire firkin of this whisky to your ship."

"An entire firkin," the big man breathed.

"I told ye I love her surprises," the skipper announced.

My eyes wide, I asked, "Does that mean I'll get a third of it?"

"Don't get too excited," the skipper advised. "I'm sure Rory'll want his cut. In fact, it'll get divided the same way the prize money does, fer every man in our crew fought hard and deserves his fair share also. Although, if ye can keep a secret, I'm thinkin' it would be best to leave the admiral out since, like ye said, it's probably best he doesn't know all the details."

Using my thumb and forefinger, I made a locking motion in front of my mouth and said, "My lips are sealed." Satisfied with my answer, they both took another drink, and during the pause, I admitted, "This is the first time I've actually earned prize money and I don't recall the process. How much would the admiral have gotten?"

"The first eighth," the skipper explained, setting his chalice on the table. "Then I get the next two, and the rest gets broken down among the crew, depending on rank and experience." Numbering on his fingers, he went on, "The officers divide an eighth, then the petty officers, the specialists, the midshipmen, and finally, the common sailors."

"So is that how it'll work with *The Sabre*?" I inquired.

"Aye," the skipper confirmed. "The Royal Navy will pay us the fair market price fer the ship and the contents, plus another five pounds a head fer the captured pirates. When all is said and done, our action today could earn every one of us more than we make in a year." Leaning forward, he raised his brows and divulged, "I'll let ye in on another little secret. Because no other ships were involved in her capture, we get first crack at the contents in her hold, and we can take everythin' we want."

"If she's a slaver," I responded, "what could she have possibly had we would want?"

"Her cannon," the skipper asserted, "and Rory has already started to take an inventory to see if any'll be an upgrade over our own. Then there's the weapons. Unfortunately, it sounds like all their flintlocks were dispersed among the pirates on the skiffs and joined them on the bottom of the sea. We did, however, find a cache of muskets we can offer in trade and a good supply of gunpowder we can use to train our men. There's a reason they hit what they're aimin' at."

"Why don't we keep the muskets?" I wanted to know.

"Because of their burnin' wicks," he responded, "makin' them touchy on land and even worse at sea. On top of it, the flash in the pan can send enough sparks flyin' to chance startin' yer own sails on fire." Arching his brows, he insisted, "I'd rather rely on bows until the day comes I can arm my entire crew with flintlocks."

"Won't that be expensive?" I asked.

Meeting my eyes, the skipper tugged at his braided goatee with his right hand and strummed the fingers of his left on the table top. His nails echoing off the wood, he lowered his voice and disclosed, "There's somethin' ye should probably know. Once upon a time, my life had been laid out fer me, and I saw a future beyond my commission. Long story short, fate intervened in the way it has a tendency to do, and though my little sloop may be the biggest ship I ever command, I've now dedicated my life to the Royal Navy."

"Why would ye do that?" I wanted to know. "I'm lookin' forward to gettin' out and gettin' my own vessel."

Sitting straight, the skipper relayed, "There's many reasons. Fer starters, I'm happy. Even if I never garner the same respect a captain of a rated vessel does, I get to see the world and I have a purpose to wake up every day. On top of it all, I won't ever have to crash into a line of enemy warships or fight in a pitched battle, and the odds are good I'll survive this war and every other one to come. Besides, the prize money gets paid out in the same amount no matter the size of yer craft." Hooking his thumb toward the big man, he stressed, "Tomas and Rory think the same way. Dangerous though it may be, they don't see a better life than the one they currently have. Therefore, we spend our money keepin' our men well trained, well equipped, well fed, and well cared fer." Waving his finger, he concluded, "I don't expect ye to do the same, ye just need to remember every time we leave port it could be our last."

Swallowing hard, I answered, "I see," and took a healthy drink.

"And don't assume our stay here will be fun and games," the skipper went on, "fer we'll spend plenty of time drillin' the crew to keep them sharp. If we're not goin' to back down from a fight, we better be prepared to get into one. It's no accident the wedge is so effective."

"Where on earth did you learn that formation?" I returned.

"The bucklers," he answered.

"The bucklers?"

"The bucklers. Back in my youth, tensions between Spain and England were runnin' high—surprise, surprise—and my skipper wanted a dozen men in his crew professionally trained. During a stop in London, he hired a former marine sergeant who had lost his leg and gave him a budget to gather weapons. To get the most out of the money, he figured it would be best to incorporate those little round shields, and he gave the group their name. Every day, they got to skip a portion of the work on the ship to practice fightin' in formation and prepare fer our defense, in case we needed it."

"Did ye?"

"Aye," the skipper mentioned, "Once. We were on our way to Jamaica and set upon by a group of pirates in a Bermudian sloop. In those years, my skipper still held on to the tradition of square sails and maintained a fully rigged ship. Completely outclassed, we were maneuvered into the wind until we floated dead in the water. While they may have known how to sail, they didn't know how to fight, and even outnumbered three to one, the bucklers sliced right through them. Watchin' it unfold, I learned the lessons I needed to learn and completed the trainin' durin' the rest of our journey. Understandin' its value, I've required it of every man under my command since. We may be small, but we're mighty." Picking up his drink, he concluded, "The same goes fer the riggin'. Always one to adapt, my skipper learned to give up on tradition and took the first opportunity he had to modify his sail plan into that of a brigantine. He didn't care if it seemed ridiculous to most, he figured it was the best way to avoid bein' captured again. Therefore, I spent my final few years under his guidance gainin' experience with gaffs, and because of it, I was happy to be assigned to *Rosie's Charm*. Foolishly clingin' to the past, the rest of my colleagues wanted nothin' to do with her."

"But hasn't it hurt yer career?" I inquired.

He took a healthy swallow, let out a happy sigh, and holding his chalice forth, declared, "That depends on how ye define hurt. They can have the higher rank. I'm happy to settle fer a finer whisky."

"And this may be the finest in the world," the big man concurred.

"I hate to be the bearer of bad news," Eugenia interrupted, "but I'm told the finest whisky is currently found in the Caribbean."

While I opened my mouth to inform her we were already acquainted with the rumors surrounding Oakies, the skipper held his left palm toward me and responded, "The Caribbean? The Caribbean is rum country. There's no way a whisky in that part of the world is better than those in Scotland."

Crossing her arms, she raised her eyebrows and asked, "Then tell me, how many men do you know who are willing to die for a Scottish whisky?" Nodding toward the flagon, she went on, "You're drinking one fit for a prince. Would you say it's worth your life?"

"Maybe," the big man grumbled, "it's as good as or better than any I've had."

"It is," the skipper agreed, "except I don't think I'd die fer it." Tilting his head toward Eugenia, he followed up, "And truth be told, I can't believe such a whisky exists. Are ye sayin' there's one we haven't heard of? What do ye know that we don't?"

Casting her eyes around the table, she leaned forward and began, "Well, I have a regular, a Venetian, who sails to that part of the world, and every time he's in Palermo, he stops in for supper on his way to a show. Maybe a week ago, he was here and told me one of the strangest tales I've heard in a long time."

"If it involves whisky in the Caribbean," the skipper inserted, "it certainly sounds like it."

"The whisky is just a part of it," she cautioned. "There's a pirate, a one-eyed Irish pirate named Clarkeson who sails a brigantine called *The Black Irish*, and according to my friend, she seized an English vessel off the coast of Jamaica simply because the captain had a barrel of her Oakies aboard."

"Oakies?" the skipper repeated.

"That's the name of the whisky," Eugenia stated, "and Clarkeson proclaimed the English were not allowed to purchase it. To drive her point home, she put the captain in a skiff and obliterated him with a volley of grapeshot."

"Her point?" the skipper commented. "She's female?"

"Obviously," Eugenia retorted, rolling her eyes. "You do know there have been other woman pirates. Haven't you ever heard of Grace O'Malley?"

"Grace O'Malley was an Irish noble," the big man pointed out. "This one sounds more like Anne Bonny. There's always been rumors that she escaped from the gallows. Maybe she's finally returned."

"I doubt it," Eugenia countered. "I heard Anne Bonny got married and settled down to raise a family somewhere in the Carolinas. Besides, Clarkeson looks nothing like her. She has jet black hair and wears a black eye patch over her right eye." Looking at the skipper, she asked, "Do you want to hear the craziest part?"

"Of course."

"She has a tall redheaded banshee at her side and a crew of dark skinned natives with bushy beards and dreadlocks. The witnesses say they appear to have been borne out of the very earth forming the islands in that sea."

"That sounds a bit odd," the skipper mentioned, "but I wouldn't call it crazy."

"They also only speak Gaelic," Eugenia followed up.

"Gaelic?" the skipper repeated. Tugging at his braid, he noted, "Hmmm, this Clarkeson does sound a bit mysterious."

Going along with the game, I chipped in, "I wonder if she's even human."

"Some say that she isn't," Eugenia offered, "and she's really a water sprite."

"Oh, come on," the skipper dismissed. "Ye don't really believe she's some sort of fairy, do ye?"

Waving her index finger, Eugenia remarked, "Normally I'd say no, only there's more to this story than meets the eye. For one, it seems every sailor who speaks Gaelic on the vessels she takes gets caught under her spell and ends up joining her crew."

Frowning, the skipper asked, "If her crew is all natives, what happens to these sailors?"

When she turned both palms over and shrugged, Big Tom insisted, "I'm sure there's a logical explanation fer it."

"There's still more to tell," she continued, "for the Spanish know which island she uses for her base and claim it's haunted. They won't step foot on it, let alone colonize it."

"A haunted island?" the skipper questioned. "Can there really be such a thing?"

"They say this one has a bay that, in the darkness of the new moon, comes alive in a living green. The Spanish believe it's the work of the devil."

"Excludin' their own treatment of natives," the skipper muttered, "the Spanish believe everythin' is the work of the devil."

"Not everybody agrees with the Spanish," Eugenia put forth, "for those who believe she's a water sprite claim the bay is really a portal to the fairy world."

"There may be a bay that glows a livin' green," the skipper allowed. "However, I doubt it's a portal to the fairy world any more than it's the work of the devil. And if the Spanish haven't given her a letter of marque, then she's nothin' more than a pirate who should be hunted down to face justice at Gallows Point."

A slight smile on her lips, Eugenia countered, "I don't think it would be that easy. According to the stories, her crew dispatched almost two hundred Spanish mercenaries the day she took her first ship."

"Two hundred?" the skipper inquired. "Don't ye think that number may be a little far-fetched? I'll give her two dozen."

Arching her brows, she turned to him and said, "If you think that's far-fetched, you probably don't want to hear what I say next."

"This is getting even better," the big man chipped in.

"Aye, now ye have to tell us," the skipper added.

Setting her eyes on us one at a time, Eugenia said, "Even knowing the consequences he was facing, a second English captain was dumb enough to try to sneak a few barrels of Oakies back to London. Somehow it came to Clarkeson's attention and almost immediately after he set out, she whipped up a tempest violent enough to drive him into a shoal."

"She whipped up a tempest?" the skipper asked.

"I said you wouldn't believe me," she reminded him, "and it doesn't matter if you don't, for in the end, once the storm had passed and his ship, *The Sea Lion*, I believe, lay exposed, *The Black Irish* was the first vessel to come along."

Upon hearing this bit of new information, I asked, "What did Clarkeson do?"

"She and her men stripped the captain naked and hung him spread eagle in his rigging to watch while they stole everything they could. When they were through, she lit the sails on fire."

"Oh, Jesus," the skipper muttered.

"They say an unnatural wind carried her cackle and his screams over a hundred miles away," Eugenia concluded.

"If she's goin' to make it a point to make an example out of innocent people," the skipper declared, "then the Royal Navy needs to make it a point to make an example out of her. They can use her body to replace Calico Jack's on Rackham's Cay and let the ravens eat it to the bones." Shaking his head, he determined, "She gives us a reason to return to the Caribbean."

"The whisky sounds like reason enough," Big Tom put forth. "We can buy a few barrels and see what we think."

Smiling, the skipper suggested, "Actually, that's a great idea. Once we purchase them, we'll let everyone know we're off to England and then she can hunt us down. It'll save us the time and trouble of findin' her." Turning to Eugenia, he asked, "Yer Venetian friend didn't happen to mention where we can get this whisky, did he?"

"Actually he did," she informed us. "There's a place in Jamaica and another on Culebra, an otherwise deserted island off the coast of Puerto Rico. Supposedly, it's within fifteen miles of Clarkeson's hideout."

"That would make it the perfect place to visit," the skipper observed, "if it wasn't in enemy territory."

"It is Spanish territory," Eugenia confirmed, "except the owner of the public house, an Irishman named Paddy, maintains his place is neutral and he has captains of all nations stop by. My Venetian friend insists it's the best spot in the world to take a vacation."

"A vacation?" I inquired.

"It's a Shakespearean term," she replied.

"Did yer Venetian friend try the whisky?" the big man wanted to know.

"No," she said, shaking her head. "He drinks wine. But he asserted Paddy raved and raved about it, claiming it's the best he's ever had. He said it was the same with the Scottish and

Irish members of his crew. They went crazy for it." Squinting, she tapped her temple and added, "There was this Gaelic phrase he said they repeated every time they took a drink."

With a quick glance at Big Tom, the skipper responded, "Uisge beatha?"

Snapping her fingers, she exclaimed, "Yes! That's it."

"Then it must be good whisky," Big Tom attested.

"Why? What does it mean?" she asked.

"Water of life," the big man answered.

"Did this Paddy mention anythin' else?" the skipper followed up.

"He says it's smooth with a woody finish and a taste like buttered corn." Shrugging, she admitted, "Since I don't know what corn is, I couldn't say whether that makes it good or bad."

"I've eaten corn," the skipper said, "and although we didn't have any butter, I imagine that would make it tasty, especially with a pinch of salt." Tugging at his braid, he posed, "I wonder why Clarkeson would bother to make such a big deal out of this Oakies, especially if she's tryin' to pass herself off as a fairy. Accordin' to legend, water sprites don't collect barrels of whisky. They collect souls of men."

"And what better way to bait them," Eugenia pointed out, "than with the finest whisky in the world?"

I nodded my head and said, "She's got a point."

"Aye," Big Tom concurred, "it would certainly work on me."

Sitting back, the skipper bowed toward Eugenia and conceded, "If anythin', ye have piqued my curiosity. When we return to the fleet, I think it's time to find a message we can deliver to Port Royale."

"Before you do," Eugenia interjected, "there is another pirate I'd like to see you capture first."

Widening his eyes, the skipper asked, "And who would that be?"

"Orana D'Groers."

Immediately, rage consumed Big Tom's features. Clenching his teeth, he seethed, "Orana D'Groers."

"Was he in Palermo?" the skipper followed up. "I can't believe he'd be welcome here."

"The Spanish gave him letters of marque," she lamented, "so the king has no choice."

"They're givin' letters of marque to everyone," the skipper complained, "and the longer the war goes on, the worse it gets."

"Who is Orana D'Groers?" I inquired.

"He's a French pirate," the skipper told me, "and a slaver."

"The worst of their kind," the big man sneered.

"He makes my skin crawl," Eugenia inserted.

"Let's hope he believes his captives will fetch a high price at the markets on the coast of North Africa," the skipper posed. "Or if not, let's hope they don't survive when they're captured."

"Why should we hope fer such an awful fate?" I wanted to know.

"He's a savage," the big man growled. "Rape and murder are the least of his sins."

"He tortures his victims," the skipper filled in, "and the longer they suffer, the more he enjoys it. Once Britain adopted a professional navy and stopped usin' privateers, the crown put a bounty on his head." Facing Eugenia, he stated, "If he's close, he's fair game. When was he here?"

"A week ago."

"Did he happen to mention where he was off to?"

"He said he was making a quick sweep along northern Italy and then heading to France."

Tugging at his braid, the skipper suggested, "That doesn't make sense. What is the point of raidin' the coast fer slaves if he was headin' to France? There's no market to sell them."

"He said he wasn't planning on taking any slaves," she revealed. "He was only looking to take ships. He was almost giddy about it. He said, and I quote, this was the first time he was unencumbered by financial constraints."

"Did he say why he wanted the ships?" the skipper inquired.

"He wouldn't tell me," she admitted, "but I had another privateer say D'Groers had passed along some information about a real opportunity for any captain willing to brave the English Channel at this time of year."

Hopefully, the skipper asked, "He didn't happen to narrow down which part of the Channel, did he?"

Pursing her lips, she let out, "No, unfortunately he didn't."

"Did he say when he had to be there by?"

"I was told the twentieth of February."

"Then that doesn't give D'Groers much time to hunt," the skipper observed.

Through snarling lips, Big Tom insisted, "We can catch him."

Dismissing his comment with a wave, the skipper stated, "We can't leave until the king gives us his reply, and if we don't have any business in northern Italy, we have no business goin' there." His attention back to Eugenia, he followed up, "If he was unencumbered by financial constraints, do ye know how he was goin' to get paid?"

"Not exactly," she replied, "except the other privateer mentioned Maurice of Saxony was involved, whoever that is, and for what it's worth, he took it seriously enough to debate making the journey." The three of us turning to face her, she held her palms forth and, obviously startled, added, "Maurice of Saxony must be someone important."

"Maurice of Saxony is perhaps the most successful general the French have," the skipper stated. "He was promoted to marshal a year ago."

"Why would the highest-rankin' French general want to hire Spanish privateers?" I asked.

"I can't know fer sure sittin' here," the skipper began, "but I'm thinkin' the French have decided to enter the war and it won't be on the British side. If Maurice of Saxony is somewhere along the channel, I'll venture to guess there's also a French invasion force somewhere near the coast."

"Which is why they'd need ships," I realized, "to transport the army."

"With all the ties between Britain and the Brittany coast," the big man noted, "I'm sure our spies would find out somethin' first, and even if they didn't, I can't believe the French would be able to land a force that big in England under the nose of the Royal Navy."

Picking up my chalice, I nonchalantly suggested, "They could if they landed at Maldon."

"In Essex?" the skipper followed up. "Why do ye say that?"

"Well, similar to our army fightin' on the mainland in Europe, our navy has gotten stretched pretty thin, and the ship I was previously aboard had been assigned to that area. With the threat of a rebellion in Scotland, however, we were sent north to support the dragoons." Shrugging, I disclosed, "No replacements ever arrived to relieve us prior to our departure, and as far as I know, none ever did."

"Then I'd bet there's holes all up and down the coast," the skipper posed.

Having finished his drink, Big Tom refilled his chalice and inserted, "Holes or not, the French would still need a large army to invade England. With all the fightin' on the mainland and the size of their borders, do ye think they'd be willin' to commit the troops?"

Watching the big man pour the whisky, the skipper suggested, "They may not have to. They may already have an army waitin' fer their arrival."

"What do ye mean?" I asked.

Swirling his chalice under his nose, the skipper took a little sip and said, "Since the French have largely supported the Stuarts durin' their thirty-year exile in Rome, it is possible the French king may have decided it's come time to collect his due."

"Are you saying yer startin' to believe the rumors of a Stuart restoration?" Eugenia inquired.

"Why not?" the skipper put forth and finished his drink. "I'm sure there's still plenty of Jacobites in England who would prefer a Stuart on the throne, and if suppressin' the Highland clans in Scotland now requires the dragoons, maybe the French king senses an opportunity. What better way to enter the war than by startin' a rebellion inside the country yer at war with?"

"That gives us a reason to get D'Groers," Big Tom declared. "We should leave at once."

"No," the skipper rejected. "We have to wait for the King's reply. We can't leave without it."

"Why?" I asked, "Especially if D'Groers is considered an enemy of the crown?"

Juggling his hands, the skipper reminded me, "Because we're a messenger ship and yer goin' to have to accept it. We don't hunt pirates, privateers, or enemy vessels. Now, if we should stumble upon one along our way, it is our duty to abide by our motto and take on the fight." Looking at Big Tom, he posed, "With Admiral Mathews and the British fleet at Hyeres enforcin' the blockade of the Spanish fleet at Toulon, D'Groers will have to avoid the Spanish coast on his way to Gibraltar. If he's takin' the time to hunt for ships first, there is a chance we can cut him off."

"I hope so," Eugenia encouraged, "and you do the same thing to him that you did to Kemi Dakit."

"Then make our plans known," the skipper divulged, "and maybe the king will give us his reply quickly so we can be off."

The last of our whisky finished, the skipper promised Eugenia he would not depart without saying goodbye, and we left her to close for the night. Wandering through the streets on our way back to *Rosie's Charm*, I listened to the skipper update the big man on his meeting with the king and then discuss trading the muskets for a few barrels of claret to auction off in London. "Everythin' else of value on *The Sabre* we'll sell here," he concluded, "and use the proceeds to throw a feast. If experience has taught me anythin', it's a well-fed crew makes fer a happy one."

"That reminds me," Big Tom stated, "the cook said we're runnin' low on limes. We need to purchase some prior to headin' out."

"Make it a point to get them tomorrow," the skipper followed up. "I don't want scurvy to be a worry. To have a chance at catchin' D'Groers, we have to be able to leave on a moment's notice."

Though I still had a limp and felt an occasional pinch when my movements accidentally tugged at my stitches, I found the pain had subsided considerably, and grinning, I put forth, "Why wait? I say we immediately head out to hunt down this Orana D'Groers and rip the bastard's arms out of his sockets."

Chuckling, the skipper suggested, "Let's have ye go to bed fer the night and see if ye feel the same in the mornin'."

"Aye," the big man concurred, "yer likely to have a different take once ye sober up."

At the outer wall, the skipper stopped and cast his gaze across the ships in the harbor, still lit up under the moon shining through a thin layer of clouds. The cool night quiet and calm, he tugged at his braid and asked, "What about Clarkeson? After we capture D'Groers, should we cross the Atlantic to hunt her down? Personally, I would love to meet a one-eyed Irish lass bold enough to teach a native crew to sail in Gaelic."

"It's not much different from what we do," Big Tom pointed out, "and we've learned that after enough repetition, the sailors get it. It wouldn't be hard for her to do the same."

"I know," the skipper responded, "which deepens the mystery. I wonder who gave her our idea."

"I'm sure it was another pirate," I insisted. "There has to be plenty of men still alive who sailed with Blackbeard or Black Bart or even Calico Jack back in the day. Any of those men could've taught her their code."

Squinting, he paused to examine my eyes and said, "Maybe yer right. Maybe it's all a coincidence."

"A coincidence?" I repeated.

In the ghastly haze, he stared right through me and, tugging at his braid, revealed, "There's a part to the story of my skipper's Clarkeson that I've only shared with very few people, and every time I hear a new tale about this one, I'd swear she knows it too. Of course, that'd be impossible." His eyes drifting out to the harbor, he settled on *Rosie's Charm* and, in a dramatic voice, delivered, "With lawyers in the vacation for they sleep between term and term and then they perceive not how time moves." At my silence, he explained, "It's a quote from the play *As You Like It*. My skipper had a copy of Shakespeare's first folio and used it to teach me how to read." Looking out to the darkness past the harbor, he swore, "And havin' planted my feet into the sand on those beaches in the Caribbean, I know exactly what that

Venetian meant. It's been a long time and we've been at it pretty good. Maybe we should consider takin' a little break. At least Clarkeson gives us a reason to go."

"The whisky is reason enough," Big Tom asserted, "but we need to hunt D'Groers first. . ."

N
W E
S

FLORIDA
(Spain)

BERMUDA
(England)

BAHAMAS
(England)

ATLANTIC
OCEAN

CUBA
(Spain)

ST.DOMINGUE
(France)

HISPANIOLA
(Spain)

PUERTO
RICO
(England)

JAMAICA
(England)

NICARAGUA
(Spain)

CARIBBEAN SEA

COSTA
RICA
(Spain)

PANAMA
(Spain)

VENEZUELA
(Spain)

The Black Irish: Clarkeson, Fergus, Ben, James, Gianis, Marcus
The Mariana: Malcolm

CHAPTER 6

October 1, 1785, Kingston, Jamaica

With half the candle on the mantel behind the bar having melted, the fifth metal pin tumbled past the frozen streams of wax that had built up down the side of the stick and fell into the pool at the bottom of the brass drip catcher. Turning his bright blue eyes toward the flickering orange flame, the old sea captain admitted, "To be sure, the skipper was right, fer when I woke the next mornin', the last thing I wanted was a fight with old Orana D'Groers, or anyone else, fer that matter." Slowly stroking his bushy white beard, he added, "And when I went fer my checkup that afternoon, it was a relief to hear the surgeon prescribe bed rest fer the next ten days."

Over the rain falling in an easy patter, Ginevra asked, "Did you ever see Eugenia again?"

"Once," the old sea captain recalled, "a little over two weeks later. Followin' the skipper's orders, the crew worked to repair *The Sabre* and get *Rosie's Charm* ready to go on a moment's notice, then we had a feast, and although I couldn't participate much, we spent our remainin' time trainin'. When the skipper finally did receive the king's reply, he felt obliged to tell Eugenia goodbye, and since the chances were good none of us would

188

survive to see another port, he gave our men one last night of revelry. But because Rory and the big man, particularly the big man, were chompin' at the bit to go, they were none too happy to be wastin' the hours, so the skipper checked in on me to see if I felt well enough to accompany him. Despite not bein' fully recovered, I was aware of my role in the stories bein' told, embellished as it was, and not wanting to miss my chance to reap the rewards, I somehow summoned the strength to tag along." A sly grin crossing his lips, he arched his brows and followed up, "Given the cost of my pleasure was pain, I suppose it would've been better had I not, yet even knowin' the consequences I was facin', there isn't a thing I wouldn't happily do again."

Wearing the same grin, Tony commented, "I'm sure there isn't."

"While the marzipan," the old sea captain went on, "was unlike anythin' I had ever had. In honor of our king, it was shaped into a single gallant red rose with white icin' on the tips, and they made one fer every member of the crew, over a hundred in all."

"Did ye catch D'Groers?" Brass wanted to know.

"D'Groers," the old sea captain repeated, "now that is another story indeed."

"I don't want to hear what happened to D'Groers," Nancy interjected. "I want to hear more about Mairi. She's the main character."

"Mairi is just peddling whiskey," John pitched in. "She can't be the main character. Main characters are heroes."

"Aye," Luke added, "and no characters are more heroic than the twins. Our grandfather met them."

Nearly choking on his rum, Jack exclaimed, "The twins? Who are the twins?" Pressing his thumb to his chest, he declared, "I've only heard two parts of this story, and I can already tell Malcolm is the hero. That's a captain I'd sail with."

Cocking an eyebrow, Tony countered, "Malcolm? You missed too many other parts. Mairi was right, if Clarkeson holds true, then Malcolm's part in this affair is coming to a bloody end. DeLogrono's role, on the other hand, I'm sure is only just beginning. No human can match the strength of a Spanish lion."

Sneering, Brass insisted, "Big Tom's the hero."

Turning his palms over and spreading his arms wide, Rags proclaimed, "None of these people were real!"

For a moment, the old sea captain tried to address each concern, but with every person speaking simultaneously, he shrugged and downed his final swallow of lager. At the other end of the bar, Jack finished his wine and, sliding his empty glass forward, accidentally rattled his gold bracelet off the wooden top. Sarah, arguing with Rags, was alerted by the subtle noise, and in the midst of the dispute, she refilled the drink. In an attempt to interrupt their back and forth, Jack intermittently raised and lowered his right hand to the height of his chin.

Finally, Sarah turned his way and snapped, "What do you want?"

With every eye falling upon him, Jack cleared his throat and started, "Well, heh-heh, it seems to me this whole thing begins and ends with Oakies, heh-heh." Hooking his left thumb toward Brass, he noted, "They had heard of it in Palermo and now Big Tom wants to find a reason to sail to the Caribbean to give it a try, heh-heh." Looking back over his right shoulder to the group at the table, he put forth, "We know the twins love it, heh-heh, which means barrels or not," he furthered, waving a finger at Nancy, "there's a demand Mairi has to meet, heh-heh." Leaning forward, he told Jack, "Since Malcolm bought some in spite of being warned, heh-heh, I'm going to say the next story should be about Clarkeson, heh-heh." Then he settled his eyes on Tony and recalled, "After all, hers was the first one he told, heh-heh. I wish I were here for the whole thing. *The Black Irish* sounds like a ship I sailed on." Holding Sarah's gaze, he tipped his head toward the old sea captain and offered, "And if I'm right, I'll buy his next round, heh-heh."

Placing his fingertips to his left temple, Rags groaned, "Jesus Christ Jack, you were never a pirate."

"That's correct. He was never a pirate," the old sea captain concurred. "Nor was Clarkeson, fer if I've said it once, I've said it a thousand times, she was a warrior fightin' fer a cause." To a crackle of lightning and rumble of thunder, he returned Jack's nod and, while Sarah picked up his empty mug, continued, "And as yer sharp mind so alertly picked up, Malcolm had to learn that lesson the hard way. . ."

Mid-November 1743, between Puerto Rico and Turks and Caicos

His flaming red hair flowing out the back of the black kerchief covering his head and his flaming red beard forked into twin braids, Fergus stood next to Clarkeson at the helm of *The Black Irish* and pointed his spyglass toward an approaching brig to the southeast. Focusing the lens on the bold black letters painted on the nameplate mounted to the portside bow, he whistled softly and told her, "The *Mariana* . . . I'll give ye credit. Ye do have a knack."

Letting her wild mane blow freely, she manned the wheel and kept her brigantine on a northeasterly course eventually intercepting the other vessel. A gleam in her dark eye, she looked at their latest quarry's billowing bright white sails highlighted against the navy-blue sky and, with a wicked smile crossing her lips, revealed, "Finding *The Sea Lion* was pure luck. Somehow that storm put us close, and we stumbled upon her. But in this case, knowin' Malcolm was headin' east to the British Virgin Islands and then north to Bermuda, I figured cuttin' between Cuba and Saint Dominique would give us a good chance to track him down."

"Still, it's a big ocean," Fergus noted. "Yer father'd be proud."

"No, he wouldn't," she retorted, shaking her head. "No matter our motives, he'd never want us to take sides in this war, and he wouldn't approve of the blood on my hands." Nodding toward the other ship, she went on, "Especially this time. Captain Stewart is a Scot and a good man. This won't be easy."

"Wasn't he advised not to buy Oakies?"

"He was," she confirmed, "and he was told to set out with *The Yorktown* or sail with a few more ships."

"Yet he didn't listen," Fergus stated, "and not only that, he made known the route he was takin'. What was he thinkin'? I can't believe he didn't keep it a secret."

Cackling more harsh than happy, Clarkeson divulged, "After the amount of whiskey he drank, he probably doesn't remember tellin' anyone."

"These sorts of moments remind me of yer father's favorite quote," Fergus observed.

"Man has two ears but one tongue," she recalled, "so he can listen to twice as much as he speaks."

"That's it. I guess nobody taught this captain that lesson."

"Well, we're goin' to teach him today in the hardest way possible. Let me know the moment he appears. He's a big man with a bushy brown beard, and he likes to show off his big biceps."

"I see him right now," Fergus reported, "starin' right back at us. What do ye expect him to do?"

"Stay on his current course," she began, "and try to slip by. He thinks he's faster and can outrun us." Firmly grasping a spindle with her right hand, she used her left to point out the three new triangular jib sails strung from their foremast to their bowsprit and furthered, "It's a good thing we were unable to salvage any canvas off *The Empire's Reach*, because we didn't have those the day we stripped what we could off *The Sea Lion*, and since nobody has seen us since, nobody knows we have them, nor how fast we've become. Now, no ship can outrun us. I bet we take her before supper."

Fergus lowered the spyglass and, sliding the tubes together, replied, "I think that may be a bit hopeful. He does have the wind at his back. My guess is it'll be a little later."

Though the *Mariana* stayed on the same heading through the afternoon, when the day faded into the evening and the outcome became obvious, she took a hard turn due east in an attempt to escape into the open ocean. Barely having to alter course, *The Black Irish* gave chase, and with the sun descending at their backs, the crew ate in turns. No longer needing a lens to identify Malcolm at his stern, Clarkeson met James, Fergus, and Ben at the helm.

Strapping his claymore to his back, Fergus inquired, "How many men are we facin'?"

Tucking her ponytail into a bun, Clarkeson answered, "No more than two dozen, but expect a good fight." She relieved Ben of the wheel and added, "He does have a couple of cannon, and I hate to say I don't know exactly where they're at."

Stepping to the right, Ben followed up, "How could he hide them?" His features obscured behind the graying dreadlocks on his head blending in with those of his beard, he wore the same black uniform the others did, and in addition to a cutlass strapped to his waist, he carried a flintlock on each hip.

"It's not that he hides them," she filled in. "It's that he uses them to balance the weight of his load and they never stay in one place. Regardless of where they end up, however, his aim is always the same. He'll keep them concealed to appear defenseless and lure us into their field of fire. Then, he'll greet the boardin' party with a face full of canister shot."

With the thin dreadlocks on his head tied at the top of his skull and those on his face at the midpoint of his chest, James stood to her left, cradling a blunderbuss in his arms. A cutlass, an axe, and a pair of daggers were stuck into his belt, and slinging the firearm over his shoulder, he asked, "How big are they?"

"Twelve-pounders," she said.

"Then he could easily wipe out half our crew," Ben posed. "Maybe we should just sink him and not take any chances."

Sliding the silver flask etched with a rose having two buds on the stem above the word *FIAT* out of the vest pocket over her heart, Clarkeson responded, "If we sink him, there won't be any survivors to tell the tale. Don't ferget, we need them to spread the word of Oakies."

"His disappearance could enhance the mystery," Fergus suggested, "the same way the storm did with *The Sea Lion*."

"His execution will make a bolder statement," she countered, "and serve the bigger purpose. Besides, this brig is a well-maintained ship. Taken intact, I figure we could use the cannon we salvaged out of *The Sea Lion* to equip her."

Frowning, Fergus asked, "Are ye lookin' to build yer own armada?"

Shrugging, she replied, "Why not? Black Bart and Henry Morgan often had several vessels under their command. We could too. Right now the Royal Navy is tryin' to increase its presence in the Caribbean. Imagine if we could tie up their entire fleet. The Spanish privateers would be free to feast on the British shippin' throughout this sea."

"Fer all we know," Fergus put forth, "Butler hasn't returned to France, let alone found the necessary support fer the prince. Keep in mind there's a reason Charles Stuart is known in Scotland as the Young Pretender."

Tilting her head to meet his eyes, she retorted, "I'm sure Butler has returned by now and his visit confirmed what we already know. There's plenty of support fer rebellion among the Highlanders. They just need someone to lead them."

"Ye make it sound easy," Fergus remarked. "The only people the clans hate more than the English are each other."

"Aye, but the English give the clans a common enemy," she pointed out, "and there's a reason Prince Charles is known in France as the Young Chevalier—they believe he has the charisma to unite them. They wouldn't commit Maurice De Saxe to the invasion if they didn't. Plus, the only troops remainin' in Britain are old men or raw recruits, and with that sort of defense, the English throne is ripe fer the pluckin'. This is the best chance the French will get to put a quick end to this war and change the course of history." Offering him a drink, Clarkeson went on, "Soon we should hear Charles has been named prince regent, and when we do, I want to be ready."

Crossing his arms, Fergus leaned forward and stated, "I hope ye don't think yer groomin' either of my sons to be the captain. I only agreed to my role in this part of yer plan so they wouldn't have one."

"Yer boys will remain where they are at," she assured him. Nodding between Ben and James, she continued, "I believe they're both more than qualified and I could pick either one, except right now I think it's best we take the *Mariana* prior to puttin' someone in charge of her. Like my father also used to say, stay focused on the task at hand." Waving her flask, she declared, "To the king."

Relenting, Fergus accepted and echoed, "To the king." He took a healthy swig and, passing it on to Ben, asked, "Are there any swivel guns?"

"Aye, he's got one on each side of the bow."

After a swallow of his own, Ben inquired, "What's yer plan?"

"We'll turn him into the wind," she began, "and goad him into firin' his cannons. Once he exposes their positions, we'll attack where they aren't."

Ben gave the flask to James and followed up, "What if he doesn't commit to firin' them?"

"Then we slide up behind her and go over the stern," she replied.

"Why the stern?" James questioned and took his swallow. Completing the circuit, he handed the flask to Clarkeson and asserted, "Twelve-pounders can be chase guns."

"Aye, they can be," she concurred, "but these are too heavy to put atop his poop deck and he doesn't have any portholes to fire them through. He'd have to place them in his cabin and fire through the window of his quarters."

"Puttin' cannon in the captain's quarters wouldn't be unheard of," Ben chipped in.

"This window is stained glass," she informed them, "burgundy to be exact, and ye can barely see through it. I personally would prefer not to break it, and given how expensive I'm sure it was, I doubt the idea has even crossed his mind. What's more, he stored his Oakies in his cabin. I don't think he's dumb enough to fire a volley anywhere near those barrels and chance blowin' himself up."

"Ye better be right," Fergus warned. "Otherwise, we'll lose more than just half our crew."

"I wish I could say fer sure," she conceded and downed a hearty pull. "Still, regardless of our plan, we better be ready fer a surprise or two. I'm tellin' ye, it's not goin' to be easy. We're probably goin' to lose some good men today."

"At least they'll have some good food in their belly and good whiskey in their veins," James commented, "which beats dyin' as a slave, starvin' on an island, or hangin' with a noose around yer neck."

"Aye," Ben agreed. He cast his gaze toward the ranks amassing on their deck and added, "It doesn't matter who ye are or where yer from. If yer fightin' fer freedom, yer fightin' as one. And even if most of them can't find Scotland on a map, should today be their last, they'll be able to say they went out on their own terms."

His attention on Captain Stewart standing alone above the blue-and-white Scottish flag at his stern, Fergus patted down his vest until he found his flask. Removing the wooden stopper, he announced, "We're gettin' close. It's time to pass out some liquid courage and get everyone ready to brawl."

Ben and James mirrored his actions, and the three waded into their men, leaving Clarkeson to guide the vessel. Passing the port side of the brig, she patiently began maneuvering it into a headwind coming out of the south until the square sails propelling the *Mariana* began flapping uncontrollably and had to be furled to their spars. Though *The Black Irish* was forced to do the same, the combination of the larger gaff on her mainmast and the added jibs on the foremast made it possible for the brigantine to round the bow of the other craft. Swooping in along its starboard side, she used the momentum to circle the back, tack into the wind, and repeat the tactic—coming even closer the second time. Giving no indication of capitulating, Malcolm rotated at his wheel and glared at her.

The bottom of the shimmering orange sun almost touching the horizon, Fergus returned to the helm and noted, "It'll be dark soon. If we don't do somethin', we could lose him in the night."

"Then let's get this over with," she determined. "Get the men riled up. If I can't get him to commit, we'll deliver a glancin' blow to her port side and swing around to attack her rear."

Ignoring the chants of "FAUGH A BALLAGH, FAUGH A BALLAGH, FAUGH A BALLAGH," Malcolm watched Clarkeson for the duration of her loop. Taking a slow curve, she crossed his front and gathered the wind in her sails to make another run. At the waist of his vessel, she narrowed her eye and commanded, "CO-BHUABDH! [Brace for impact]." Those closest to her grabbed the rigging and repeated her cry, sending it rippling through her crew. Ordering, "LAIMH CHEART! [right turn]," she spun the wheel to the right, and the brigantine clipped the brig hard enough to knock Malcolm off his feet. Crying, "LAIMH CHEARR! [left turn]," she spun the wheel the other way and headed in a winding arc to the left. Tracing a tight figure eight, *The Black Irish* came in directly behind the *Mariana*. Clarkeson yelled, "BEIR AIR! [grab hold]," and slammed her bowsprit into his stern, fracturing a web through the whole of the burgundy window.

"FAUGH A BALLAGH!" Fergus bellowed.

Under the cover of the musketeers, the boarding party cast their lanyards and secured the two ships together. Rising within the jumble of ropes, Malcolm grasped the bulwark and, seeing the first wave starting to ascend, shouted, "NOW!" Suddenly, the cracked glass shattered completely and two iron barrels emerged from his quarters.

Her eye wide, Clarkeson screamed, "FERGUS! CHASERS!" Abandoning the helm, she ran down the deck repeating, "SEACHAIN! SEACHAIN! SEACHAIN! [duck]."

Everyone she passed immediately dove for cover, but the din of the battle swallowed her warning, and Fergus prepared to climb with the second group. Sprinting the remaining distance, she leapt off her feet and smashed into his lower back.

Two enormous blasts erupted, enveloping both ships under a thick cloud of acrid smoke. Aboard the *Mariana*, the clanging of steel rang out. Beneath the haze creeping over *The Black Irish*, a few coughs accompanied some moans. When a member of her crew tried to rise, he realized his left arm was mangled and both legs were missing below the knees. His piercing cry shattered the eerie silence, and the rest of her men began to clamber to their feet. Because the faint orange glow of the setting sun was barely visible through the dark shroud, the healthy sailors had to follow the groans to find their wounded comrades. With the fighting on the *Mariana* morphing into shouts of pain and then ceasing altogether, several of the merchantman's crew appeared at the conjoined bulwarks. Axes in hand, they hacked at the tethers binding the ships together and sent them whipping across *The Black Irish*.

Tackled from behind, Fergus landed headfirst below the bulwark, and Clarkeson tumbled over his body, ending up face down across his lower legs. Seeing a red streak matting her hair, he scrambled to his knees and flipped her onto her back.

Anger blazing in her eye, she roared, "Go take this ship!"

A flicker of a smile on his lips, he surged to his feet, drew his claymore, and holding it high, boomed, "FAUGH A BALLAGH!" Returning his call, James materialized out of the smog, and the surviving members of their boarding party rallied to them both. The cannons having disappeared into the cabin, they flung a second array of lanyards. Clarkeson ran down the deck of her ship, found Ben, and together, they assembled a makeshift firing line. Pointing to the sailors severing the ropes, she ordered, "Kill them first, then train yer fire inside that window. I don't want to see those barrels again!"

Ben nodded and started the cycle. In violent bloody puffs, their targets fell away. Redirecting their aim, they poured a steady stream of rounds into the cabin, protecting Fergus and the men scaling the side. Wielding a shortened claymore, Malcolm led his remaining crew into the fray. He struck the first person cresting the bulwark below the ear, cleaving his head in two and sending the body tumbling back into the mob.

Lost in the chaos, Fergus made it over and called, "FAUGH A BALLAGH!" James fired the blunderbuss and cleared the space for their men to assemble the wedge. Mercilessly, they cut Malcolm's sailors down and forced him to retreat to the wheel. A few of his men gathered with him, and despite several crimson slashes throughout his clothing and a darkening patch on his left thigh, he stood at the forefront of the defenders, swinging his sword in a mighty spiral.

Staring down the tip of the blade, Fergus barked "STAD!" and the wedge came to a halt. Glaring at Malcolm, he asserted, "Waving that thing isn't goin' to do ye any good. Yer better off puttin' it down."

"Once I drive it through yer heart, I'll be happy to," Malcolm retorted. "Or are ye too much of a coward to fight me man to man?"

Laughing gruffly, Fergus slid his bloody claymore into its sheath and, drawing a flintlock, remarked, "I'm wise enough to know it's better to just shoot ye dead and be done."

"Typical pirate," Malcolm spat, "a man of no honor."

Raising his pistol, Fergus responded, "There'll be no honor among the sharks feastin' on yer body either. Any last words?"

Slipping in on his right, Clarkeson appeared and inserted, "Well, well, well, what do we have here?"

Without looking away, Fergus stated, "This one wants to be shot."

Meeting Malcolm's eyes, she tilted her head and asked, "Is that true, Captain? Ye want to be shot?"

Holding her gaze, he seethed, "I'd rather die with my sword in my hand than be made one of yer spectacles."

His attention on Malcolm, Fergus shrugged and commented, "See, I told ye. Would ye like me to pull the trigger, or would ye like the honor?" Risking a quick glance toward her, he frowned and followed up, "Do ye know yer bleedin'?"

The top of her bun dangled underneath her right shoulder and, touching the left side of her head, she replied, "I am? Where?"

"Right there," he said. Glaring at their captive, he added, "Ye don't feel it?"

Removing her red, wet, sticky fingers, she rubbed them in circles on her thumb, wiped them on her vest, and put forth, "No, not yet."

Clenching his teeth, Malcolm grumbled, "Too bad my aim wasn't a little more to the right."

"Can I kill him now?" Fergus inquired.

Letting her wicked smile return, she instructed, "No," and in a songlike fashion, continued, "James, would ye be kind and let me borrow yer blunderbuss? I'd like to keep these gentlemen under guard while ye take a few of our men and search our new vessel. Bring everyone ye find to me." Smiling, he slid the firearm off his shoulder, quickly packed another load of metal pellets down the barrel, and handed it to her. Sneering, she pointed the flared muzzle at Malcolm, cocked the hammer, and vowed, "Satisfyin' though it'll be to make ye watch us plunder yer ship, it'll feel even better to steal yer crew right before yer eyes."

Twenty minutes passed until, in a single file, James brought four bound prisoners of European descent and forced them to the deck at her feet. She returned his weapon, placed her hands on her hips, and throwing out her chest, declared, "Yer captain wants to die at his helm, and rest assured I'm goin' to oblige him. Furthermore, and regardless of his feelin's, ye can bet it'll be quite a spectacle." Letting out a harsh cackle, she went on, "Luckily fer all of ye, no one has to share his fate. Nevertheless, I wouldn't want the world accusin' me of not lettin' ye choose yer own destiny, so yer all gettin' one last opportunity to prove yer loyalty." Sweeping her arm toward Malcolm, still holding his sword at the ready, she suggested, "If ye'd like to stay a part of his crew, go ahead and raise yer hands. He can make his little claymore useful and cut yer binds free."

For an entire minute, she remained silent and waited for someone to move. Finally, she switched to Gaelic and announced, "Good. Yer will to fight is impressive. Yer exactly the type of men I'm lookin' fer." A trail of blood creeping down her cheek, she smirked and continued, "I know they say I'm a murderer and cutthroat, but the truth is I'm a warrior and I'm fightin' fer freedom. Yer freedom. Our freedom." While a few of the captives met her eye, she winked at the few faithful holdouts and furthered, "I suspected fightin' a clan of Scots would prove costly and it was—I lost good men today. I need good men to replace them." Producing her flask, she stated, "I'm not askin' ye to starve. In fact, ye'll eat better than ye currently do." Unscrewing the metal cap, she added, "I'm not askin' ye to suffer, fer most nights ye'll sleep on a cot under a roof." Holding it forth, she proclaimed, "And I'm not askin' ye to sacrifice, fer ye'll always drink the finest whiskey the world has ever known."

She took a swig and, switching to English, surmised, "As fer the rest of ye, to prove my compassion, I'm givin' ye a pardon. It's not yer fault yer captain broke me rules. Goin' home, we'll be passin' the British Virgin Islands. If ye don't do anythin' stupid on the way, I'll send ye off in a skiff close to Road Town with a firkin of Oakies. I'm told the rest of the world is catchin' on to its worth. If yer smart, ye'll save half to sell and probably make enough to build a ship of yer own." Turning her gaze on Malcolm, who had placed the tip of his claymore into the deck and now leaned on the hilt, she asked, "What do ye think? How many of yer men are mine?"

His face contorted behind his scowl, he let his sword fall to his feet and, responding in Gaelic, answered, "Perhaps all of them." Seeing James raise the blunderbuss, he maintained her native language and insisted, "Though, to men like these, nothin' will prove the worth of yer integrity like killin' me in cold blood." In English, he yelled, "She can claim she's not a murderer or a cutthroat all she wants. Let her actions speak louder than her words. Should she execute me, I hope one of ye returns the favor and slits her throat durin' her sleep." Holding her stare, he concluded, "She'll deserve no less honor."

Staying in Gaelic, Clarkeson told him, "Well put, Captain. I knew we were in fer a few surprises today, and this is certainly one. Are ye sayin' ye want to be a part of somethin' bigger?"

Shrugging, he replied, "I'm sayin' I'd like to have the same choice they have."

"If ye choose to live," she reminded him, crossing her arms, "ye follow me orders. Is that somethin' ye can handle?"

"That depends on what yer orderin' me to do," he shot back. "I'm no pirate. None of us are."

Raising her brows, Clarkeson looked up at Fergus, who opened his palms and curled his lips. To a trail of blood dripping out of her wound, she tilted her head to her left and murmured, "Maybe we just solved a problem."

Removing his kerchief, he wrapped it around her temple and responded, "Maybe."

She grimaced and, passing her flask to Malcolm, inquired, "Do ye have a surgeon?"

Accepting her offer, he nodded to a bald man with a meaty stomach, wrinkly skin, and glasses, huddled in the mix of captured sailors on the deck. "Right there," he said and took a drink. Swallowing, he glanced at the flask, then Clarkeson, then to the flask again, and handing it back, mentioned, "Uisge Beatha. That is fine whisky."

"Uisce Beatha," she repeated. "It's out of my personal cask." After downing another swig, she told Ben, "Take the captain and his surgeon to *The Black Irish* and keep them under watch. Turning her eye on Malcolm, she went on, "We'll see if yer man can keep ye alive, and if he does, we'll talk about yer future tomorrow."

Nodding to the sodden kerchief, Fergus posed, "Speakin' of stayin' alive, that cut needs to be tended to."

"I'll get to it," she dismissed, "once we get everythin' squared away."

"No," he persisted, shaking his head. "A head wound is nothin' to trifle with. If ye pass out, there's no tellin' if ye'll wake up again. Now go. I can take care of this ship."

Though she responded by rolling her eye, she did return to *The Black Irish*, where her surgeon, Gianis, had opted to set up a triage in the shade of the bulwark along the port side of the main deck. Permitted to keep his white hair short, he had thin shoulders, pale skin, skinny arms, soft fingers, and a peg in lieu of his right foot. Dressed in a black tunic with a white apron splattered in red, he knelt to peer under the saturated bandage covering a man's stomach. Giving his aide a somber look, he shook his head and moved on to the next casualty in line, whose shattered femur jutted out through the skin below a tourniquet tied around the top of his left thigh.

"What can I do for ye, Captain?" a soft voice asked. Flinching, she turned to her right to find Marcus, Gianis's second aide, trying to see where she was hurt. Slender, he had light-brown eyes, dark skin, a patchy black beard, and spirals of tight cornrows winding over his scalp. Tilting his head, he saw the wet kerchief and asked, "What happened?"

Waving her hand, she said, "It's a scratch. I did it trimmin' me hair before the battle. It doesn't even hurt. Fergus made me come here to have it looked at."

Gingerly, Marcus removed the makeshift bandage, and fresh blood trickled out. "It's more than a scratch," he determined. His voice popping, he reapplied some pressure and asserted, "Gianis needs to give this a look."

"Leave him be," she commanded. "He's got bigger things on his plate. I'll be in my cabin. Ye can send fer me when he's done takin' care of everyone else."

Marcus crossed his arms and, smiling gently, told her, "If I were to do that, I'd be keelhauled, and whatever was left of my hide would end up at the forefront of the next boarding party." Waggling his finger, he insisted, "And trust me, I'd be no good in the middle of the fighting. Whether ye like it or not, ye're going to wait right here. I'll be back."

While his aide fed his latest patient several consecutive ounces of whiskey, Gianis whistled and cleaned his bone saw with a rag soaked in rum. At Marcus's touch to his shoulder, he looked at Clarkeson, set his tools down, and immediately came over to see her. A gleam in his eye, he examined her injury and, smiling curiously, marveled, "Well, mmhmm, this is a good one."

"It's nothin'," she growled. "Go take care of that other man first. He's in far worse shape than me."

Gently probing her temple, he murmured, "Oh, he'll be fine. We're giving him enough whiskey to pass out. Even then, he's sure to wake up. They don't really go under until the pain sets in, mmhmm. Now let me have a look-see."

Wincing, she suggested, "I really don't think it'll need anythin' more than a few stitches. To be honest, I didn't even notice it right away."

"I think you may be right," he mumbled, probing the flesh. "I can't feel any fragments, although it's impossible to be sure with all this hair. I'm sorry to say, mmhmm, but I have to make Marcus shave some of it."

"With what other people are losin' today," she replied, "I think I'll be fine."

Beaming, Gianis flared his nostrils and remarked, "That's the spirit. Have a seat."

Alone, she settled in on the starboard side. Marcus returned with a rag in a bucket of boiled sea water, a flask of rum, and a thin razor blade folded into a bone handle. Squatting at her side, he asked, "Would you like an ounce of whiskey first?"

Producing her flask, she told him, "Save yers fer the others. I've got plenty."

Marcus let her drink several belts and started wiping away the dried blood. His voice soothing, he urged, "It is best if you breathe deeply for me. I don't want you to pass out." She silently followed his orders, and rinsing his hands in the water, he warned, "I'm going to clean it with rum now. It's going to burn. Would you like to bite down on something?"

"No," she snapped and took another healthy swallow. "Just tell me about our losses. That'll give me plenty to chew on."

Pouring alcohol directly on her cut, Marcus began, "In that case, his volley was effective. So far, it cost us seven dead and twice that wounded. Unfortunately, there were quite a few who were pretty much obliterated, and we can't be sure of the exact number of casualties until Fergus returns with the boarding party."

Over the sound of Gianis's saw cutting through flesh, she clenched her teeth and asked, "How many of the wounded will live?"

"For most of them," Marcus answered, "it's tenuous at best. I think we'll be lucky to save half." As the saw blade hit the bone, he paid no heed to the muffled screaming and rapidly shaved a patch of hair surrounding a jagged furrow near her temple. Then, he applied a clean dressing and, continuing to talk, sat down on her right.

Sweating profusely, she tilted her flask to her lips, emptied it, and said, "All yer yappin' is makin' the pain worse. Go tend to somebody else."

"I can't. I have to keep ye awake," he responded.

Working quickly, Gianis finished amputating the fractured limb within minutes. His patient unconscious, he let the aide cauterize the stump, stood, stretched his back, turned around, and gimped over to Clarkeson. "Your turn, mmhmm," he put forth. "Lie on your right side. Do you want something to bite down on?"

Doing his bidding, she insisted, "I'd rather be able to talk. I hear ye've been busy today."

"I have," he confirmed, reexamining her wound, "and you've been fortunate. I can't find anything to dig out, mmhmm."

Widening his eyes, he smiled curiously and determined, "It seems you somehow really do have the luck of the Irish."

Sweat ran down her forehead, and wiping her brows, she muttered, "Thank God fer small miracles."

Pinching the gash together, he went on, "Of course, this is more of a laceration than a cut, mmhmm. I'm afraid you'll have a scar."

"Better to have a scar than lose a leg," she snarled. "Now be done with it. The sun's almost set, and ye still have plenty of work ahead of ye."

"In that case," Gianis started, "take a deep breath, mmhmm."

As the needle pierced her skin, Clarkeson balled her fists and inhaled. With the suture being pulled through, she let it out and mentioned, "Marcus told me the number of casualties. Do ye have any idea of how many will survive?"

Tying a knot, Gianis divulged, "A good half were hit in the belly or the head, and there's not much I can do to save them. If the ones with head wounds don't wake up in a day, I've learned they probably won't."

"What'll happen then?"

Adding another stitch, he told her, "I'll slit their throats and throw them overboard, mmhmm. If I don't, their bodies will continue to function, and they'll soil themselves, increasing the risk of infection for the rest."

"What about those with belly wounds?" Clarkeson wanted to know.

"To ease their suffering," he murmured, "the best thing to do is give them enough whiskey to pass out and take care of it then, mmhmm. Otherwise, all their moaning and screaming would be bad for morale."

Clenching her jaw, she asked, "And the rest?"

"Well, I've got a few more appendages to saw, broken bones to set, and plenty more stitches to sew," he stated, "especially, I'm sure, once the boarding party gets back, mmhmm."

Her teeth clamped tight, she posed, "Ye sound like a tailor."

"I doubt I could do their job," he muttered. "Tailors have to sew in a straight line, mmhmm." Hooking the needle, he glanced down at her and ordered, "Stop holding your breath."

"Aye, aye, Captain," she retorted and slowly exhaled. "Fer what it's worth, we captured the surgeon of the *Mariana*. I'll send him to help the moment he's done patchin' up Captain Stewart."

His eyes seemingly popping out of his skull, Gianis inquired, "You didn't execute the other captain?"

"No, not yet," she replied, "he's gettin' a chance to join us. If he survives tonight, I'm goin' to make him an offer tomorrow."

Casting an easy wave to the wounded men surrounding them, Gianis raised his brows and asked, "Even after all this?" Sliding the needle back through her skin, he suggested, "I wonder if this head wound is more severe than I think, mmhmm."

Smiling weakly, she commented, "Especially after all this. He got us good, and fer that alone, he deserves some respect."

Tying off the last stitch, Gianis returned, "Do you think you can trust him?"

Sitting up, Clarkeson shrugged and admitted, "I don't know. I guess we'll find out. To be honest, his injuries were pretty severe. We'll see how good his surgeon is."

"He'll get a chance to prove himself helping me, mmhmm," Gianis assured her. "I'll have him treat the ones I can't. Maybe he knows something I don't. If not, oh well, it won't matter anyway, mmhmm." Wrapping a fresh bandage around her head, he went on, "Now listen to me. I don't want you nodding off. No matter how slight they may seem, head wounds can be fatal, and I'd hate to have to do what I'd have to do if you didn't wake up, mmhmm. Get comfortable. You're staying right here where I can see you."

"Yer busy."

"Marcus will be watching. He'll keep you awake."

Stifling a yawn, she gently pressed the fingertips of one hand to the left side of her head and, with the other, removed her flask out of the pocket over her heart. Holding it forth, she remarked, "Good job, Doctor Surgeon. Now whether ye like it or not, I'm goin' to my cabin to fill this up, and I'm stayin' there. It's not that my head aches. It's the pinch of the cut that hurts. I'll be fine. If you're really worried, send Marcus to check on me every so often." Meeting his eyes, she allowed, "Even I know that'd probably be best."

Reluctantly, he gave her a nod, and she climbed down the nearest ladder to the gun deck. Built for speed, *The Black Irish* was a bit more than eighteen feet at the widest point and tapered to the stern, leaving very little room for her quarters. Her vessel facing east, she opened the hatch of her cabin to the sun setting in a final burst of scarlet through the three narrow vertical windows looking out the rear of her ship. A pair of wooden barrels sat cradled in a frame below them and a trio of chairs lay haphazardly strewn about. To her right, a table was nailed to the bulkhead, and to her left, a curtain—woven in a red, white, and blue tartan—had been strung the length of the space.

Clarkeson straightened the mess, removed her eye patch, and stripped out of her sullied clothes. Inside a drawer at the base of the frame of the cradle, she found a steel basin and filled it with water out of one barrel. She added a healthy splash of whiskey out of the other and did her best to scrub the grisly remnants of the battle off her body. Donning a fresh outfit, she filled her flask, took a swallow, and slid open the curtain to reveal her bed. Upon collapsing into it, she laid her head on the pillow and fell fast asleep.

It was well into the night before both vessels were squared away, and they headed south for home. Forced to tow the *Mariana*, they tacked back and forth into the wind on a course to the British Virgin Islands. Because Marcus had a knack for showing up within fifteen minutes of her drifting off, Clarkeson spent the entire time in and out of consciousness. Finally, at the darkest hour, she insisted the best thing he could do for her was to stop worrying and get some rest.

The next morning, she woke to Fergus gently shaking her shoulder and whispering, "Come on, hon. It's time to wake up."

Rising on one elbow, she looked outside to the golden sun breaking through the few ethereal clouds drifting in the violet sky. "Where are we?" she asked.

Giving her a mug of coffee, he answered, "A hidden cove in one of the deserted islands near Tortola. I thought it would be best to stop here and see what yer plannin' next. If we're goin' to drop off any survivors at Road Town, we'll do it when we leave."

Carefully accepting his offer, she held the mug between both hands and cautiously took a sip. Easing out of bed and walking to the table, she admitted, "I haven't thought that far ahead." She sat down facing the entry, tucked her left leg under her right, and furthered, "I want to wait until I talk to Captain Stewart first."

Sitting in the chair opposite her, Fergus raised his eyebrows and inquired, "What are ye plannin' to say to him?"

Cradling her cup, she blew off the steam and put forth, "I'm goin' to give him his options."

Tilting his forehead, Fergus raised his eyebrows and remarked, "I'm sure he's well aware of his options."

"Aye, I'm sure he is too," she concurred, "but if he's to sail fer me, I'd prefer it was because he believed in the cause, not because I'm holdin' a knife to his throat."

"I doubt yer goin' to convince him to take ships and execute captains," Fergus warned. "At this point in his life, I'm sure he's had plenty of opportunities to get letters of marque."

"I agree. I don't think he's suited fer that role anyway," she asserted. "If he joins us, I think I have somethin' better in mind."

"What's that?"

"Gettin' rid of the loot," she stated. "We've still got all the molasses *The Empire's Reach* had aboard. I was thinkin' we could trade it fer weapons and then he could smuggle them to Scotland. Neither of us can do it without bein' recognized, but since nobody will know he's joined us, they'd have no reason to question him." Softly patting her bandage, she followed up, "What kind of condition is he in?"

Bobbing his head, Fergus said, "He fought a good fight, and he's got the wounds to show fer it. His surgeon needed a few hours to take care of them all."

"Will he recover?"

Shrugging, he suggested, "It's the same fer him as it is fer us. If an infection doesn't set in, he should be fine."

"Has he been fed?"

"He's still asleep."

She stood up and returned to her bunk. Retrieving her flask, she poured a healthy sploosh into her mug and stated, "Well, when he wakes up, make sure he gets plenty of whiskey. If he aches like I do, I'm sure he'll need it."

Fergus nodded and asked, "When do ye want to see him?"

"What's the weather like?"

"Beautiful. Another day in paradise."

"Then since there's no way anyone can know what happened, we don't need to rush gettin' back. After yesterday, our men could probably use a little break anyway. Let's do some fishin'." A slight smile on her lips, she faced Fergus and ordered, "Send a huntin' party ashore too. We'll have a feast to welcome the newest members of our crew."

"This is British territory," he reminded her.

"There's hardly any Brits around," she responded, "and I doubt those that are have any idea we're here. It may be better to take our time and head out this evenin' anyway. If we sail through the night, we'll be home no later than tomorrow mornin'."

"What do ye want to do with Captain Stewart in the meantime?"

"Keep him fed and slightly drunk," she directed, "and we'll let him listen to his men enjoyin' themselves. Maybe it'll make him a bit more agreeable when the three of us sit down fer supper."

Stroking his forked beard, Fergus mused, "Maybe, or maybe it'll make him that much more contentious."

"Perfectly fine with me," she sighed, "then it'll be easier to kill him and move on."

They spent the morning and the early afternoon anchored in the cove, waiting for the foraging parties to return. Subsequently, the aroma of several feral pigs roasting over a fire began wafting throughout the brigantine. While the musicians played their instruments, the rest of the crew gathered on the main deck to pass the hours, eating, drinking, and singing bawdy songs of a life at sea. That evening, when the festivities ended and they prepared to hoist anchor, Clarkeson prepared for her guest.

Through the windows at the back of her quarters, the colors of the setting sun ran the gamut from deep purple to bright fuchsia across the horizon. To help illuminate the room, she lit the dozen candles already spread around the space. At the table, she touched her burning switch to the wick of a thick white beeswax candle placed between a stainless steel flagon and a matching ewer. Like the dishes and the goblets in the three settings, they bore the same etching of a heraldic rose with two buds on the stem over the word *REDI*. As the flame reflected off the polished surfaces, she sat in the chair facing the entry and let her dark hair fall down over the top of her baby-blue smock. The white square bandage protecting her wound was held in check by a thin strip of cloth wrapped around her head, and finagling her tresses, she did her best to cover them both. At a rapid succession of knocks, she fixed a black patch over her right eye and called out, "Come in."

With Fergus at his back, Malcolm stepped into the threshold and scanned her cabin. He had changed into clean black pants, a new burgundy vest, and a white sleeveless shirt exposing the multitude of stitches crisscrossing his arms. Rising, Clarkeson cackled happily and, in Gaelic, said, "Don't worry. I'm not Edward Longshanks. Killin' ye here wouldn't make a good spectacle, and quite honestly, I don't want the mess to clean." Seeing his gaze linger on the curtain, she went on, "That's where I sleep. Don't fret. There's nothin' to interest ye behind there." When he settled his attention upon her, she turned over her palms and offered, "Welcome to my table, Captain. Take a seat. If yer hurtin' like I am, ye need it." Doing his best to hide the pain, Malcolm slowly limped to the chair opposite hers. Smirking, she let him know, "I'd present me hand, but I'm afraid ye'd bite it off."

"I wouldn't bite it off," Malcolm responded. "I just don't think ye'd appreciate the courtesy."

Cackling harshly, she stated, "Yer correct. I'm no noble and it's not often I meet someone who can figure me out so quickly." As Fergus occupied the seat to her right, she poured everyone an ounce of Oakies and, topping each off with water, followed up, "But like yerself, I'm sure, I do appreciate a full belly."

Shrugging, Malcolm replied, "Especially if it's my last meal."

Holding her goblet forth, Clarkeson proclaimed, "At least ye know ye'll enjoy the whiskey. Who knows, we may come to find the end of the day doesn't necessarily have to also mean the end of yer life. Uisce beatha." Repeating the toast, both men tapped their drinks to hers, and to the echo of the high-pitched chime, they all took a sip.

Before anyone could speak again, a stout man entered with an oval tray on one hand and a folding stand in the other. His skin was tan, his straight dark braid reached the middle of his back, and though he hadn't shaved in the past two months, his cheeks were bare. He set his burden down next to Clarkeson and removed the cover atop a large steaming steel bowl. Inside, a gumbo consisting of shrimp, beans, tomatoes, and onions had been seasoned with salt, pepper, garlic, and basil. He stirred it several times and then ladled equal portions into three cups. Upon passing them out, he set the extra soup and two small platters on the table. The first had a stack of circular flatbread, and the second contained several fresh limes cut into wedges. Silently, he picked up his tray, tucked it under his arm, and looked among the group.

Giving him a nod, Clarkeson mentioned, "Thank ye, Mo."

Responding with a bow, he turned and exited.

"He's not a man of many words," Clarkeson told Malcolm. "Bein' a Taino, his language is completely different, and even James is strugglin' to communicate with him. Lucky fer us, he doesn't have to speak to tell us what we can and can't eat on these islands or, even more importantly, to teach the chef how to prepare it. He showed him cassava, the root they ground into the flour used to make those crackers. In fact, ye could say Mo contributed to almost every recipe fer this meal." She picked up a lime wedge and, squeezing it over her cup, suggested, "I'm not sure if any addition to our crew has ever made the men happier."

"I hope ye don't expect me to cook," Malcolm returned and lifted his spoon to his lips. "I'm much better at eatin'."

Watching him savor his mouthful, she held up another wedge and advised, "It's even better if ye add a bit of fresh juice."

Shaking his head, he remarked, "Limes make everythin' too tart."

Clarkeson glanced at Fergus, who shrugged and picked up his own. Her concentration back on Malcolm, she inquired, "What if I could teach ye how to keep yer vessel free from scurvy, Captain?"

Dipping a cracker into the broth, he retorted, "I'd be all ears. Who wouldn't?"

"Then ye should listen to me."

"Are ye sayin' ye know some secret the rest of world doesn't?"

"It's not really a secret," she explained. "Ye see, in 1734, a Dutch physician discovered the cure and published a book about it. Givin' him passage, my father bought a copy and actually read it. I guess the rest of the world has yet to."

Setting his spoon down, Malcolm pressed, "And how exactly do limes cure scurvy?"

"I don't know," she admitted. "I didn't get to read the book, but I can say after that voyage they were a part of my father's every journey and I've never seen a case."

Malcolm looked to Fergus and asked, "Is this true?"

Breaking up a flatbread and mixing the pieces into his gumbo, Fergus swore, "I was there for the conversation he had with the doctor, and yes, scurvy has never been a problem since."

Meeting Clarkeson's eye, Malcolm followed up, "Did yer father teach ye to sail?"

"He did."

"Was he the one who taught ye how to be a pirate?"

"My father was a good man and an honest merchantman," she snapped.

"If he was such a good man," Malcolm responded, "why are ye on the course yer on?"

Arching the brow above her patch, she growled, "Because the captain of an English frigate wrongly accused my father of smugglin' and killed him in cold blood. He then sank our ship and abandoned the rest of us in the flotsam. Somehow, I survived. Is that a good enough reason fer ye?" When Malcolm didn't answer, she smiled, held up a lime, and concluded, "Now, would ye like to change yer mind? Tart or no, anythin' beats scurvy."

Breaking up the moment, Mo returned with a platter of stuffed corn husks. Picking one up, she discarded the outer leaf to reveal a tortilla underneath. "These are called guanime," she stated, "and ye never know what's inside them." She took a bite, swallowed, and curled her lips into a tight circle. Letting out a succession of quick breaths, she reached for her goblet and drank several gulps. "Be careful," she warned. "There's peppers mixed into the pork and beans, and wow, they give it a kick." Nibbling at it again, she noted, "There's a bit of pineapple too. Mmmmm . . . it's both sweet and spicy."

Helping himself, Malcolm said, "It sounds unique."

"Our entire diet is," she replied, "I'm tellin' ye, every time Mo goes out into the jungle, he comes back with somethin' different to try."

Malcolm consumed one and emptied his goblet washing it down. Picking up the flagon, he offered some whiskey to Clarkeson and Fergus. They both refrained, and he poured himself several ounces. Topping it off with a splash of water, he began, "I'm guessin' I'm here fer some reason other than to learn what's edible in this part of the world, and if possible, I'd like to enjoy the rest of my meal. So if ye don't mind, I'd prefer we get to the point."

Meeting his eyes, Clarkeson admitted, "I'd prefer we get to it also. If yer goin' to sail with me, I want it to be because ye believe in the cause we're fightin' fer."

Nodding to the flagon, he retorted, "And what cause is that? Keepin England free of Oakies?"

"Only until Charles Edward Stuart sits on the throne."

"Charles Edward Stuart?" he repeated. "Yer a Jacobite?"

"I am," she confirmed, "and the more trouble I can get into over here, the more help I give yer countrymen over there."

Sighing, Malcolm shook his head and put forth, "The rumors of Stuart restoration haven't stopped in the thirty years since the Old Pretender's failed attempt back in 1715."

"This time there's more to the rumors," she filled in. "What if I told ye the French have already started layin' plans fer an invasion, and to make it happen, all the prince has to do is unite the clans?"

"Then I'd tell ye to give up," Malcolm asserted, "and quit while yer ahead. I've smuggled enough weapons into the Highlands to know the clans want them to fight with each other more than they do the English."

"That may be so," she concurred, "but the English do give them a common enemy and the prince represents a common standard to fight under."

"Let's say fer argument's sake he could win them over," Malcolm allowed. "He still wouldn't have the manpower to fight an all-out war. Regardless of how tough the Highlanders think they may be, the British have trained, experienced, disciplined soldiers. They'd have no problem squelchin' an unruly mob."

Pressing her right finger to the tabletop, she responded, "And that may be the case if their armies were in England, except right now they're spread out over Europe, and in reality, a single decisive strike could flip the throne."

"Perhaps," Malcolm challenged, "but should Charles Stuart seriously pose a threat, the Royal Navy could return every single British soldier long before he took Edinburgh, let alone London." Meeting her eye, he concluded, "And I have no desire to be a martyr any more than I do a pirate."

Mo reappeared and delivered three large serving dishes. Removing the cover of the first, Clarkeson pointed to the marinating fillets of red snapper and mentioned, "Escabeche. When yer chef is Spanish, it's a part of every meal. He actually lets it soak for a day in vinegar, olive oil, onions, garlic, and pepper." While Fergus lifted the top off the second, covered in crispy slices of tender pork, she furthered, "He calls this one Mediterranean Porco. He rolls each roast in a blend of salt, pepper, garlic, and oregano then sears the sides, locking in the flavors prior to slow cookin' them on a spit over low heat." Under the third, corn was stacked in a pyramid bathed in melted butter. "And if ye don't know already what that is," she summed up, "I'll give ye a hint: it'll remind ye of yer whiskey, minus the woody finish. Go ahead, dig in." Smiling, Clarkeson watched Malcolm load his plate and waited until his mouth was full to ask, "Have ye ever heard of Maurice de Saxe?"

"Maurice de Saxe?" he sputtered. "The French general?"

"I believe he's been promoted to marshal," she corrected.

"Marshal, general, of course I've heard of him," Malcolm told her. "He may be the most famous officer they've ever had."

Her smile morphing into a sneer, she revealed, "He's also been picked to lead the invasion. With the size of their borders, do ye really believe the French would commit their greatest leader if they didn't think it was possible to pull off?"

Cutting through his pork, Malcolm shook his head and returned, "The British have spies up and down the Normandy coast. They'll discover any invasion force and see to it the Royal Navy is waitin' in the Channel to sink it."

"There's where we come in, Captain," she said. "The Royal Navy is spread out worse than the army, and there's entire stretches of coastline that aren't patrolled anymore. With the help of the Scottish rebels, the French would need no more than ten thousand troops to restore Charles Stuart to the throne." Shrugging, she stated, "A force that small could sneak across and land right under their noses."

Holding his goblet between his hands, Malcolm sat back in his chair and took a healthy drink. Letting out a long breath, he met her eye and inquired, "Even if it were to succeed, what good would it do?"

Arching her eyebrow, she stated, "It would free yer countrymen."

Rubbing his temples, he retorted, "Free them from what?"

"Tyranny."

"Tyranny? It sounds like all yer doin' is exchangin' one tyrant fer another. What's the point?"

Squinting, she shot back, "Ye don't think it'd be better fer yer people if a Scot were wearin' the crown?"

Blinking, Malcolm stroked his beard with his right hand and strummed the fingers of his left on the table. Without giving her an answer, he asked, "How do ye know all this?"

"I could've gone to Dunkirk to help with the invasion."

"Why didn't ye?"

Lifting her goblet, she downed the remaining contents and said, "There's plenty of roles in the rebellion, and I have my own to fill. Personally, I believe it's best I stay here and do what I'm doin'."

"Does that mean yer lookin' fer me to ferry French troops?"

"No, I doubt ye'd make it in time," she put forth, "and I think yer better suited fer a completely different function."

"Such as?"

"The vessels I take may not be full of gold and silver," she began. "However, a fluyt can hold a substantial amount of molasses, and right now, we have enough to possibly equip five hundred men. I want ye to help make it happen."

"That's it?"

"There's a little more," she continued, "fer once ye purchase the provisions, I need ye to go to Scotland and get it to the rebels."

Crossing his arms, he replied, "So ye want me to be a smuggler."

"Don't give me the doe-in-the-woods routine," she grumbled. "I may not know ye very well, but I do know yer not that innocent."

Spreading his arms wide, he noted, "Ye've got plenty of men under yer command, why not one of them?"

"Because they don't know business," she responded, "and I can tell ye do. Sure, I could send someone else, and yes, he'll be able to complete the task. The problem is he won't know how to get the best deal." Leaning forward, she went on, "That's yer duty. Believe me, it's easy fer me to find men willin' to kill."

"If I were to agree, where would I go in Scotland?"

"Are ye familiar with Glenuig Bay, along the western coast?"

"Familiar enough," he maintained, "and with my crew, I'm sure I'd have no problem findin' it."

"Ye no longer have a crew," she remarked. "Those who survived have become a part of mine."

"That was quick."

"I know what I'm doin'."

Lifting his goblet, he proposed, "Then I'll be happy to sail with yer newest replacements."

With a harsh cackle, she asserted, "Nice try, Captain. If ye take me up on my offer, I'll pick most of the sailors ye set out with."

"Which one will be holdin' the dagger to my back?" Malcolm retorted.

Narrowing her eye, she declared, "None of them. If someone has to, I'd prefer ye be honest and I'll kill ye now."

Silently, they stared at each other until Malcolm emptied his goblet and picked up the flagon. Realizing they had finished the whiskey, he set it down and asked, "What if I say no?"

Waving to the remaining scraps on the platters, she returned, "Then I hope ye enjoyed yer last meal." Flaring her nostrils, she furthered, "And yer last drink."

"Do I have any time to think it over?"

Crossing her arms, she glared at him and stated, "I plan on bein' back at me island tomorrow morning. Since ye'll be buried at sea, ye have until then."

"Fair enough," he allowed and pushed back his chair. Standing up, he held his left palm toward Fergus and added, "Easy, big man, I'm not ready fer another fight, and I've been on enough ships in my time. I'm sure I can find my little cabin on my own." He limped to the hatch, bit his bottom lip, and turned around. Returning to the table, he picked up the empty flagon, carried it to the barrels below the window, and filled it with whiskey. Walking back to the hatch, he said, "I do have one more question."

"What's that?" she wanted to know.

Holding her gaze, he put forth, "Why is an Irish lassie so hell-bent on seein' a Scot on the throne? I'd figure ye'd want another Paddy, like yerself. . ."

The Scottish Rose: The skipper, Big Tom,
Rory, the old sea captain

CHAPTER 7

October 1, 1785, Kingston, Jamaica

With the steady rainfall morphing into a heavy downpour, the sixth metal pin fell from the side of the candle on the mantel behind the bar and landed quietly in the soft wax at the base of the stick. Forced to raise his voice over the storm, the old sea captain boomed, "To be sure, I don't know what took more courage, callin' Clarkeson a Paddy or seizin' a flagon out of her personal cask." Lightning struck nearby, and during the particularly angry clap of thunder, he took a moment to finish his last few swallows of lager. Setting his empty mug on the bar, he followed up, "When I asked Malcolm what he was thinkin', he said he had no desire to become somethin' he didn't want to become and no way of knowin' if he could trust her. Bein' the next mornin' could've been his last, he figured he had nothin' to lose, fer if she'd had a problem with what he did, he was probably a dead man anyway."

Raising his rum to his lips, Jack asked, "So Malcolm joined her?"

Stroking his beard, the old sea captain replied, "To answer that question is to start another story."

"What about Gianis, heh-heh," Jack chipped in, "the surgeon, heh-heh? Does he join her too?"

Her smile warm, Nancy put forth, "He's already a part of her crew. He's her surgeon. That's why he stitched her cut."

"Laceration, heh-heh," Jack corrected. "Boy, do I remember those days, heh-heh."

"Jesus Christ Jack," Rags interrupted, shaking his head, "for God's sake, you weren't a surgeon. You were an undertaker. The only bodies you sewed together were already dead." Letting out several gravelly guffaws, he added, "And it's a good thing too. Had they been alive, ugly scars would've been the last of their worries."

Grinning mischievously, Tony inserted, "Speaking of scars, while I find it isn't normally the case, I'll wager Clarkeson's only enhanced her appeal."

"Where are the twins in all this?" John wanted to know. "Tortola isn't far from home—"

"Yes, I can't believe they didn't catch her," Luke followed up, "although I'm sure she knew better than to tangle with them."

"That's right, that's right," his brother agreed.

Ignoring the siblings, Lina declared, "For some reason, I feel like someone important is missing."

"Ye couldn't be more right," the old sea captain told her, "fer the French haven't arrived yet, and in a story of heroes, their entrance brings perhaps the greatest one of them all." Widening his eyes, he raised his right index finger and went on, "To be sure, the tale doesn't really begin until then."

"Until when?" Sarah questioned. She glanced back to the mantel and, seeing four pins remaining in the side of the candle, exclaimed, "Oh my God, I didn't realize the time." Yelling, "Last call," she gave the rope a hearty tug, and a single peal reverberated over the storm.

"Last call?!!?" Rags groused, "It can't be last call already. Your grandfather would have never called last call with a full bar like this. No wonder this place isn't packed like it used to be."

"Oh shut it," Sarah barked, "My grandfather set the rules the day he first opened, and for forty-three years, we've always rung the bell at six pins."

"Then I'm afraid I'll never get to answer all yer questions," the old sea captain mentioned, "at least not in an hour."

The thunder and lightning mingling with the falling rain, Sarah looked to the ceiling and observed, "Well, you can wrap up what you can tonight, and since I doubt this storm is going to pass anytime soon, you can come back tomorrow and pick up right where you left off." Meeting the old sea captain's eyes, she followed up, "Unless you don't want to return."

Twirling his empty mug, the old sea captain responded, "With how generous everyone has been, I don't think there's anywhere on earth I'd rather be." A gleam in his eye, he cast his gaze across the crowd and furthered, "So as long as all of ye want to listen to this old man prattle on, I'm happy to continue."

Placing his left hand on Rag's shoulder, Tony remarked, "It's been better than listening to this old man prattle on."

"I want to know what happened to D'Groers," Brass stated. "Whose turn is it to buy?"

Crossing her arms, Sarah commented, "Rags is the only one who hasn't."

Rags closed his eyes, dropped his chin to his chest, and shook his head.

Leaning against the wall in the gap leading behind the bar, Nancy told him, "What? What's your problem? It is your turn to buy."

Pressing his palms to his forehead, Rags growled, "Well, never let it be said the old Ragman didn't pick up his share of the tab. I guess I'll go ahead and get his last one, even if everything he's saying is horseshit."

"Rags!" Sarah snapped.

Smiling sweetly, Nancy noted, "See how easy that was?" Turning her soft almond-shaped brown eyes on the old sea captain, she suggested, "Earlier, you said if there was a rule your skipper lived by, it was to keep your bartender happy. If this is to be the last story of the night, then I think it should be about Mairi."

"He also said great minds think alike," the old sea captain returned, "and yet again, he's proven right. Unfortunately, we're not to the last story yet."

Sarah topped off his lager and, setting it down, asserted, "I already called last call." Arching her brows, she placed a hand on each hip and, leaning forward, told him, "With how long each story has been, you only have time for one more."

"While normally that's the case," the old sea captain conceded, "some parts to this tale need to be broken into smaller bits, and if everythin' is to make sense, prior to endin' the night with Mairi, it would be best to fill ye in on Malcolm's fate. Before I do, however, I should skip ahead to the February of the following year and satisfy the curiosity of the big man at the other end." The lightning and thunder waning in the distance, he looked at the flame dancing atop the candle on the mantel behind the bar and began, "Fer, to be sure, I'll never forget the day I finally had the strength to climb up to the main deck. It was late in the mornin', and though the sun shone bright in the navy-blue sky, there was a sharp bite in the gusty breeze. Grateful to have some scruff, I joined my mates at the very instant the skipper sighted *The Emballeur* . . ."

Mid-February 1744, the Mediterranean Sea, between Corsica and France

His spyglass to his eye, the skipper peered to the north and announced, "Orana D'Groers. Tomas, I'll give ye credit. Ye do have a nose fer pirates."

Guiding the wheel of *Rosie's Charm*, Big Tom clenched his jaw and, flaring his nostrils, bore his murderous stare on a little convoy barely visible against the horizon.

"Unfortunately," the skipper continued, "it looks like he caught his limit. I count four vessels taggin' along behind him." Glancing at the big man, he noticed my arrival and, smiling wide, stated, "Well, well, well, look who finally slept off his hangover and decided to join us. Yer timin' is impeccable."

It had been almost a month since the last time I stood at the helm, and although it was impossible to know for certain, my extended absence may have had something to do with the festivities during our last night at Eugenia's. The morning we set out, I felt fine, but a few days later, I began to run a fever and felt several sharp, stabbing pains piercing my wounded left thigh. Having been present the moment the surgeon lifted the bandage, the skipper surveyed the angry red ring surrounding the cut and proposed, "Well, I've got good news. I maintain the same pension system Black Bart did fer his crew, and it pays any sailor who loses a limb in battle a lump sum fer his retirement. Should yer leg need to be sawed off, we'll consider ye a casualty and ye'll qualify."

Immediately the surgeon began a regimen of cleaning the infection with vinegar and rum three times a day. Thankfully, my fractured tooth had been removed and the swelling in my jaw had subsided, for I made it through the duration of each session biting down on my own personal thick brown leather strap. Ten mornings passed until, finally, I awoke to the pain lessening and, much to my relief, the fever breaking for good. Underneath my dressings, we discovered the tissue had also lightened to a healthier pink, and given a medical release, I managed the journey topside.

Prior to our departure, Rory had been assigned the command of *The Sabre* and, in the event the oars were needed, given half the crew. Luckily, a good Marin wind coming from the northern coast of Corsica propelled both ships, and they currently sailed parallel to our port side. Considering the king's reply was to be delivered directly to the admiral of the British fleet blockading Toulon, I thought our course would head east around the southern tip of Sardinia and then north to Hyeres. During our journey, however, it apparently followed a meandering arc west of our destination and closer to the border separating the French and Italian coasts.

Now, as I regained my bearings, the skipper handed me his spyglass and said, "Here, see if ye can figure out which one is his flagship."

I focused the lens and homed in on a flotilla of five vessels taking advantage of a mistral wind blowing off the southern shore of France. Forced by the conditions to sail at a thirty-degree list, the procession consisted of a third-rate ship of the line, an old three-masted galleon, a two-masted fluyt boasting a forecastle, and a pair of two-masted fishing ketches. Cursorily, I examined each one and finally settled on the man-of-war at the head of the column. Over one hundred fifty feet long with three masts all supporting a fighting platform and five spars, she was able to rely exclusively on her mainsails to sustain the speed of those trailing behind her. Her tilt keeping her portholes closed, it was impossible to accurately count her number of cannon, though I estimated she had the capacity for sixty to sixty-five.

Even more ominously, at her stern I made out a large green flag flaunting a bright gold D in the middle.

"I'm guessin' the biggest," I reported.

"Aye," the skipper confirmed. "Feast yer eyes on old Orana D'Groers, the scourge of the Mediterranean."

"He's not afraid to fly his true colors?" I asked.

Almost chuckling, the skipper responded, "Heh, with a ship that size, he doesn't have to be. There's a reason that design is called a French '74. She's armed with seventy-four cannon."

Nearly choking, I shot a look at the skipper and repeated, "Seventy-four cannon?" I did some quick math and, my eyes widening, determined, "She's got to have a good three hundred men aboard."

His goatee braided, the skipper gave it a tug and responded, "At a minimum. According to Tomas, there's closer to five."

"Five?" I exclaimed, "That means we're outnumbered six to one."

Sighing, the skipper told me, "And it'll be even worse once Rory leaves."

Swallowing hard, I returned, "Once Rory leaves? What do ye mean once Rory leaves? Where's he goin'?"

"To Hyeres," the skipper filled in. Putting his right hand on my left shoulder, he explained, "The repairs we made were only meant to get *The Sabre* to Port Mahon. She still needs a good amount of work to be battle ready. If she were to get sunk now, we'd miss out on the prize money and then all the pain ye've suffered would have been fer naught. I'd hate fer that to happen." He inhaled deeply, located Rory at the other helm, and ordered, "It's time to send him on his way." A signal flag raced up our mainmast, and watching the galley-hybrid change course, he noted, "Pray this swift wind takes them the entire distance, and they don't need the oars. The sooner Rory gets the message to the admiral, the better off we'll be." Turning his attention to *The Emballeur*, he gave me a shrug and put forth, "Ye see, it's all part of the plan."

My heart beginning to thump, I replied, "Part of the plan? What plan?"

Tilting his head my way, the skipper tapped his left temple and mentioned, "Hmmm, I forgot ye were feverish and weren't there when we came up with it."

Sweat soaked my palms, my hands trembled, and I felt my stomach drop. Doing my best to keep my voice steady, I cleared my throat and proposed, "Yer welcome to fill me in right now."

"To be honest," the skipper divulged, "it's still pretty fluid. Like ye already established, we're heavily outnumbered, and even worse, we don't have the element of surprise."

Vigorously, I nodded my head and agreed, "No, no, we don't. Nor do we have any help on the inside."

"He's learnin'," the big man pointed out.

"He is indeed," the skipper acknowledged. Proudly, he slapped my back and furthered, "Since D'Groers needs to reach the western coast of France in the next two weeks, I figure he doesn't have the time to waste on us so, and while ye may not like hearin' this, I'm not lookin' to go all cocksure into battle, especially since we'll have to tack into the wind to cross his bow. Instead, I think our best course of action is to stay the course we're on and see how badly he wants to get to his destination." Lowering his voice, he added, "I suppose there is a chance we'll engage her. I just don't want ye to get yer hopes up. It's all goin' to depend on how he reacts."

Feeling a tingle in my lower jaw and saliva pool under my tongue, I forced myself to swallow a few times and inquired, "Ye don't think he'll surrender, do ye?"

Laughing, the skipper told Big Tom, "Get this fellow." Slapping my back again, he went on, "No, no need fer ye to worry he'll surrender. With the crimes he's committed, D'Groers knows he's got a short noose waitin' at Execution Dock."

"The shorter the better," Big Tom growled, "I hope he writhes a good five minutes."

Giving the skipper his spyglass, I lamented, "Then it's certain he won't make this easy."

A gleam in his eyes, the skipper vowed, "Oh, ye can bet old Orana will fight to the bitter end."

In an effort to slow my heart and hide my apprehension, I patted my pockets until I found my flask. Regrettably, my share of the King's Firkin had already been consumed, and I had to survive on the daily rum ration. Always sugary and sweet with a slight burn, I took several swigs to calm my nerves and asked, "Does this mean we're goin to face *The Emballeur* on our own?"

Gesturing over his right shoulder to Big Tom, the skipper said, "Well, our only other option is to tell him we're goin' to let D'Groers get away." I hastened a look at the big man, and angrily grinding his teeth, he snapped his beet-red eyes upon me. Strangely, angry pulses began pounding in my head and drowned out every other sound. Quickly, I turned to the skipper and, the noise diminishing, I heard him add, "Maybe I'll delegate that task to ye. I don't think I have it in me."

Desperately, I covered my brows and spun in a complete circle, scanning the wide open deep-blue sea. With the exception of *The Sabre* disappearing to the northwest, the horizon was clear in every other direction. My heart falling into my guts and my groin contracting tight, I downed half my remaining rum and inquired, "What if D'Groers decides to attack us?"

Smiling mischievously, the skipper returned, "Then we'll play cat and mouse."

"I'm guessin' we're the mouse."

"Well, given the size difference, we can't be the cat," he responded, "but that doesn't mean we're easy prey. The way I see it, if he's got five ships under his command, his crew has to also be spread pretty thin, and he won't be able to shoot a full volley at once."

"Even so, half a single broadside would double our firepower," I pointed out.

"True," the skipper concurred, "only we've never heard he actually takes the time to train his men, and we figure the odds are good they'll have a hard time hittin' anythin'. If we can sneak in and get one good barrage in on her waterline, we can make a difference." Pointing to our triangular sails, he added, "Remember, we do have one big advantage—he can't tack like we can. If necessary, we can always turn into the wind and get away."

My heart beating in my chest, I simultaneously felt a cool sweat beading on my forehead and the blood draining out of it. Feeling a bit dizzy, I grabbed a mainstay for the rigging and held on.

The skipper grasped my elbow, helping to steady my balance, and asked, "Are ye all right?"

Wiping my brow, I sputtered, "Aye, I ah . . . it's just . . . I ah . . . I just ah . . . it's the wound."

"Ah yes, the wound," he repeated, "That makes sense. The way ye're handlin' it, I forget it's even there."

I let out several long slow breaths and, regaining my composure, inquired, "Is it more likely we'll sink *The Emballeur* or board her?"

"Sink her," the skipper stated.

"And yer good with missin' out on the prize money," I mentioned.

Slapping Big Tom on the chest, the skipper inserted, "Do ye get this fellow?"

"Prize money," the big man grumbled.

"I'll tell ye what," the skipper followed up, "should we get the chance we'll board her. The absolute last thing I'd want is fer ye to miss out on any prize money."

Given how hard it was to walk, let alone climb or run, I responded, "Who'll be leadin' the charge?"

"Yer more than welcome to," he let me know, "fer in the end it won't matter. It'll take all hands. Nobody wants to be captured anyway. Trust me, ye can't imagine what D'Groers would do to that cut on yer thigh."

We stayed on the same heading throughout the day, and when the sun began to descend on the evening, *The Sabre* had long since disappeared. Meeting the mistral winds head on, we tacked back and forth on a course crossing the front of our enemy. After my final checkup, I limped to the helm in time to overhear the skipper telling Big Tom, "It looks like we were right. D'Groers is plannin' on passin' Hyeres at night." His flask in his hand, he took a swig and, handing it to the big man, continued, "It makes sense. The captured ships are flyin' false colors and won't garner any consideration. If he must, he can leave them and, sailing at full speed, quite possibly sneak *The Emballeur* all the way past Port Mahon before sunrise."

"We won't let that happen," the big man asserted. He savored a drink and, letting out slow breath, suggested, "At a minimum, we'll create enough noise to draw some attention and do enough damage that someone else can finish the job."

Nodding to me, the skipper put the stopper in his flask and muttered, "We better wait until then to give him any of this.

"What's that supposed to mean?" I inquired.

Measuring the distance between *Rosie's Charm* and *The Emballeur*, he mentioned, "We don't need anyone lookin' fer a fight until we know we're gettin' into one."

The chilly gale penetrated my woolen coat, and with the pain of my cleaning still fresh, I was in no mind to stir up any trouble. I simply wanted a swig to warm my bones and ease my suffering. Irritated, I retorted, "I still don't get what yer tryin' to say. Bein' from the Stornoways, I was weaned on whisky, and it's never affected me one way or another."

"Wow, the rumors really are true," the skipper told the big man. "He really is oblivious."

"That's usually the case," Big Tom attested. He nodded to the flask and added, "I swear, we should be rationed that instead of rum. The Royal Navy would be unstoppable."

Shaking it, the skipper posed, "I bet that's why Clarkeson's men fight the way they do. Maybe Oakies is the secret to their tenacity."

Narrowing his eyes, the big man furthered, "Maybe that's why she wants to keep it out of the hands of the English. Now, I definitely think we should cross the Atlantic to purchase some, if fer no other reason than to see what effect it would have on us."

"If we cross the Atlantic," the skipper attested, "we're goin' to do more than purchase a few barrels of Oakies." Looking to the west, he curled his goatee around his finger and put forth, "We're also goin' to catch Clarkeson. Beyond the bounty, I'd love a chance to have dinner with her."

In what could only be described a complete look of total and abject fear, the big man shook his head and hissed, "Oh no."

Scowling, the skipper put forth, "Oh stop, it's not what ye think. It's simply that I want to hear her story. I'm tellin ye, there's more to it than meets the eye."

"Why?" I asked. "What makes her different from every other pirate?"

"Well fer one, I already told ye she's the second one I've heard of to use that name," he reminded me.

"In Ireland, I'm sure it's not that uncommon," I observed.

"Aye, but I feel there's a connection between the two that I can't put my finger on."

"Do ye think they could somehow be related?"

"I doubt it," the skipper replied, "fer though he had quite the clan, Clarkeson really wasn't much of a pirate. If he was anythin', he was a moonshiner."

"A moonshiner?" I questioned.

"Go ahead, tell him the story," Big Tom stated. "Given the circumstances, it's a good one to pass the time."

"I suppose yer right," the skipper concurred. He turned his gaze on me and, with a serious look, stressed, "Before I do, there is somethin' ye need to respect—outside of Rory and Tomas, most everyone who knows this tale is dead. Should we survive to see tomorrow, I expect it to remain that way. It could save my life."

Furrowing my brows, I gave him a curt nod and returned, "I understand," even though I really didn't.

Looking to the vermillion sunset, the skipper let out a long sigh and, pressing his braid to his bottom lip, began, "Durin' my youth, my skipper lived accordin' to the sayin' 'Man has two ears but one tongue so he can listen to twice as much as he speaks,' and on every voyage, he would set aside a few cabins fer wealthy passengers so he would have some people to talk to. He felt that was the best way to continue to learn, and to be sure, it was at his table that I was taught limes prevent scurvy." His smile turning sad, he kept his eyes on the western horizon and continued, "Ye see, he had a gift and he could endear himself to anyone. Many times his guests would do more than simply chat about their lives. They'd often end up spillin' secrets they would never tell another soul. Old man Clarkeson was no different."

"Did ye meet him?" I asked.

"No, my skipper was a young captain at the time," he filled in, "and in those days, he sailed a small craft ferryin' people to the major cities around Britain. One night on the way to Dublin, he sat with Clarkeson on the top deck under a full moon and they shared a flagon of blended Irish whisky. At the darkest hour, his new acquaintance told how, though he had been raised Catholic, he remained a slave to temptation, and in his eighteenth year, he fathered five sons over six months."

"Five sons in six months," I blurted out, "that's impossible! No woman could bear five children that quickly."

"Well, no woman could settle him down," the skipper went on, "fer his boys had four different mothers, with one havin' a set of twins. Ye see, bein' a likeable fellow and quite funny, ye could say he had a way with the ladies."

"He most certainly did," I noted.

Holding his left palm toward me, the skipper remarked, "Whatever faults Clarkeson may have had, he loved his kids and did his best to raise them, all of them. He built a place on a plot at the edge of a bog that served as a catchment fer a small river nearby and, in the beginnin', did his best to survive farmin' what little land he could. It worked fer awhile, except his boys grew bigger, his brood grew larger, and one year, it became apparent he couldn't grow enough food to provide fer everyone."

"If he had that many mouths to feed," I pitched in, "I can see why he would consider piracy."

"Actually, he gave moonshinin' a try first," the skipper corrected, "fer his boys had reached the age to help and would venture into the bog to poach what they could. One day, a few of them were out and found a large spot firm enough to support a kiln. With the whisky tax destroyin' the industry in Ireland a few years before, Clarkeson figured he could produce his own and sell it illegally. Scraping together the parts to construct a still, he planted barley the next spring, and whether it was right or wrong, his idea worked, fer he fared so well he gained weight the followin' winter."

"It was the same fer a lot of moonshiners," Big Tom interjected.

"And like the rest," the skipper furthered, "Clarkeson would have happily lived that way forever except a bad harvest a few years later left him with barely enough whisky to survive the winter, let alone to offer in trade."

"That would be a huge problem," the big man stated.

Giving me finger guns, the skipper went on, "There's one little detail ye need to know. Clarkeson was easily one of the hairiest men in the county and always sported a full, thick beard covering his face. Chips off the old block, his boys were no different and early in their teenage years they were all capable of growin' their own. By adulthood, their own mothers were havin' a hard time tellin' them apart, and though Clarkeson didn't have much, he did have his wits. Stuck in a bad situation, he devised a plan. Every fall, farmers would pole their harvests to the market on barges down the river near his home, and knowin' the best places to hide, he and his boys would lie in wait to ambush one. When an unsuspectin' victim came along, three of them provided a distraction on one bank to allow the other three to slip off the opposite bank and climb aboard. Then, they'd simply push their victims into the water, and once in control of the vessel, they'd all quickly get it to a spot where it came closest to the bog, transfer the bounty to some rafts, and disappear into the mist."

"Even if the local sheriff didn't catch them red-handed," I determined, "I can't believe he didn't know who had perpetrated the crime."

"He did," the skipper confirmed, "and with his witnesses in tow, he would show up a day or two later. Only he was never able to make any arrests." When I furrowed my brows, he laughed and told me, "Ye see, Clarkeson would always greet the sheriff wearin' a smile and pretend to take the accusations seriously. Once they had been made, he'd feign outrage and go on to claim he was doin' his best to raise his sons to become good Catholics like he had become. Assurin' everyone he'd turn in his own blood rather than see any of his boys burn in hell, he'd bluster on and on about how their incarcerations would only make his life easier, fer he'd have less mouths to feed."

"If that was the case, what was the sheriff waitin' fer?" I wanted to know.

"Well, Clarkeson's sons would march out in a line with their cheeks shaved as smooth as they were the day they were born," the skipper put forth, "and ye can imagine the looks of confusion, fer the victims always said their attackers had full beards, not baby faces. Because he'd see their hesitation, Clarkeson would ask, 'When exactly did ye say this took place?' and regardless of their answer, he'd insist, 'That's impossible', before pointin' to one of his boys and sayin', 'That day was little Paddy's muther's birthday, and out of respect, I make them all shave every mornin' the entire week. I do it fer each of their mums. It helps us them tell 'em apart. I may not have much, but I do have respect fer the women who gave birth to me clan.'" Shrugging, the skipper turned both palms over and concluded, "Since he couldn't prove otherwise, the sheriff would inevitably have to let them all go."

Incredulously, I responded, "Are ye kidding me?"

Shaking his head, the skipper laughed again and swore, "Honest to God that was the story he told. He'd also always blather on and on that there were bog people livin' in the swamp and that he or his boys had happened to see them the very day of the crime. Bein' the sheriff had no desire to go trampin' back there to investigate, Clarkeson got away with it fer a time."

Stroking the stubble on my chin, I suggested, "Somehow that seems believable. Did he ever get caught?"

"Almost, fer his propensity to grow hair wasn't the only thing his sons inherited and his brood grew exponentially. In the beginnin', their raids were sparse, and they didn't draw much attention to their exploits. The larger the family got, however, the more frequent their attacks became. With Clarkeson's boys somehow stayin' out of jail, rumors began swirlin' he was usin' his illegal whisky to pay off the sheriff, and the local laird showed up to investigate." Turning his palms over, the skipper revealed, "The day he arrived, the entire family happened to be present, and seein' all those little ones runnin' around half naked, the laird came to the realize if he were to arrest Clarkeson, he'd likely create even worse trouble fer himself in the future. To spare the headaches, he recognized the existence of the bog people, and in exchange fer the protection of the river, he awarded Clarkeson a viceregal license to legally sell his whisky."

Frowning, I pointed out, "Clarkeson and his boys were the bog people."

Giving me a wink, the skipper noted, "Which made it easy fer them to fulfill their duty. To the townsfolk, there were plenty of other details that seemed a bit sketchy, fer it was well known both the laird and the sheriff personally collected the tax every year. In the end, though, Clarkeson was able to build a little pier on the river leadin' to a tradin' post on the shore where he and his boys did their business, and havin' lived frugally fer such a long period, he was quite prepared to become successful. Once legitimate, he found ways to squeeze every drop out of every barrel, so to speak."

Having finished his story, the skipper quietly looked to the west and the sun descending into the auburn horizon. Letting my gaze venture toward *The Emballeur*, I spotted her crew climbing within her rigging. Suddenly, she took a heading directly toward us, righted in the water, and I watched her full complement of sails unfurl. My heart pounding in my chest, I sputtered, "Ah, skipper, ah, ye better get a look at this."

Turning his attention in the same direction, the skipper reached into his pocket and produced his flask. "Hmmm," he began, removing the stopper, "I guess D'Groers is willin' to call my bluff." Offering me a drink, he admitted, "Even worse, this is earlier than I was countin' on. It looks like we need a new plan."

Gratefully accepting, I took a healthy swallow. Malty and meaty with a peaty burst, I felt like I bit into my first taste and the moment the raw burn hit my belly, the pain in my thigh seemed to vanish. My muscles swelling, I let out a long slow breath and, smiling, asked, "Is this an inappropriate time to inquire where ye find whisky this good?"

Respectfully, the big man nodded to the skipper, who looked at me, raised his eyebrows, and replied, "I suppose there's never an inappropriate time to talk good whisky. We bought this barrel in Palermo off a Scottish captain from Port Ellen."

"It's an Islay," Big Tom contended.

"Bein' from Stornoway," the skipper followed up, "ye may not have ever tried one before. You're probably used to Island whiskies."

"This is definitely peatier than what I grew up on," I affirmed.

"It's typical fer Islays," Big Tom explained, "and part of the tradition in that region."

"If there's one thing the big man is an expert on," the skipper testified, "it's whisky. Ye'll never meet anyone who knows more. He's tried every one the world has to offer."

"Except Oakies," I clarified.

"Except Oakies," the skipper repeated, "and I bet it'd only take a single taste fer him to crack the secret of the finish."

"Maybe they use some sort of special barrel," I suggested.

"That wouldn't matter," the big man told me. "Part of the reason ye burn peat in the kiln is to cover any residual flavors the alcohol may pick up later. Have ye ever drunk a batch shipped in a cask made of pine?" Shaking his head, he curled his lips and spat, "Within a week, it tastes like somethin' ye'd use to scrub the deck."

"Maybe these barrels are different," I countered, "maybe they don't affect the taste."

"Ye still don't get it," the big man explained, "the barley is dried out in the kiln long before it becomes whisky. No matter what kind of barrel ye use, the peat will overwhelm everythin'."

Nodding to *The Emballeur*, the skipper interrupted, "He can tell ye the rest of the process later. Right now I think it would be best to focus on the task at hand."

Swallowing hard, I looked to the man-of-war bearing down on us. With the wind filling her sails, her portholes opened one by one, and two rows of cast-iron cannon barrels emerged down her sides. Feeling the blood coursing through my veins, I inquired, "Is this when we start playin' mouse?"

Shrugging, the skipper disclosed, "To be honest, I was hopin' it didn't get this far. I guess we'll see what happens next." I tried to hand him the flask, only he nodded to it and said, "Help yerself. We're goin' to need it."

I drank another healthy swallow, and thankfully, my hands stopped trembling. Estimating we would be engaging the approaching vessel in less than an hour, I took a third swig, narrowed my eyes, tilted my head, and remarked, "A third-rate should be worth some serious prize money."

"Here we go," the skipper inserted.

"It doesn't take much," Big Tom followed up.

Unconcerned with their comments, I absentmindedly placed my hand across my brows and turned in a circle scanning the horizon. Suddenly, to the northwest, I caught a flash of light. It disappeared just as suddenly, and unsure if it was simply the sun shimmering off the water, I cupped both hands around my eyes. Holding my breath, I noticed another flash, then a third, and then a series of several more.

"There," I mumbled, "there it is again."

Hastening a look in the same the area, the skipper asked, "There what is again?"

Pointing to the spot, I told him, "I'll bet there's a ship over there." Almost regretfully, I added, "Perhaps several."

Fluidly, the skipper raised his spyglass, extended the tubes, and held it to his eye. A smile slowly creeping across his face, he announced, "Whew, Rory came through. He had me a bit worried. I knew he wasn't happy, but I didn't think he'd drag it out this long." Trading me the flask for the spyglass, he ordered Big Tom, "Turn us south. Let's get the wind at our back and get out of here." On cue, our two gaff sails swung out over our port side, and *Rosie's Charm* circled in the other direction.

I located a little flotilla, and homing in on the bright red Cross of England adorning the mainsail of the closest vessel, I asked, "Rory? I thought you sent Rory with the message to the admiral at Hyeres."

"I sent him with a message," the skipper confirmed, "but not the king's reply. That would've been suicide. If I had, ye can be sure we'd be facin' *The Emballeur* alone."

Making out two fourth-rates, two sixth-rates, and two frigates, I retorted, "That doesn't make any sense."

"That's because ye still don't understand our role," the skipper stated. "We're a messenger ship, we're nobody important." Grinning, he divulged, "But the messages we transport often are, and because of Tomas's nose fer pirates, I felt confident we'd hunt D'Groers down. Therefore, in case we did, I wrote out a second message for Rory to deliver to the admiral."

"What did it say?" I wanted to know.

"We're under attack, and it's unlikely the king's reply will safely arrive," he concluded. "I gambled they'd send the help needed to ensure it does."

"And the help would capture D'Groers," I realized, lowering the spyglass.

"Well, what did ye think," the skipper replied, "that we were really goin' to attack a third-rate by ourselves? That would be crazy. I told ye from the get-go not to get yer hopes up. Furthermore and fer the record, if I'm plannin' on gettin' into a fight with a bigger opponent, I wouldn't send Rory away. I'd want him at my side more than ye."

"I did find the notion somewhat questionable," I admitted.

"Which is why I figured it was best to split ye two up," the skipper revealed. "Once he starts, he's contagious. Ye know how the Irish can be."

"Insane," Big Tom broke in.

My heart no longer racing, I remembered where our position would be on a map and said, "How did he get away with tellin' them our location? It's obvious we weren't obeyin' our orders."

"Oh, it's due to a libeccio off the Corsican coast that blew us off course," the skipper answered.

"I don't recall any libeccio," I told him.

His face contorting, the big man stated, "Ye were feverish when it happened."

"I must've been," I concurred and quickly looked to our approaching comrades. A bit disappointed, I murmured, "It's too bad we won't be a part of the battle and earn our share of the prize money."

"Actually," the skipper corrected, "we don't need to actively participate in the fight to get an equal cut. We only need to be in sight of the action. Even better, we'll also get paid fer the other four vessels. Although there'll be lots of hands in this pot, we should still make a nice tidy amount."

"At a minimum, we'll be able to afford to drink the finest whisky all of next year," the big man remarked.

Furrowing my brows, I looked between them both and inquired, "Are ye tellin' me that we'll get the same pay as the sailors who are in the thick of it?"

Nodding several times, the skipper returned, "That's correct."

"It doesn't seem fair," I suggested.

"I don't make the rules," he came back. "I just play by them. If they want me to captain a little ship in this big navy, then I'll leave the combat to the big ships in this big navy. They're better suited fer it anyway." Tilting his head toward Big Tom, he rolled his eyes and commented, "Sheesh, I guess the new fellow here really did want to mix it up with D'Groers. Maybe Rory is right. Maybe there is some Irish in him."

"No," the big man countered, "there can't be. He's from the Stornoways. It's more likely there's Scandinavian."

Tugging at his braid, the skipper recalled, "Aye, that's right." He smiled crookedly, looked at me, and proclaimed, "Tomas, do ye know what this means?"

"What's that?"

"There must've been a Viking raid on his hamlet long ago and it planted the seed fer one of those warriors who go psychotic in battle. What are they called again?"

"Berserkers," the big man answered.

"Ah yes, berserkers," the skipper repeated. "Now we know why he's fit right in. . ."

The Black Irish: Clarkeson, Fergus,
Ben, James, Gianis, Marcus

October 1, 1785, Kingston, Jamaica

Staring at the flame dancing atop the candle on the mantel behind the bar, the old sea captain slowly stroked his beard and mentioned, "Of course, not everythin' went accordin' to plan, fer old Orana D'Groers noticed the little fleet sooner than we had hoped and was able, fer a little while, to outmaneuver his pursuit. Finally, close to midnight, the British ships had boxed him in, and we watched the encounter in the flashes of cannon fire." To bursts of lightning striking outside, he glanced at the windows and followed up, "To be sure, outgunned though he was, D'Groers fought the fight the skipper had warned he would, and lookin' back, I'd say he never gave up, fer the battle didn't end until his mizzenmast came crashing down on his helm." He turned to face the room, and numbering on his fingers, went on, "It broke both his legs, crushed his left arm, and pinned his right shoulder to the deck. Thank God too, fer when the sun rose the next morning, every ship was damaged, and both the fourth-rate tied to the port side of *The Emballeur* and the sixth-rate tied to the starboard were deemed unseaworthy. It was a good thing we were close to Hyeres and they could all be towed to safety."

"Did D'Groers survive?" Brass wanted to know.

"Aye, that he did," the old sea captain confirmed, "and to be sure, they cut off his limbs to be certain he'd face justice in London. Regrettably, we weren't there to see him hanged. However, accordin' to the stories, old Orana entertained the crowd twisting and turning fer a good two minutes. At the time, it was considered the longest anyone had ever done the Marshal's Dance. Then they put what remained of his body in gibbets on the banks of the River Thames as a warnin' to anyone tempted to follow in his footsteps."

"Heh-heh, now that must've been a sight to see," Jack declared.

While Rags put his hands to his temples, the old sea captain continued, "Beyond our share of the prize money and the bounty on D'Groers's head, the admiral rewarded us with that great big green-and-gold flag. In recognition of our feat, the skipper nailed it to the deck, and our crew walked over it until the D wore completely away. Indeed, I don't know if I've ever seen a more beautiful sight." Lifting his mug to his lips, he noticed the candle had melted halfway to the next pin and determined, "Uh-oh, it looks like a half hour has passed by."

Her arms crossed, Sarah inserted, "And you said you have two more stories to tell. If you're planning on keeping your bartender happy, they had better be quick."

Stroking his beard, the old sea captain looked at the flame and stated, "I may cut it a bit close, but I promise it'll be worth it. In this next part, we'll go back a couple of months to the morning *The Black Irish* returned home, fer it was do-or-die time fer old Malcolm . . ."

Mid-November 1743, off the southern coast of Vieques, Puerto Rico

Standing alone at the bow of *The Black Irish*, Malcolm let his long hair and bushy beard blow freely in the swirling headwind. Directly to the north, the sunrise crept across a lush thin sliver of land with its highest summit located on the western side and a central ridge of rolling hills ending at a second peak near the eastern tip. A brewing thunderstorm farther to the northeast silhouetted the isle in an amber aura, and to crooked bolts of lightning bursting amid the volatile bank of approaching clouds, the brigantine led the captured brig toward a large bay cut into the eastern half of the rugged southern coastline.

At the stern of the ship, Clarkeson surfaced through the hatch behind the helm. Her black patch covering her right eye, she wore a black kerchief on her head with a double knot at her right temple and the tails grazing her cheek. Dressed in her usual dark outfit, she wound her long braid around the left side of her neck and, keeping her gaze on Malcolm, advanced slowly down the main deck. Cradling his claymore, Fergus appeared next, followed by James, and then the remainder of her crew silently filled in along the way. Upon reaching her captive, she stopped, put her hands on her hips, and cleared her throat.

Malcolm turned and spent a few moments finding the smattering of men sprinkled among those behind her who, only a few days prior, had been sailing under his command. At their refusal to meet his eyes, he narrowed his and settled on hers.

"He's Catholic," she stated.

Frowning, Malcolm responded, "Come again?"

"He's Catholic," she repeated. "Ye had a question fer me and I'm givin' ye me answer. I'm supportin' Prince Charles because he's Catholic, and I believe my people will be better off with a Catholic on the throne."

Rolling his eyes, Malcolm let out a groan and asked, "So this is a holy war?"

"It's not a crusade," she replied, "but ever since the last Jacobean rebellion, England has been relentless in its persecution of Ireland. They've done everythin' they can to take away our land, our heritage, and even our language."

Sighing, he put forth, "And ye think a Catholic is goin' to restore it? Religion is just another way fer the kings to retain their power and control their peasants. Look at the whole of Europe right now. We all supposedly believe in Jesus Christ and yet we're all killin' each other in his name." Raising his brows, he inquired, "What if I tell ye I'm not Catholic? What if I tell ye I'm one of those Protestants ye hate?"

"What if I tell ye I don't hate Protestants," she returned, "and that I don't care how ye pray or who ye pray to?" Gesturing toward her crew, she noted, "Most of these men aren't Christians, and with the way they've been treated by the Spanish, I doubt they'll ever be." Nodding to the island at their fore, she furthered, "This is a new world, Captain, and those that inhabit it first are the first to set the rules. Where I stand, I say everyone is free to worship however they want and whoever they choose, ye just can't force someone else to do the same." Pointing to his chest, she asserted, "Yer even welcome to pray to Thor if ye'd like."

Crossing his arms, Malcolm retorted, "And that works?"

"Sure it works," she insisted, "why wouldn't it? Yer an educated man. Ye have to have heard of the Romans. They let the people they conquered keep their gods and even went on to adopt many as their own. Feel free to do the same. Worship one or worship a bunch, I don't care. If it helps win the war, ye can dedicate a shrine to Julius Caesar."

Stroking his beard, Malcolm mused, "I guess it did work fer the Romans."

"Now ye see why I want ye to join me," she picked up. "Ye can keep an open mind and think fer yerself. Fer the cause to succeed, we need men like ye to be a part of it."

"Havin' an open mind doesn't make me a Jacobite," he countered.

Arching the eyebrow above her patch, she told him, "The truth be told, I sometimes wish I had somethin' nobler to fight fer than a king in a distant land, but right now, that's the best there is and I do believe his victory is the greatest hope we have to bring peace to the world."

"And if he wins, what happens next?" Malcolm wanted to know.

"Come again?" she responded.

Shrugging, Malcolm explained, "Well, should he lose, yer facin' the noose at Gallows Point, and with a little more notoriety, they may even hang yer bones in gibbets on Rackham's Cay. Should he win, however, then I figure yer expectin' to be pardoned and not be punished fer yer crimes. In the unlikely event that happens, what will ye do then?"

Shaking her head, she divulged, "I haven't thought that far in advance. I'll probably be dead before either scenario takes place."

"I'm not plannin' on dyin'," he attested, "and I do think that far ahead. Is this expected to be a lifelong commitment?"

Tilting her head to the left, she suggested, "Right now, my plan is to see the prince victorious. If I should survive to see that day, then perhaps I'll use the vessels under me command to start me own shippin' company."

"What if I want a fleet of my own?" he followed up.

"Then by all means, go ahead and build it," she told him.

A gust of wind blew a lock of hair across Malcolm's face, and brushing it back, he turned his attention toward the shore. Close enough to see the white sandy beaches interspersed within the clumps of emerald mangroves, he peered into the wilderness and mentioned, "It looks deserted."

"It's supposed to," she replied. "I don't want anyone knowin' where I'm at."

Meeting her eye, Malcolm remarked, "Should the English decide yer a problem, they'll send the ships to find ye."

"Let them. This is a Spanish territory. They'll be facin' a bigger threat than the one I can muster."

"What if the Spanish come lookin' fer ye?"

"Why would they? Tacitly, I'm on their side."

"They don't mind ye settlin' on their land?"

Cackling more harsh than happy, she stated, "The Spanish believe this place is cursed, and I'm perfectly happy to perpetuate the myth. That bein' said, I still believe they'd never allow an English force to conduct a raid so close to Puerto Rico."

"Maybe fer now," he allowed, "but if the Royal Navy really wants ye, they'll come burn ye out, the Spanish be damned."

Brushing him off with a wave, she pointed to the highest mountain and revealed, "Which is all part of the plan. There's an observation post up there, and if I choose, I can be long gone prior their arrival."

"What if they slip in at night? They could easily form a blockade and trap ye."

Suppressing a yawn, she rolled her eyes and said, "Perfect. That'll leave them fewer vessels to patrol the coasts of Britain."

"How do ye expect to survive? It's not like ye can count on any reinforcements."

"It's an island," she reminded him, "it provides everything we need. We've even planted corn to ensure we'll be able to distill our own whiskey. The English will run out of provisions before we will."

"What if they don't settle fer a blockade? What if they send in the marines?"

"I hope they do," she snarled with a harsh cackle. "It'll give us plenty of targets to shoot dead on their way to shore. I'll happily turn this entire place into one gigantic meat grinder."

"Sooner or later, ye'll run out of gunpowder," he noted, "and the English won't."

Spreading her arms wide, she sighed, "Ye just don't get it, do ye? I already told ye I don't plan on makin' it to the end. I only want to do me part in gettin' there. Whether it be takin'

English merchantmen or tyin' up a whole fleet of men-of-war, if I can divert enough resources of the Royal Navy to allow the prince to land his invasion force, I'll have made a difference. And if, somehow, I see him on the throne and get me pardon, then just like that," she furthered, snapping her fingers, "I'll be a hero in Britain."

"So the Young Pretender is aware of ye?" Malcolm wanted to know. At her silence, he looked to a rocky outcrop at the entrance of the harbor and asked, "What do ye expect me to do if he loses and I return to find ye surrounded?"

Suddenly the lightning flashed, the thunder rumbled, and scattered droplets of rain began to fall. Observing the coming storm, she asserted, "In the event the prince fails and ye arrive to see this island under a cloud of smoke, then I hope ye smile and wave and go on with yer day. I'd hate it if ye martyred yerself on me behalf. I don't need yer blood on me hands." Giving him a wink, she concluded, "Besides, just like Anne Bonny, I have a way of slippin' in and out of trouble. Odds are, they'll probably be wastin' their time." Flaring her nostrils and curling her lips, she snapped, "Now enough talk, I want to spend this gale fast asleep on a soft bed under a dry roof. It's time to take care of business." She nodded to Fergus, who slid his claymore out of the sheath, and stated, "I answered yer question. It's time ye answer mine. Are ye joinin' me crew or not?"

"No final meal?"

"No sense in wastin' good food on a dead man."

"What about one last swig of Oakies?"

"No sense in wastin' good whiskey either." She turned her left palm over and, waving her fingers, demanded, "Come on, let's have it. I haven't had me coffee yet."

Staring into her eye, Malcolm ran his fingers through his beard three times and muttered, "I guess it's official. I'm the first captain in Clarkeson's armada."

Cackling more happily than harshly, she repeated, "Clarkeson's armada. I like it. It has a nice ring to it." She produced the silver flask etched with a rose having two buds on the stem above the word *FIAT* and, holding it forth, declared, "To the king across the sea."

"To the king across the sea," Malcolm echoed, and with the crew cheering wildly, they both took a healthy swallow.

Beaming, Clarkeson held Malcolm's gaze and told him, "Go ahead and have another, Captain. I can't tell ye how relieved I am ye came to yer senses." Waiting until he had tilted the flask to his lips, she added, "But there is one little thing we do need to clear up."

Letting out a happy sigh, Malcolm passed the flask to Fergus and asked, "What's that?"

In one fluid motion, she drew a thin dagger hidden up the sleeve of her left forearm and sliced it under his chin, trimming off the bottom third of his beard. Gawking at Clarkeson, Malcolm flinched and caught the severed whiskers against his chest. The blade jutting out the base of her fist, she waved it before his face and warned, "Should ye ever call me a Paddy again, ye don't need to worry about anyone plungin' a knife into yer back. Instead, ye better bet I'll run this one across yer throat. . ."

BELIZE
(Spain)

AMBERGRIS CAY

Oakies

N

W   E

S

Belize Town

The Scottish Rose: Mairi, Connor, Angus

October 1, 1785, Kingston, Jamaica

The lightning and thunder fading away, the old sea captain watched rivulets of melting wax run down the final three inches of the candle on the mantel behind the bar. Stroking his long bushy white beard, he mentioned, "To be sure, had Clarkeson cut a quarter inch deeper, old Malcolm wouldn't've called anyone anythin' ever again."

His rum finished, Jack set the empty glass on the bar and stated, "I'm surprised he still sailed with her. I don't know if I'd let any woman shave my beard."

"He had said what he said to provoke her," the old sea captain filled in, "and knew he had it comin'. Besides, he had already fallen under her spell. If Clarkeson wanted ye, she had ye. Ye couldn't deny her." Waving his right hand toward Sarah, he proposed, "Much like, I'm sure, our good bartender here."

"Don't waste time flattering me," she cautioned, crossing her arms. "You hardly have any left."

Meeting her gaze, he swirled the contents of his mug and replied, "I hardly have any lager either, so I guess it's good I don't need much of both. To be sure, a promise is a promise, and in keepin' the bartender happy, it's time to bring an end to the night." He took a quick sip, and, focusing his bright blue eyes on the flickering orange flame, began, "Tomorrow we'll revisit the day Malcolm arrived on Clarkeson's island, but fer now, we're jumpin' ahead a few weeks, close to the same time *Rosie's Charm* departed Palermo on our quest to find Orana D'Groers. Fer right around then, Mairi had completed her rounds and was returnin' home to her own little island off the coast of Belize . . ."

Early January 1744, east of Belize

Wearing a black shirt with black pants, Mairi stood alone at the bow of *The Scottish Rose* and gingerly scratched her left temple under the bonnet woven in the red, white, and blue tartan. Ahead, the sun set in a range of rose to ruddy and cast long shadows over a bright green tropical island approximately ten miles off the coast of Belize. Barely one mile at its widest point, it ran north for almost twenty-five until a channel at the top edge provided a natural boundary to the Yucatan peninsula. Officially it was a part of the Spanish Empire, only they had found nothing more than the blackish waxy lumps of ambergris coughed up by whales on its shores and left it uninhabited. Nevertheless, with a barrier reef offering an abundant source of food, an underground reservoir supplying fresh water, and Belize City giving access to corn grown in Mexico, it fulfilled all the basic needs required to operate a distillery. Two years earlier, she had scouted it on the advice of the Baymen, and the moment she stepped into the tranquil turquoise surf surrounding the white sandy beaches, she knew she was home.

Now, she brought her spyglass to her right eye and scrutinized a narrow strip of land located on the southern portion. Amid a dense thicket, she spied a covered platform cresting the treetops and cloaked in fresh branches harvested out of the surrounding woods. Though Connor settled in to her left, she continued to scan the forests atop the hills to the north and south. Focusing the lens, she told him, "I can pick out the elevator, but even knowin' where the two lookouts are, I can't find them."

"Do ye think they've seen us?" he asked.

"I'm sure of it," she stated. "They can see everythin' fer miles in every direction. Should we ever be attacked, their signal fires will give us plenty of time to prepare."

"What will we do if there's a raid?" he wanted to know.

"Leave in a hurry," she replied. "Ideally, there'll be a ship available, and everyone can be away to Belize Town."

"What if there isn't one?"

Lowering her spyglass, she slid the tubes together and put forth, "Then we'll take Earnest into the jungle and keep him alive until we're rescued. His life is worth more than the rest of ours put together, includin' mine."

"And let the pirates have the whiskey?" Connor questioned.

Waving her right index finger, she retorted, "Oh no, ye can bet anyone who enters the warehouse uninvited won't leave it again. The alcohol in those barrels is cask strength and a single spark would blow the whole thing up." She inhaled deeply, let out a weary sigh, and concluded, "Though it may hurt, I'd rather personally light the fire and see the perpetrators burn alive than let them steal a single drop."

They came around the southern end and reached a series of cays disguising a harbor cutting into the western coast. Navigating into its mouth, they went north and, for several miles, followed the narrow strip of land buffering the Caribbean. Sailing roughly half the length, they reached a little cove where a pier extended from the shore and a second schooner was tied to the closest side. The vessel spotlighted in the waning daylight, it was one hundred feet long, and her two masts were tall enough to support a second smaller trapezoidal gaff sail at the top. A few hundred yards farther on, an additional empty pier ended at the landing for a single-story rectangular building constructed deep into the encompassing copse.

To its right, a row of five more buildings—lit up in the florid sunset—shared common walls and featured windows along their eaves large enough to allow a view of the forest in the background. The two on the left climbed like steps up to the tallest in the center, and a single slanted roof descended down the pair on the right. Behind the highest point, a tower with a covered platform concealed under freshly cut boughs stood between dual cisterns resembling oversized wooden barrels.

Her attention on the moored schooner, Mairi told Connor, "Oh good, *The Whiskey Rebellion* is here."

They continued to the farther pier, and while they secured their ship, the one person in the distillery permitted to have facial hair came out to meet them. Mairi's height, he had ebony skin, dark-brown eyes, short curly black hair, and a thick mustache combed out wide at the corners of his mouth. His tan shorts were cut off at the knees, and he wore a dingy white sleeveless shirt that made it obvious his muscular right arm hung lower than the left. He gave her a warm smile and, in a deep baritone voice, declared, "Oh, is it good to see you. With everything going on, I worry it will never happen again." Nodding to *The Whiskey Rebellion*, he added, "Your timing is impeccable. MacGregor's headin' out tomorrow."

Cackling more happily than harshly, Mairi gave him a tender hug and responded, "Well, Earnest, like my father used to say, timin' is everythin'. Why's he leavin' so soon?"

"There's news," Earnest answered, "and he's needed in Scotland."

Ending their embrace, she raised her brows and repeated, "News? What kind of news?"

"Not the kind for me to tell," Earnest returned. "I wouldn't care anyway." With Connor in tow, they began walking toward the shore, and with a bright grin crossing his face, he revealed, "I do, however, have somethin' exciting to relay."

"What's that?"

"He brought the materials to build a second fermentor. Once it's set up, we should be able to produce two batches a week."

Her eyes wide, Mairi exclaimed, "Two batches a week! I don't see how we can possibly produce two batches a week. We don't have the barrels to store it in!"

"MacGregor has been collecting his share," Earnest reported, "and between the both of you, we should have plenty."

"Ye make it sound easy," she lamented. They reached the landing and turned right toward the boardwalk leading to the row of buildings. At the corner of the warehouse, she glanced to the casks stacked against the side wall and stated, "I'll be happy if half of those we found this time out are serviceable. I only grabbed them in case ye figured out a way to clean these out."

"We'll figure out what we need to figure out when we need to figure it out," Earnest assured her. "Right now, we have other, more important, considerations." Giving her a wink, he furthered, "Didn't you tell me your father always said something about being all work and no play?"

Grinning sheepishly, she said, "I suppose yer right. Did ye tap the firkin?"

"The instant you were sighted."

"Ye haven't tried it yet?"

Shaking his head, Earnest replied, "Not yet. MacGregor wouldn't even consider the idea without you present. Had you taken a day longer, we would've had to wait until April or May for another chance to give it a taste."

Frowning, she pointed out, "MacGregor's the owner. He doesn't need my permission."

"The tradition started with the three of us together," Earnest reminded her, "and you know how he is with tradition."

Nodding, Mairi agreed, "I suppose some are better left untouched. How long has it been since the last time?"

"Almost five months," he filled in, "which puts it at fourteen."

"Then it's more than a year old. I can't wait. It only gets better with age."

The boardwalk came to a fork where it either continued straight to the first building or veered left between the entire line and two more single-story structures flanking the tower. The first a workshop built out of wood, it had a thatched roof with brick chimney in the center and its own small cistern at the far end. The second was nothing more than a large tent covering a dozen round tables surrounding a stone chimney in the middle. Ignoring the aroma of heavily seasoned seafood gumbo wafting in the air, they kept on the path until it cleared the entire compound. Turning toward the Caribbean side of the island, they finally came to a stop at a small cabin nestled in the trees and overlooking the sea.

On the front porch, a single man sitting at a table surrounded by four chairs watched the stars come out over the water. He had tied his slicked-back gray hair into a ponytail, waxed his silvery mustache into swooping curls at the corners of his lips, and grown his silvery goatee a good foot off his chin. Dressed in a white shirt under a black vest with black pants, he wore a red rose pinned to the lapel over his heart and a gold band on his left ring finger. Seeing Mairi, he stood, smiled, and spread his arms wide.

Without saying a word, she rushed forward, and though he was several inches taller, lifted him off his feet.

Gasping for air, he grunted, "Careful, if ye break this old man in two, yer liable to put an end to my clan."

"It's been a hundred and fifty years since the English branded the MacGregors outlaws," she responded, "and if that hasn't broken ye, I doubt a young Scotswoman who grew up in Port Glasgow has a chance."

"Aye, except the English only made us angry," he countered. "I'll never say the same about ye."

Setting him down, she stated, "I warned ye the day ye saved my life to get used to this hug. Ye should be grateful, yer the only person who gets it."

Squeezing her tight, MacGregor put forth, "It's an honor greater than knighthood." At her happy cackle, he lamented, "Oh, Mairi, five months is too long to make these old eyes smile. I wish I didn't have to leave tomorrow mornin'."

Raising her eyebrows, she let him go and followed up, "Earnest said ye have news. What is it?"

Giving her a wave, MacGregor responded, "We have plenty of time to get to that." The table was set with a glass flagon, a bowl of water, and four chalices (all etched with a single rose having two unopened buds on the stem over the word *Revirescit*), and sweeping his arm toward the spread, he went on, "First things first, we need to have a toast." Picking up the flagon, he poured an ounce of whiskey in each glass and asked, "How's business?"

Producing a leather purse, she rattled the coins inside and asserted, "In my wildest dreams I never imagined the plan could go any better. Ye men are too easy."

"Maybe it's simply that yer a genius," MacGregor noted. "If it wasn't fer yer idea, I'm not sure this whole thing would be possible."

Nodding to Earnest, she insisted, "He's the one who makes this possible. I just play my role."

Gesturing to MacGregor, Earnest chipped in, "We all play our role. Had he not envisioned this place, I'd still be a slave."

"Then I guess we'll credit the universe fer bringin' us together," MacGregor furthered, "and givin' us the chance to change the course of history." He picked up a chalice and, holding it forth, asked, "Have ye heard how much a barrel of Oakies is expected to fetch at auction in London?"

"Not specifically," Mairi answered, "although with the way captains are goin' mad over it, it better be a small fortune."

Chuckling, MacGregor passed out the remaining glasses and revealed, "They say the first man brave enough to successfully bring one across the Atlantic could expect to get its weight in silver."

Arching the eyebrow over her right eye, Mairi repeated, "Its weight in silver?"

Laughing, MacGregor tilted his head and confirmed, "Aye, its weight in silver and if it's worth that much, I say it's time we expand. Did Earnest tell ye his good news?"

"He told me ye brought the cypress to build a second fermentor," she snapped, "except he didn't tell me where we're supposed to get the extra barrels to fill. Have ye come up with a solution fer that little problem yet? Or should I expect they'll simply fall out of the sky?"

"Earnest is right," MacGregor sighed. "Yer all work and no play." Raising his glass, he swirled it under his nose and ordered, "Fer the next hour, yer takin' a break, and we're goin' to enjoy the finest whiskey the world has ever known. Chances are good we'll never get to do this again."

Connor and Earnest glanced at Mairi, who, doing her best to suppress a smirk, uttered, "If ye say so, old man."

Giving her a double take, MacGregor raised his chalice over the bowl and declared, "To the king across the sea."

Echoing, "To the king across the sea," they all touched their drinks to his, and the slight tinkling rang over the gentle lapping of the waves hitting the beach.

Mairi took a sip and, patiently savoring the flavor, rolled hers around her tongue. She swallowed, circled her lips, and let out a long, slow "Uisge beatha."

Their delight palpable even in the darkness, MacGregor, Earnest, and Connor all responded, "Uisge beatha."

Almost giggling, Mairi asked, "Earnest, how long until we have some of this to sell?"

"If everything works out," he returned, "I should have a few barrels ready in June."

"In June," she repeated. "Well, if Oakies is currently worth its weight in silver, then this'll be worth its weight in gold." Arching both eyebrows, she cackled harshly and, raising her glass, declared, "I know they say the first man, but when that day comes maybe I'll be the first captain to make that journey across the Atlantic. After all, it's not like Clarkeson's goin' to stop me. . ."

EPILOGUE

October 1, 1785, Kingston, Jamaica

With the seventh pin falling from the side of the candle, the old sea captain cast his bright blue eyes on the flickering orange flame and suggested, "I guess I've run out of time." Lifting his mug to his lips, he downed the last of his drink and added, "I guess it's a good thing I've also run out of lager. Too bad I don't have some more of both, because in my opinion, the story hasn't even started yet."

"Don't fret," Sarah inserted, "because in my opinion, it is time to close. They can all come back tomorrow, and you can pick up right where you left off. I know I'll be here." She turned and tugged the rope dangling from the bell tower. The rain light, a loud peal rang over some thunder far in the distance, and directing her attention to the room, she ordered, "For now, everyone needs to finish up."

"It can't be time to go," Rags snarled. "I'm telling you, none of the kids want to work these days."

Over the jumble of protests following his, Sarah crossed her arms and snapped, "I don't want to hear it. I've spent most of my night with all of you, and I'm looking forward to spending some time at home with my family. I suggest you do the same."

Waving both hands toward the door, she insisted, "Now go, all of you. I'll see you tomorrow."

His rum gone, Jack set his empty glass down and lamented, "I don't want to go home. I like this family better."

"Yeah, heh-heh," the other Jack followed up, "and I can't remember how to get there."

"Jesus Christ Jack," Rags put forth, "you can follow me like you always do." Sneering, he rose and, looking at Sarah, growled, "But with the way they treat their best customers, you may have to figure out something else. I don't know if I'll ever set foot in this joint again."

Rolling her eyes, Sarah remarked, "If I could only be so lucky." Glancing at Tony, who set his empty wine glass on the bar, she nodded toward the two old men shuffling down the center aisle.

"Of course," he assured her. Covering his heart with his right hand and twirling his left, he asserted, "They will arrive at their destination more safely than a maiden in DeLogrono's charge." Bowing to the old sea captain, he proclaimed, "My compliments to you, good sir. For of all the pints I've purchased over the years, I'm not sure if one has made me happier. I am truly captivated by your tale and can't wait to hear how it ends."

Still seated, the old sea captain took a quick drink, and nodding to Tony, he swallowed and replied, "Why, thank ye kindly, good sir. I look forward to gettin' there."

The couples rising from the table, Luke told their group, "Since we're trapped on this island until the storm passes, we should also return."

"I'd definitely like to know what happens to the twins," John affirmed.

"And I want to know what happens when France gets involved," Lina stated.

"I think we should revisit Palermo," Ginevra murmured.

Pushing his stool back, Brass asserted, "I want to know what Big Tom thought of Oakies."

Standing in front of the casks, Nancy picked up, "Oakies," and narrowing her eyes, she uttered, "Wait a second—"

"Wait until tomorrow," Sarah interrupted. Nodding to the people at the door donning their cloaks, she suggested, "I'm sure everything will be made clear then. Right now, they need to leave." She rounded the end of the bar and, herding everyone forward, pressed, "Let's go, get home while there's a break in the rain. The way the weather has been, it won't be long until it starts pouring again."

Letting the cool night air creep inside, Rags stood in the entry and looked to the sky. "She's right," he groused. "Come on, Jack. If we hurry, we may not get soaked."

"Yeah, heh-heh, let's hurry," Jack concurred. "The last thing we want to do is get soaked, heh-heh." Poking his head out, he glanced both ways and asked, "Now, where do I live again?"

"Jesus Christ Jack," Rags snarled, "you live across the street, in the apartment next to mine."

"Of course, heh-heh," Jack returned, and they disappeared into the darkness.

Behind, Tony told Jack and Brass, "I'm not sure who I love more, Mairi or Clarkeson."

Shaking his head, Brass responded, "Women are bad luck on a ship."

"Which is part of the reason I prefer the land," Tony maintained.

"You wouldn't if you were married to my wife," Jack interjected, and one by one, they all stepped outside.

Leaning against the jamb, Sarah yelled, "Just remember who you all love the most. Now get home safely and I'll see you at six. Don't be late." She pulled herself inside and, waiting for Luke, John, Lina, and Ginevra, went on, "You know I'm open when you hear the bell ring, although feel free to arrive a few minutes before then. Everyone else does."

Smiling, Lina vowed, "We'll be here early."

"Even if they're not," Ginevra added with a wink.

"Which means we don't have a choice," the brothers concluded simultaneously.

Upon their exit, Sarah locked the door, walked behind the bar, and poured her own mug of lager. Coming back to the other side, she sat next to the old sea captain, took several healthy swallows, and let out a long sigh. Meeting his bright blue eyes, she asserted, "You know, there's no better beer than the first one at the end of the shift."

He tapped his mug to hers and stated, "I'm not sure if wiser words have ever been spoken."

Nodding to his drink, she replied, "Sometimes the wisest words are left unsaid. I'm glad you knew to keep your mouth shut when Nancy filled your mug. It gives us some time to talk in private. Do you have a place to sleep tonight?"

Looking away, he stammered, "Well, I...uh . . . I...uh . . . I suppose I have yet to find a bale of hay under a dry roof. Ye don't happen to know of one ye could recommend, do ye?"

Grinning, she offered, "I recommend ye stay in the back where we store our extra barrels. There's some hooks in the walls and enough space to stretch a hammock across the room. I imagine anyone who's sailed the world would be comfortable sleeping on one of those."

"I've put in many a night swingin' back and forth."

"Good," she followed up, "because I'm willing to give you three meals and three pints a day during your stay. In exchange,

I expect you to keep your story going until that storm breaks. If you're going to get paid anything more, it's up to you to earn it."

"I understand."

Glowering at him, she warned, "And don't get any crazy ideas. Like Mairi, I also have a dagger, only mine is real and I'll trim more than your beard."

Widening his eyes, the old sea captain held his left palm forth and remarked, "I would expect nothing less."

Reaching out her right hand, she waited until he grasped it and proposed, "Then we have a deal. With this weather keeping everyone shut in and bored, let's hope word of your story spreads across the city and brings in some business."

A gleam in his eye, the old sea captain gave her a wink and remarked, "To be sure, not only do ye work every bit as hard as yer grandfather did, yer every bit as savvy as he was too."

COMING SOON:

BOOK 2

OF

THE OLDE ROSIE CHRONICLES

"THE KING'S FIRKIN"

Rosie's Charm: The skipper, Big Tom, Rory, the old sea captain

CHAPTER 1

October 2, 1785, Kingston, Jamaica

Burning brightly, the flame spontaneously consumed the fresh wick atop the white beeswax candle on the mantel behind the bar, and a sweet aroma immediately invigorated the entire place. With the first melting droplet winding its way through the ten metal pins evenly spaced down the left side of the stick, Sarah, standing before the three different-sized casks in the cradle below the mantel, continued her grandfather's forty-three-year tradition and tugged on the knotted rope dangling from the bell tower above her head. A steady rainfall echoed through the pitched roof, and over the random patter, a clear metallic ring announced Henry's was open for the evening. Suddenly, lightning flashed through the wooden shutters protecting the arched windows flanking the entrance and briefly illuminated the stained glass inside the five casements lining each side wall. The ensuing thunderclaps boomed, resounding in the confined room, and the reverberations rattled the glasses stacked in neat rows on the shelves built into the cradle. Unfazed, Sarah glanced upward, took one last deep breath, and to the trailing rumble, turned to face the familiar murmur of a gathering crowd.

Waiting when she arrived for the evening, Rags now sat in his regular spot on her right, two stools off the end, and sipped on a glass of fresh water. A custom wide-brimmed cream hat hiding his crinkled features, he sported a cream suit with a cream bow tie and a silver crucifix on a silver chain. To her left, at the opposite end, the old sea captain had pivoted in his seat and, leaning against the exposed brick, conversed with the two couples occupying the table at his back. To listen intently, the pair closest, John and Ginevra, faced each other while the pair across, Luke and Lina, sat on the edge of their chairs.

Despite the weather, both Lina and Ginevra wore low-cut form-fitting black gowns tight on their tall slender frames, large diamond wedding rings, and a plethora of gold jewelry—including hoop earrings, herringbone necklaces, and rope bracelets. Ginevra, dark and subtly olive, had painted her lips scarlet and tied her two braids into a bow at the base of her neck. Lina, whose rich brown eyes sparkled in the subdued lantern light, went without makeup and let her russet ponytail lie in the middle of her tanned shoulder blades. Though Luke's shirt was yellow and John's was blue, the brothers donned matching black suits and silver wedding bands with blue-green amethysts in bezel settings. Their mannerisms, like their light-brown eyes and pale skin, were nearly identical, and their silvery blond hair was cut short in the same clipped style. The remaining four tables between theirs and the door were empty, as were four of the five on the other side of the aisle, but Nancy, the serving maid, waited on six people who had recently settled in at the one directly behind Rags.

The rain began to pour, and the door opened to a woman wearing a forest-green cloak. She rushed in, Tony followed, Brass came next, and quickly, he shut out the storm. His black cloak sodden, he took it off and hung it up on a peg to the left of the entry. Making his way to the end on Sarah's right, he slipped by Nancy, circled Rags, and came to his usual perch looking down the length of the bar.

Serving his mug of lager, Sarah said, "You're early."

Scooching forward, Brass cast his penetrating light-brown eyes upon her and, in his raspy voice, replied, "I wanted to be here at the start." Clad in a plum sweater tight on his muscular torso, he had shaved his tawny head bald and sculpted his thick sable muttonchops to meet at his upper lip. A pair of silver hoops pierced his left earlobe, a variety of silver skull-shaped rings covered his fingers, and a bracelet made up of tiny silver skulls wound around his right wrist. Flexing his defined chest, he directed his gaze at the old sea captain and followed up, "I feel like I'm missin' somethin, and it's been botherin' me all day."

To the right of the entry, Tony helped the lady remove her cloak, took his off, and hung them up together. Even soaking wet, his dark mustache remained waxed straight off the corners of his lips, and his goatee came to a point on his wide chin. The hood had kept his wavy, gray-streaked black hair dry, and he let it hang free to shroud the top of his red leather vest. Underneath it, the first three buttons of his black velvet long-sleeve shirt were undone, and in the midst of his dark chest hair, a large Spanish gold coin dangled on a thick braided gold chain. With his right hand on his companion's lower back, he escorted her to the spot three from the old sea captain's and pulled out two stools. She sat first, and gently, he helped her slide in until she could rest her elbows on the aged mahogany top. Caressing her shoulder, he placed his left foot on the brass rail at the base of the bar and twirled his left hand. The large ruby in his gold pinky ring glittered in the flickering light, and giving Sarah a nod, he said in a slight Spanish accent, "A glass of your finest claret, por favor, and whatever the maiden would like."

Tilting her head toward the lady, Sarah inquired, "And what can I get for you?"

Full-figured, she had a heavy ebony braid that she flicked over her left shoulder so the end came to a rest at the frilly black lace lining the top of her dress. Emerald green, it fit snugly, came to a V at her ample cleavage, and followed the shape of her body to the frilly black lace in the hem at her knees. Her eyes set wide on her round face, she bore a slightly crooked nose and, under her right cheekbone, a faded scar in the shape of a half-circle. Squinting, she smiled raucously and, in a heavy Irish brogue, replied, "Tony says ye carry rum imported from Barbados. Is that true?"

Without turning, Sarah knocked on the top of the little rundlet to her left and answered, "It is. And it's the best you'll find in all of Jamaica."

The wrinkles at her temples furrowing, the lady smiled wider and followed up, "Oh goody, I love Barbadian rum. This is such a treat. Give me a double with a splash of water and a slice of lime, if ye please."

"Of course," Sarah replied. She looked at Tony and added, "Are you going to be a gentleman and introduce us?"

Bowing slightly, he responded, "My apologies. This is Labhrain. She helps her father run Patrick's Holiday, a tavern off the docks near my warehouse."

"Call me Labby," Labhrain interjected.

Filling their order, Sarah commented, "It's my pleasure to make your acquaintance, Labby." She set down her drink and went on, "I've heard of your place, and I'm told it can be a rough crowd. I have to ask, how do you handle it?"

Holding up her two powerful hands, littered with faded cuts and bruises, Labby smacked her weathered right fist into her equally toughened left palm and disclosed, "If someone's gettin' out o' line, I give him a little whack upside the head with me shillelagh. If that doesn't do the trick, I'll knock him out and let the press gangs know I've got another recruit fer 'em." Her smile morphing into a sneer, she continued, "And by the time the troublemaker wakes, he'll be a hundred miles out at sea aboard a ship in the Royal Navy. Trust me, I've no qualms seein' some arse off to the other side of the world. I've done it hundreds of times. In fact, they say I'm a bit of a celebrity at Port Royale." Giving Sarah a wink, she concluded, "But don't believe everythin' ye hear. It's not all feuds and fights. We do have our fair share of laughs. Ye should come down fer a visit. I'll keep ye safe."

"I'm sure you would," Sarah remarked. "Unfortunately, I can't let a hurricane close me down, and since my father's not alive to help, I won't get a day off until my younger sister gets a little older." Interrupting their conversation, Nancy appeared in the gap to the left of Brass and called out the beverages she needed. Enduringly happy, she had bound her black hair into pigtails and always seemed to have a radiant shine in her almond-shaped light-brown eyes. Like Sarah, she wore a white shift, black vest, and black bow tie.

Working quickly, Sarah filled a variety of glasses and set them on Nancy's wooden tray, then at the sound of the door opening, she noticed a man at the entry removing his baby-blue cloak. Wiry, he was clean-shaven and had an oversized gold bow binding his silky brown ponytail. Dressed in a fitted yellow satin shirt with thin vertical sky-blue stripes tucked into his white leather trousers, he effortlessly strode to the bar and slid out the stool to the left of Tony. His eyes matched the sapphire set in the gold ring on his right hand, and nervously, he strummed his fingers on the weathered top until Sarah gave him a nod. Smiling easily, he returned her gesture and, in a melodious French accent, inquired, "Is it true that you serve claret here?"

Knocking on the barrel in the middle of the cradle, marked with a scripted vermillion *CLT,* Sarah replied, "We do. It's the finest claret produced at the finest estate in the entire Bordeaux region of France, and everyone says it gets better during its journey across the sea."

"It most certainly does," Tony concurred.

Letting out a sigh of relief, the Frenchman sat down and replied, "Oh thank God. Technically it may not be Bordeaux. However, given the circumstances, it will suffice. May I please have a glass?" Glancing at Tony, he shook his head and admitted, "This storm has stranded me for several days now, and out of boredom, I have drunk almost all my best wine. If it does not pass soon, I am afraid I will have none remaining for my voyage home."

"Should you run into that problem, stop by my warehouse prior to your departure," Tony responded, "and I will be happy to solve it for you. May I ask your name?"

"Andre," the Frenchman replied.

The door opened, and a stout, barrel-chested man with a full head of silver hair entered. He took off his heavy navy-blue peacoat and hung it next to Brass's cloak. Though his knee-high black leather boots were soaked, his cobalt broadcloth vest, stiff maroon shirt, and pearly white breeches remained dry. Purposefully, he strode to the spot to the right of Rags.

Turning his watery eyes upon him, Rags let out a grumbly chuckle and noted, "Well, well, well, if it isn't the Commodore. To what do we owe the pleasure?"

His square head set deep into his broad shoulders, the Commodore had thick rolls at the base of his neck and faint pockmarks dotting his cheeks. Staying on his feet, he turned his bright blue eyes on Rags and, in a gruff British accent, replied, "I have some business in the city regarding my estate, and I was hoping to see a play tonight. Unfortunately, the theater is closed."

Nodding toward Sarah, Rags remarked, "With the exception of Henry's, everything is closed. What did you expect in the middle of a hurricane?"

Waving both hands, the Commodore snapped, "Hurricane, bah, this doesn't compare to the one in '80, much less the one in '26. Now that was a hurricane." He tapped Rags's shoulder and added, "Do you remember the damage it did to Port Royale?"

"I was six years old," Rags responded.

"Well then, let me say, being barely fourteen, I had only just begun my service in the Royal Navy," the Commodore announced, "and to this day, I can still recall how it sunk fifty ships in the harbor. What a mess that was to clean up."

Giving Andre his glass of wine, Sarah asked the Commodore, "The usual?"

Nodding toward the rundlet, he inquired, "Has Tony convinced you to sell my brand of spiced rum?"

Shaking her head, she returned, "You know how I feel. I sell the rum my regulars request."

Waving both hands again, he muttered, "Bah, Barbadian rum. You are aware that swill is nothing special. The only reason it's expensive is because, unlike us, they still haven't recovered from the hurricane that came through five years ago and they simply can't meet the demand. It has nothing to do with the quality or the taste." He frowned and, looking down on Andre, concluded, "With how incompetent they are, one would almost think Barbados was a French colony and not English. You watch, it won't be long until Jamaican rum makes everyone forget about that rotgut they make."

Shrugging, Sarah told him, "And the day it happens is the day I'll make the switch. Now, would you like to try the competition?"

Shaking his head, he let out a sigh and responded, "No, I'll stick with the usual. Once I decided to make the trek to Kingston, I began craving a few mugs of your lager." He turned his palms over and added, "I also plan to purchase a few hogsheads to take home."

"I'll need a week to get them ready," Sarah replied, "but I'll warn you now, the price has gone up."

"The price has gone up!" the Commodore exclaimed.

"I don't want to hear it," Sarah snapped. "There's some sort of Indian war going on in the colonies that's cut the supply of barley and it's gotten more and more expensive to import. Maybe if some wealthy landowner started growing it here in Jamaica instead of sugarcane for his rum, we wouldn't be in this situation."

Brass let out a low whistle, Rags chuckled, and positioned in the gap leading behind the bar, Nancy interjected, "I told you Sarah is just like Mairi."

"I think she's tougher than Mairi," Tony chipped in.

Narrowing his eyes, the Commodore asked, "Mairi? Who's Mairi?"

"Mairi is the brains behind Oakies," Nancy stated.

"Oakies? What's Oakies?" the Commodore repeated. Tapping Rags' arm, he asked, "What are they referring to?"

Waving his left hand, Rags replied, "Ahh, don't ask. That old man at the end of the bar has been feeding them a bunch of balderdash."

"Actually, he's been tellin' a pretty good story," Brass whispered.

"A story?" Andre picked up. "I like a good story. What is it about?"

"Whiskey and pirates," Tony let him know, "with a little Shakespearean flair. The hero is a Spanish bull named Ricardo DeLogrono."

"Don't believe him," Brass interrupted. "The real hero is a Scot named Tomas." Glowering, he added, "But ye can call him Big Tom."

"Big Tom isn't the hero," John exclaimed.

"The twins are," Luke followed up.

"If ye ask me," Labby pitched in, "the hero is the Irish lass named Clarkeson, the most beautiful pirate to ever sail the Caribbean." Cackling out loud, she added, "Tony says somethin' about her reminds him of me."

Shaking his head, Rags told the Commodore, "See? I tried to tell them none of those people were real. You were alive back then. Maybe they'll listen to you."

"Hmmm," the Commodore noted, "I certainly don't recall any pirate named Clarkeson." Rubbing his chin, he leaned forward, looked down the length of the bar, and stated, "Let me guess, in the end we're going to find out she was really Anne Bonny."

Slapping his hand to the bar, Rags followed up, "That's exactly what I said."

"And yer both wrong," the old sea captain insisted. "Clarkeson was no pirate. If I've said it once, I've said it a thousand times, she was a warrior fightin' fer a cause."

"When does this story take place?" the Commodore inquired.

Stroking his bushy beard, the old sea captain cleared his throat and began, "It starts in October of 1743, on the very day Clarkeson took her very first ship, *The Empire's Reach*. It was her very first act in support of Charles Edward Stuart."

"The Young Pretender?" the Commodore questioned. "She was a Jacobite? How on earth could the Scottish rebellion in '45 be connected to a pirate in the Caribbean?"

"She believed stirrin' up trouble over here," the old sea captain explained, "would help the cause over there."

"Clarkeson is just a distraction," Nancy broke in. "I'm certain the real story is about Mairi."

"Clarkeson was a distraction indeed," the old sea captain confirmed.

"And where were you in all this?" the Commodore wanted to know.

"I was an officer in the Royal Navy," the old sea captain filled in, "aboard a sloop of war fightin' in the Mediterranean."

"Hmmm," the Commodore determined, "I must admit I can't know for certain if any of this was real, for during those years, I too was a young officer in the Royal Navy, stationed aboard a vessel in the Mediterranean—a first-rate, to be exact. I'll never forget those days. I was on the admiral's ship, and we were assigned to the fleet in Hyeres blockading the combined Spanish/French force trapped at Toulon. Indeed, over the course of the battle, I earned several commendations for my bravery, and though it was an inglorious defeat for the British, my performance led directly to my rapid rise through the ranks. I would be given the command of my own rated ship within the year." Grasping his bare chin, he noted, "Hmmm, I haven't spoken of those deeds for some time." Tapping Rags' shoulder again, he suggested, "If you're pining for the truth, I would be happy to regale them for everyone."

"Please no," Rags grumbled.

"Aye," Brass concurred, "keep them to yourself."

Standing straight, the Commodore retorted, "Well, if this Clarkeson had posed such a significant threat, she would not have been the responsibility of a ship in our theater of the war. They would have placed a bounty on her head and commissioned someone stationed at Port Royale to hunt her."

"Correct you are, sir, and to be sure, they tried, yet no captain in the Caribbean proved worthy enough to catch her," the old sea captain declared. "Eighteen months would pass until we finally received our orders."

"Since you tracked D'Groers," Tony picked up, "I'm surprised you weren't sent immediately."

"Findin' D'Groers was a feat," the old sea captain responded, "yet believe it or not, it paled in comparison to my skipper's next accomplishment." Covering his heart with his right hand, he concluded, "And while he may not have done what he set out to do, he did enough to set us on our fateful course."

"What could have possibly been greater than capturin' *The Emballeur*?" Brass wanted to know.

Licking his lips, the old sea captain strummed both hands on the bar and replied, "Oh, if I were to answer yer question, I'd be gettin' into another story."

"Well, I don't think you should start with a story about your skipper," Luke chipped in.

"Nor do I," John added. "I think it should begin with the twins on Paddies island."

"Paddies island?" the Commodore inserted.

"Culebra," Tony filled in, "and I would agree, for I would think any story on Culebra would also involve DeLogrono."

Suddenly, Brass tapped the edge of a silver coin on the bar and silenced the room. With every eye turning toward him, he slid it forward and told Sarah, "If the next story told has to do with Big Tom, then I want to buy his first round. And he can keep the change."

Raising her eyebrows, Sarah turned right to the hogshead with a capital H branded above the tap and filled a mug of lager. She set it down in front of the old sea captain, who picked it up, took several healthy swallows, and tilting his head toward Brass, remarked, "Why, thank ye kindly, good sir." Glancing around the room, he mentioned, "Though I'm happy to leave the decision to all of ye, I have to wonder if it's a little too early to start. There's a few people who were here last night that haven't arrived yet, particularly that fellow Jack. He kept sayin' how much he wished he were here at the beginnin'."

Frowning, Sarah responded, "Jack? Don't worry about Jack. Jack has to sneak away from his wife. If he gets out, it won't be until later."

"That's not the gentleman I was referrin' to," the old sea captain clarified.

"Oh, you mean Jesus Christ Jack," Nancy returned.

Snapping his fingers, the old sea captain said, "Aye, that's him."

Letting out several deep, grumbly chuckles, Rags repeated, "Jesus Christ Jack. I wouldn't worry about that Jack either." Holding his right hand parallel to the bar, he wobbled it and followed up, "He's starting to lose it. I don't know if it's from a lifetime of burying dead bodies, but in the last few years, he's gotten really bad. He probably won't remember last night anyway." Looping his finger around his ear, he went on, "Besides, it's best he shows up a little later. Once he gets a few in him, he really goes off his rocker."

In the distance, the lightning flashed, the thunder grumbled, and slowly stroking his bushy beard, the old sea captain directed his bright blue eyes to the flame dancing atop the candle on the mantel behind the bar. Watching a few more rivulets of melting wax meander down the stick, he took a deep breath and determined, "Then maybe it is best if I do begin, fer it starts many years ago with quite the circuitous course around Scotland . . ."

Mid-December 1744, Port of Inverness

His visage fierce, Big Tom swirled his glass under his nose and declared, "Campbeltown." Dressed in our finest, in his case a custom fur-lined black leather vest over a fitted purple long-sleeve shirt and a heavy wool kilt woven in a purple-and-gold tartan, we had recently arrived at an upscale public house and settled in at a smooth, shiny square table made of teak. He sat on the opposite side, and in the shadowy light of the lanterns hanging on the wall at my back, his long brown hair blended in with his thick dark muttonchops. The burning flames reflecting in his eyes, he glared at me and stated, "By the smell alone, it should be obvious to everyone this isn't Oakies."

Seated to my left, the skipper responded, "Easy, Tomas, not everyone has yer affinity." Though he too wore a kilt woven in a purple-and-gold tartan, he had donned a long white wig that dangled before his eyes, a golden silk shirt, and a royal-purple broadcloth jacket trimmed in solid gold buttons, cuff links, and epaulettes. He had also, of course, assumed his signature look, with his mustache waxed into horns at the corners of his lips and his goatee tied into a braid several inches long. A thin leather strip bound the end, and giving it a tug, he went on, "I doubt very many people in this town have ever tried anythin' other than a Highland or maybe a Speyside, and I'm sure it's quite easy to pass off a Campbeltown fer somethin' else. Keep in mind, it took a few times around the country until I could distinguish them all." Turning to me, he nodded to my drink and asked, "What do ye notice?"

This was actually the third public house where we were sold a flagon of Oakies that, once again, proved to be counterfeit. Similar to the previous two occasions, my compatriots had determined the legitimate origin of our purchase, and they were now giving me a chance to denote the subtle nuances pinpointing its identity. While I had consumed plenty of whisky growing up on the Outer Hebrides, I gave little regard to the taste and was completely unaware the flavor was considered distinct to one of six regions native to Scotland. Despite my lack of experience, I had been demonstrating an innate capacity to pick out the unique attributes of the other five, and the reformation of my palate was progressing extraordinarily well. Nevertheless, I sensed the big man's unsettling stare, and as my heart beat harder in my chest, I felt my palms begin to sweat. Personally, I still preferred the more traditional uniform—a navy-blue peacoat with gold lacing, white facings, and white breeches—yet it had been a year since the skipper forbade me to shave, and my facial hair had become rather shaggy. Using my left hand to stroke my beard, I lifted the glass in my right and peered through the crystal-clear liquid.

It really all started the prior February, after the apprehension of D'Groers, when we reached the fleet at Hyeres blockading the combined Spanish/French force at Toulon and delivered the king's reply to the admiral. Acknowledging our role in the capture of *The Emballeur*, he had personally signed one voucher for our share of her prize money and a second worth the full value of *The Sabre*. Subsequently, we were ordered to transport a dignitary to Port Mahon, and the skipper was able to cash them both in at the base. Initially, we had planned to give our crew a full two weeks of leave. However, on the twenty-second, the enemy fleet attempted a breakout, and in addition to a good number of their vessels making it to safety, the Royal Navy suffered significant losses. Tasked with delivering the bad news to High Command, we ended our celebration prematurely and immediately headed home.

In April, we had arrived in London to rain and learned that at the same time as the Battle of Toulon, a French invasion force commanded by Field Marshal Maurice De Saxe had neared Dungeness off the coast of Kent. Luckily, a storm in the Channel had destroyed a good number of their transports and the surviving vessels had retreated to Dunkirk. Confirming the skipper's suspicions, a formal inquiry determined its presence and purpose was to support a Jacobean rebellion. The looming threat of a second attack made the protection of England a priority, so instead of returning to our previous duties, we were reassigned to help patrol the shores of Britain.

No longer sailing the Mediterranean meant our two-masted sloop of war, *Rosie's Charm*, no longer needed oars, and she was thus allotted a full complement of twenty-two cannon, with ten twelve-pounders on her sides plus a pair of nine-pound chasers in her stern. Sent to the shipyards at Chatham to have her weaponry refitted, we used the opportunity in a dry dock to careen her eighty-foot wooden hull, replace her four canvas triangular gaff sails, and restring the miles of hemp rope necessary to operate her rigging. Stuck residing in the barracks made it hard to find moonshine, let alone any good whisky, and we often had to choose between drinking our rum ration or gin, the local favorite. Seeing the big man refused to consider the former, we acquired the latter on the condition he was first allowed to see the still. "Shady establishments will substitute turpentine fer juniper berries," he had warned, "and I'll be damned if I'll fall fer that trick."

Unimpressed, I found the English liquor to be very dry with an almost medicinal disposition, and I longed for our preferred alcohol of choice. Thankfully, the improvements to our ship were completed in less than three weeks, and the moment she was ready, we were directed to help reinforce Edinburgh. Enjoying the warm sunny weather the day we set out, I stood at the helm next to the skipper and expressed my enthusiasm for our ensuing change in spirits. Seeking to temper my expectations, he suggested, "Don't get too excited. We may have a hard time findin' any good whisky to drink."

"Why?" I questioned. "Edinburgh is the capital of Scotland. At a minimum, we should be able to find some good moonshine."

Scrunching his face, he said, "Aye, we'll be able to find moonshine, but it's more likely it'll taste like the city."

"What's that supposed to mean?" I returned.

Behind us, at the wheel, Big Tom chipped in, "It means it'll taste dirty. Do ye remember the swig ye took out of Rory's flask the day we took *The Sabre*?"

Positioned on our left, Rory cackled harshly and followed up, "He looked like he was breathin' fire." His sandy-brown hair cut short and his cheeks bare, he was dressed in a black wool sweater with his usual blood-red scarf and emerald-green kilt. As I glanced over my shoulder, he let a cruel smile cross his lips and added, "Maybe me blow to his jaw knocked him senseless."

Though my recollection of the battle was somewhat hazy, the gleam in his sandy-brown eyes brought me back, and instantly, I recalled the harsh piney burn with the heavy smokiness masking the faint taint of rotten eggs. Shuddering, I shook my head and replied, "There's some things I'll never forget. If that's our only option, maybe I will stick with rum."

We had reached our destination on a cloudy evening in June and, leaving Rory to his own devices, the three of us visited the skipper's favorite public house near the wharf. Packed full of sailors, it was a long rectangle consisting of a timeworn wooden counter running the length of the wall to our left and a narrow aisle taking up the remaining space on our right. Following Big Tom through the crowd, we found enough room at the back to be able to stand in a row, with the skipper in the middle of me and the big man. To our surprise, the barkeep offered to sell us a flagon of Oakies, albeit at a high price, and we happily accepted, for the stories of Clarkeson had made us want to try it. Unfortunately, Big Tom took his first sip, looked inside his cup, and proclaimed, "Islay."

Shrugging, the skipper commented, "At least it's a good Islay."

On his right, I had asked, "Islay?"

"This whisky may not be a product of Edinburgh," the skipper explained, "but it's definitely not Oakies. It probably came from the Kilarrow House, on the southernmost island of the Inner Hebrides."

"How do ye know?" I inquired.

Topping off our brass chalices with water, he met my eyes and put forth, "There's a lot more to whisky than ye think. Instead of gulpin' it down to numb yer pain or numb yer soul, pay attention to the taste and get to know the character. If yer patient, it won't take long and ye'll recognize the flavors specific to the six different regions." He nodded to his left and insisted, "Indeed, to Tomas, the aroma alone can often give it away."

Heeding his advice, I allowed my first sip to roll around my mouth. Primarily peaty and smoky, it was seasoned with the sea, and upon swallowing, I caught them both intently watching my reaction.

"Well," the skipper wanted to know, "anythin' stand out?"

Striving for something acceptable, I managed to say, "Once I got past the initial hit, I'd say there was a bit of brine and some seaweed." Simultaneously, they raised their brows and looked at each other. Smacking my lips, I had added, "And perhaps a bit of fish?"

"Kippers," Big Tom confirmed, "a true sailor's drink." Smiling a wretched grin, he stated, "Ye should be proud of yerself. Ye have a tongue fer this."

Tugging at my sleeves, I responded, "I told ye long ago, I was weaned on whisky. I'm sure I'm a natural."

Ignoring my comment, the skipper waved the barkeep over and inquired, "Is this really Oakies?"

"I believe so," he answered, "it's not like anythin' I've ever drank."

"Do ye know where the owner got it?" Big Tom followed up.

"A Dutch captain offered it in trade a few days ago. He claimed he reached the Hebrides with a dozen barrels in only six weeks."

"Six weeks?" I questioned. "That's impossible."

Shrugging, the barkeep related, "He said he kept havin' nightmares Clarkeson was chasin' him and he didn't sleep more than an hour the entire journey. To get here faster, he dumped the rest of his cargo. He says that's the biggest reason it's expensive."

"If he's Dutch," the skipper picked up, "why would Clarkeson cause him to worry?"

Leaning forward, the barkeep revealed, "According to his story, when the French got involved in the war, she also expanded her role and started targetin' British allies. Soon after, she captured a Dutchman carryin' three barrels of her Oakies that he intended to auction in London."

"Did she execute him?" Big Tom asked.

Shaking his head, the barkeep returned, "No, she seized his ship and told him to let the world know his countrymen, like the English, were no longer welcome in her sea."

He went to serve another guest, and swirling my chalice, I mentioned, "I don't care if the old devil Davy Jones was chasin' him, there's no way that captain crossed the Atlantic in six weeks."

"It's more probable he was never even in the Caribbean," the skipper contended, "and more likely he heard the latest on Clarkeson during his stop at the Kilarrow House. I bet he figured her story gave him a good reason to bump up his price."

Glad to be drinking something the big man considered a true Scottish whisky, we consumed several more flagons that night, and assigned to a flotilla providing a picket guarding the harbor, we regularly came back in during the next three weeks. Finally, an army colonel needing expedited passage to Aberdeen changed our routine, and on a crisp cloudy October afternoon, we arrived at our next stop. Our charge safely delivered, the skipper brought the big man and me to a small pub in the back of a two-story building. The owner, a squat lady with gray hair tied in a bun, gave him a hug and offered us a flagon of Oakies. Though it was costly, she was convincing, and we consented to pay the extra. Sadly, the big man took his first sip, shook his head, and glowering at me, stated, "This should be easy."

Unable to direct my attention away from his harrowing look, I found what was once a source of pride had morphed into one of pressure and felt my heart beat harder in my chest. To settle my nerves, I took a full thirty seconds to savor my first taste. Much softer and considerably less peaty or smoky than the Islay, it had the same coastal influence with a somewhat oily, peppery finish and was particularly comforting hitting my belly. I cast my eyes on his and observed, "Somehow, it reminds me of home."

Smiling and slapping his hand on the table, Big Tom asserted, "And well it should. This whisky is an Island, and Island whiskies are inherent to the Outer Hebrides. Who knows, it could've been distilled near yer home in Stornoway." Tapping his copper cup to the skipper's, he suggested, "I think we found a keeper."

Tilting his head to me, the skipper remarked, "Now that is a compliment indeed."

We toiled a full month, making rounds between Aberdeen and Edinburgh until finally being dispatched north with an urgent letter for Fort George. On a cold evening in December, too late for the skipper to meet the recipient of the message, we landed at the Port of Inverness, and the three of us went to a public house on par with Eugenia's in Palermo. A rectangular brick building, it featured the image of a leprechaun carved into the center of the heavy oaken double doors, a glass window on both sides of the entry, a slate roof, and a cobblestone chimney at each end. Inside, between the two fireplaces, three empty communal tables stretched the length of the floor, and to our left, a granite bar long enough to seat twelve had been angled to take up the entire far corner. On its right, next to the gap leading behind it, another row of six shiny square tables made of teak were positioned like diamonds against the back wall. Able to accommodate four, they were all unoccupied, and waving to the barkeep, the skipper led the way to the one closest to her.

Upon our entrance, she had been standing in front of the cradle for five wooden casks of different sizes while facilitating the back and forth among the three patrons spread out on the stools. Her eyes sparkling like emeralds, she recognized our little party and exited the conversation to come give us each a warm embrace. A flaming-red braid snaked over her left shoulder, ending at the top of her turquoise gown, and she wore a gold chain with a polished heart-shaped green marble pendant dangling between her breasts. Once we had sat down, she leaned over, smiled, and in Irish Gaelic, whispered, "I've got a little secret fer ye boys. If yer willin' to pay a bit more, I can get ye a flagon of Oakies."

For some reason, we gave the idea little thought and enthusiastically accepted her proposal. Only after a single whiff, Big Tom had discerned the whisky wasn't what we had hoped for, and now, having declared it was actually a Campbeltown, he stared at me. The burden of my past success weighing heavy, I felt my heart pounding in my chest and sweat pooling in my palms. To temper my nerves, I swirled my glass under my nose and inhaled the husky aroma. It was comforting, especially on a chilly night, and with my eyes closed, I took a healthy swig.

While I was greeted with the peaty smokiness found in every true Scottish whisky, I also noticed an uncommon flavor underscoring the standard salty, earthy brine I had become accustomed to. It was particular, if not peculiar, and when I swallowed, it gave me a warm fuzziness all over. Slowly, I licked my lips and suggested, "I feel like I pulled my favorite sweater over my head."

Smiling, the big man slammed one palm to the table and, patting my shoulder with the other, declared, "That's the wet wool, and the taste is inherent in every Campbeltown. My father always swore the warmer it was, the finer the whisky. Do ye know what he dubbed the moonshine made on that island?"

Unable to look away, I feebly returned, "What?"

"Wet dog," Big Tom divulged, "and if it was rotgut, he'd say 'This is one mangy mutt.'"

I heard the skipper snicker and realized I had been holding my breath. Letting out a nervous chuckle of my own, I quickly responded, "I take it yer father's the one who taught ye about whisky."

"Aye," the big man affirmed, "fer whisky bein' all he knew, it was the only thing he could teach me."

Though I had always felt uneasy asking the big man about his past, given his respect for my newfound ability, I thought it would be appropriate to follow up, "What did he do? Collect the excise tax?"

The big man's sordid guffaws loud enough to echo in the empty place, they got the attention of the few men seated at the bar. As every set of eyes turned to him, he paid the scrutiny little heed and, shaking his head, told me, "My father called the excisemen gaugers, and no, he was anythin' but. Fer a time, he actually worked in a distillery. It was the same one that employed his father and grandfather, and like them, he started when he was young enough and small enough to climb into the stills to clean them out. As he got bigger, they gave him every job he could handle, and had the tax on malt in 1725 not killed the entire industry, he would have become their first master distiller under the age of thirty." Crossing his arms, he added, "It was a shame he didn't get the chance, fer in those days, Lowland whisky was considered the best in the world, better even than the King's Firkin we had in Palermo."

I remembered back to our evening at Eugenia's and the flagon we were rewarded. Recalling the flavor was slightly smoky with a sweet floral tinge, I compared it to that of the swill I had out of Rory's flask and, shaking my head, replied, "I'm not sure I can believe that."

"It's true," he insisted, "and if it wasn't fer the tax, it would've stayed that way."

"How could a tax change everythin'?"

His glass empty, Big Tom poured himself another round and stated, "It made whisky too expensive to drink." Seeing me furrow my brows, he went on to explain, "The downfall actually began in 1707, when Great Britain was formed under the Acts of Union. At the time, malt was taxed at a higher rate in England,

and the House of Commons pushed for a corresponding hike in Scotland. Resisting the idea, many Scottish nobles attempted to have the treaty abolished and dissolve the Union. Unfortunately they lost the vote, and in 1725, the crown forced the issue. Almost overnight, the common person couldn't afford whisky anymore, and in less than three years, most of the distilleries in the Lowlands had closed. Men like my father, who only knew one thing, were left no other choice than to turn to moonshinin'." Shaking his head, he took a sip and concluded, "Makin' it illegally made it hard to meet any sort of standards, especially in the cities where the gaugers were constantly on the prowl, and it didn't take long until the vast majority of moonshine became nothin' more than rotgut. Although anymore, callin' it rotgut may be insultin' to rotgut."

"I'm surprised the people didn't riot," I inserted.

"Oh, they did," he confirmed, "and my father enthusiastically joined in. His actions brought him to the attention of the gaugers though, and once they knew who he was, they were constantly at his heels."

"Then why did he stay in Edinburgh?"

Holding his glass between his hands, the big man sat back and revealed, "He didn't have much choice. When the distillery closed, he had the option to help the owner set up shop in the New World and he would've gone, except with a pregnant wife and four children under the age of eight, he was afraid we all wouldn't survive the journey and he decided it was safer to stay." His eyes drifting to the lanterns, he furthered, "Until my mother gave birth, his plan was to set up shop anywhere available, be it an old barn or the back of a shipyard, and make all the whisky he could until the law caught wind of it. Then he'd move on."

"How would they find out?"

"The smoke mostly," Big Tom began, "fer durin' the day, they'd see it, and at night, even under the shine of the moon, they'd smell it." Grinning mischievously, he divulged, "My father always claimed his best hideout was in the back of a bakery, where the aroma of the baking bread provided cover. I remember those three months bein' his longest in any one place."

"Why did he leave it?"

"Well," the big man put forth, "if the smoke is the biggest giveaway to moonshinin', someone's big mouth is a close second, and sure enough, with the number of people workin' in the kitchens, the word got out. The day it was raided, they almost caught my father, and he had to abandon his copper still. That's when he realized we needed to leave the region fer good."

Enthralled, I had to follow up, "Where did ye go?"

"North," he answered, "to Dufftown. Fortunately, my uncle was a well-known barber-surgeon who called on a rich clientele, and one of his regulars was a wealthy landowner with an estate on the River Spey. Since this man preferred whisky over rum, he was lookin' fer someone like my father who was willin' to move to his farm and produce it." Leaning forward, he insisted, "Regardless of the risks the travel presented to my pregnant mother, she wanted to go, fer it was an opportunity to get the stability needed to raise a family that wasn't possible movin' all over the city."

"Is that where ye learned how to make moonshine?"

Immediately, I regretted the statement, for he narrowed his eyes and snapped, "I was barely seven when I started helpin' him and already knew how to make moonshine." He took a healthy swallow and, with his countenance softening, went on, "No, in Dufftown I learned the true meaning of uisge beatha."

Grasping for words, I stammered, "Doesn't . . . doesn't uisge beatha mean water of life?"

"In English it does," he responded, "but when it comes to the spirit of whisky, it means much, much more."

Furrowing my brows, I admitted, "I don't get what yer sayin'."

His sudden look searing my soul, he snarled, "And if I have to explain it, ye won't."

Swallowing hard, I held my glass forth and said, "I only ask because ye've opened my eyes to a whole new world."

He stared at me for a moment, then downed the rest of his drink and growled, "If it wasn't fer yer gift, I wouldn't tell ye a thing. Ye better not take it or this story fer granted."

Covering my heart, I vowed, "They'll be woven into my soul."

He placed three fingers to the side of his glass and, filling it to the equivalent level, began, "Dufftown was a completely different world. The landowner used one of the river's tributaries to power his millstone, and he had built two barns a few hundred feet down the bank. The first had a kiln in the middle with large tubs to steep the barley on one side and a stone malting floor to germinate it on the other. The second housed a cast-iron kettle, a cypress washback, and a sparklin' new six-foot-tall pot-bellied copper still. I'll never forget the sight of my warped image climbing to the point at the top or the metallic echo when my father tapped the side. 'Tomas,' he proclaimed, 'I finally get to teach ye how to craft true Scottish whisky.'" He paused and, to the flickering yellow light of the lanterns dancing on the tabletop, asked me, "Do ye know how many ingredients are used to craft true Scottish whisky?"

Frozen, I admitted, "No."

"Three," he stated, "water, malted barley, and yeast. And to that point, I had never been to the country and seen water more clean or pure. In Edinburgh, even prior to the malt tax, it was always a bit murky, and later, when we were forced to make moonshine, it was downright putrid." Shaking his head, he curled his lips and furthered, "Worse yet, we rarely had enough barley, and to compensate, we'd add rotten carrots or rotten fruit or any other available sugar source to the mash, which meant we also had to double the peat in the kiln to cover the awful taste."

"That explains Rory's," I noted.

"Aye," Big Tom agreed, "that and a few other things. In Dufftown, however, the landowner wanted the finest whisky and allotted us the choicest grains to make it. The day of the harvest, my father filled his hands, held them to his nose, and told me, 'Tomas, this, combined with the yeast, is the essence of life in the Speyside region, and it'll form the character of every batch we make.'"

Absentmindedly stroking my beard, I tilted my head and asked, "Where did ye get the yeast?"

Sitting back in his chair, he spread his arms wide and returned, "From the very air ye breathe. In the city, we'd set out a little bit of rotten fruit with water and use the mold that grew on top." Shivering momentarily, he admitted, "Because we weren't concerned with how it would affect the quality, we didn't bother to test it first." He took a sip and went on, "But it was quite the opposite in Dufftown, where we had a variety of orchards at our disposal, including apple, pear, and plum. There, we picked fruit fresh off the branch, muddled it, and set it on a table underneath the very tree it came from. A few days later, we scraped off the yeast and baked each strain into a loaf of bread."

"Bread?" I repeated.

"Aye," he filled in, "fer we had cultivated twelve samples, and it was the easiest way to try them all. Once we selected the three we liked the most, we made three separate batches of whisky and had the landowner choose his favorite."

"Was there really that much of a difference?" I wanted to know.

A faraway smile on his face, he put forth, "More than ye can imagine, fer the grains were grown in different fields and contributed their own nuances. Plus, we could burn the correct amount of peat in the kiln, so instead of dominating the other flavors, the smokiness served to enhance them. I couldn't believe the variation in taste. With every sip, the landowner even started to recognize the pasture that sourced the barley."

My mouth watering, I leaned forward and inquired, "What were they like?"

His eyes beaming, he picked up his glass and stated, "The first was sweet and earthy, the second was rich and bold, and the third was light and grassy."

Widening my eyes, I had to ask, "Which one did he pick?"

Snorting, he answered, "None. He told us to keep makin' them all."

We both took a drink, and relishing the fuzziness warming my veins, I noted, "Yer explanation fer the flavor of a Speyside makes sense, but it doesn't explain this Campbeltown. Wet wool isn't somethin' that grows out of the ground."

"Have ye ever visited the area?" the big man returned.

"Once," I stated, "a few months after I was assigned to my first ship. We had been caught in a storm and forced to stop to use one of the shipyards to make emergency repairs."

"What was the weather like?"

"Rainy and chilly."

"Of course it was," the big man remarked. "It's always rainy and chilly in Campbeltown. What else do ye remember?"

"Rollin' green hills covered in herds of sheep."

Smirking, he followed up, "Did anythin' stand out about the people?"

"Not really," I mentioned, "they were all too busy to be bothered."

Raising his brows, he responded, "Even in spite of the damp and cold?"

"Like it didn't exist."

Holding his glass toward me, the big man posed, "Then tell me somethin . . . to people rugged enough to work in those conditions, do ye think there's anythin' better than putting on yer favorite sweater in the mornin'? And, once yer job is done, what could be cozier than a whisky that warms yer soul at night?"

Blinking, I muttered, "Somehow that makes perfect sense."

"It's the same in every region," he went on. "A farmer by the River Spey will want to taste the earth, a sailor in the Hebrides the sea, and when it comes to a shipbuilder in Campbeltown, he'll want very thing that keeps him comfortable all day."

"And it's those differences that define the true meanin' behind uisge beatha," the skipper inserted.

My look a confused jumble of questioning and understanding, I nodded slightly, downed my last swallow, and set my glass on the table. Refilling my beverage, I asked the big man, "If life was good in Dufftown, why did ye leave?"

"The gaugers, like always."

"I'm surprised they tracked ye that far away."

"Well," he divulged, "had my father been content with only makin' whisky, they probably wouldn't have bothered."

"Why, what else did he do?"

"He was possessed with the fever of the riots," the big man let on, "and he openly spoke of revolt. To make matters worse, my mother gave birth on the journey, the baby died, and he forever blamed the malt tax fer our situation. Aware of what the Stuarts preferred to drink, he believed they'd make the changes to the law necessary to restore the industry, and he let everyone know he hoped to see another Jacobean rebellion in his lifetime. Sooner or later, the magistrate would hear of his talk, identify him, and we'd be on the move again. We left the Spey side and traveled through the Highlands, then the Islands, until finally reachin' Campbeltown. Along the journey, my remaining two brothers and my mother perished, leavin' my father to take care of me and my younger sister alone. In his contempt, he went from bein' bitter to downright hostile." Shrugging, Big Tom proposed, "We all probably would've been better off if he had chanced the trip to the New World."

Swirling my glass, I had to respond, "Where did ye go after Campbeltown?"

"He took me to Islay."

"What happened to yer sister?"

"She stayed behind. She helped moonshine too, and like me, she could make the cuts when she was twelve. A shipbuilder with a son her age had wanted to open a distillery in the New World. Figurin' she could be his master distiller, he offered to arrange their marriage, and believin' she would be safer, my father agreed to it."

"I gather it was fer the best," I surmised.

"It wasn't," he stated.

Thinking it was a good idea not to probe any further while still wanting to continue our conversation, I quickly inquired, "How long did ye stay in Islay?"

Sighing, he replied, "By then, my father had been branded an outlaw, and we barely had the time to make a half-dozen batches. Without any more regions to hide in, he took off on his own to Ireland."

"Ye didn't go with him?"

"Nope, I was fourteen and tired of runnin'," the big man responded. "Instead, I returned to Edinburgh and apprenticed under my uncle. Fer two years, I shaved the children of his clients, and had I stayed, I probably would've inherited his business."

"Then why would ye join the navy?"

Glowering, he clenched his teeth and seethed, "I wanted to kill pirates."

Fortuitously, the owner, a portly Irishman with a balding spot in the middle of his gray hair and a white beard the length of his torso, slid into the empty chair facing the skipper. Pointing to our flagon, he noted, "Well, would ye look at that? Me granddaughter sold ye some Oakies. She's got a gift. I'll tell ye now, she'll be the one takin' over when I'm done. I've already started lettin' her handle some of me negotiations." Nodding to the skipper's drink, he asked, "How do ye like it?"

"It's good," the skipper replied, "but it's not Oakies."

Both frowning and maintaining his smirk, the owner returned, "And ye've had Oakies?"

Shaking his head, the skipper admitted, "No, I haven't had Oakies. However, I have spent time in Campbeltown, and this whisky tastes a lot like the whisky I drank there." Nodding to the big man, he added, "Tomas agrees."

Raising one eyebrow while lowering the other, the owner followed up, "And how does Tomas know Oakies doesn't taste like a Campbeltown?" His smirk transforming into a smile, he nodded to the barkeep and said, "I'll tell ye, Almhath made the deal and she swears by it. Who am I to believe? Maybe I should call her over, and ye can give her yer thoughts."

A fearful scowl distorting his features, the skipper shot back, "I'm . . . I'm not givin' Almhath my thoughts on anythin' other than how beautiful she is. Personally, I'd prefer if she didn't hear we even had this conversation."

"Where'd she get it?" Big Tom wanted to know.

"A captain come through on his way to London," the owner filled in. "He claimed to have bought it at an Irish pub near Puerto Rico."

"If he was on his way to London," the skipper remarked, "why didn't he sell it at an auction house? We've heard a barrel of Oakies can fetch its weight in silver."

Holding up two fingers, the owner corrected, "Twice that. And I asked the same thing. He said he didn't want Clarkeson findin' out what he done and usin' the portal to come hunt him down."

"Portal?" the skipper questioned. "What portal?"

"The one on her island that glows a living green," the owner filled in. "They say she can use it to come and go anywhere on the earth she pleases."

"I hope ye didn't buy that," I interjected.

His smirk morphing into a sneer, he met my eyes and stated, "Bein' she's a water sprite and given the fate of the previous captains who defied her, are ye sayin' yer dumb enough to risk it?"

When I opened my mouth to rebut his claim, the skipper held his right palm to me and observed, "I'll say this, she does seem to have conjured up some sort of magic. Everywhere we go, everyone believes any whisky with a taste different than the local stuff is Oakies."

"In Edinburgh," Big Tom picked up, "we had an Islay instead of a Lowland. In Aberdeen, we had an Island instead of a Speyside, and now here in Inverness, instead of a Highland, we're drinkin' a Campbeltown."

His eyes darting around the table, the owner lowered his voice and divulged, "She didn't have to cast a spell fer that. Her legend alone has made Oakies famous, and now every shrewd captain is usin' it to cash in. I've never seen anythin' like it." Sighing, he added, "If ye get to Campbeltown, ye'll probably get to drink a good Highland. Lord knows we haven't had a decent one in weeks." Leaning forward, he concluded, "And the ones we have had have been so bad ye could barely taste the heather."

"Heather?" I inquired.

"Aye," Big Tom inserted, "when it blooms durin' the early summer and early autumn, the Highlands are covered in blankets of it." Raising his glass, he added, "And like the wet wool in this Campbeltown, the flavor of heather gives away a Highland whisky."

"The King's Firkin is a Highland," the skipper pointed out.

Thinking back to its floral nature, I mentioned, "I guess it did have a certain purply texture. Is that why it's so sweet?"

"Not necessarily," the big man said, "I heard it's shipped in barrels originally filled with French claret and it picks up the residual sugars on the way."

"That's true," the owner confirmed. Raising both brows, he tilted his head forward and followed up, "Talk about a whisky that's become impossible to find. Even Almhath can't track any down."

"Well," the skipper informed him, "should we stumble across it on the other side of the country, we'll be sure to get ye some."

It would be a while until we moved on, however, and our next few months were spent ferrying messages, troops, and the occasional official between Fort George and Edinburgh. During our journeys, we stopped off everywhere along the way, and in finding it becoming easy to discern the differences in the whiskies we drank, I was looking forward to trying something new. Finally, in April we were sent to Stornoway with a message for Kenneth Mackenzie, who would have been the sixth Earl of Seaforth governing this region had his father not supported the Old Pretender back in 1715 and lost his title. On the afternoon of our arrival, we were caught in a sudden downpour, and instead of reporting directly to headquarters, the skipper thought it best to bide our time at his favorite public house until it passed.

"Does it have whisky?" I inquired. "Because if not, I know of a place that makes their own and disguises it with honey and herbs. They call it their spiced rum."

Grinning, he told me, "This should be interestin'."

Coincidentally, his favorite place happened to be my favorite place and the most popular on the island. Housed in an old stone church constructed out of limestone blocks, it had a curved sign with "The ROB ROY" painted in bold red letters over its two wooden doors and a pair of stained-glass windows coming to the same high pitch as the thatched roof. Inside, three communal tables replaced the pews and ran perpendicular to a stage that replaced the altar. Every seat was taken, and every person was watching a juggler balance a lit candle on his head while flipping nine daggers into the air. I looked at the corner on our right, where a small walnut bar supplanted the confessional. Years of names, dates, initials, and drawings were scrawled into the top, and noticing the three stools were empty, I suggested, "If ye don't mind havin' to turn around to watch the show, we can sit over there."

"Actually," the skipper replied, "in my mind, Alison is the only show in town."

Alison, the barkeep, had worked there for years and often managed the business at the same time she tended the three casks cradled behind her. Though she was my age, little wrinkles had formed at the corners of her piercing dark-brown eyes, and a few silver streaks ran through her jet-black pigtails. Dressed in an ebony dress with a lacy white corset, she sported a collection of metal piercings in her ears, an assortment of metal rings on her fingers, and a jumble of metal chains hanging to various lengths around her neck—the longest touching the edge of a scar at the top of her cleavage. Recognizing the skipper, she rounded the gap to our right and, wrapping her arms around his waist, demanded, "Why has it been ages since ye stopped in to see me?"

"Duty calls," he responded, "and the war took us to the Mediterranean."

"Has duty returned ye fer good?" she wanted to know.

"It's returned us today," he answered, "hopefully fer longer than the last time."

While moving on to hug the big man, she guessed, "And I'm sure ye'll be wantin' the usual."

A slight smile on his face, the big man murmured, "Of course."

She gave him an extra squeeze, slipped out of his embrace, and meeting my gaze, hesitated. "Is he with ye?" she asked them. "Under that beard, I didn't recognize him at first."

"Aye," the skipper let her know, "he's my latest executive officer."

Pointing at my nose, she growled, "I don't care what yer rank is or how long it's been. The rules haven't changed. Ye only get two." Waving her finger, she stressed, "And I don't care who yer sailin' with. I'm the captain of this ship, and ye better respect it. If ye get out of hand, ye'll beg to be flayed."

Behind her, the skipper and the big man gave me the most awful looks. Shrugging, I told them, "What? So I may have been a bit rambunctious in my youth."

Crossing her arms, Alison warned, "There better be no rambunctiousness tonight, or ye won't see another one." Glancing at the skipper, she asked, "Do ye know what he gets like?"

Shaking his head, the skipper told her, "Believe me, his reputation preceded his arrival to my crew, and yes, he's certainly lived up to the expectations it set. Quite honestly, he's actually rather handy to have in battle. He just needs some cannons goin' off to prove it." Hooking his thumb to the big man, he went on, "But don't worry, Tomas is used to keepin' the peace. Nobody is goin' to be a problem, especially in yer presence."

Her glare softening, we settled in with me in the middle, the skipper to my left, and the big man to my right. She returned to her station and, knocking on a hogshead in the cradle, announced, "This big one is ale, the little firkin at the other end is our special spiced rum, and the barrel in between is water." Stepping before me, she leaned on her forearms and, watching our eyes, whispered in Gaelic, "Fer those of ye who may prefer an alternative, I've got good news. If ye have the means, I can offer ye a flagon of Oakies."

Eerily similar to the night in the Port of Inverness, we gave little heed to the expenditure and cheerfully accepted. Crouching down, she tapped a rundlet hidden in the belly of the barrel of water and measured out several ounces into a copper flagon. She then retrieved a trio of tin goblets hanging in the rack below the bar and poured us each a healthy splash. No longer ascribing my sweaty palms or pounding heart to being anxious, I picked up my drink and enthusiastically swirled it under my nose. Aromatic and earthy with a hint of citrus, the scent radiated through my cheeks, and smiling wide, I touched my cup to theirs.

Over the metal ting, the skipper declared, "Here's to a fourth region in Scotland."

Extraordinarily smooth, the first sip imparted an underlying balance of smoke complementing bursts of lemongrass juiciness with a hint of peat lingering in the aftertaste. I closed my eyes, and envisioning the sun setting on an ancient river winding through fields flush with ripened barley, I mumbled, "Speyside."

Slamming his fist on the bar top hard enough to rattle the cups underneath, the big man exclaimed, "It's more than a gift! Yer a true prodigy!"

Every person in the room turned to look our way, including the juggler, and both the candle on his head and the daggers in the air clattered to the stage. Crying out, he presented his right arm to the crowd, absent his right hand.

"Aw, Jesus," Alison sneered. Scowling at Big Tom, she swore, "I don't care how ye feel fer me. If I've got to clean up his blood, I'll cut yer throat!"

To the ensuing gasp, the juggler wiggled his fingers out the end of his sleeve and teased, "Got ye." During the resulting burst of laughter, he gathered the daggers, replaced the candle, and restarted his show.

Opening his palms to Alison, the skipper remarked, "Ye don't have to kill him, ye just have to understand, our mutual acquaintance has a keener sense fer whisky than anyone we've ever met."

Her look giving me a shiver, she responded, "Given how much of it he's drank, that's not a shock."

"That's what I keep tellin' them," I concurred.

"It makes sense you could identify an Island," the skipper pointed out, "but it doesn't with this Speyside. Given we haven't tried one yet, how did ye know?"

"Well, fer one, there's no flavors attributable to the sea, rulin' out another Island, Islay, or Campbeltown," I began, "and without the purple floralness, I knew it wasn't a Highland. More than anythin' though, the second I closed my eyes, I imagined a scene taken out of the big man's childhood story."

His eyes a bit watery, Big Tom mentioned, "I'll bet this one was distilled up the road at the Elchies Manor."

"Are ye sayin' that's not the real Oakies?" Alison wanted to know.

Shrugging, the skipper replied, "Unfortunately it's not." When she put her hands on her hips, he furthered, "Don't get me wrong. It's a fine whisky, but it didn't originate in the Caribbean."

"We can tell by the taste," I inserted.

"It's been the same all over Scotland," Big Tom continued. "Where did ye get it?"

"An Englishman who came in a week ago," Alison related. "He told everyone he and two Dutch captains got together and they each bought twenty barrels in Jamaica with the idea that if they set out at the same time, Clarkeson couldn't catch them all." A smile wavering on her lips, she let out a deep breath and put forth, "He said she seized the first one before they reached Saint Kitts and got the second outside Bermuda. Luckily fer him, a hurricane formed, and skirtin' the northern edge, he was able to elude her."

"He skirted the northern edge of a hurricane?" the skipper questioned. "And that didn't seem a little far-fetched?"

"Bein' he was English, he said didn't have a choice," she replied, "fer he knew if she caught him, he'd end up dead. Had he been Dutch, he might not have risked it, for she doesn't execute their captains, although one recently did die when she attacked his ship and his crew mutinied." No longer suppressing her grin, she furthered, "She told the survivors that the Dutch, like their English allies, are nothin' but a bunch of cowardly gin drinkers. She even said it twice."

"Cowardly gin drinkers?" the skipper repeated, "and she said it twice?" Leaning forward, he let out a low whistle and suggested, "Ohhh boy, if she's goin to go off and offend the spirit of two countries, she must really be spoilin' fer a fight."

"I doubt the Dutch are goin' to give her one," the big man returned.

"Yer probably right," Alison picked up. "The Englishman said the only reason the two Dutch captains got on board with his plan was because they knew they could surrender to her."

Smirking, the skipper pointed out, "As it is, I'm surprised he got away. We were told she's a water sprite and can control the weather."

"Aye, and they say she has a portal on her island she can use to go anywhere in the world," Alison furthered. "I'm not sure if I believe she's a fairy, but I will say I love hearin' her stories. Everybody does. At this rate, she's becomin' more famous than Anne Bonny and more iconic than Grace O'Malley." Leaning forward, she glanced at us individually and insisted, "The English better hope Clarkeson doesn't decide to magically come over here and unite the clans. Prince or no, Charles Edward Stuart has nothin' on her."

With a break in the show, her servers made their rounds and came to fill their orders. Left to ourselves, the skipper leaned forward to tell Big Tom, "The last thing Britain needs is a pirate stirrin' up trouble in the Caribbean. If she isn't stopped, she's likely to spark another rebellion on the other side of the world.

How long ago was Howe dispatched to Port Royale? She should be his first priority."

"It's been at least a year," he replied.

"Howe?" I inquired.

"He's the captain of *The Yorktown*," the skipper informed me, "a brand-new third-rate ship of the line, and he was ordered to put an end to the privateerin' in the West Indies. Knowin' he would be primarily facin' Bermudian sloops, the admiral sent him to spend a few weeks sailin' with us to get a feel fer what to expect."

"If he wasn't such a pompous ass," the big man growled, "he would've paid attention and caught her by now."

"Maybe her ship is faster than his," I suggested.

Rolling his eyes, the skipper retorted, "Catchin' a pirate has nothin' to do with speed. He simply needs to know where to find her."

"The island she uses fer a base is considered Spanish soil," I reminded him. "He can't simply go and trap her."

"If he used his brains," the skipper countered, "he wouldn't have to."

"What would ye do?" I wanted to know.

"She's got to sell her loot somewhere," the skipper stated, "and with how savvy she's been, I'll wager she does it in plain sight."

"Not if she's missin' an eye," I asserted. "Someone would recognize her."

"I'll bet she can see out of both eyes perfectly well," the skipper maintained.

"Then why would a woman wear a patch over one?" I asked.

"Because she's smarter and cleverer than ye," he responded and took a healthy swallow. Looking to the big man, he asked, "Not that he would've listened, but do ye remember if I told

Howe the story of Old One-Eyed Pete? The more I hear Clarkeson's stories, the more I think of him."

"Who's Old One-Eyed Pete?" I interjected.

Smirking, the skipper emptied his goblet and, setting it at the far edge of the bar, replied, "He was a pickpocket who preyed the docks in Port Glasgow, and his name aside, he actually had two very good eyes." Waving his right index finger, he continued, "Ye see, he would wear the best clothing and finest jewelry he could afford until a passenger ship came in. Then he'd don rags atop his outfit, tousle his hair, dirty his cheeks, hobble around with a fake limp, and of course, slip a little black patch over his right eye. In an instant, ye'd think he was a common beggar."

"Why go through the trouble?" I asked.

"To blend into the crowd," the skipper filled in, "and be able to slip in and slip out undetected. Most of the time, his marks didn't even notice him, but on the few occasions they did, he'd sprint to the nearest corner, and once out of sight, he'd remove his costume and tumble to the ground to make it appear he was run over." Chuckling, he pointed his left thumb over his shoulder and concluded, "When his pursuit caught up, he'd tell them, 'The thief ran that way,' and while they continued their chase, he'd wander back into the crowd like nothin' happened."

"That is pretty savvy," I had to admit.

"And if ye ask me, Clarkeson is savvy enough to use the same tactic, only in reverse," the skipper stated. "If I were Howe, I'd go to every public house in the Caribbean. Even in the whole of the sea, there can't be very many female ship captains. With men bein' men, I guarantee the one they consider the most attractive will be well known, and I bet if ye find her, ye find yer pirate."

At the conclusion of our second round, the storm eased, we paid our tab, threw in a bit more extra than usual, and went on our way. Known as Lord Fortrose, Kenneth Mackenzie had already regained some of his family's estates, and hoping to restore his family's name, he was determined to prove his loyalty to the crown. In case the information he would be receiving required an urgent response, the skipper ordered us to round up our crew and prepare our ship for an immediate departure. Sure enough, he soon returned carrying a sealed package, and that evening, we set out for Fort William. With the big man at the wheel, the skipper, Rory, and I stood at the helm of *Rosie's Charm* and watched the twinkling lights of my hometown disappear into the night.

"Thank God that storm gave us a chance to say hi to Alison," the skipper noted. "She would've been pissed if she had heard we were in port and didn't stop in."

"Let's hope she's not angry we didn't return to say goodbye," Big Tom put forth.

Shrugging, the skipper responded, "It may not matter. We could all be dead long before we get a chance to see her again."

"I may prefer it that way," the big man muttered.

Built in 1654 to subdue the Highland clans, Fort William was located inside the western coast of Scotland at the end of Loch Linnhe and was stout enough to hold out during the Jacobite uprising of 1715. On an unseasonably chilly morning in the middle of May, we reached the nearest docks, and the skipper having the big man and me tag along, we made our delivery. Because his local public house was a few miles outside of town, he thought it best if, in addition to wearing our finest, we should be armed, so he tucked an axe into his belt, the big man strapped the claymore to his back, and I carried a cutlass on my hip. Unfortunately, the commander's schedule was full, and we weren't dismissed until late in the afternoon. Our walk exhausted the remaining daylight, and our destination, cast in the bright red glow of the setting sun, was a round building with vertical wooden siding and a stone chimney rising through the middle of the thatched roof. A gravel pathway led to a single door, and inside, three rings of tables circled a hearth occupying the center of the floor. Small groups of people were scattered in the spots closest to the fire, and noting our weapons, they begrudgingly accepted our presence. Giving little heed to their frigid reception, the skipper led the way to our left and a winding narrow aisle that ended at a pair of parallel counters dividing the rear of the room.

Lines had formed on each side, and in practiced movements, a trio of sisters with bright blue eyes and long grayish-brown hair worked in the space between. While the oldest stirred the various kettles placed on a grill mounted along the edge of the hearth, the middle tended the five casks cradled at the opposite side, and the youngest filled each order prior to collecting the payment. At the final table in the outer ring to our left, an old man sat in the outside chair facing the workers and read a book in the light of a single candle. His hair was white, his skin was wrinkly, and his beard hung well past his chest. Dressed in a black cloak over a maroon sweater, he wore a kilt woven in a red-and-green tartan highlighted by yellow squares. When the skipper slid a copy of *Don Quixote* into the glow of the flame, he kept his gaze on the page he was reading and stated, "I thought I made it clear yer to give me a day's notice prior to yer arrival." His eyes icy blue, he slowly looked up at us and followed up, "I need the time to send my daughters away."

Grinning, the skipper returned, "Then I'd have to eat yer cookin'."

Upon marking his page, the old man snapped his book shut and retorted, "Ye seem to ferget, I'm the one who taught them how."

Shrugging, the skipper replied, "Aye, but there's a reason they don't let ye anymore. Besides, I figured if they're here, I can be assured to leave alive. Since the cancelled invasion last February, the tension in this region is palpable, and I don't think even ye could save me."

Picking up the skipper's gift, the old man said, "Had ye not remembered to bring this, I might not have bothered to try. Take a seat."

With Big Tom on his right, the skipper settled in directly opposite the old man, and I took the spot on his left. His youngest and middle daughters came out to greet us, and covering his chest, the skipper murmured, "Which one of ye are keepin' my heart safe?"

Smiling, the middle one leaned over to give him a hug and asked, "The usual?"

"Of course," he told her, before turning to the old man and mentioning, "Unless yer goin' to say ye've got some Oakies to sell us. Everyone else has."

A gleam in his eye, the old man stroked his beard and answered, "I wouldn't bother to try." He gave us a wink and furthered, "And don't believe what anyone else is telling ye either. To my knowledge, a barrel of Oakies has yet to cross the Atlantic." Taking a flask out of a pocket inside his cloak, he went on, "But regardless of what some Irish pirate has to say, I still consider true Scottish whisky to be the finest in the world, and it's yer good fortune to know I can boast havin' the best of the best." Turning to his daughters, he asked, "Would ye please be kind enough to bring me my favorite glasses and an ewer of water?"

Not only did they do his bidding, they also brought us each a piece of bread and a bowl of hearty mutton soup with barley, carrots, split peas, cabbage, and leeks. While we ravenously ate, the old man poured an ounce of whisky into four crystal chalices. Polished and clear, they each bore the word *Revirescit* above several scripted verses of a hymn etched in Latin. The moment I finished eating, I picked mine up and, closing my eyes, swirled it under my nose. To a slight floral aroma and the smell of a smoldering campfire, the image of a Scottish hillside covered in living patterns of purple, red, gold, and even some silvery gray flashed through my mind. Immediately, I glanced across the table. The skipper gave me a smirk, and to my surprise, Big Tom didn't scowl.

Raising his cup, the old man offered, "Would anyone like to make a toast?"

With a shrug, the skipper suggested, "Long live the king," and though the old man hesitated, we all took a drink.

The first taste unbelievably smooth, it was mildly smoky with a sweet, fruity, almost purply flavor, and I felt like I was standing on a mountain while a refreshing summer storm washed through a field of blooming heather. Realizing I was familiar with the taste, I furrowed my brows and looked through my glass.

"He's figurin' it out," the skipper observed.

"He's got a gift," the big man insisted.

"I know I've had it," I admitted, "but I can't place it."

"That's not a surprise," the skipper determined. "Ye were pretty beat up that night."

Glancing between us, the old man inserted, "Are ye sayin' this isn't the first time ye drank this whisky?"

"Aye," the skipper let him know, "we had it in Palermo a year ago. It was our reward fer doin' the king of Naples and Sicily a favor."

"It must've been some favor," the old man responded.

Slamming my hand to the table, I blurted out, "The King's Firkin."

"That's correct," Big Tom confirmed.

"Is there any way ye can sell us some?" the skipper asked the old man. "I told a pub owner in Inverness if I found any, I'd get it for him."

Shaking his head, the old man lamented, "Unfortunately, this is all I have."

"Is there a possibility I could buy some off the person who sold it to ye?" the skipper followed up.

Shaking his head, the old man remarked, "Who said I bought it? It could be a friend of mine from Glenfinnan had a legal issue at the fort and it was his payment fer my help resolvin' it." Lowering his voice, he continued, "And while I suppose I could give ye directions to his public house, I wouldn't recommend ye try to find it. Even my daughters couldn't protect ye up there."

"Glenfinnan?" the skipper questioned. "Why on earth would a public house out in the middle of nowhere have the King's Firkin?"

"I didn't ask," the old man stated, "and I'd rather talk about somethin' else."

We topped off our cups with water, and for the next hour, the skipper relayed our journey tasting the whiskies around Scotland until the topic settled on Oakies. Using Alison's opinion that Clarkeson could unite the clans, he changed the course of the conversation toward the likelihood of another Jacobean rebellion. "We've spent most of our time at sea," he went on, "and I wouldn't pretend to know what the chances are." Meeting the old man's ice-cold eyes, he added, "What about ye? I can imagine there's a person in Britain who has a better idea."

Stoically, he took a swig, let out a deep breath, and divulged, "I doubt a young Irish pirate, beautiful though she may be, could bring peace to these lands."

"What about Charles Stuart?" the skipper returned.

A slight smirk on the corner of his lips, he shrugged and let out, "Who knows? His father did it thirty years ago."

"The Young Pretender has never set foot on Scottish soil," the skipper pointed out.

Sitting back in his chair, the old man finished his drink, cast his gaze across the table, and offered, "Aye, but there's a reason the French call him the Young Chevalier."

He didn't speak on it anymore and we departed soon after, for the night had rolled in and we had quite the walk ahead of us. The very next morning, we were ordered to give an army major passage to Stornoway, and we set out to a warm sun in the bright blue sky. Retaining his purple-and-gold regalia, the skipper ordered Big Tom, Rory, and me to wait at the helm until he finished giving our passenger a personal tour of our vessel. Watching them climb up the ladder at the bow, the big man put Rory on the wheel and told me, "Come on. The skipper just gave us a signal. Somethin's up."

"Where are we goin'?"

"To his cabin. Whatever it is, he wants to keep it a secret."

Like every ship built for speed, *Rosie's Charm* narrowed at the stern, and although it was the same length as our wardroom, the captain's quarters were relatively cramped. Still, there were three rectangular windows opposite the door, a table accommodating four in the middle of the room, and against the bulkhead to our right, a desk with a well-worn rocking chair. To our left, he had enough space for a full-sized bed and, in the far corner, the cradle for his personal rundlet.

The skipper met us, and pouring a healthy swallow into three small wooden cups, he revealed, "Our guest grew up in Glasgow and says he hasn't spent much time on a ship. He admitted he doesn't have any sea legs and he's wary of the legends surroundin' the Blue Men of Minch. I assured him unless there was a terrible storm, we wouldn't be goin' near the Shiant Islands and their notoriously rough waters." Passing a drink to the big man, he smiled mischievously and divulged, "Too bad it seems like the wind is pickin' up and blowin' us in their direction. It'd be a shame if he ended up below decks before this afternoon."

"Why?" I asked.

Tugging on his braid, he hung on to my cup an extra second and, meeting my eyes, answered, "Because I'm comin' up with a plan. And it looks like yer finally goin' to get to shave. . ."

Appendix A

SHIPS AND THEIR CREWS:

Chapter 1
The Black Irish: Clarkeson, Fergus, Ben, James, Gianis, Marcus

Chapter 2
The Scottish Rose: Mairi, Connor, Angus
The Wasp: Mark
The Hornet: Mathew
La Bonita Senorita: Ricardo DeLogrono

Chapter 3
Rosie's Charm: The skipper, Big Tom, Rory, the old sea captain

Chapter 4
The Scottish Rose: Mairi, Connor, Angus
Mariana: Malcolm

Chapter 5
Rosie's Charm: The skipper, Big Tom, Rory, the old sea captain

Chapter 6
The Black Irish: Clarkeson, Fergus, Ben, James, Gianis, Marcus
Mariana: Malcolm

Chapter 7
Rosie's Charm: The skipper, Big Tom, Rory, the old sea captain
The Black Irish: Clarkeson, Fergus, Ben, James, Gianis, Marcus
The Scottish Rose: Mairi, Connor, Angus